PERSEVERANCE

PERSEVERANCE

A WYN PRICE MYSTERY

P.A. TREMBLAY

Copyright © 2025 by P.A. Tremblay
Cover and Interior Design by Daniel Pyle

ISBN: 979-8-9929981-1-5

Tales on the Rocks Publishing LLC

For Topper, Alex, Katie, and Logan,
who all encouraged me to go on,
and for Sammy. Especially for
Sammy—and he knows why.

ONE

I was headed back to the Perseverance police station, listening to Eminem and mulling over my cactus infestation problem, when the doe stepped out onto the highway.

It was already past lunchtime, and I was in no mood to appreciate the wonders of Wyoming wildlife, so I leaned on the horn of my 1998 Crown Victoria police cruiser to encourage her to move along.

She took several tentative steps before halting in my lane and twitching her delicate taupe ears.

"Oh, come on." My stomach rumbled as I braked to a hard stop, anticipating the leftover lasagna waiting for me in the fridge at the station.

A whoop from the cruiser's siren might've encouraged the doe to move along, but it would have been tragic if it propelled her into the grill of the Dodge Ram pickup truck that was barreling towards us and showing no signs of slowing.

Then I saw it. A tiny spotted fawn struggled on spindly legs to mount the road from the deep ditch on the other side of the highway. I held my breath as the Dodge roared by in a blur of chrome and diesel fuel fumes, bass throbbing from the stereo.

After the truck passed, the fawn was nowhere to be seen, and my heart sank. Then his head popped up in the tall grass of the ditch as he scrambled back to his feet. The draft from the vehicle had knocked him backwards, but he was determined to join his mother and in a courageous burst of speed, he mounted the lip of the road and skittered across the blacktop to her side.

For a moment, both stared at me, undaunted despite a close brush with two and a half tons of cowboy metal. Then, with the fawn at her side, the doe bounded off the highway and disappeared into a thicket of willows.

The police band radio crackled. "Wyn?"

It was Connie Walsh, the Perseverance Police Department dispatcher. "Wyn, are you there? The Edgemont County Sheriff's Office called. Someone out in Brightwater Canyon is requesting a welfare check on an elderly widow."

I swore under my breath and reached for the microphone handset attached to the dusty dash of the cruiser with Velcro. "Why can't the sheriff's deputy handle it? You know, Barker, or whatever his name is."

"Deputy Bartel is up at Union Pass. They got a report of a fire up there this morning."

"Oh, for Pete's sake. Where is Chief Vanderberg? I thought he took all the overflow calls from Edgemont County dispatch."

"The chief is having lunch with the Kiwanis Club today."

If I was honest with myself, I didn't have any other pressing police business on that fine June day in Perseverance, Wyoming. Until Connie called, my plans for the rest of the day involved eating lunch at my desk followed by another long slow patrol through town.

"Okay, fine," I said, spinning the cruiser around in the road with a resigned sigh. "Give me the details."

In the fifteen miles between the city limits of Perseverance and the exclusive enclave of Brightwater Heights, the landscape transformed from cactus and sagebrush to lodgepole pine forest as the highway climbed into the foothills of the Wind River Range. The sheer scale of the scenery had a way of swallowing you whole, like you could disappear into it if you had a mind to.

I turned off the pavement onto a gravel road with a posted speed limit of twenty-five miles per hour that meandered along a picturesque stream shaded by cottonwoods, then descended into a red stone canyon with twisting curves. In places, the canyon walls fell back from the road, revealing glimpses of grand estates tucked among the towering pine trees.

After about five miles, a carved wooden sign announced the entrance to Spruce Hollow Gulch, and I punched the code Connie gave me into the keypad of the security gate and followed the winding dirt road until it branched off onto Meadowlark Lane.

Evelyn Randall's home was a sprawling structure in the classic lodge style, featuring a log façade, copper roof, and wrap-around veranda. Set back from the road up against the foothills of the Wind River Range, it was the sort of house a Wyoming senator owned as a backdrop for his campaign photos so he could pose on the front veranda, white teeth gleaming as he lounged on the porch swing next to his pretty brunette wife, surrounded by a private army of strong, good-looking children.

I parked the cruiser in the circular gravel driveway and surveyed the area before approaching the front door. Dense stands of pines and spruce encircled the house, obscuring the neighboring homes and creating a sense of seclusion accented by the twitter of songbirds.

After my first knock didn't elicit a response, I knocked again, louder this time. "This is Officer Price of the Perseverance Police Department. Is anyone home?"

Still nothing.

I tried the door handle. It was unlocked, and I pushed the door open. "Hello? Mrs. Randall?"

But I already knew Mrs. Randall wasn't going to answer. The sickly sweet stench of rotting flesh wafting down the hallway told me everything I needed to know.

That stink became imprinted on my senses when I found my first dead body as a rookie cop over ten years ago. It always filled me with dread. Even after I showered, the smell plagued me, like the scent particles were stuck to my skin, or maybe the membranes of my nose. Either way, it was an odor I never forgot.

The rubber soles of my black oxfords *squick-squicked* on the glossy wood floor as I made my way down the hallway, emerging into a spacious great room with floor-to-ceiling windows on the north side and a soaring log truss ceiling above.

At the foot of a floating staircase, illuminated in a pool of molten gold by the midafternoon sun slanting through the skylights, lay a crumpled body.

She was face down, legs splayed out at awkward angles, and one arm was twisted up behind her back. The other arm extended out in front of her body, palm up in supplication. Inches from her outstretched fingers lay the stem of an amethyst-hued *Iris missouriensis*, a species of native wild iris, withering under the intense light of the sun.

I squatted to get a better look. Her head was twisted to one side and bruising was visible on her exposed cheek and neck. From her wiry gray hair and liver spots on her arms, I estimated she was in her late sixties or early seventies, which described Evelyn Randall.

She wore a salmon pink silk blouse with cropped denim pants and one tan moccasin. Her other foot was bare, and I glanced up at the massive floating staircase above me, wondering if she lost the other shoe in a fall down that thing.

I pulled my cell phone out of the case on my belt and grunted in disgust. No cell service. Out in rural Wyoming, cell towers were few and far between.

Near the entrance to the great room was a telephone on a carved wooden table and rather than trudging back out to my cruiser to use the police band radio, I punched the station's number into the push-button handset and waited for Connie to pick up.

"Perseverance Police Department, Connie Welch speaking."

"Hi Connie. It's Wyn."

"Oh, hello Wyn. I didn't recognize the number."

"There's no cell service in Brightwater Canyon, so I'm calling from Evelyn Randall's landline. Anyway, I have a body and I need the Edgemont County Coroner."

"Oh no. Is it Evelyn Randall? What happened?"

"It looks like she fell down the stairs, but we'll have to wait for the coroner to give us his official opinion."

Connie coughed. "So you know, the coroner isn't one to keep regular business hours. I'm just saying you might wait a while."

"Okay," I said, suppressing my exasperation. It wasn't her fault that everything in Edgemont County ran like a rusted Ford Model T. "Listen, I need you to do me a favor. Call Gracie and ask her to pick up Dancy. I won't make it back to town before her daycare closes."

My neighbor Gracie McKenna waitressed at the Six Sisters Truck Stop, but she worked the early morning shift, which freed her up to babysit my two-year-old daughter on those rare occasions when work prevented me from picking Dancy up from daycare.

"Sure, I can do that," Connie said, "and I'll do my best to get the coroner out there pronto. If I can't track him down, I'll call his wife."

"Thanks. By the way, did you know Mrs. Randall?"

"Oh heavens, no. Like most of the citizens of Perseverance, I'm casually acquainted with a few of the Brightwater Canyon glitterati, but none well enough to score dinner invitations to their grand mansions or anything like that. It's far too pricey for locals."

If this house was a typical example, that was no doubt true. With its soaring ceilings and handcrafted wood, it was a model home for an architectural digest. Not that any of that mattered to Evelyn Randall anymore.

"One last thing before I let you go," I said. "When Chief Vanderberg wanders back to his job at the police station to do some actual work, tell him he owes me one."

She snorted in amusement. "I'll call Gracie, but you'll have to tell the chief yourself."

"Okay. Thanks, Connie."

I shouldn't have gotten lippy about Perseverance Chief of Police Lars Vanderberg, but he was spending more time schmoozing than working those days. While he was swanning around like the Mayor of Whoville, I was in the boonies playing lackey to the losers over at the Edgemont County Sheriff's Office.

I scribbled some notes before wandering through the great room, pausing to admire the view of a meadow dotted with patches of purple penstemon and yellow wallflowers through the windows.

On the mission table behind the leather sofa, a framed portrait featured a happy couple with their arms around each other. In another photo, an older version of the same woman posed on a rocky summit and flashed a peace sign for the camera, her beaming face ruddy with exertion.

Behind the staircase, a hallway led to a sumptuous master suite with a sitting room next to an executive study appointed in dark wood. Farther down the hall, an airy white granite and chrome kitchen adjoined a formal dining room and mudroom.

Except for a half-eaten tuna salad sandwich and a pickle stem on a plate next to the stainless steel sink, the kitchen was immaculate.

I passed through the dining room, exiting on the left side of the staircase, and circumnavigated Evelyn Randall's body to ascend the stairs.

At the top, a polished occasional table stood against the wrought-iron railing overlooking the great room. It wasn't quite flush against the railing—which irritated me—and then I noticed another wild iris crushed under one of its legs. Mrs. Randall must have dropped it right before she fell.

The rest of the room was occupied by a brushed-suede sectional sofa facing a flat panel television at one end and a home office and craft area at the other. Doors at both ends of the loft area led to additional bedroom suites.

The front door banged open, followed by heavy footsteps.

A voice carried to the loft. "Officer Price, are you in here?"

"Yes, sir." I trotted down the stairs.

County Coroner Ricky Gleason kneeled on one meaty knee beside the body with his back to me, pulling on blue latex gloves. He snapped the wrist of the one on his right hand as he surveyed the scene. Yellow sweat rings stained his short-sleeved white dress shirt, and it was untucked in back, exposing the tops of his hairy buttocks.

Overweight and balding, I estimated Gleason was in his mid-forties. His fleshy face was unshaven, and at close range he smelled of sweat, whiskey, and stale cigar smoke.

He craned his neck around to look at me, eyes widening. "You're the new town cop, huh? I heard they hired somebody from California."

I could guess what he was thinking. He was expecting a man. A crusty, potbellied burn-out with an opioid problem, not a thirty-something blonde chick who looked more like a high school cheerleader than a law enforcement professional. At one time, his reaction might have amused me, but then it simply made me weary.

He broke eye contact and resumed examination of the body.

"Hmm." Pressing her head to one side, he lifted an eyelid with his thumb. Then he reached underneath and flipped her body over. Her head hit the floor with a *thunk*.

My throat tightened.

He pointed to the purplish discoloration on the side of her face and arms. "Rigor mortis is waning, and based on lividity, I'd say she dropped dead on this very spot within the last two days. She was an elderly woman, so it was likely a stroke or heart attack."

I motioned to the floating staircase looming above us. "But—"

"I'm ruling it death by natural causes." He hoisted himself up and towered over me, which isn't hard since I'm five feet two in my service oxfords. "You got a problem with that, *officer*."

He was dealing with the wrong cop if he expected me to back down. I made my reputation in law enforcement by standing up to misogynists like Gleason.

I didn't budge, though the stink of his breath alone was enough to make me flinch. "She could have fallen down those stairs. It's somthing we should consider, *sir*."

"Your opinion doesn't count, sweetheart. Last time I checked, city cops don't rule on cause of death. The county coroner alone has that authority, and I say it was natural. Now stand aside." He shouldered past me and lumbered down the hall.

A few minutes later, his broad rear end emerged from the hallway, wrangling a bent gurney. He maneuvered it close to the body and kicked a reluctant hinge. "Help me get her on this thing."

I slid my arms under her thighs and ankles as Gleason pulled the body into a sitting position and wrapped his arms around her chest. At his nod, we lifted together and placed her on the gurney.

He threw a grungy sheet over the deceased and buckled her down, then mopped his brow with a heavy forearm. "You notifying kin?"

Before I could sputter a reply, he propelled the squealing gurney down the hall and out the open front door.

I trailed behind, watching from the doorway as he rammed the gurney into the dusty black Suburban with "Edgemont County Coroner" stenciled on the door in gold letters.

The gravel churned up by his tires pinged off the grill of my cruiser as the SUV sped away.

"Of course I don't mind notifying kin, Coroner Gleason. Of course it's no bother. Glad to oblige, *sir*," I said in a mocking voice to the receding taillights.

It was a forty-minute drive to the police station, and the paperwork for County would consume an hour at minimum, which meant I needed to hustle to make it home before Dancy's bedtime.

I marched back through the putrid-smelling house to a mail and key organizer on the wall near the mudroom. While I was grabbing a set of likely looking keys from one hook along the bottom of the organizer, a large pink envelope with "Mrs. Evelyn Randall" written on it in neat cursive caught my eye. The return label was from Ms. Olivia DeWitt in New York City. I pulled the envelope out and slipped the card free.

"Dear Aunt Evelyn, I hope your birthday is amazing. Love, your niece Ollie."

I jotted down the return address and crammed the card and envelope back into the mail slot before jogging to the front of the house where I flung open the front door and bounced off the barrel chest of a man standing outside, his arm poised to knock.

"Whoa!" I put up a hand to push myself away.

He was well over six feet tall from the top of his straw Resistol to the tips of his Lucchese ostrich boots and, despite being in his late fifties to early sixties, in robust physical condition.

"Good afternoon," he said in a resonant baritone.

"Uh, good afternoon. I'm Officer Wyn Price, and you are?"

"My name is Robert Sandoval. I live over that ridge back there." He pointed, eyeing me as if he caught me looting the place. "The coroner's SUV drove by while I was visiting a friend and I stopped by to see if I could help. What's a Perseverance police officer doing out here in Brightwater Canyon, Officer Price? This is the Edgemont County Sheriff's jurisdiction. Where is Deputy Bartel?"

I resisted the urge to spank Sandoval with a verbal warning to mind his own business. His dignified bearing commanded respect, and if there is one thing I learned in my career as a police officer, it is that insulting people who exude importance—however satisfying in the moment—is never productive in the long run.

"Deputy Bartel had other duties to deal with, Mr. Sandoval," I said in a pacifying tone, "and the sheriff's office asked the Perseverance PD to assist with some business here in the canyon."

His tanned forehead wrinkled in contemplation. "What business would it be that involved Edgemont County Coroner Ricky Gleason? Is Evelyn all right?"

"Unfortunately, Mrs. Randall is dead, sir. The sheriff's department received a call from a neighbor requesting a welfare check on her, which they passed on to city dispatch, and I responded to the call. After entering the residence, I found her body."

Sandoval's face clouded. "That is too bad. Evelyn was an esteemed member of our community, and we will miss her, but in the end, we all must face our almighty creator. Call me if I can be of further assistance. I'm in the book."

He spun on his stacked heel and departed without a tip of his hat.

I locked the house and climbed into my cruiser, muttering to myself. *Arrogant prick. What was that 'face our almighty creator' hogwash?*

As I cranked the ignition, Eminem's "Not Afraid" blared out of the radio, and the old Ford roared to life with the aroma of burned oil.

Before heading home for the night, Chief of Police Lars Vanderberg dropped by the police station, where I was filling out county reports in ballpoint pen and cursing the day in the not too recent past that I became a police officer in Perseverance, Wyoming.

Tall, fair-haired Vanderberg was a captain on the Chicago police force before coming to Perseverance five years ago, so he didn't get too excited about anything that happened in pocket-sized Perseverance. Besides being laid back, he laughed at my caustic humor, which made him a pretty good boss in my book.

When he saw me at my desk, he stopped in his tracks. "What are you still doing here, Price?"

"Paperwork for Edgemont County."

"I didn't know a call came from county dispatch. Anything exciting?"

"There was an unattended death in Brightwater Canyon. A Mrs. Evelyn Randall."

"I'll be damned. Where the hell was Deputy Bartel?"

"He was called out to a fire at Union Pass. A neighbor called county dispatch and asked for a welfare check—"

Vanderberg frowned. "Which neighbor?"

"Uh." I shuffled through my notes. "Mrs. Maggie McGuiness—"

"Damn it. If the sheriff's office wasn't such an unmitigated disaster." He rubbed his lantern jaw.

It was common knowledge the sheriff's department was a train wreck. The problem began about a year ago when Edgemont County Sheriff Bucknell "Buck" Lanier died in a drunk-driving accident. Afterwards, his senior deputy up and skedaddled rather than assume the reins, which left dotty old dispatcher Betty Reynolds and overburdened and underpaid Deputy Clifton Bartel in charge of the sheriff's day-to-day operations until the next election.

"Did you call the county coroner?" the chief said.

"I called Connie as soon as I found the body and asked her to contact Coroner Gleason. He arrived about an hour later and determined Evelyn Randall died of natural causes."

Vanderberg brightened. "Natural causes, huh? Great. I mean, it's very sad she passed, of course, but it's not our problem. The County paper-work is a formality. It can wait until tomorrow, so don't burn the mid-night oil over it. Go home. In fact, do you know what? You can put the forms on my desk, and I'll finish them myself in the morning."

"Okay. There's one more thing. Gleason also asked me to notify next of kin."

"That figures," he said with a scowl. "Who is the next of kin?"

"Mrs. McGuiness told Connie the subject wasn't originally from around here. She and her husband moved to Wyoming from New York years ago, but I got this from a birthday card." I gave him the piece of notepaper with Olivia DeWitt's address on it. "This woman is her niece."

He studied the piece of paper. "I've got contacts in New York law enforcement. I'll give one of my buddies a call and ask him to pay this woman a death notification visit, okay? You don't need to worry about it."

"Thanks, chief," I said, shoving the forms into a folder.

He sauntered towards the door, then remembered something and turned back. "Don't forget that Wednesday night is the staff meeting. Did you get a babysitter yet?"

"Not yet, chief, but no worries. I am working on it," I said with a forced smile.

"All right, I'll leave you to lock up, then. Goodnight."

After he was gone, I mumbled something I wouldn't want my mother to hear.

The chief instituted the monthly staff meetings at the Silver Spur Saloon to engage the Perseverance Police Department in team building, irresponsible social drinking, and sucking up to the townsfolk. He called the exercise "getting to know our constituency."

Of all the quirky local rituals this job entailed, meetings at the Spur were the ones I loathed the most. A few months ago, I left early to avoid punching an inebriated constituent who mistook me for a dance hall girl instead of a police officer. After that debacle, I concocted every conceivable excuse to be absent from the meetings. Last month, I fabricated a story about not being able to find a babysitter, but I knew the chief wasn't buying it.

It was after eight o'clock, and I was famished and exhausted when I stumbled into my little mustard yellow house on Cinnamon Street with the dirt and cactus lawn. My neighbor Gracie was on the sofa, cuddling my daughter on her lap.

"Here's Mommy, our favorite crime-fighting superhero," Gracie said, in the same Mickey Mouse falsetto she used with her ancient tabby cat, Sarge.

Her wispy blonde curls in disarray, Dancy giggled when I scooped her up to cover her face in kisses.

I grinned at Gracie. "Thank you for picking Dancy up from daycare.

I don't know what I would do without you, girlfriend. Please let me pay you this time, okay?"

For a split-second, she pretended she might refuse, but then caved. "Okay, but only because I'm saving up for the National Finals Rodeo in Vegas."

It took an effort not to laugh.

Authentic buckle bunny Gracie had never married, but the former rodeo queen's appetite for cowboys—the younger the better—was insatiable. Although stray grays were glinting in her long strawberry-blonde locks and a push-up bra bolstered her cleavage, she was still a crowd pleaser. Every local man with a pulse would give his right arm for one night with town sweetheart Gracie McKenna.

I remembered my conversation with Vanderberg earlier. "Oh, hey, can you babysit Dancy Wednesday night? We have a staff meeting."

"A staff meeting? You mean a night out cavorting with your fellow law enforcement officers? You expect me to miss the one night you go out and enjoy yourself like any other red-blooded single woman?"

"I don't enjoy it. It's forced camaraderie, but Vanderberg made it pretty clear it's mandatory. Now that you mention it, though, it would be more fun if you were there. Besides, with your dazzling presence, the local yokels might leave me alone."

"That's debatable. Why do you keep saying no to that cutie, Dylan Webster?"

I ignored her. I wasn't about to have another pointless argument about Dylan.

"Okay, forget it." She rolled her eyes. "Anyway, I know a junior high girl who would jump at the chance to get out of her parent's house and babysit Dancy for an evening. Don't worry, she's a good kid and her folks are upstanding pillars of the community and all that. I'll call her and set it up."

Before I could grill her on the babysitter's qualifications, she headed to the kitchen.

"C'mon," she said. "You can tell me what's happening in the exciting world of Perseverance law enforcement while I reheat some tater tot casserole for you."

I settled into a chair at the kitchen table with Dancy on my lap and let her play with my cell phone until Gracie handed me a plate of steaming casserole. Then she got a couple of Saddle Bronc Brown Ales from the fridge and slid one across the table to me.

In between bites and swigs, I regaled her with my adventures in the Brightwater community, leaving out the confidential police bits and embellishing other parts to make her laugh.

"Well, I've heard some mighty weird things about the goings-on in Brightwater Canyon," she said with a belch when I finished.

"Oh yeah, like what?"

"Well, for one, the folks who lived there before Robert Sandoval came to Edgemont County didn't like when he moved in and started throwing his weight around."

I nodded in agreement. "Based on my first impression, Sandoval seems like a pretentious ass."

"Some say he used his influence to stack the board of the Brightwater Canyon Homeowner Association. Then the board became aggressive with residents and started scaring off buyers. Ambitious locals used to dream of affording a ranchette in the canyon, but nobody fancies living there now."

"What kind of stuff does the board do?"

"They spy on owners and other shit," she said, warming to the topic. "Once they sued a guy for owning llamas because the board didn't approve of them beforehand, claiming the llamas were an exotic species or something. They also harass people who want to build on their own property.

"One guy had a contract in Brightwater Canyon for a custom barn with a heated tackle room. He completed two-thirds of the framing before the Association got a restraining order against the homeowner because the building site was ten feet south of the spot the board approved. The lawsuit dragged on for years until the disgusted owner sold the property for less than it was worth and moved back to Missouri."

Dancy was asleep in my arms and I got up from the table, careful not to wake her.

Gracie followed me down the hall into Dancy's bedroom. "When folks get fed up and try to sell, the Association scares off prospective buyers and then makes a lowball offer to the owners."

After I put Dancy in her crib, I shoed Gracie out and closed the door. "Enough talk about homeowner associations. Let's watch a couple of episodes of *Grey's Anatomy*."

"I'm game if you are, but don't you work in the morning?"

"Yes, but Vanderberg offered to finish the paperwork for the county, so I'm going to get in a morning workout before I slide behind the wheel of my trusty Crown Vic and cruise Main Street like a boss."

"Livin' the dream," said Gracie, grabbing the television remote control and throwing herself on the sofa.

Evelyn Randall hovered inches from my grasp at the top of a winding staircase. Her eyes were milky, and her mouth sagged open to reveal a black, swollen tongue. For a brief instant, her icy hands clutched mine, but she let go and tumbled backwards in a shower of amethyst iris blossoms.

I awoke with a start, my heart pounding.

Back in San Diego, sometimes I would wake up in a cold sweat, unable to breathe, and my husband Jason would take me in his arms and hold me, but that was a long time ago.

I stared at the floral-patterned rectangle on the wall made by the moonlight shining through the lace curtains.

The stem near Evelyn Randall's hand was a wild iris, which was a delicate flower and withered quickly without water. When I was young, my grandmother would put them in a cut-glass vase as soon as I came home with a handful of them. I imagined Evelyn was looking for her own vase when she died.

After several deep breaths, I rolled over and fell back to sleep. This time it was Jason who was standing at the top of the staircase and I reached for him, but he shoved me away and I fell, swallowed up by the darkness below.

TWO

I eased the cruiser into a parking spot outside the Perseverance Cafe and shifted into park, regarding the heavy-set woman standing on the sidewalk near the entrance. With her shiny ebony hair twisted into a tight knot at the nape and her black eyes, I guessed she was a Northern Arapaho from the Wind River Reservation.

Although she kept her head down, I recognized her as the police department's cleaning lady. I couldn't remember her name. Every few seconds, she raised her eyes to scan the street, but when I lifted my hand in greeting, she looked away.

A few minutes later, a white sedan with a pink Perfect Touch Cleaning and Maid Service decal on the side stopped at the curb near the cafe and the heavy-set woman got in.

"Wyn?" Connie's voice came over the radio.

"Hi Connie, what's up?"

"Olivia DeWitt has called three times in the last hour."

"Olivia DeWitt?"

"She's Evelyn Randall's niece, and she wants to talk to you. I planned to wait until you came back, but she isn't giving up."

"Okay, I'll head back," I said. "By the way, you know the suspicious

Native American woman Mrs. Cox complained was loitering outside her cafe? It was the police department's cleaning lady, what's-her-name."

"You mean Josefina?"

"Yes, Josefina. It looks like she was waiting for her ride. She's gone now, but tell Mrs. Cox not to be such a xenophobe."

"Sure. I'll do that," she said, but we both knew she wouldn't.

"How did Ms. DeWitt get my number?"

Connie's brows knitted in thought. "Vanderberg called one of his friends in New York this morning to do the death notification, but I doubt he mentioned you by name. She could have gotten it from Betty at the sheriff's office."

"Okay. Well, I guess I'll find out what she wants." I dialed the number on the yellow sticky note and waited.

"Hello?"

"Ms. DeWitt? This is Officer Wyn Price with the Perseverance Police Department. I'm returning your call."

"Officer Price. I appreciate you calling me back."

"No problem, ma'am. I am sorry for your loss." I meant it, but I always found it difficult to speak with the bereaved without sounding wooden.

"Did you know my aunt?"

The image of Evelyn Randall from my dream the night before popped into my head unbidden. "No, I didn't know her."

She *tsked* in irritation. "Well, I am in shock. I simply cannot believe she dropped dead of a heart attack. Aunt Evelyn was in excellent health. We joked she would outlive me, and the last time I spoke with her—last week, I believe it was—she said she was making a daily trek down the hiking trail behind her house to see the wildflowers blooming."

I thought about the withered iris near Evelyn Randall's outstretched hand, but remained silent.

"The officer who came to my house said the coroner will send my aunt's body to a local mortuary," she said. "Do you know which one?"

"Perseverance has but one, Allman Funeral Home, but the coroner will contact you as soon as they transfer your aunt's body. Unless someone claims the body within five days, the coroner's office will arrange for burial at the county's expense. Did your aunt have any children or siblings?"

"No, I'm her sole living relative and I will pay for the funeral. Will there be an autopsy?"

"That is the coroner's decision, Ms. DeWitt."

"My Aunt Evelyn was as healthy as a horse, you know, and tough. She could still stand up to jerks who tried to intimidate her...."

She trailed off for a moment. When she continued, her words were clipped. "I want to know why my aunt died, Officer. It's within my rights to demand an autopsy."

"That is correct, Ms. Dewitt. I can inform the coroner that Mrs. Randall's next of kin is requesting an autopsy." The instant I spoke the words, I wished I could suck them back in like a string of spaghetti. Gleason already made it clear Evelyn Randall's death was not my concern.

"Thank you, Officer Price. Please let me know what you need from me in order to move forward."

"Yes, Ma'am, I'll call the coroner's office right away." I hung up the phone with a groan of consternation.

"You crammed your foot in your mouth that time," Connie said, not looking up from her romance novel.

I sighed and dialed Gleason's number.

After five rings, a woman answered. "Coroner's Office." Her tone was peevish.

"I'm Officer Wyn Price from the Perseverance Police Department. Is Mr. Gleason in?"

"He's in." She clamped a hand over the mouthpiece, but I could still hear her yelling in the background. "Ricky! Ricky! It's business. Officer Price or somesuch."

She came back on the phone. "He's comin'."

I waited.

"Y'ello." Gleason sounded like he just woke up, though it was already past ten o'clock in the morning.

"Uh, this is Officer Price. We met yesterday at the Randall residence out in Brightwater Canyon."

"Yeah, yeah, what do you want?"

"I received a call from Evelyn Randall's next of kin, Olivia DeWitt. Ms. DeWitt is inquiring about an autopsy."

"Oh, for chrissakes, what the hell for? Like I said yesterday, she had a heart attack or a stroke. She was an old lady. What's an autopsy going to tell us we don't already know? No point in wasting the county's money." He lapsed into a fit of coughing.

I said nothing. If the coroner decided an autopsy wasn't necessary, it was his prerogative, but next of kin could request an autopsy and he knew it.

He finished hacking up a lung and came back on the line. "Where did she get that idea, anyhow? Was it your idea to ask for an autopsy?"

"No. Ms. DeWitt sounded quite confident of her rights, with no advice from me."

I wouldn't admit that I didn't attempt to talk her out of it. Something about Evelyn Randall's frail, plaintive hand reaching for the iris blossom bothered me. If she were my aunt, I would feel responsible for her, too.

He grunted. "Anyway, it's too late. We already sent the body over to Allman Funeral Home."

I raised an eyebrow. Gleason's Suburban was at Smokey's Tavern when I came back into town last night and I would bet a brick of gold Evelyn Randall's body was still in the back of it. The lazy slob had a raging hangover and didn't possess the fortitude to think about autopsy arrangements.

"Your call," I said, "but I don't think Ms. DeWitt is going to give up. She sounded pretty darn adamant—and well-informed, if you know what I mean. I doubt she will let this go without making a fuss."

"All right, all right. I'll send over the paperwork, get her to sign it and lemme see what I can do, okay?"

"Thanks." I said with a touch of sarcasm.

Why couldn't he get his own paperwork signed? What was I, his secretary?

I hung up and redialed Olivia DeWitt's number.

My navy and white Ford Crown Victoria police cruiser, or Crown Vic for short, had seen better days. The stained front bench seat sagged like a broken-down sofa, and it drove like a swaying barge, but the stereo was outstanding, and it could fly like a demon when I asked it to, which wasn't very often to my regret.

I didn't mind being back on patrol duty, except it gave me too much time to ponder the sad series of events that landed me in the boondocks of western Wyoming.

My husband Jason left me before our daughter Dancy was born and soon afterwards, I parted ways with the San Diego police force, but that was an ocean of heartache ago, and now here I was in Perseverance living the Mayberry life and driving Andy Griffith's car.

At the end of Main Street, I took a right and meandered through Perseverance's largest campground on the banks of the Wind River. It was still early summer, but I noted a couple of RVs and fifth wheels that weren't there a few days ago.

Tourist season was coming, and the locals claimed the population of Perseverance would double in size when city folks flocked to the nearby campgrounds and dude ranches. More visitors increased the probability that greenhorns might rub up against the pricklier locals, resulting in misunderstandings requiring police intervention, and that would interfere with my daily routine of endlessly cruising around in circles and listening to Eminem.

According to the bombastic spiel Mayor Dippert gave me when I took this job, the scenic little hamlet of Perseverance was on the verge of extinction twenty years ago, but the city council leveraged its reputation as an authentic western locale into a vacation destination.

Some people who came here on holiday stayed, lured in by the beautiful views, low housing costs, negligible taxes and low crime. The resulting population boomlet meant the town needed more cops, and that was how I ended up here.

I returned to the police station and walked the three blocks to downtown. My destination was the Barrelman Art Gallery next to the Perseverance Cafe, but before I reached the gallery, Robert Sandoval and two men came out of the cafe, deep in conversation.

"And here is one of Perseverance's finest," Sandoval said when he caught sight of me, as if I were a stage actor entering on cue.

I smiled and bobbed my head while sizing up his companions. The younger one could have been a model for J Crew, while the other, with his silver hair and patrician features, was straight off Wall Street. Judging by their expensive business suits and impeccable grooming, I reckoned they weren't from Wyoming.

"We take the safety of our citizens and visitors seriously," Sandoval said to his associates. "Our local law enforcement officers serve the public with commitment and enthusiasm. Yesterday, Officer Price here was in Brightwater Canyon, assisting one of our elderly residents at the behest of the Edgemont County Sheriff's Office."

The silver-haired man turned his head to murmur in his companion's ear, then he chuckled. Something about the timbre of his laughter made my hackles rise.

"I beg your pardon?" Sandoval said, keen to be in on the joke.

The man smirked and said in a deep Texas drawl, "I was wondering if you will use the dollars coming in from development to hire full-sized officers."

I bit my tongue at the taunt and shot him an insincere grin.

Sandoval stared at the man, attempting to gauge the relevance of his remark. After a few moments of uncomfortable silence passed, he resumed his oration on the merits of Perseverance, leading his guests down the sidewalk to the courthouse.

As they moved past me, the younger man made eye contact and mouthed the word, "Sorry." He had striking hazel eyes and smelled like money.

I stepped into the Barrelman Art Gallery.

The owner, Buddy Dunwoody, was leaning on the counter and chewing a toothpick. "Who do you figure those two carpetbaggers are parading around with Robert Sandoval?"

"I don't know them," I said.

"My guess is he's trying to sell them property," he said. "That's all we need, more outsiders buying up all our rangeland. Pretty soon, the federal government and out-of-state investors will own this entire state. There ought to be a law against it if you ask me."

"Mm," I said, hoping to avoid a prolonged discussion with Buddy, who was a bit eccentric.

He pointed at me with the toothpick. "When I was a working man, cowboys trusted me to be the human shield between them and two thousand pounds of testosterone-fueled bovine. Laws to protect the west should be like that."

"Like a rodeo clown?"

"Yup."

An acclaimed Western artist, Buddy was once a professional bull-fighter and rodeo clown. The name of his studio, the Barrelman Art Gallery, was a nod to the clowns known as barrelmen who distracted the bull with comedic antics after a cowboy dismounted—or was bucked him off. It was a dangerous profession, and some folks whispered he was kicked in the head by one too many bulls.

I got down to the real reason for my visit. "Buddy, summer season is almost here. If you have an alarm system or security cameras, I suggest you make sure they are in working order within the next couple of weeks."

He harrumphed and extracted a twelve-gauge pump-action shotgun from underneath the counter, holding it up to show me. "I got all the security I need right here."

If he wanted to protect his property with a firearm, it was his constitutional right, as long as he didn't hurt any innocent folks.

Besides, I suspected he was trying to wind me up. I grew up in a small town and I understood the role of a town cop. Ninety percent of my job was to be seen so the good folks of Perseverance could smile and greet their friendly law enforcement officer as I strolled down Main Street—the thin blue line between them and crime. Not that any serious crime to speak of transpired in that sluggish burg.

"Okay, Buddy. Call me if you have questions—"

"—you're only a phone call away." He waved me off with a grin.

I left the gallery and walked a block and a half down the street to Trujillo's Hardware.

Teresa Trujillo was with a customer, but she smiled when she saw me come in. "Hello Officer Price. I'll be right with you."

"Hi Teresa. No hurry," I said, wandering over to the paint section.

Dancy's room needed to be repainted, and a color called Wild Iris caught my eye.

Teresa peered over my shoulder. "Can I help you find some paint, officer?"

"Another time," I said. "I stopped by to say hello and remind you to check your security system before summer."

"That's Alex's department, but I will remind him."

"Okay, well, if you need anything, I'm a phone call away."

If Teresa opened the front door of her hardware store and yodeled, the entire police department would hear her since the station was across the street. However, I said this to all the downtown merchants.

Teresa folded her arms and gave me a sidelong look. "I heard Mrs. Randall died."

The remark caught me off guard. "Uh, yes, did you know her?"

"No, not personally. She stopped in last week to purchase binoculars and became angry when we didn't have any. Those rich canyon people think Perseverance shopkeepers should cater to their every whim. What happened? Did she drop dead of old age?"

I made a show of consulting my watch. "Oh, my goodness, would you look at the time? I better get back. Don't forget to tell Alex to run a check on your security system."

As I exited Trujillo's Hardware and crossed the street to the police station, my cell phone buzzed with an incoming email notification. It was the signed autopsy request form from Olivia DeWitt. With a few taps, I forwarded it to Gleason.

THREE

I woke up feeling on edge. It could have been trepidation about the staff meeting that night, or maybe it was because I hadn't heard from Gleason about Evelyn Randall's autopsy.

Either way, a workout would help me work off some of the stress, so I hoisted myself out of bed, pulled on my old San Diego PD sweats, and shuffled out to the backyard to punch something.

Before I discovered kickboxing, I was a runner. Then a fellow officer on the San Diego force suggested I take up the sport to build upper body strength. The exhilaration of landing a blow to a solid object with my fist or foot hooked me, and I never looked back. The first non-essential item I purchased after arriving in Perseverance was a secondhand kickboxing bag on Craig's List. As soon as I got home, I drew Jason's face on it with a black marker.

It wasn't as satisfying as sparring with human opponents, but regular sessions kept me in respectable shape and "Jason" put up a passable resistance.

I was forty-five minutes into my workout when Dancy woke up, so I gave the bag one last jab-cross-uppercut combination and went inside.

Most mornings, my toddler daughter ate nothing for breakfast except

Goldfish crackers, fruit snacks, and bananas, but that didn't stop her from demanding things we both knew she didn't want and dissolving into a nuclear meltdown if I didn't comply. As a grand finale, she pulverized the uneaten food and smeared it into every nook and cranny of her highchair and cranial orifices. *Parents* magazine assured me this was a passing phase.

Dancy had my fine blonde hair and wide blue eyes, but the shape of her lips and mischievous personality—the defiance and devilish cackle when she was in trouble, for example—were pure Jason. How she mimicked the father she had never known was a mystery to me. Maybe there was truth to that cellular genetic memory gobbledygook.

"C'mon, sprout, it's off to daycare for you," I said, making a last swipe at her face before hauling her out of the highchair and heading out the door.

Connie was reading her romance novel at her desk when I arrived at the station a few minutes before nine o'clock. "Good morning, Wyn."

"Did you go home, or have you been sitting there reading trash all night?" I said on my way to the breakroom to put my lunch in the refrigerator.

Connie let out a peel of laughter. She had the sort of infectious laugh that made people who heard it want in on the joke. She had been a third grade teacher at Perseverance Elementary for twenty years before Alan Sloan, the chief of police prior to Vanderberg, discovered her extraordinary ability to multitask and offered her a job with the police department. Indefatigable and organized, she had been the station's dispatcher, office manager and anchor for the last fourteen years.

"It's been slow," she said, following me into the breakroom, "and I've got nothing to do except read since the chief is always out of the office. I reorganized all the files and cleaned out the cupboards in the breakroom. I even went through Justin's desk."

We both shuddered. Part-time police officer Justin Stokes wouldn't recognize a trash can if you put it over his head. The cleaning woman took the brunt of it, but once I was standing nearby when he opened the bottom drawer of his desk, and it looked like he was growing penicillin cultures down there, except I knew Justin wasn't that smart.

"At this rate, you'll finish that smutty book by noon," I said.

Two incoming lines lit up, and Connie shot me an accusing look.

I pretended to sympathize and hastened to my desk.

After she picked up the first call, she said, "Wyn, I've got Olivia DeWitt on the line. She says she has information for you."

"Information for me?"

Connie bobbed her head. "That's what she said. I can take a message and tell her you'll call her back."

"No, put her through." I took a gulp of coffee and lifted the receiver. "Hello Ms. DeWitt, this is Officer Price."

She launched into her narrative without preamble. "I received a call late last night, officer. I considered not answering it, but I couldn't resist the opportunity to vent my anger at the idiot on the other end. It was Robert Sandoval, who insisted he was a friend of my late aunt—which I knew to be a lie—but I was curious about his intentions and allowed him to continue.

"In short, he wanted to take my aunt's property in Brightwater Canyon 'off my hands'. Those were his words, as if it were a snake-infested bog in Mississippi. He offered me $400,000—a third of what it's worth—and acted as if he were doing me a favor, the dolt. As soon as I declined to consider his insulting offer, he attempted to intimidate me."

"What did Mr. Sandoval say?"

"He called me 'Little Lady' and said he was sorry we couldn't come to a cordial agreement and that I wouldn't get a better offer. He said he hated to see me get a raw deal."

"Did he elaborate?"

She sniffed. "By that time, I had reached the limits of my patience. I informed him I wasn't interested and not to call me again since he did not have the money to make an honest offer. Then I hung up on him."

"Did he say anything else, or threaten you in any specific way?"

"No. That was the extent of our conversation."

"Based on the information you have given me, Ms. DeWitt, a crime has not occurred. Mr. Sandoval may have been obnoxious and insulting, but that isn't illegal."

"I realize that, but his patronizing tone irked me and I thought you should know. My aunt said he was a bully and now I can see why," she said with exasperation. "Anyway, I was expecting you might have some information for me about the autopsy, officer."

"I forwarded your autopsy request to the county coroner as soon as I received it. He'll call you with the results."

"Thank you, Officer Price, and please, call me Olivia."

"Of course, Olivia, and if I hear anything, I will let you know. Good-bye." I replaced the receiver and raised a dubious eyebrow in Connie's direction.

"Speaking of the Coroner," she said, "Gleason called. Again. He wants you to get over to the morgue ASAP."

"Me? Did he say why?"

"No, but he called twice before you got here, asking for Chief Vanderberg. He called again while you were on the phone with Olivia DeWitt. I advised him there was no one else here except you and he decided he would talk to you instead. He didn't say why."

"Okay, let me finish this and I'll head over there." I took another gulp of coffee. It was already cold. I tilted my head at the chief's office. "Where is Chief Vanderberg?"

"He's on sheriff's business in Fort Washakie."

Fort Washakie was on the Wind River Indian Reservation. American Indian tribes lost the right to prosecute non-Indians for crimes on the reservations in 1978, which meant any time a non-Indian got into trouble on the reservation, the tribal police called in the Edgemont County Sheriff to handle the matter.

I said, "I bet the chief will be glad once the forestry division contains the fire at Union Pass and he can turn the sheriff's department affairs back over to Deputy Bartel, don't you?"

Connie looked at me in surprise. "You didn't hear? Some looky-loo ran a fire barricade and when Clif tried to stop him, the idiot dragged him a few yards before he halted."

"Is Deputy Bartel all right?"

"I spoke to his wife this morning. She said his ankle was broken, and he suffered several nasty scrapes and bruises, but with some rest, he'll be fine."

I scrunched my nose. "So much for Vanderberg getting relief from Bartel. Maybe they should raise our pay and combine the sheriff's office and the police department."

"Now Wyn," Connie said, chuckling, "you know there's a snowball's chance in hell of that happening."

The coroner lived in a neglected house in the nicest neighborhood in Perseverance, which wasn't saying a lot. Branches from the dying elm trees littered the overgrown lawn and faded orange lounge chairs huddled together for comfort on the front porch.

A plywood sign with "Morgue" hand-printed on it in red marker was nailed to the weathered front door, and an arrow pointed to the left.

The furnishings of the morgue's front office comprised a small desk, two cracked green leatherette chairs, and a wall rack with stuffed with old issues of *People* magazine. It smelled of Pine-Sol and Lemon Pledge.

The door behind the desk was cracked open, revealing a dark corridor. I ventured through it. "Gleason?"

"Yeah," Gleason's voice came from an open door farther down the corridor. "We're back here."

Gleason and an elderly gentleman I didn't know waited in a well-lit examination room. They were both wearing pale green scrubs, and a sheet-covered body lay on a stainless steel examination table in the center of the room.

"Glad you could join us, Officer," Gleason said with a hint of annoyance. "I tried to contact Chief Vanderberg, but it would seem he is otherwise engaged."

"Yes. Sorry," I said.

Gleason pointed to the older gentleman. "This is Doc Appleton. Before he retired, he owned a pathology practice in Jackson. He's going to be our medical examiner today."

The smiling doctor raised a rubber-gloved hand and waved, as if we were at a cocktail party for University of Wyoming alumni.

"You can stand there." Gleason directed me to a spot across the examination table from the doctor and shoved a surgical gown and plastic face shield into my arms. It was then I realized I was attending the autopsy.

"Whenever you're ready, Officer Price, we can begin," Gleason said, with a hint of impatience.

I hastily donned the gown and face shield.

When he was satisfied I was protected, he nodded to the doctor. "Okay. Let's get on with it."

Doc punched a button on the voice recorder. "Subject is a well-nourished white female. Seventy-five years old, sixty-three inches tall, and weighing approximately one hundred and ten pounds at death. Generalized rigor mortis is present, but waning. Livor mortis is anterior and fixed. The body is cool to the touch. There is exterior bruising to the body and extensive skeletal fractures, of the skull in particular, which may have occurred ante or postmortem and are consistent with a body tumbling down a stairway."

Gleason sniffed, refusing to meet my gaze.

Doc Appleton pressed the scalpel into the white, wrinkled skin and it parted like bread dough. For an octogenarian, his hands were remarkably steady.

Piece by piece, the doctor disassembled Evelyn Randall. At first, he did so with violence, cutting away her ribcage with an implement resembling pruning shears, then removing her internal organs with tender care. After each extraction, he examined the organ tissue and commented on it for the benefit of his observers and the voice recorder.

During our phone conversation, Olivia DeWitt insisted her aunt was in exceptional health for a woman of her age, and disregarding the injuries sustained in the fall, the condition of her internal organs supported that claim. The doctor observed that her heart muscle showed no signs of a cardiomyopathy, which elicited a grunt from Gleason.

Doc emptied the stomach contents into a steel pan and poked around. "Not much to see here. It had been a while since she had eaten."

"I found a plate with a leftover tuna salad sandwich and pickle on it in the kitchen," I said.

"Well, if that was her last meal, at least four hours passed before she died. Now let's look inside her cranium."

He removed the top of her skull and cut away the dura, then lifted Evelyn Randall's brain out of the cranial cavity and placed it on a scale. "1078 grams. Other than the expected trauma from the fall, the brain appears normal."

Slicing off a piece of the gray gelatinous blob, he laid it on a glass slide and analyzed it under a microscope. "I don't find evidence of infarction of the brain tissue, which leads me to conclude she did not have a stroke." He turned back to the body. "Now, on to the neck, which exhibits significant exterior bruising. This is not abnormal in a fall, but I wouldn't consider it commonplace. Let's look at the internal tissues."

Doc showed signs of tiring, but then his movements became rapid and precise. "Look—see the bloody strap muscles? There is significant intramuscular and subcutaneous hemorrhaging—"

He dug his fingers under the tissues of the neck, feeling for something. "—ah! See this?"

I bent forward. "Fractured hyoid?"

"Yes. The larynx has also been fractured." He made incisions with a knife, grabbed the entire throat apparatus, and pulled it out of the body. Then he stuck his fingers into the neck cavity, feeling for something. "The neck is not broken."

He lifted one of the dead woman's eyelids and looked at her eyeball with a magnifying glass. "It is as I suspected, look."

I stepped closer to observe the pinpricks of blood on the whites of her eyes. "Petechiae. Here, too, Doc." I pointed out what looked like a rash on her cheeks.

"The larynx and hyoid bone are fractured," he said, "but the subject's neck is not broken. Hemorrhaging is present in the tissues of the neck, which also displays unusual exterior bruising. Petechial hemorrhaging is evident—"

I interrupted him. "—all of which suggest a vice-like pressure caused these injuries rather than the blunt force trauma of a fall."

Doc Appleton nodded in agreement, his face grim.

Gleason grumbled under his breath.

The doctor gave him a sideways glance. "I began this autopsy with the hypothesis that the subject suffered a stroke or heart attack, but the healthy brain and heart tissues disqualify a natural health event. Injuries to the brain sustained in a fall could have caused death if it weren't for the fractured hyoid and damage to the neck tissues—which occurred ante-mortem. This leads me to believe the subject wasn't killed in the course of a fall and that the skeletal fractures and bruising on the trunk and extremities were instead sustained postmortem."

Face like a thundercloud, Gleason crossed his arms over his considerable gut. "In plain English, Doc."

"Bruising and fractures from a fall have a particular pattern. We call them blunt force trauma. But neck bones broken during strangulation have their own unique pattern." Doc made a vice-like squeezing motion with his right arm. "Her throat injuries signify human force, and since no ligature marks are present, I conclude the manner of death was manual strangulation."

I flipped up my face shield. "You are saying someone murdered Evelyn Randall?"

Doc Appleton's expression was grave. "Yes, that is my conclusion. It will take a couple of weeks to issue the final report, but the preliminary findings aren't apt to change."

Gleason made a choking sound.

I felt lightheaded, and it wasn't from the smell of blood and formaldehyde. "Okay. Mrs. Randall was upstairs. Her attacker grabbed her—" I wrapped the neck of an imaginary victim in the crook of my right arm.

"—and she struggled to pry his arm away." Doc lifted one of the dead woman's hands. "I swabbed her for DNA, but found no debris under her nails. However, I noticed several fingernails were torn off on both hands."

I thought for a moment. "She tried to break the hold." I mimed trying to claw an arm away from my neck. "Then her attacker let go and threw her—or she fell—down the stairs."

Doc bobbed his head. "That sequence of events would be consistent with the physical facts. No doubt she lost consciousness within seven to fifteen seconds if the grasp was tight enough. With constant pressure, she would have died within five minutes."

"What about the time of death?"

"Difficult to say with precision." He clasped his hands together. "Given the level of decomposition, I would say she was dead over twenty-four hours when you found her."

"So, Saturday or Sunday?"

"Mm. Didn't you say there was a leftover sandwich at the scene? It was her lunch, then. She was an elderly woman, so if we account for a slower metabolism, I will venture to say she died late Saturday afternoon or early evening."

"Thanks, Doc." I stripped off the paper gown and handed it to Gleason. "Are you notifying next of kin?"

He glared at me.

I rushed out of the morgue, pushing aside Josefina who was struggling through the door with a bucket of cleaning supplies in her arms.

"Excuse me," I said without looking back.

On the way back to the police station, I called Vanderberg's cell, but it went straight to voicemail, so I left a message urging him to call me back right away.

Justin and Connie were playing cribbage at Connie's desk when I burst into the station, out of breath.

"The chief still isn't back?" I said.

Connie looked up. "I haven't heard from him since this morning. You look a little pale, Wyn. Are you okay?"

"Yes. No—I need to speak to the chief. It's important."

They both regarded me with anticipation, but I wasn't ready to spill the details until I talked to Vanderberg.

Justin returned to the game, counting his crib and pegging out.

Connie glared at him. "Well, the chief will be at the Staff Meeting tonight, Wyn. Oh, and he wanted me to remind you that your attendance is mandatory."

"Yes, he made that pretty clear," I said. "But it's almost five o'clock, so I'm going to run home and make dinner before the sitter arrives. I'll see you at the meeting."

I had little appetite after the autopsy, but I needed to get something in my stomach before I added alcohol.

"Mm-hmm," Connie said, dealing the next hand.

•   •   •

Vanderberg wasn't at the Spur when I arrived, so I joined Connie and Justin at a table near the bar.

On a typical Wednesday during the off-season, the crowd was quiet and well-behaved, but judging by the decibel level, this was not an ordinary Wednesday.

"There you are," Connie said with her usual enthusiasm. "I told Justin you would be here."

Justin drained his glass and muttered a greeting.

In his late twenties or early thirties, Justin Stokes was pudgy with a thick mop of black hair. Before Vanderberg hired him two years ago as a part-time officer, he was the assistant manager at the QwikMart. Gracie swore Justin still lived in his parent's basement and played video games for entertainment, which explained why he was inept in social situations until he had a few beers under his belt and his humor tended towards jokes from junior high school.

Gracie, in tight jeans with her voluminous hair loose around her shoulders, was pretending to play darts in the raucous back room of the bar, but in truth she was holding court with a mob of male bar patrons, one of whom was the younger man I saw with Sandoval the day before. Despite the fact that he was wearing boots and Wranglers, he stood out from the resident hayseeds like Ryan Gosling at a barn dance.

The jukebox boomed above the din, and I fidgeted with my coaster, praying that Cassidy, the gawky teenager Gracie found to babysit Dancy, was trustworthy.

When the chief showed up an hour later, I attempted to get his attention without causing too much of a fuss, but Justin buttonholed him the moment he sat down at the table and prattled into his ear while the chief scanned the crowd and feigned interest.

Connie was at the jukebox, fixing to play "Friends in Low Places" again so everyone could sing along.

Up at the bar, Dylan Webster caught my eye and winked, raising his beer in a silent toast. I had a headache the size of Montana from the formaldehyde that I inhaled at the morgue, but I flashed him a smile and looked away before he read anything into it.

A few barstools away from Dylan, Buddy Dunwoody was nursing a bottle of Budweiser. It was unusual to see him in the Silver Spur on a weeknight, and he didn't appear to be enjoying himself.

When Justin realized Vanderberg wasn't listening to a word he said, turned to me. "What's the story about this Brightwater Canyon death? It was Evelyn Randall you found, right Wyn?"

Disconcerted by the shift in conversation, I stuttered. "Um. Yeah. Evelyn Randall. Uh, I found her body a couple of days ago."

Justin said, "There's something about the whole Brightwater Canyon community that doesn't smell right. What do you think, chief?"

Vanderberg didn't seem to hear him. He was trying to catch the waitress's eye to order another round of drinks for the table.

I ignored Justin and leaned forward. "Chief, I need to speak with you about something. Do you have a minute? It's pretty important. We could go outside where it's not so noisy—"

"What can I get you folks?" The red-haired waitress had to raise her voice to be heard above the din of the bar.

The chief instructed her to bring another round to the police department table with a circular motion of his arm and then pointed to the bar. "And supply those fine gentlemen with another round and put it on my tab."

Once the waitress departed, I raised my hand, hoping to lure Vanderberg into a conversation, but he was looking past me towards the bar, where two middle-aged men in cowboy hats nodded in his direction. He took a gulp of his Diet Coke and got up to speak with them.

Connie completed her jukebox mission and plopped down next to me. "Are we talking about the Randall case?"

I shook my head. "No—"

Justin cut in. "I'm willing to bet Robert Sandoval had something to do with it. It's like that time a year ago when we tracked a meth operator to the territory west of Brightwater Canyon. We swore Sandoval was behind it, but he and his greasy cronies stonewalled us every chance they got. They didn't refuse to cooperate outright, but they were evasive, which frustrated our investigation. Then the sheriff's office poked their noses into it. You can guess what happened after that."

"Nothing," Connie said, engrossed by the story, though she already knew how it ended.

I opened my mouth to put an end to the discussion, but Justin talked over me, his tone rising.

"You're damn right nothing." He puffed out his chest in indignation.

Connie nodded at me with a raised eyebrow. "The scuttlebutt was that the sheriff was on Sandoval's payroll."

I glanced around, praying no one noticed the indiscretion of the exchange.

Everyone knew about the rampant corruption of the sheriff's office under Sheriff Buck Lanier, but there were some townsfolk, many of whom were Silver Spur regulars, who considered his exploits legendary, almost worthy of admiration. When he crashed his Tahoe, killing himself and two unidentified females, he had a blood-alcohol content over twice the legal limit, which added to his outlaw cachet.

Justin looked morose. "Next thing you know, the Wyoming Division of Criminal Investigation was involved. And then poof—it all went away. It's obvious Sandoval bought the DCI off. He has the money."

I made a face. "That's hard to believe. Do you think it's plausible the DCI is taking illicit money from Sandoval?"

"Do you know who Robert Sandoval is?" Justin stabbed a finger on the table.

I wanted to ignore him, but against my better judgment, his intensity aroused my interest. "Fine. I'll bite. Who is Robert Sandoval?"

Keen to be part of the conversation, Connie said, "He was the CEO of Blackhammer, wasn't he? That big contractor out of Denver. Isn't that right, chief?"

Vanderberg was back, but he wasn't listening because a couple of bar patrons had stopped by the table to chat and shake his hand. I stared at him, sensing something was afoot but not able to put my finger on it.

Justin took up the tale again. "Blackhammer got into some kind of hot water, and they cut him loose. Anyway, he ended up here, a big swinging-dick in a little country town. That was fifteen years ago. The word is he runs the county, and he sure as hell runs Brightwater Canyon."

"You mean the homeowner association?" I said. "I hear they have quite a reputation. Is he the chairman of the association board?"

Justin cackled. "Oh, hell no. Sandoval would never stoop to that.

He's the guy behind the curtain pulling the strings." He raised his hands and parodied the actions of a puppeteer.

Abruptly, Vanderberg stood up from the table, making a show of straightening his uniform before striding to the center of the saloon. A smattering of applause burst forth as he held up his hands, smiling like P. T. Barnum opening the circus. Then someone made a shushing noise and the crowd, wondering why their festivities were interrupted, grew quiet.

"I suppose you're all wondering why I called you into my office today," Vanderberg said, a smile splitting his face.

A couple of people guffawed.

"It's terrific to see so many familiar faces down here tonight. And that's what makes Perseverance and Edgemont County so special, the people. Those of us who live here care about each other and the collective concerns of the community—namely tourism, education, job opportunities, responsible development, infrastructure, cross-jurisdictional cooperation, and public safety." The chief ticked the points off on his fingers.

Except for two drunks near the dart board arguing over the proper way to quaff a Jägerbomb, the assembled crowd listened with rapt attention.

"But while the Edgemont County Commissioners, Mayor Dippert, and the Perseverance City Council have been working shoulder to shoulder with the community to address these issues, there is one critical piece of the puzzle missing. And we all know what that is."

A murmur coursed through the crowd and Vanderberg let the thought marinate before continuing.

"The Edgemont County Sheriff's Office is an embarrassment. You don't need me to tell you that. Everybody here knows it. Years of corrupt management, disregard of the law, and outdated processes have resulted in the egregious waste of your taxpayer dollars and exposed our close-knit community to drugs and crime."

This prompted boos from the crowd in agreement.

"This county deserves a sheriff's office that stands on a solid foundation of honesty and professionalism. We must put an end to corruption and the waste of tax dollars. Edgemont County needs an experienced law enforcement officer at the helm who has the skills and strength to enforce these changes.

"That is why tonight I am throwing my hat in the ring to be the next sheriff of Edgemont County." He pulled his navy hat out of his back pocket and tossed it into the air for dramatic effect.

The saloon erupted in foot-stomping and whistles, but Vanderberg wasn't quite finished.

"For five years, it has been my absolute pleasure to serve as the Perseverance Chief of Police. Since the unfortunate passing of our last sheriff, I have also served as the de facto law enforcement official for Edgemont County, so most of you know me well. You know my work ethic. I was a captain in the Chicago metropolitan police force before joining the Perseverance Police Department. In Chicago, I spent most of my time locking up thieves, murderers, and rapists.

"When elected sheriff, I will hire qualified law enforcement officers and create a budget-conscious and responsive department with the goal of improving public safety throughout Edgemont County and keeping your families and property safe. Now you honorable citizens want to get back to socializing and drinking—"

Someone said, "Yeah!"

"—and I won't bore you with the full list of my credentials and commendations, but I am asking for your vote in November. Thank you for coming to the Silver Spur tonight to support me."

More cheers and hand clapping followed. A crowd of well-wishers gathered around Vanderberg, pumping his hand and slapping him on the back.

I rounded on Justin and Connie. "Did either of you know about this?"

Justin ignored the question, getting up to join the cluster of people congregating around the chief.

With a contrite air, Connie spread her hands. "I guessed something momentous was brewing with his frequent travel to golf tournaments and whatnot, but I didn't know his specific aim until last Monday. He asked me to keep it under wraps until he made the announcement here tonight."

The crowd was already beginning to thin out. Buddy Dunwoody

drained his beer and slipped out the door without looking in the chief's direction. It was then I noticed Robert Sandoval standing near the exit.

Teresa Trujillo and Barb Mitchell, the owner of the Van Gogh Coffee Shoppe, approached our table and plopped down on the chairs vacated by Vanderberg and Justin.

When I looked up again, Sandoval was gone, and I searched for him in the crowd, but he was nowhere to be found.

Barb gestured to the chief with her can of rosé wine. "Chief Vanderberg is gonna be pretty busy from now until November."

Teresa and Connie clucked in agreement.

"What does this mean for you guys, Connie? Can the police department function with the chief running two law enforcement units and a campaign?" asked Teresa.

Connie heaved an exaggerated sigh. "The Perseverance Police Department staff will endeavor to keep the wheels on until the November election, right Wyn?"

I took a sip of my beer.

Teresa looked uncertain. "But what if he wins?"

Without waiting to hear Connie's answer, I got up and nudged my way through the knot of men surrounding Vanderberg, who cast disapproving glances at my intrusion.

I ignored them. "Chief, I need to talk to you."

Justin snickered, but Vanderberg didn't bat an eyelash. "Gentlemen, please allow me to introduce Perseverance's newest police officer, Wyn Price. She's from California."

As soon as they heard the words "newest" and "California", some of them raised their eyebrows. Combined with my gender and short stature, it was obvious this information didn't generate a favorable first impression.

My face flushed.

"Price, I understand you have something pressing on your mind," the chief said, "but I have important business to discuss with these gentlemen. Go have some fun with your friends. I promise we'll talk first thing in the morning." He tipped his head towards Connie, Teresa, and Barb, who were staring at me like I had sprouted horns.

"Yes, sir." I ground my teeth as I slunk back to the table and sat down.

Dampened by my foul mood, the conversation languished until an exuberant Gracie showed up, more than a little intoxicated. She slapped the table with both palms. "Y'all aren't talking shop over here, are you?"

Before anyone could deny it, she gestured to the harried waitress. "Annie, a round of tequila poppers for my girlfriends."

The women whooped with glee, and the rest of the evening dissolved in a blur.

FOUR

I fiddled with a Perfect Touch Cleaning pencil and tried to figure out what I missed at the scene of Evelyn Randall's death while I waited for Chief Vanderberg at the station the next morning.

Connie's earlier efforts to engage me in banter had been rebuffed, so she was eyeing me with suspicion over the top of her paperback.

After what seemed like an eternity, the front door of the station swung open.

"Good morning." The chief removed his signature navy cap with "Perseverance PD" embroidered in white letters on the front and "Chief" on the back, and smoothed down his shock of sandy hair. "Is there coffee?"

Connie jumped up. "We drank the last of it, chief, but I'll make a fresh pot."

"No, it's okay, Connie. I'll get it," he said.

Vanderberg liked to have a cup of gourmet joe in his hand before engaging in morning conversation. He had spent his own money equipping the station with a fancy coffeemaker and was a snob about coffee bean origins, roasts, and processing methods. In fact, he preferred his own brew to the trendy coffee place across the street.

I waited until he came out of the breakroom before I accosted him halfway across the squad room. "Chief—"

"I know, I know. You have something you want to talk to me about." He swept a hand towards his office.

Without waiting for him to take a seat, I dropped into a guest chair and made my announcement. "Evelyn Randall was murdered."

Vanderberg's eyes widened. "Murdered? Are you certain? Is this the coroner's opinion?"

"Yes. Well, it is the medical examiner's opinion that Mrs. Randall was, beyond a doubt, murdered. The cause of death was manual strangulation. The facts suggest her killer strangled her upstairs and threw her body down the staircase."

He passed a hand over his face. "You said she died of natural causes."

"That was Gleason's initial conclusion, but when I found her at the scene, I thought—" I paused, unsure if I should mention my reservations about how Mrs. Randall died. To my shame, Gleason and I both looked like fools after I let him bully me into accepting his version of events.

Vanderberg frowned. "What's the matter? If you disagreed with the coroner's conclusions, why didn't you say anything?"

"I tried, but he made it clear he wasn't interested in hearing my views on the matter. Besides, although I didn't agree with his assessment, it didn't look like a murder scene. I assumed she had taken an accidental fall on the stairs."

"Is this new opinion final? What about the pathology results?"

"Dr. Appleton sent tissue samples to a pathology lab, but he doesn't expect pathological testing to change his conclusions. He seemed pretty confident."

The chief hunched forward and folded his hands on the desk. "When you entered the Randall residence, did you find evidence of a break-in or struggle? Broken glass? Furniture that was out of place? Scuff marks?"

"Nothing obvious. The house appeared to be in perfect order despite the front door being unlocked." I scratched my head. "But it seemed odd there wasn't a vase."

"A vase?" The chief raised an eyebrow.

"Yes. My first impression was that she was upstairs when it happened." I squinted, conjuring up the scene in my mind. "A flower stem was lying on the floor by her hand, and there was another one upstairs by the table, which suggested she was holding the flowers when she fell, but there was no vase in sight. It didn't seem important, but now it seems odd."

"I'm sorry. I'm not following you."

"They were wild irises. *Iris missouriensis*, to be exact, also called Rocky mountain iris or western blue flag. They don't last without water."

The chief puckered his brow. "Maybe she didn't intend to put them in water."

"Evelyn Randall was an outdoorswoman. She wasn't the sort of woman who would pick fragile wildflowers and let them die. There should have been a vase. Perhaps Mrs. Randall or her killer broke it in the struggle, but there was no trace of it..." I trailed off.

The chief waited as I mulled over the possibilities.

"Unless the killer got rid of the evidence." I drummed my fingers on the arms of the chair. "It takes nerves of steel to clean up after a violent crime, which means he probably wasn't a common thief or vagrant."

"Damn. Well, this changes things." Vanderberg twirled his pen, then swiveled his leather chair to look out the window.

"Where do we go from here, chief? Somebody needs to follow up—"

Vanderberg interrupted me. "Do we have any suspects?"

"No. But Olivia Dewitt—"

"Who?" He pivoted to face me.

"You remember, Mrs. Randall's niece, Olivia DeWitt? Yesterday she said Robert Sandoval was harassing her about selling the Randall place to him."

"Sandoval has been harassing her?"

"Okay, harass is too strong a word. Sandoval called Ms. DeWitt and made an offer on the Randall property which she felt was too low. He implied she wouldn't get a better offer, which she took for intimidation."

"That's it?"

"Yes, I think that's the gist of it."

The chief leaned forward. "What do you think? Is her complaint valid?"

"No. Not from what she recounted to me, anyway. Sandoval was being opportunistic, which isn't surprising given his reputation. From what I hear, he's a supercilious asshole."

Vanderberg narrowed his eyes at my choice of words. "From what you hear?"

"Well, that and first-hand experience. He was snooping around out at the Randall place on Monday, asking questions and acting all self-important. Once I informed him that Mrs. Randall was dead, he didn't seem too broken up about it. He made some weird remark about everyone needing to face their creator, or some such nonsense."

"You didn't find it unusual? Sandoval turning up like that?"

"In retrospect, yes. But at the time..." I trailed off.

The chief's brow furrowed. "Okay. I want you to go back out to Brightwater Canyon and secure the crime scene, then talk to Mrs. Randall's neighbors."

A thrill of excitement shot through me, then fizzled as quickly as it came. "But this is an Edgemont County case, isn't it? I assumed Deputy Bartel would take it from here."

"Deputy Bartel was injured providing support at the wildfire up at Union Pass. Perseverance PD will cover the county's calls a little longer while he's laid up."

"Yes, Connie told me, but—"

"Don't panic on me, Price. This is your chance to dust off your city slicker resumé and try your hand at managing a homicide investigation Wyoming-style. Take Stokes with you and show him the ropes on gathering evidence—you know, the usual stuff. He needs the experience, and he's been asking for more hours."

"Who will take the patrol shifts?"

"Both of you will remain on call in case police intervention is required, but..."

He didn't finish his sentence. We both knew the possibility of anything happening in Perseverance that demanded the immediate presence of law enforcement was slim to non-existent.

I chewed my lip and stared into my coffee cup, making a mental list of the resources I needed to a complete a thorough investigation.

Vanderberg, mistaking my silence for apprehension, rose to perch on my side of the desk. "I know this wasn't what you signed up for when you came to Perseverance from San Diego. You're worried your investigative skills are rusty."

Although it wasn't his intent, his assessment of my state of mind and readiness to take on this case offended me. My investigative skills were restless, not rusty.

"If I wasn't so busy running two law agencies and this damn campaign." He raked both hands through his abundant hair. "I don't want you to be stressed out about this, Price. Bring everything you find here to the station, and I'll help you interpret it."

"I'm not—"

Vanderberg stood up and opened the door, showing with a gesture that I should use it. "Don't worry, Price. It will be challenging, but not impossible. I will guide you every step of the way and together we'll get through it. In the future, I promise the sheriff's office won't drag you into its messes again, okay?"

"Chief," Connie said, "Dolores Donovan from Perfect Touch Cleaning is on line four for you."

"Got it, Connie, thanks. Would you call Stokes and tell him we need him at the station?" He turned back to me. "Tread lightly, Price, and keep a tight lid on this for now. Don't step on any sensitive toes until we understand what happened."

"What about Robert Sandoval?"

He made a calming motion and lowered his voice. "I intend to question Robert Sandoval, but you need to be patient while I rearrange my schedule and sort some things out. Now, if you will excuse me, I need to take this call."

After the chief's door closed, Connie said, "The town is abuzz this morning with the news of Mrs. Randall's murder, Wyn."

I hadn't told anyone that Evelyn Randall was murdered until a few minutes ago, which meant either Gleason or Appleton was a blabbermouth. My money was on Gleason.

Then I remembered Justin's comments the night before at the saloon. "Connie, Justin mentioned something last night about Sandoval being involved. I thought he was drunk and talking nonsense, but did he already know she was murdered?"

"Not in so many words, but Doc Appleton drove down from Jackson yesterday morning and went straight to Coroner Ricky Gleason's house. That means an autopsy, which Chief Vanderberg would be required to attend as interim sheriff. But since the chief was incommunicado, Coroner Gleason insisted you hop right over there. Four hours later, you came back asking for the chief, as white as a sheet, and wound tighter than a spring. We simply put two and two together afterwards."

I tipped my head from side to side, clearing it of the convoluted logic of small-town gossip. "And then you told the whole town?"

"No! No, I didn't tell anyone, Wyn, I swear it. It was Justin, and he alleged someone 'who should know' confirmed it."

"Gleason."

"That would be my guess. Ricky Gleason never was much on following the rules, you know, when he's drunk in particular."

"Since you and everybody else in this town seem to know more than I do about it, who do you think killed Mrs. Randall?"

It was a sarcastic remark, but judging by Connie's rattled expression, she thought I was serious. "Oh heavens, Wyn, I don't know, and I am pretty sure nobody else does, either, except the killer, of course." She blanched. "Oh my God, someone I know could be a murderer."

"Call Justin, Connie."

"Right."

While she called Justin, I located the metal crime scene equipment case in the storeroom and hauled it to my desk. Inside was a nice digital camera and an acceptable selection of forensic supplies. In the front pocket, I found the 2013 edition of *Crime Scene Investigation: A Guide for Law Enforcement*, which, judging by the stiff binding, had never been used.

Connie tried occupying herself with her book, but gave up. "Sorry Wyn, but I'm still too wound-up to let the subject drop. I heard you and the chief talking about bringing Robert Sandoval in for questioning."

"That's confidential."

"Oh! Of course. I would never disclose police business, Wyn, but if you don't mind my saying, Robert Sandoval has a lot of influence among the city and county big shots."

She paused, casting a furtive glance at the chief's office door, but before she could continue, a call came in on the emergency line and she snatched it up. "Perseverance Police Department. What is your emergency? Oh, hello Mrs. Barker."

It was the town pest, Elvira Barker, so it was a safe bet it wasn't a real police emergency. More likely it was a pothole or blocked culvert. It might even be a plugged-up toilet or a suspicious squirrel. With Mrs. Barker, anything was possible. She drove Connie crazy, but I suspected the old woman's calls to the police station were the social highlight of her day.

"Thank you for calling, Mrs. Barker," Connie said. "I'll let Jerry Hanson at Public Works know about the raccoon carcass, but for now, I suggest driving on the opposite side of the street. Okay. Goodbye."

Justin stumbled into the station, unkempt and looking a little green around the gills.

"Glad you could make it, Justin," I said. "The chief wants you to shadow me on the Randall murder investigation."

"Yeah, I know." His voice was a harsh croak.

I closed the crime scene case and hefted it off the desk. "Good. Are you ready to roll?"

"I need a cup of coffee first."

"Fine. I'll be in the car. Connie, we'll be in Brightwater Canyon most of the day, but we're on call. If anything comes up and you can't get us on the police band, try the landline at the Randall's house."

"Right. Good luck," she said. "Let me know how I can help."

"Thanks." At the door, I turned back. "There is something you can do, Connie. I need a whiteboard. Do you think you could arrange that?"

"Teresa might have one at the hardware store. If not, I'll order one from Amazon."

I shifted the heavy case and nibbled my lip. "I'd like to have it today. Would someone at the school have one we can borrow?"

"Great idea. I'll call my friend Bev Peterson. She's the head custodian of the Perseverance School District." She snatched up the phone receiver, no doubt relishing an opportunity to gossip more about the case.

The white-capped volcanos of the Absaroka Mountain Range glittered in the morning sun as we drove out of Perseverance on our way to

Brightwater Canyon. Justin slurped his coffee and stared at the dashboard in silence.

If he wanted to be uncommunicative, that was fine by me. I had enough on my mind without dealing with a pouty millennial.

My last homicide case in San Diego still weighed on me because I didn't get the chance to solve the murder of Veronica Martinez, who had been beaten, raped, and stabbed three times before her killer dumped her body in a parking lot in Logan Heights. I was closing in on the dirtbag when they took me off the case.

They never caught the perpetrator, and the case grew cold, but by then I wasn't on the San Diego police force anymore. Instead, I was at home with a newborn, unemployed, and struggling with depression. Jason was already gone and Veronica's murder, like so many things I once cared about, ceased to matter. I liked to pretend it was all Jason's fault, but I shared in the blame for what went wrong. Solving Evelyn Randall's murder was my chance to redeem myself.

Before we were a mile out of town, Justin fell asleep slumped against the passenger window and began to snore, the half empty coffee mug tipped sideways in his hand. I wasn't counting, but he drank enough beers the night before to sink a boat of sailors, which meant he would be worthless today.

My cell phone buzzed. It was from area code 212, New York. There wasn't anyone I knew from New York except Olivia DeWitt.

I parked the cruiser near the bank of mailboxes at the entrance to Brightwater Canyon and answered the call. "This is Officer Price."

"Officer Price. I have been trying to reach you, but my calls keep going straight to voicemail."

I pulled the phone away from my ear to look at the screen, but it showed no missed calls. Of course, it wasn't unusual for messages to show up hours later.

"I apologize for that, Olivia. Cell phone service out in these parts is unreliable."

"It's not important. What does matter is that *you* are to investigate my aunt's murder." She emphasized the word "you," as if discussing something odious.

Surprised by the perceived slight, I struggled for a suitable response.

"Hello, Officer, are you still there?"

"Yes, I'm still here. At the request of the sheriff's office of Edgemont County, the Perseverance Police Department is taking over the inquiry into your aunt's death, and Police Chief Lars Vanderberg asked me to lead the investigation."

"Well, I hope you know what you're doing, Officer Price. The dispatcher tells me you are new to the department."

"Dispatcher? Do you mean Connie Welch?"

"Yes, of course I mean Connie Welch. She said you have been on the job for less than ten months." She paused. "Have you ever investigated a murder before?"

I stifled a sarcastic laugh. "Yes, ma'am—*Olivia*—I've investigated a few."

"A few? In Perseverance, Wyoming? I would be amazed if that hamlet experiences more than a few murders in a decade."

"No ma'am, in California. I was a homicide detective with the San Diego force for five years before I joined the Perseverance police force."

I wanted to tell her I closed five of the six homicides I was assigned in the year before I got pregnant and received a commendation from the city, but I didn't. Of course, after that, everything imploded, and the San Diego PD was glad to see my backside. It wasn't necessary for her to know that, either.

"I see," she said. "Connie said you have a suspect."

So much for Connie's insistence that she would never discuss a murder investigation with outsiders. Maybe in her mind the family of the deceased wasn't included in that definition, or she couldn't resist sharing juicy information.

"I'm not at liberty to discuss specifics, but we are pursuing all leads. We'll call you as soon as we have any new information we can share."

"Fine. I guess that will do. Good day, officer."

"Wait, I have a few—"

She disconnected before I finished. I would have to call her back. I redialed the number and tapped the steering wheel while it rang. When she didn't answer, I left a message.

Justin eyed me. No doubt he heard the entire exchange.

Without looking at him, I said, "What?"

"Nothing."

I jammed the Crown Vic into gear.

A short distance inside the Spruce Hollow gate, a red Ford Super Duty and a black Chevy Silverado were parked abreast on the narrow gravel road, leaving no room to pass on either side. Although the male occupants noticed the cruiser's approach, they ignored us and continued to chew the fat.

After several minutes ticked by and they were in no hurry to let us pass, I prodded them with a toot of the cruiser's horn and the Ford crawled forward, opening the minimum amount of space required for the cruiser to squeeze through between the pickup trucks.

I waved in thanks as we passed, but the driver scowled at me from under his black cowboy hat and refused to return my greeting.

"Do you know those two?" I asked Justin.

"Frank McGuiness and Don Verhulst."

"Are they always that friendly?"

"I wouldn't read anything into it. They don't get much traffic in the canyon."

His condescending tone set my teeth on edge, but I let it go.

At the Randall house, Justin ambled to the front door while I grabbed the crime scene case out of the trunk. Placing the case on the veranda swing, I took out latex gloves and shoe covers and held them out to him.

"Is this stuff necessary? The scene is already contaminated," he said.

"You can wait in the car if you prefer."

He snatched the gear and pulled it on.

When I unlocked the door, the smell of death flooded down the entry hall in a surge. Unbidden, the image of Evelyn Randall's naked, eviscerated body on the autopsy table flashed into my mind, like a lurid polaroid snapshot.

One of my colleagues in the San Diego PD homicide division—a cantankerous old codger named Dutch who taught me almost everything I knew about solving murders—drilled it into me that no matter how many autopsies I attended, I should never forget what a person looked like on the stainless steel autopsy table, before and after the autopsy.

The "after" in particular. He said if I let that thought "molder" in my mind, it would help me catch killers.

Justin stepped inside the house and gagged. "Holy crap."

"Don't worry, you'll get used to it," I said. "Come on."

The midday sun was shining through the skylights as we entered the great room. I halted and stared at the floor where the body had been. The withered iris—the one out of the reach of Evelyn Randall's lifeless hand—was gone.

I threw my arm out, stopping Justin in his tracks. "Don't come any farther."

"What—"

"Just wait a minute." I put down the heavy crime scene case and turned in a circle, searching for anything that might be out of place since my last visit.

Crisscrossing the lower level with Justin on my heels, I continued to search for signs of disturbance, but nothing stood out until we reached the kitchen.

The plate with the remains of the victim's lunch on it had disappeared.

I pulled open the dishwasher. It was empty.

Justin poked my arm. "Are you gonna tell me what's going on?"

"Hold on," I said as I led him through the dining room and up the floating staircase.

At the top, the table was pushed flush against the railing, and the iris stem under the leg was missing.

I bent over until I was at eye-level with the tabletop. Not a smudge or speck of dust marred the smooth honeyed surface. Backing away, I turned and circulated through the loft, using a methodical visual scan of the furnishings and layout to detect subtle changes, but like downstairs, nothing jumped out at me.

Angry and at a loss for words, I scrubbed my face with my hands.

Justin stood on the landing at the top of the stairs, watching me. "What is it, Wyn?"

After I regained my composure, I pointed to the table. "The stem of a wilted wildflower was under the leg of this table, and another blossom of the same variety lay on the floor near the body downstairs. In the kitchen, a plate with Evelyn Randall's half-eaten lunch on it was the counter next to the sink. All those things are gone. The whole place looks like it's been cleaned up."

"You think the killer came back and covered his tracks?"

"I don't know. It's possible."

"Then what's the point of searching for evidence? We won't find anything."

There were two cardinal rules of murder investigations. The first one stated a law enforcement officer should not jump to conclusions and the second one required that a murder investigation be carried out in a prompt and professional manner.

I violated the first when I allowed Gleason to browbeat me into accepting the cause of death as natural, and the second when I failed to perform a full investigative sweep of the house when I found the body. In the words of famous homicide investigation expert Vernon Geberth, "Do it right the first time. You only get one chance." Vernon would be very disappointed in my handling of this case thus far.

Justin inched backwards down the stairs. "Let's head back to the police station and tell Chief Vanderberg."

A small knot of panic swelled in my throat, and I fought to control it. *One foot after the other, Wyn.*

I gave a shake of my head. "We stay and process the crime scene. If we're thorough, we'll find evidence even if we have to turn this entire house inside out and upside down. I want you to begin by taking pictures of the scene. Photograph every room from every angle, beginning in the entry hall. Do not touch or move anything. If you see anything unusual, give me a shout. The digital camera is in the case downstairs. Go."

He pressed his lips together and stared at me.

I returned his glare. "If you prefer to sleep your hangover off in the car while I process the scene, Justin, be my guest. Besides, you would simply get in my way."

He clenched his hands, then spread them. "Okay. What are you going to do?"

"I'll sketch the scene and try to remember everything from the day I found the body. When you're done taking pictures, we'll go over every inch of this place together and look for clues that might lead us to Evelyn Randall's murderer."

Without waiting for an answer, I brushed past him and went downstairs to get the sketch pad out of the crime scene kit.

Justin came into the kitchen while I was adding the missing lunch plate on the layout I had drawn. I noticed he didn't have the camera with him.

"Have you photographed the entire house?" I asked.

He opened the refrigerator. "Yeah. It wasn't hard."

"Did you take a picture of that?" I motioned to the contents of the refrigerator.

"You mean the inside of the fridge? Why would I do that? I was looking for something to eat. I'm hungry."

"It's a crime scene, Justin. Even the contents of Mrs. Randall's fridge might yield a piece of valuable information."

He slammed the door shut and propped himself against it, crossing his thick arms over his chest. "How much longer will this take?"

"As long as it takes. We still need to sweep for prints and trace evidence."

He observed me as I continued to sketch. "I heard you were a hotshot homicide detective out in Cali." From his manner, he didn't believe it.

Jason and his Hollywood Marine Corps buddies used to call California "Cali". I guess because saying "California" was uncool. Something about hearing "hotshot" and "Cali" in the same sentence reminded me of a sweltering summer day on Del Mar beach, cheering while tanned, muscular jarheads clobbered each other in beach volleyball.

"Who told you that?"

He shrugged. "I dunno. Vanderberg. Or maybe it was Connie."

I closed the sketch pad with great care. "With the help of an excellent supporting team, hard work, and luck, I wrapped up a good number of murder cases."

"He told me you had some kind of breakdown, and the San Diego PD sacked you," he said, his lip curling.

I crossed the kitchen and stood so close to him I could smell his sour breath as I trapped him against the refrigerator.

Eyes wide, he uncrossed his arms and stood up straight.

Part of me longed for him to open his stupid trap again so I could put my fist in it, but it was his lucky day and my self-control prevailed.

"Are you ready to learn evidence collection techniques, Justin?" I said, keeping my tone even. "We can be back in town by late afternoon if we work together."

He twitched his head in the affirmative, but refused to look at me.

"Great. As soon as you photograph the contents of the refrigerator, we can start. Oh, if you're starving, there are a couple of candy bars and a bag of peanuts in the glove box of my cruiser for emergencies. Help yourself."

We inspected every surface inside the Randall house for latent prints and swept every nook and cranny for trace evidence. Except for fingerprints on the empty garbage bins in the garage, we found little of significance.

The effects of the late night at the Silver Spur Saloon were catching up with us, and I was prepared to call it a day when we found Mrs. Randall's hiking boots in the mudroom. The boots were about my size— a six. Turning one of them over, the dried mud embedded in the heavy treads reminded me of what Olivia DeWitt said about her aunt's love of hiking.

I opened the back door and stepped into the afternoon sun, grateful for the fresh air that carried away the cloying stink of the house.

A flagstone path sloped away from the house and disappeared into a shady gulch lined with shimmering aspens and gigantic pines.

Justin hovered on the threshold, squinting at the outdoors.

"Dust the outside door handle for prints," I said to him before moving farther down the stone path.

Where the flagstones ended, a well-worn dirt trail meandered downhill through the undergrowth, suggesting Evelyn Randall used the path regularly.

I turned back to Justin, who was craning his neck to peer over the edge of the flagstone path without leaving the safety of the doorway.

"Oh, hell no," he said. "You are not dragging me down there."

I stifled a snort. "I want to see where it goes, but I won't be gone long. You can dust the outside doors and windows and then pack up. As soon as I get back, we'll head to town."

Eager to have some time alone and stretch my legs, I set off down the path.

The pines and aspens on either side became sparser until they petered out and gave way to shrubs and cottonwoods as the trail descended into a deep gulch. At the bottom, a small, icy stream ran through the floor of the ravine, fed by the snowmelt from higher elevations. Dark throated shooting stars and sticky purple geraniums flourished in the shade of the trees flanking the brook.

Someone wearing hiking boots left a series of distinct footprints in the soft earth around the water. The prints crossed the stream, headed west and then doubled back, heading east. Across the stream, a faint path zigzagged through the sparse vegetation on the gulch's western slope.

I laid my pen next to one imprint and snapped a picture with my mobile phone before crossing the creek to inspect the track ascending at an angle from the floor of the gulch. The prints disappeared into the vegetation in spots. If they were Evelyn Randall's, I admired her physical condition because it wouldn't be an easy climb at any age.

By then it was late afternoon, and I still wanted to interview one or two of Mrs. Randall's neighbors. Besides, I told Justin I would make it quick, and he would champ at the bit if I didn't come back soon, so I pivoted and retraced my steps.

The back door was locked when I returned and I found Justin on the porch swing on the front veranda, staring off into space.

He started when I came traipsing around the side of the house. "Geez, you scared me."

"I see you locked up already. Were you able to lift any prints?"

"Yup. There were some smudged prints on the outside door handle, but I got one flawless handprint—I mean, I think it's flawless—off the glass of the door."

"That's great. Good thinking, Justin."

"Did you find anything down there?" He inclined his head towards the trail.

"Not much, except some footprints. I think they're from Mrs. Randall's hiking boots we found inside, but I took pictures anyway."

He stood up and yawned. "Good. Let's get out of here."

"We still need to canvass the neighborhood."

"Oh, come on. It's almost four o'clock and these folks aren't going anywhere. We can talk to them tomorrow."

A biting reminder that this was a murder investigation sprang to my lips, but I couldn't muster the energy to deliver it. Tomorrow I would convince Vanderberg to let me ditch Justin. I could get more done if I weren't dragging him around behind me like a petulant child.

"Okay," I said, "but we at least need to talk to Maggie McGuiness. She's the woman who called county dispatch for a welfare check on Evelyn Randall."

From the Randall place, I drove along the road looking for a marker or mailbox bearing the number 1158 Meadowlark Lane, which was the McGuiness address.

Justin pattered his fingers on his knees and yawned.

As we neared the gate to Spruce Hollow Gulch, two Australian Shepherds darted out in front of the cruiser, barking. Nearby, a middle-aged woman wearing jeans and a barn coat stood at an open gate, shouting at the dogs to come back. The address marker on the gate post said 1158 Meadowlark Lane, so I pulled the cruiser over and got out.

The dogs rushed to meet me, but it soon became obvious they were harmless as they frolicked about with tongues lolling, overjoyed to make my acquaintance.

Their owner, however, regarded me with suspicion. Her black hair was pulled into a ponytail and she had a pale, pinched face. Despite the warm June day, she was huddled inside her coat.

"Are you Maggie McGuiness?" I asked.

Her eyes flicked from me to Justin, who had gotten out of the police cruiser to stand behind me.

"I'm Officer Price." I offered my hand. "Do you have a moment? We would like to ask you a few questions about Evelyn Randall."

She pressed her lips together and ignored my outstretched hand. "Why? I wasn't friends with her. I don't know anything that will help you."

"It will only take a few minutes—"

"No. I told you I didn't know the woman. There is nothing to discuss. Now if you'll excuse me, I have chores. Come on Pippi, come on Sheila, let's go home." She closed the gate and darted away, the dogs racing in front of her.

I trudged back to the cruiser, ignoring the smug look on Justin's face. "We caught her at a bad time, that's all. We'll approach her again tomorrow. I reckon we're both tuckered out after last night, so let's get out of here."

"About time," he said with a growl.

But when we reached the intersection of the county road and Spruce Hollow Gulch, our exit was blocked by a herd of Black Angus cows streaming through the gate. Riders on horseback were driving the cattle through the narrow opening from the county road, while others on the Spruce Hollow side kept the herd together and turned it south.

There was no rushing a herd this size, so I pulled over, switched off the cruiser's engine, and rolled down my window. Justin pulled his navy cap down over his eyes and prepared to take a nap.

One rider noticed us and reined her roan horse away from the herd to approach the cruiser, bringing her mount to a halt near my window. "Good afternoon, Officer," she said, hunching down to look at me. "I hope you don't need to get out on emergency business. We're moving two hundred and fifty head to summer pasture on the south side of the canyon."

She had a weathered face and a thick braid of graying brown hair.

I waved a hand. "It's not an emergency. We can wait."

She kept her attention on the cattle operation. "Are you out here investigating Evelyn Randall's murder?"

"That's right. News sure travels fast in these parts."

"It does if it's bad. I'm Irene Brockman of Brockman Ranch, by the way. Evelyn was a friend of mine."

I got out of the car and Irene swung down from her saddle, dropping the reins to let her horse graze. She extended a tanned hand, and I took it, noting the strength of her grip.

"I'm with the Perseverance Police Department," I said. "My name is Officer Wyn Price. Since Deputy Bartel is not available to take on additional cases, I'm leading the investigation."

With a wry smile, Irene gestured to the Perseverance PD door decal. "Yeah, I figured that was the deal after I heard about Clif. That poor man has the worst luck. I also heard Chief Vanderberg threw his hat in the ring for the sheriff's job."

"Yes, Ma'am."

She eyed me for a moment, then jerked her head in the general direction of Meadowlark Lane. "She knew something. I'm not sure what, but I suspect it had that bunch so worried they made sure she didn't tell anybody else what she knew."

"What bunch are you talking about?"

"I'm talking about the Homeowners Association of Brightwater Canyon and Robert Sandoval. Evelyn called me last Saturday night to tell me she discovered what was going on in the canyon, but she refused to discuss it over the phone though I pressed her. She sounded a little scared, but excited, too. She wanted to get together, but I was too busy." Irene looked down to scuff the sole of her boot against the dirt. "I told her I would stop by this week after I got the cattle moved to summer pasture. That was the last time I talked to her."

"If you were to hazard a guess, what do you think she was talking about?"

The older woman pursed her lips, avoiding my gaze.

"Look, Irene, Mrs. Randall is dead. We're trying to find out how it happened. Folks are eager to share gossip and hearsay, but without concrete evidence our case is dead in the water, so if you have information that can help us, you need to tell me."

"I'm wary like everybody else, Officer," she said. "Sandoval and his cabal of cronies in the homeowner's association are a domineering presence out here in the county. They're rich, greedy bastards and it's risky to get on their bad side because they will force any foolhardy soul who opposes them out of the way—with a sledgehammer."

"Give me more than that, Irene. I can't arrest someone for murder because folks don't like them."

Her eyes flicked to mine, then away again. "Check out who is snatching up property in Brightwater Canyon, officer. I think you'll find Robert Sandoval and his pals have been as busy as beavers."

With a farewell tip of her head, she mounted her horse and chased after the herd as it disappeared over the ridge.

"I don't know why you're making such a big deal out of it," Gracie said. "It's merely an adult night out with me and two handsome, fun loving Texas businessmen. You don't have to think of it as a date."

She was sitting on the floor of my living room painting her toenails a tacky shade of red called American Beauty while I paced and Dancy fussed in her crib in the bedroom.

"Are you listening to me?" Gracie asked, the nail brush poised in midair.

I stopped pacing. "Uh, yes, of course I am listening. The answer is still no. I can't go out with you and your new friends. I'm in the thick of an investigation—and don't get nail polish on my rug."

"Why does your job have to interfere with an evening of socializing? The chief can't expect you to work on the case twenty-four seven. I mean, what are you supposed to do? Skulk around the canyon at night, spying on people with infrared goggles while you listen to that gangsta rap?"

I set my jaw. "Eminem is not gangsta rap."

She rolled her eyes heavenward. "This isn't about your taste in music, it's about having a little fun and making friends of the male persuasion. Listen, I don't know what disastrous event caused your marriage to Jason to fall apart, but not all men are all jerks. For your sake and Dancy's, maybe it's time for you to move on."

"I think you should go home, Gracie."

Exasperated, she clambered to her feet with the wads of cotton still stuck between her toes and hobbled out the front door without bothering to close it behind her, yelping when she stepped on a cactus as she cut across my lawn.

FIVE

The rickety wooden blackboard leaning over my desk was scratched and clouded by hard use, which occurred well over a century ago by the looks of it. But a fresh box of white chalk rested on the tray, affixed with a yellow sticky note that said, "Best I could do," in Connie's neat cursive handwriting, and embellished with a smiley face.

I extracted a pristine stick of chalk from the box and sketched a timeline of the events linked to Evelyn Randall's death across the top of the board. In the middle, I printed her name in large block letters and wrote Robert Sandoval on one side and Olivia DeWitt on the other. Under Olivia's name, I wrote "heir?" Across the bottom of the board, I listed the three crucial aspects of a crime—motive, means, and opportunity.

As I admired my handiwork, Vanderberg handed me a mug of hot coffee.

"Thanks, chief. I didn't hear you come in." I took a grateful sip of the fresh brew.

He gestured to the blackboard. "Interesting investigation board. I haven't seen one of these in years, but it's a good way to visualize the chain of events and stay organized."

I nodded. "Hopefully, it will help Justin understand the process."

Connie hurried into the station, the mail under one arm. "Sorry I'm late, Chief. I hadn't seen Darlene since she got back from her vacation in Florida."

Darlene was the postmistress at the Perseverance Post Office.

"Not a problem, Connie. I made a pot of coffee," he said. "Come on, Price, let's reconvene in my office."

"How did it go yesterday?" he asked, settling into his chair.

"From bad to dreadful, I'm afraid," I said. "After Gleason and I removed the body late Monday afternoon, it appears someone entered the Randall house on Tuesday or Wednesday and wiped it clean."

The chief straightened and leaned forward. "Go on."

"On Monday, I observed a flower on the floor near the body and another at the top of the stairs. There was also a lunch plate with what I presumed was Mrs. Randall's lunch on it in the kitchen. But when we arrived at the Randall residence yesterday, the flowers were gone, and the plate was washed and put away. We documented the missing evidence, but there wasn't much to begin with."

"You found nothing useful at all?"

"No, sir—nothing earthshaking, at least, but I diagrammed the murder scene and sketched in the missing details. We also swabbed for DNA. However, I'm not holding out much hope for any revelatory results, considering the thorough cleaning that took place. We lifted some partial fingerprints from the trash bins in the garage, but found the most promising piece of imprint evidence on the exterior window of the mudroom door. It was the complete impression of a large hand."

"Huh." Vanderberg chewed the inside of his lip. "You know, Price, this entire investigation is ass-backwards. I know the jurisdiction issue doesn't make it easy—damn Edgemont County. But you didn't secure the crime scene, and that screwed up the chain of custody. If this state of affairs existed anywhere other than backwater Perseverance, the court would disregard our evidence and dismiss any case we can build from it on pure technicality."

"I admit I made mistakes, chief, but I'm confident we can still solve this case."

"I appreciate your willingness to take responsibility for your own errors." He waved a hand. "We've all slipped up at one time or another, but as they used to say in Chicago, 'Lars Vanderberg's officers do everything by the book'. From this point forward, we employ solid, old-fashioned police work to close this case. Are we on the same page?"

I sat up straighter. "We are, chief."

"Good. What are your plans for today?"

"I'm headed back out to Brightwater Canyon this morning to canvass the neighborhood. Someone must have seen something that can help our investigation."

Vanderberg opened one of his desk drawers and rummaged around. "I have a map of the canyon divided up by property sections in here somewhere. Ah, here it is." He pulled out a sheet of hot pink paper and passed it to me. "We drew it up a couple of years ago for a fire mitigation crew. Sections with names written next to the numbers are residences. The others are unoccupied land. We have more detailed maps, but this should be sufficient for a simple door-to-door canvass."

"Thanks." I perused the crude hand-drawn map of Brightwater Canyon. "This might help us track down any potential witnesses."

The corner of his mouth twitched. "Good luck convincing them to talk to you, though. It's like pulling teeth to extract information from homeowners in Brightwater Canyon, and the Association doesn't like Perseverance cops poking around out there."

"Yes, I gathered as much. We ran into Maggie McGuiness on the road on our way out, but she was evasive and wouldn't answer my questions."

"Do you think she knows something?"

"Maybe—or she doesn't like outsiders. I'll talk to her again. I also got a promising lead from a woman named Irene Brockman. She was a friend of Mrs. Randall's and alleged Mrs. Randall might have uncovered unsavory information implicating Robert Sandoval. She didn't know what it was, but suggested I look into recent Brightwater Canyon property transactions. I figured I would go down to the courthouse and talk to Myrna Flowers."

"Let me know what you find out. In the meantime, I'll send the prints and swabs to the state crime lab, but they're drowning in a backlog of work. It could be weeks before we get the results."

I stood to leave.

"How did Stokes do yesterday?" he asked.

"Uh, well, he discovered the handprint on the window of the back door—"

"Good. I'm glad to hear he's stepping up to the plate. You should let him take the lead on one or two interviews with the neighbors today—after he sees how it's done, of course."

Connie knocked on the door and opened it without waiting for a response. "Chief, Mayor Dippert is on line one for you."

Vanderberg put his hand on the handset. "You're doing great, Price. Don't forget to keep me in the loop."

I followed Connie to the squad room and wrote a note about property transactions under Robert Sandoval's name on the blackboard.

"I see you put the chalkboard to use," she said. "What does all this mean?"

"It's called a link chart or investigation board. They aren't really used much, but they can help an investigative team picture the components of the crime."

"Why is Olivia Dewitt's name up there like Robert Sandoval's? Is she a suspect?"

"If she is her aunt's sole heir, then she stood to gain on the sale of the property, which could explain why she was so upset that Sandoval offered her a below-market price. Or she could be the beneficiary of a life insurance policy if Mrs. Randall had one. In any case, we need to talk to her. Which reminds me Connie, please—"

The door of the station banged open and Justin lurched in. When he noticed us, he pointed to the back. "I'm going to..."

He disappeared into the breakroom. Minutes later, he shuffled back out carrying a mug and tripped over a trash can, sloshing coffee all over my desk.

"I'll wait in your cruiser," he said on his way out the door.

Connie ignored Justin's behavior. "What were you saying, Wyn?"

I wagged my head in resignation. "Never mind. It's important to conceal this board when we're not working on it or if guests are present. Could you find a sheet or blanket that would fit the bill?"

"I think we have some emergency blankets in the storeroom."

"That'll work," I said.

• • •

Justin drained the last of his coffee and dropped the travel mug on the floorboard of my cruiser. "What's the plan?"

His eyes were bloodshot, but his uniform was clean, and he smelled of Irish Spring soap.

I handed over the map Vanderberg gave me. "We're going to start by canvassing Mrs. Randall's neighbors on Meadowlark Lane because they are the most likely to have information that can help us. Then I want to speak to the people who live along the Spruce Gulch road. There's one entrance into that community. Our murderer either lives in Brightwater Canyon or they used that road to gain entry."

He made a noise like an irked teenager. "That's going to take days."

"Not as long as you think. Four homes are on that loop, one of which is the Randall property, and another five front Spruce Gulch."

"This is a waste of time. Why don't we cut to the chase and arrest that bastard Sandoval?"

The thing about Justin Stokes was I wanted to throat punch him after I spent more than an hour alone with him. I pulled over on the shoulder of the road.

"Why are we stopping?" he asked.

I turned to him. "It's time for another lesson in proper crime investigation technique, Justin. A good investigator doesn't harbor a preconceived notion of who did it. Without solid evidence, we will not jump to conclusions for the sake of convenience. Do you understand?"

Justin clenched his hands into fists on his thighs and jutted out his chin, staring at the dashboard.

"This murder investigation is not a game," I said. "If we screw it up, Evelyn Randall's killer could escape justice. You may not like Robert Sandoval—hell, maybe he did it—but it is critical you keep an open mind." I bit the last words off.

He chewed his lip and ground his boot on the floor mat.

Leaning across him, I shoved open the passenger door. "I don't have time for your bullshit. If you can't follow simple instructions without melodrama, you can hoof it back to town."

He exhaled and pulled the door shut. "Okay, how does canvassing work?"

I eased the cruiser back onto the highway and directed him to the backseat with a tip of my head. "The canvassing sheets are in that binder. We have to fill out a sheet for every residence we visit, even if we don't talk to anybody. I'll conduct the first couple of interviews, then turn it over to you."

He grabbed the binder and flipped through it. "You're kidding, right?"

"You're local. The folks might respond better to you."

"Brightwater Canyon snobs won't have anything to do with us locals. They come out here to Wyoming and build their big old fancy houses on our choicest land and then complain about everything from the cattle to the governor."

"Are you saying it's an 'us versus them' thing? No one in Edgemont County cares because Mrs. Randall was murdered within the boundaries of Brightwater Canyon?"

He lifted his shoulders. "They keep to themselves, and we keep to ourselves, but that doesn't stop them from grousing about us locals nonstop—and most of it unjustified. It was bad enough when the sheriff's office had a full staff, but Clif says responding to their petty complaints is about all he has time for anymore."

"Clif? Do you mean Deputy Bartel? Is he a friend of yours?"

Justin clamped his mouth shut and looked out the window.

Turning into the first driveway on Meadowlark Lane, I pointed to the map in his hand. "Whose place is this?"

"It's owned by someone named Bennett, according to this."

The Bennett's terracotta hacienda was tucked behind a mesa a quarter of a mile from the road. We didn't see until we were right on top of it. Decorated in a desert theme with green metal cactus sculptures, giant multicolored salamanders, and boulders of red sandstone, the front yard resembled a children's playground on LSD.

Our knock was answered by a breathless, sixty-something woman in workout gear. "Yes?"

A voice boomed from within the house. "Who is it?" An instant later, a tall, white-haired man with an artist's paintbrush in one hand appeared.

"We're Officers Price and Stokes," I said. "We're with the Perseverance Police Department. Are you Mr. and Mrs. Bennett?"

The man glowered. "What do you want?"

"We're investigating the death of your neighbor—"

"Yes. Yes. We're aware of the situation, but Bob assured us it's nothing to worry about," he said.

I cocked my head. "Bob?"

Mrs. Bennett said, "Bob—Robert Sandoval."

"You found out about Mrs. Randall's murder from Robert Sandoval?"

She waved a hand. "Oh, no, no. We got an email from the homeowner association, but Bob stopped by yesterday to set our minds at ease. Such a kind, wonderful man. I don't know what we'd do without him."

Mr. Bennett squinted at me. "He said to expect someone from the sheriff's office."

"The sheriff's department asked the Perseverance Police Department to take the lead on this one. Were you acquainted with Mrs. Randall?"

"Not well. We saw her at the annual meetings. That's about it," he said.

His wife made a dismissive gesture. "She was a pest and rabble-rouser, always trying to stir up trouble against the homeowner's association—"

Mr. Bennett cut in. "—and Bob Sandoval."

Without skipping a beat, Mrs. Bennett said, "I can't believe anyone would have a bad word to say against Bob. The man is a saint. He would give you the shirt off his back. Because of him, Brightwater Canyon is an exceptional place to live, and he makes certain the board puts the homeowners first. He oversaw the upgrades to the canyon's infrastructure—"

"—which has increased our property values year after year," her husband said, cutting in again. "We have Bob Sandoval to thank for that."

Justin muttered something under his breath.

"Getting back to Mrs. Randall," I said. "You believe she was causing trouble for the HOA and Mr. Sandoval? Can you tell me more about that?"

With a wave, Mr. Bennett dismissed the question. "I don't recall the specifics. It was silly nonsense."

"Or maybe she had dirt on Sandoval and the HOA board and they wanted to shut her up," Justin said, "Which is how she ended up dead. So if you're covering for your friend Sandoval and know more than you're telling us, that could make you an accessory to murder."

Mr. and Mrs. Bennett gaped at him and I shot him a scathing look, but before I could smooth things over, Mr. Bennett ordered us off his property and closed the door in our faces.

We returned to the cruiser, but Justin's door was still open when I put the car in gear.

"Whoa! Calm down, will you?" he said, pulling his right leg in and slamming the door. "I was trying to move things along is all."

If I looked at him, I would throat punch him. "You didn't hear a word I said earlier, did you, Justin? Next time you can keep your mouth shut, or you can stay in the car. Now give me that map."

The Randall property was surrounded by unoccupied lots according to the fire mitigation map, which meant the house next to the Bennett's was the closest residence on the northeast side of Meadowlark Lane, but the map provided little information about the owners other than the initials "LSI".

The LSI property was an impressive multi-gabled mansion of river rock and timber tucked in a thick stand of pines at the end of a long, curving driveway. Although the front lawn was professionally land-scaped, no flowers or ornaments graced the immense front entrance area except for giant plume-like grass growing in copper urns on either side of the door.

After no one answered when we rang the doorbell, Justin cupped his hands around his eyes to peek into a window.

"Can I help you?" asked a man's voice behind us.

It was the young businessman who was with Sandoval outside the cafe a few days ago. He was taller than I remembered, and more attractive.

"Good morning. I'm Officer Price and this is Officer Stokes from the Perseverance Police Department," I said. "Are you the owner of this place?"

"Uh, no. I am a guest. The name is Tug Stratton." He held out his hand.

I took it but couldn't help wondering what the hell kind of name "Tug" was.

Instead of letting go of my hand, he continued to hold it. "Didn't we meet on Tuesday, Officer Price?" Like his colleague, his drawl had the deep twang of a Texan, but it wasn't as pronounced.

"Yes, in passing, but it is nice to meet you again, Mr. Stratton." I pulled my hand away. "Where can we find the owner?"

Tug's gaze flickered back and forth between me and Justin. "What's this about?"

"We're investigating an elderly woman's murder that occurred down the road from here," Justin said, planting his fists on his hips, "and we don't have all day to stand around and exchange pleasantries, so why don't you tell us where the owners are?"

"This property is owned by my employer, Lone Star Investors of Dallas, Texas," Tug said, "I'm Senior Managing Director of Portfolio Management for Lone Star and my colleague Johnny Butler, who you also met the other day, Officer Price, is Senior Vice President of Fundraising."

Stratton's fancy title didn't impress Justin. "What are you doing here in Brightwater Canyon?"

"I don't see how that's any of your business." Tug's amiable demeanor was evaporating.

Before Justin made the situation any worse, I offered Tug a charming smile to ratchet down the tension. "I hope you and your associate have been enjoying your stay, Mr. Stratton. There's nothing like springtime in the Rockies. Have you and Mr. Butler been in Wyoming long?"

"We flew into Jackson Monday afternoon and arrived in Perseverance around seven thirty that evening."

I gestured to the security cameras overlooking the courtyard and the front door. "Do these cameras pick up activity on Meadowlark Lane, like vehicles driving by?"

"I don't know. I can give you the name and number of the property management division at LSI. You can ask them." His manner was no longer pleasant.

Justin snorted. Tug shot him a hostile look.

I cleared my throat to draw Tug's attention away from Justin. "That's great. I'll take you up on your offer."

He took his wallet out of his back pocket and extracted a white business card embossed with a metallic red, silver, and blue star. "The number of our corporate headquarters is at the bottom. When you call, ask for the property management team. You can give them my name if they inquire."

"We'll do that," I said. "I appreciate your time today, Mr. Stratton."

He turned on his heel and entered the house, slamming the door behind him.

Justin's lip curled in derision. "Why did you fall all over yourself for him? I thought you said to keep an open mind. I mean, that guy could be a suspect, right?"

"Not if what he says about arriving Monday is true, and we verify it—which you will do by calling the Jackson Airport." I passed him the business card. "Then you can call Lone Star Investors and inquire about Mr. Stratton and Mr. Butler when you speak to the property management people about those cameras. Be discreet, Justin. And as far as handling Mr. Stratton with care, remember you'll catch more flies with honey than you will with vinegar."

Bewildered, Justin took the card.

I disregarded his confusion. "The likelihood of finding a close neighbor who saw something useful to our investigation is plummeting. Let's see if Maggie McGuiness is at home. Maybe she'll be more forthcoming if we're standing on her doorstep."

In a stroke of luck, the McGuiness's white crossbuck gate was open as we approached, and I steered the police cruiser through it without hesitation.

Unlike the previous residences we visited in Brightwater Canyon, this place was situated in an open meadow and looked like a working ranch rather than an executive estate. Horse stables with large paddocks flanked a rambling cream brick house and a familiar red Ford Super Duty pickup was parked in front.

"There's Frank McGuiness." Justin pointed to a big man forking hay off a wagon into one of the paddock feeders.

I climbed out of the police cruiser and walked in McGuiness's direction, with Justin following a few paces behind.

When he saw us, McGuiness jumped off the wagon and strode forward to meet us, pitchfork in hand.

"Mr. McGuiness? I'm Officer Price with—"

"I know who you are. Now get the hell off my property." He gestured with the pitchfork as he closed the distance between us. "If you ain't got a warrant, you ain't got no business here."

I put my hands up. "Take it easy, sir—"

McGuiness's face was turning a nasty purple color. "I said get off my property."

I backed up several paces, keeping a wary eye on McGuiness. Behind me, the cruiser door slammed. So much for Justin having my back.

Then my butt bumped up against the warm metal of the Crown Vic and I scrambled in, turning the key in the ignition while I pulled the door shut.

"I should have warned you about Frank," Justin said.

"You think?" I gave the old Crown Vic some gas before McGuiness could put his pitchfork through the trunk. "Is he always that cantankerous?"

"He's a nasty piece of work. Clif says it's best to steer clear of him."

"You could have said something before he nearly forked my trunk. An irate dude chasing my police cruiser with an agricultural tool is a first—even for me."

Justin snickered, and I turned my head so he wouldn't see me trying to suppress my smile.

The interviews of the other canyon residents were replays of our conversation with the Bennetts, as if everyone was reading from the same script. Those who had heard of Evelyn Randall portrayed her in a negative light, but almost all seized on the opportunity to put in a positive plug for Robert Sandoval.

One resident, a spry old character by the name of Jameson Warner, mentioned seeing a light-colored sedan he said he didn't recognize on the canyon road, which was almost no help since he admitted he didn't know what other residents drove. He couldn't remember what night it was, but thought it was suspicious because they were "driving so slow".

On our way back to town, I said, "Sandoval sure has devout admirers. Those folks we talked to today all believe he is the greatest thing since sliced bread. A saint if you could believe Mrs. Bennett."

Justin scowled. "It sounded to me like Robert Sandoval coached them—making sure they all got their stories straight, and I find it mighty suspicious he got to them before we did."

"Maybe he was only trying to reassure them, but it's something we will ask Sandoval about when we talk to him."

Justin's face split into a wide grin. "All right. We can head over to Sandoval's ranch now. It's a long drive, but I remember how to get there."

I was keen to talk to Sandoval myself, but it would be a disaster to let Justin get anywhere near him. "Vanderberg made it crystal clear that he wants to be there when we interview Sandoval. Besides, we have a ton of legwork to do, so we're going back to town. While I follow up on the lead from Irene Brockman and call Olivia DeWitt again, I want you to contact Lone Star Investors and Maggie McGuiness. Convince Maggie to come to the station and give us a statement, or we're going to harass her until she does."

Justin's face glowed with enthusiasm. "Will do, boss."

SIX

As its name specified, the City and County Building on Main Street housed both the municipal and county government offices. Residents referred to it as "the new courthouse" because it was built in the eighties after safety concerns prompted the city to condemn the old building. With its sleek profile and black glass windows in the minimalist Scandinavian style, it was completely out of place in funky Perseverance.

I waved to Jessie and Carla in Motor Vehicles before climbing the wide staircase to the County Clerk's office on the second floor. No one was at the reception desk, so I sauntered down to the Records Department, but it was locked.

"Were you looking for me, Wyn?" A plump silver-haired woman in a black polyester pantsuit bustled towards me, keys jingling in her hand.

"Yes. I beginning to fear that you overslept," I said with an impish grin.

Efficient and well-liked, County Clerk Myrna Flowers ruled the courthouse with a firm hand and, according to Connie, ran unopposed in every Edgemont County general election for the last twenty years. She also kept the County Commissioners under control by making sure they didn't embarrass themselves or ruffle any important feathers. It was far trickier than it sounded.

She cackled with amusement. "So what brings you to the courthouse today, other than to expose my slothful habits?"

"I'm searching for information on the Brightwater Canyon development, Myrna. If you could point me in the general direction of the relevant property records, I'd sure appreciate it."

"What are you looking for?" Myrna asked, sorting out a key to unlock the Records Department.

When she pushed open the door and flipped on the light, my jaw dropped. The floor-to-ceiling shelves were crammed with boxes and bundles of documents alternated with row upon row of tiny wooden drawers. A microfiche machine the size of a Volkswagen beetle dominated the center of the room.

She caught me eyeballing the archaic equipment. "We're working on digitizing our records, but it takes time and money. Unless you're familiar with our filing system, it would be much faster and easier if I did it for you rather than making you spend hours digging through the records yourself."

I agreed with her assessment. Unless a person was familiar with the County's filing system, it would take days to find useful documents in those stacks of paper.

"I'm looking for property sales in Brightwater Canyon for the last fifteen years," I said. "Who owns the property now and the date they bought it, to be specific."

She cocked her head to one side.

"It's a lead I'm following up on for the Evelyn Randall case."

"Oh! I see. The gossip around town is that she was murdered."

I looked at my oxfords. "Yes, ma'am."

She caught the hint and changed tack. "How much detail do you need? If you want legal descriptions and copies of deeds, that will take a while. If ownership changes and approximate dates are sufficient, there is a simpler way to get that information."

"Simple works for me. Let's start with that."

Opening a long wooden drawer, Myrna flipped through sleeves of microfiche. When she found what she was hunting for, she placed the sheet of film into the fiche machine and adjusted the focus. "These should do the trick."

She pressed the print button, and the machine clunked and growled like it was giving birth before spitting out a sheet of paper. The process was repeated until she had printed fifteen sheets.

I took the pieces of paper she handed to me and scanned through them. "What am I looking at here?"

"These are Brightwater Canyon parcel ownership maps for the last fifteen years. The HOA files them annually under an agreement with the county. They mark the parcels with the owner's names. If you compare the maps year over year, the changes in ownership during the year should be apparent."

"What's this? Brightwater P-t-r-s?" I pointed to an annotation on a parcel.

"Brightwater Partners. That's the legal name of the buyer, but it's one of Robert Sandoval's shell companies."

Before I could ask another question, Myrna held up her hand. "It's lunchtime. Rather than begin a lengthy discussion in this musty old storeroom, I propose we go out for lunch, and I'll tell you everything I know about Brightwater Partners and Robert Sandoval."

"You're on," I said, putting the papers in the pocket of my case binder.

Despite its newfound popularity, the old-fashioned practice of community lunchtime lived on in Perseverance. From noon to one o'clock, the bars and restaurants were the only businesses open downtown. Everything else, from the bank to the courthouse, was closed.

Myrna and I left the City and County Building and crossed Main Street to the Perseverance Cafe.

Established in 1928, the cafe was an institution, and although tourists and newcomers frequented the restaurant, it was the local regulars who kept it in business. You wouldn't find any nouvelle cuisine on owner Evangeline Cox's menu, but if you were hankering for a patty melt or a hot beef sandwich mounded with creamy mashed potatoes smothered in gravy, the cafe was the place to go.

Other patrons were already waiting to be seated when we arrived, but Myrna made eye contact with Mrs. Cox, who was behind the cash register, and then headed straight to a booth near the kitchen.

The red leatherette seats were cracked and patched from heavy use and my butt slid into the indentations left by thousands of backsides before me. I loved this place. It smelled of smoky grease and reminded me of a diner where my dad and I used to eat in Harding County, South Dakota.

A few minutes later, Dottie, the waitress, hobbled over, slammed two glasses of water down, and threw the sticky menus beside them.

It was a miracle she could walk at all. The heavy support hose she wore was stretched in such tight bands around her swollen, veined legs it looked painful. Bobby pins held her long gray hair in place, and her hands were liver-spotted and gnarled from decades of hard work.

"I'll be back," she said with a rasp. She wasn't the friendliest waitress in town by any stretch of the imagination, but if you ate at the Perseverance Cafe, you consented to put up with Dottie.

After scanning the menu, Myrna got down to the purpose of our conversation. "What is now the Brightwater Canyon Subdivision was once the Lumineux Ranch. At one time, the Lumineuxs were some of the biggest cattle operators in Wyoming and owned a sizeable chunk of Edgemont County. Old Bud Lumineux founded Perseverance in the late eighteen hundreds as a camp for his cattle hands—"

Dottie's arrival interrupted her story. "You decide?"

Myrna said, "I'm on a diet, so I'll have the club sandwich with cottage cheese instead of fries."

"To drink?"

"Oh, a Diet Dr. Pepper," Myrna replied.

"Give me the usual," I said. I always had the patty melt, French fries, and a Coke.

Dottie nodded and gathered up the menus.

Myrna picked up where she left off. "It was Bud Lumineux who built the first Perseverance Courthouse—the one they tore down in 1982— and the Catholic Church. He encouraged local businesses to build by lending them money at low rates. That was before they organized the bank, of course, but the point is the folks hereabouts loved and respected Bud Lumineux."

Dottie brought the drinks and left without a word.

Myrna took a sip of her Diet Dr. Pepper. "Bud's oldest son, Duke, was well respected, too. He ran the place after Bud died. He was Bud's son by his second wife Pearl—she was a Knutsen. Bud's first wife died of consumption."

"Consumption?"

"That's what they used to call tuberculosis. Anyway, Duke was a renowned cattleman, but he was also an incorrigible ladies' man. Despite this, he and his wife Rose had eleven kids—the poor woman—four boys and seven girls. In the mid-sixties, he built Rose a big fancy mansion in Denver. Some said it was a sweetener to dissuade her from divorcing him for his infidelity and taking him to the cleaners. She moved to Colorado and never returned to Edgemont County.

"The kids were a bunch of hellraisers. Well, at least the boys were. Rose saw to it her girls behaved themselves and got topnotch educations. All the daughters accompanied Rose to Denver and never showed their faces again in these parts. I heard several of them married into Denver high society and did quite well for themselves.

"The boys were another story altogether. Their daddy was rich, and they thought it entitled them to do whatever they pleased, which involved drinking, trying to get girls pregnant, and wrecking their fancy cars. Gary, the youngest, killed himself in a rollover accident south of Wilderness. That was in seventy-six or seventy-seven. I don't remember."

"Club sandwich, patty melt." Dottie stated the obvious as she slid the plates in front of us. "Can I getcha anything else?"

We both shook our heads in the negative.

Before leaving, Dottie contorted her face into a terrifying expression meant to resemble a smile.

Myrna eyed my patty melt and French fries. "I don't know how you can eat like that and stay so trim."

"I'll have to kill myself kickboxing in the backyard for a couple of days," I said, tucking into the patty melt, "but it's worth it."

"Good heavens, kickboxing?"

"Mm-hmm. I used to run. Then I bought this old punching bag and—" I stopped myself. She didn't need to know I had drawn Jason's face on the cracked vinyl with a marker. "Anyway, you were telling me about Duke's kids."

Myrna took a moment to regather her thoughts. "Well, after Duke died, the surviving boys fought over who would run the ranch. It turned into a blazing feud that would drag on for ten miserable years."

"Wasn't the Lumineux property big enough for all of them?"

"A reasonable person might have thought so, but instead of dividing it equitably, they slugged it out in court, paying exorbitant fees to attorneys and creating familial rifts that would never heal. And while the brothers squabbled, the ranch went to hell. One dreadful winter, over a quarter of the Lumineux herd was lost and the following year cattle prices tanked, so by the time they settled their differences, the place was worth a lot less than it was at the time Daddy Duke died."

"I can't believe Duke didn't leave a will." I stabbed the air with a French fry.

"It's more common than you think. Either he thought they would work it out on their own or the prospect of a no-holds-barred feud between his remaining boys—survival of the fittest and all that—amused him. In the end, his youngest son Charlie finagled a deal to buy his brothers Leon and Vincent out, but by then he was deep in debt and the ranch was in shambles."

I leaned forward. "How does Robert Sandoval figure into this sweeping saga?"

"I'm getting to that," Myrna said, holding up a hand. "It turned out Charlie didn't care if the place falling apart, because he never planned to run it as a working ranch. Instead, he intended to develop the property into a swanky subdivision and make a fortune selling it off in forty-acre ranchettes. He named it Brightwater Canyon and sunk a chunk of money into roads and other minor improvements, but he didn't sell more than a handful of the parcels before he ran out of funds."

She leaned in and lowered her tone. "Here's the part that will interest you, Wyn. Charlie needed to bring in a partner, someone with the cash and connections to make Brightwater Canyon a success. It wasn't easy, but at a private poker game in Denver, he met a multimillionaire who was looking for a real estate investment."

"Let me guess—Robert Sandoval."

"Yes. Sandoval convinced Charlie they could make a fortune together, so Brightwater Partners was formed and development in Brightwater Canyon exploded. They brought in power lines, upgraded the roads, and built a fire station. The lots were selling like hotcakes, but it wasn't long before Charlie suspected his partner was making deals on the side and cutting him out of the action."

"What did Charlie do about it?"

"Given his history, you would think he fought like hell. But he didn't. Instead, he picked up and quit Edgemont County altogether. Afterwards, Robert Sandoval formed the homeowner association and to ensure the HOA stays under his control, he handpicks the directors. Of course, it helps that he's the majority owner of Brightwater Canyon through the partnership."

"Wait," I said, "I'm confused. What happened to Charlie? Did he disappear without a trace?"

Myrna's expression was pained. "Wyn, bear with me, please."

Dottie slapped the ticket on the table and seized our plates. "You finished? Mrs. Cox can take your money at the cash register up front."

We ignored her.

Myrna took a deep breath. "Charlie and I used to be close, and I've kept in touch with him over the years." She threw me a warning look that said, *don't go there.* "I'm not sure how Sandoval drove him away, but Charlie always said he considered himself lucky to worm out of the devil's bargain with Sandoval—but it was by the skin of his teeth. That's about everything I can tell you."

I was a little disappointed. The conversation was fascinating, but I was no closer to establishing why Robert Sandoval might have been involved in Evelyn Randall's murder.

Myrna fidgeted with her napkin for a minute, then took a pen out of her purse, scribbled something on the distressed paper and shoved it across the table. "It's Charlie's address in Billings. He doesn't have a phone."

Waving away my questions, she said, "I know what you're thinking, Charlie is another bitter loser with an ax to grind and you may be right, but he spent over five years at the same trough with Robert Sandoval and he might help you."

She looked at her silver wristwatch in alarm. "Whoops! That hour flew by. We should have lunch more often. I'll get the check." She patted my arm and left.

I nursed my Coke, ruminating on what Myrna told me, but when Dottie noticed me hanging around, I bolted before she could ask if I wanted anything else.

Justin and Connie were studying the blackboard when I returned from lunch.

"Did Olivia DeWitt call back?" I asked.

They both shook their heads.

"Justin, did you get in touch with Maggie McGuiness?"

"I left a message on her home phone," he said. "If she doesn't call back, I'll keep hounding her until I get a hold of her."

"Okay. Keep me posted."

Justin pulled a chair up to my desk and sat down. "I verified Stratton's story, but the woman in charge of property at Lone Star Investors said the security system is designed to monitor the LSI property, so the cameras are programmed to pick up movement on the estate, but not on Meadowlark Lane."

I tipped back in my chair and crossed my arms. "That's discouraging."

"But she's reviewing all the camera footage for the timeframe of the murder, and she'll let us know if anything unusual jumps out."

Connie snickered. "You should have heard Justin buttering her up. Who knew he had a silver tongue?"

Justin's face reddened. "I took your advice, Wyn. You know about the honey and vinegar—"

Connie cut in. "After I explained what the adage meant."

"Well, excellent job, Justin," I said. "Next, I want you to talk to the directors on the HOA board and see if they felt threatened by Mrs. Randall. Perhaps one of them can tell us why she was stirring the pot."

"I'm on it." He jumped up and moved to his desk.

Either he was taking this seriously or he was avoiding patrol duty. I hoped it was the former, but if it was the latter, I couldn't say I blamed him.

Connie pointed to a gray blanket on my desk. "I found something I think will work to cover the blackboard, Wyn."

"Thanks, Connie. Which reminds me—I've been meaning to discuss something with you and Justin. Perseverance is a close-knit community, and it's natural for people to be curious about Evelyn Randall's murder, but the details of the investigation and information on this board must be kept in the strictest confidence." I made eye contact with both of them. "That means you can't discuss it with anyone, not even your friends or family, and especially not with any person whose name is on this board, got it?"

"Yes, Ma'am," Justin said, dialing a number on his desk phone.

Connie sniffed at the insinuation, but nodded.

Satisfied I had made my point, I said, "Okay, let's get—"

The station door flew open, and a tall, sophisticated woman swept in. Her champagne blond hair was cut and styled to perfection, and she wore Gucci sunglasses and nude patent leather Christian Louboutin pumps with her tailored white suit.

Connie stared, her mouth agape.

Justin dropped the phone receiver.

I threw the blanket over the blackboard before greeting our guest. "May I help you?"

"I am Olivia DeWitt. Is Officer Price in?" She took off her sunglasses and scanned the shabby little station.

"I'm Officer Price," I said, scrambling around my desk. "What a surprise. I was about to call you again."

She took my hand in her cool, firm grip. "I apologize for not returning your calls, Officer Price, but I had some important business in the area, so I thought I might kill two birds with one stone, as they say."

I gestured to a chair. "Please, have a seat. Can I get you a bottle of water or a cup of coffee? Chief Vanderberg is a coffee aficionado, and since he bought the station a grinder, the coffee is always fresh."

She inclined her head. "I will take coffee, please. Thank you."

As I was handing her a steaming mug, the chief came back from lunch.

"Chief," I said, "this is Olivia DeWitt, Evelyn Randall's niece. Olivia, this is Perseverance Police Chief Lars Vanderberg."

Vanderberg extended his hand. "It's a pleasure to meet you, Olivia. How is the coffee?"

She remained seated, but took his hand. "Likewise, and the coffee is delicious."

"My condolences for your loss," he said. "Officer Price will call the coroner's office to ask when they will release the body so you can get on with funeral arrangements."

Olivia demurred. "I've already taken care of it, Chief Vanderberg. As soon as I arrived in town, I visited the coroner and arranged for my aunt's body to be cremated and her ashes sent back to New York. There will be no memorial service."

"I understand," he said. "Well, again, our sympathies. Your aunt was an enthusiastic member of the Edgemont County community."

Connie touched Vanderberg's elbow. "Excuse the interruption, chief, but an officer with the Bureau of Indian Affairs is holding for you on line one."

Vanderberg said, "Right. Well, if you'll excuse me, Olivia, I'll leave you in the capable hands of Officer Price. It was nice to meet you."

After he left, she leveled her gaze at me. "Now that pleasantries are out of the way, let's get down to business. I'm here to discuss the progress of the investigation."

Olivia was manipulative by nature—that much was obvious from our previous interactions—however, I needed some answers and was in no mood to be accommodating.

"I can't release any information that might compromise the case," I said, "but we are pursuing some very encouraging leads."

"That sounds like a sidestep. I hoped more progress had been made by this stage."

I spread my hands. "It's the best I can do, I'm afraid. We're a small department with limited resources. However, I'm glad you stopped in because I have questions for you."

"For me? Well, I'll help in any way I can."

"Who is the beneficiary of your aunt's estate?"

She hesitated. "I am—not that her remaining property is significant enough to be called an estate. There is the house and perhaps miscellaneous collectibles."

"No cash or investments?"

"My Uncle Phil's prolonged illness drained their resources, I'm afraid. Evelyn had a bit of cash in reserve, but it didn't exceed more than a few hundred thousand dollars."

I wrote the amount on my notepad and underlined it. "In your estimation, together with the house, the total value of her estate is around what?"

She shrugged. "Perhaps a couple million dollars, give or take."

"And you will inherit *all* of that?"

"All of that?"

Her tone was amused, but I kept my expression neutral.

Then understanding dawned on her face. "You consider me a suspect. You think I had my aunt murdered for her money."

"A couple million dollars is a lot of money. People have killed for far less."

Righteous anger, real or contrived, is the most common reaction to an accusation, and that was the emotion that played across Olivia's face, but then she drew a deep breath and composed herself.

"Officer Price, I was devoted to Aunt Evelyn. My mother and father died when I was quite young, and she was all the family I had. However, I expected to provide her with financial support in her old age and as far as the money I will receive from her estate—well, let's say it is of little consequence to me. I had no reason to want my aunt dead, and I had nothing to do with her murder."

"What about life insurance?" I asked. "Did Mrs. Randall own any substantial policies and who benefits in the event of her death?"

"She owned a whole life policy, but I am not the beneficiary. Half of the insurance policy proceeds goes to The Nature Conservancy and the other half to The Cancer Research Institute. But you don't have to take my word for it. My attorney can send a copy of the policy and Aunt Evelyn's will to you."

"That would be beneficial."

She took an engraved business card out of her Hermès handbag and handed it to me. "This is my business card. If you have questions, please call me at this number. If I am not available, my secretary will make sure I call you back."

"I appreciate that, Olivia. There is one thing I forgot to mention. We haven't released the crime scene yet, but once we do, I'll hand over a set of your aunt's keys to you so you can go through her personal possessions."

"Thank you, but I won't be trekking out to Brightwater Canyon," she said, disdain flashing across her aquiline features. "My aunt's love of rustic life never appealed to me. I haven't visited her home in Brightwater Canyon, and I don't intend to do so now that she is gone. When you release the house, I'll hire a professional to pack up the house and have them stop by for the keys."

"Of course. Were you planning to return to New York today?"

Although my question was innocuous, she shot me a shrewd look. "I'll be in Jackson Hole at the Four Seasons until Sunday. Unless, of course, you are advising me not to leave town."

We considered each other for a moment. I figured she knew I couldn't require her to stay put without a court order.

"No, that's all right," I said. "I have all I need for now. Thank you for coming in and answering my questions today, Olivia."

She rose to her feet and set the mug on my desk. "Goodbye Officer Price."

Once she was gone, Justin let loose a low whistle. "What did you make of that piece of work? Was she out of place or what?"

"Like an atheist at Mass."

The chief poked his head out of his office. "Price, do you have a minute?"

When I stepped into his office, he said, "I got a call from Betty Reynolds over at the sheriff's office. She insists you have been harassing the residents of Brightwater Canyon and that a couple of them are threatening to file a complaint against you and Stokes."

"Are you kidding?"

"Nope. They claim you were snooping around and making accusations for no reason other than to intimidate the good citizens of the Brightwater Canyon community."

"That is ridiculous, chief. You know I couldn't intimidate anybody.

Frank McGuiness was pretty upset when we showed up unannounced and ordered us off his property, but since we intend to question Maggie McGuiness anyway, I didn't see any reason to force the issue."

I decided not to mention Justin's tense exchanges with the Bennetts and Tug Stratton.

Vanderberg chuckled. "Don't sweat it. I've dealt with these folks before and they can be drama queens, but I wanted you to know that you stirred the pot a little. How did the canvassing go?"

"Not a lot of joy there except for one old fella, Jameson Warner, who thinks he saw a suspicious white or tan sedan one night—he couldn't remember exactly which night—on the Brightwater Canyon Road. Nice man, but he had to be in his nineties with glasses a half inch thick. Plus, his memory seemed flaky, so I'm not sure it's worth pursuing."

"You're right, he doesn't sound credible," the chief said. "Besides, that road is a public access thoroughfare. Unless he saw the sedan Saturday night on Meadowlark Lane, it would be tough to link it to Mrs. Randall's death."

"Those were my thoughts as well, but I'll keep it in mind. You never know when a random tip can tie a case together. Most of the other neighbors we spoke to noticed nothing out of the ordinary the evening of the murder and admitted to nothing more than a passing acquaintance with Mrs. Randall."

"Huh. Do you think they were being truthful?"

"As far as I could tell, but here's something interesting. The residents consider Robert Sandoval the most virtuous man on the planet. Several people called him the 'salt of the earth' and a 'give you the shirt off his back' kind of guy. After the HOA board sent out an email informing them of Mrs. Randall's death, Sandoval himself visited several of the residents yesterday, under the guise of assuring them everything was under control."

Vanderberg considered this, stroking his jaw. "The canyon folks have always been staunch Sandoval supporters, which makes it is imperative you remain courteous and cautious, Price. We don't want to upset the illustrious residents of Brightwater Canyon beyond what is necessary."

"Of course, but we should talk to Sandoval."

"I'm as keen as you are to haul Sandoval in for questioning, but I want to question him myself. Give me time to clear my schedule, okay?"

I bit my lip. "Okay."

He switched subjects. "Olivia DeWitt showing up unannounced surprised me. Did you know she was coming?"

"Nope, not a clue. I was as shocked by her arrival as you were, chief."

"Is she still a suspect?"

"She's a slippery one and I couldn't get a good read on her. She claims she loved her aunt, and that the money from Mrs. Randall's estate is chump change, but we should still verify her statements and maybe do some digging into her background."

"That sounds reasonable. What other angles are you working?"

"I got some interesting information when I talked to Myrna Flowers."

"What did you find out?"

"A group called Brightwater Partners purchased almost every parcel sold in Brightwater Canyon since 2010. Guess who owns Brightwater Partners?"

It didn't take long for him to guess. "Robert Sandoval?"

"Yup. Myrna suggested I speak to Charlie Lumineux. Charlie was a partner in Brightwater Partners until Sandoval squeezed him out. The problem is, he has no phone, and he lives in Billings."

He raised one brow. "Charlie Lumineux, huh?"

"Myrna thinks he may have more information on Sandoval's dealings that Irene Brockman was talking about."

The chief nodded. "Then you should talk to him. You can take Stokes with you."

The thought of spending ten hours alone in the car with Justin made my gut ache. "Uh. I was planning to have Justin start the background on Olivia and make some calls. I have a close friend in the Billings Police Department who can tag along when I talk to Lumineux. We need to catch up, anyway, and Justin would feel like a fifth wheel."

Vanderberg thought about it. "Okay, but I don't want you talking to this Lumineux character alone, understand?"

"Roger that. If it's all right with you, I'm going to head home and make it an early night. I need to get on the road to Billings tomorrow before sunrise."

Vanderberg waved me away. "You're dismissed."

"Billings? Why in hell's bells do you need to go to Billings?"

Gracie was sprawled on my sofa, watching *Grey's Anatomy*. It was the dumb singing episode, otherwise she wouldn't be listening to me at all instead of half-listening. She was still pissed at me for being bitchy to her while she was painting her toenails last night.

"I have to talk to someone that might have information about the Randall case," I said again.

She looked perplexed. "Why don't you call him?"

I rolled my eyes. "He doesn't have a phone. Will you take Dancy to daycare in the morning?"

"Okay, okay. I'll let Rusty know I'll be late."

I twisted my hands together. "There's something else I want to ask you, Gracie. The murder investigation is heating up and if something comes up at the last minute, it's possible I won't get off work before the daycare closes. For the foreseeable future, I need you to pick Dancy from daycare every day. Can you do that for me?"

"As long as you're paying me, girlfriend." Gracie rubbed her fingers together but didn't take her eyes off the television.

SEVEN

Detective Rodney Lewis was waiting for me at the door of the Billings Police Station when I rolled into the parking lot, smiling so broadly I thought his face would split.

As soon as I got out of my police cruiser, he enveloped me in a bear hug. "Geezus, Wyn. It's been too long."

Rodney and I attended rival high schools in South Dakota and were classmates in the Criminal Justice program at the University of Wyoming. He joined the Billings Police Department following graduation, and we bumped into each occasionally while I was with the Rapid City police force, but lost touch after I followed Jason to California.

"I heard about San Diego," he said. "It must have been awful. I wish I could have helped—if I had known..."

He trailed off, sounding so forlorn I almost felt sorry for him.

I hugged him harder for a brief second before letting go. "It's okay. I got over it and I've moved on. Anyway, it's awesome to see you, L-Rod. Thanks for agreeing to help me out."

"No one has called me that in ages," he said with a laugh. "You want to interview one of our residents, right? Got an address?"

I handed him the piece of paper with Charlie Lumineux's address on it.

He snapped the paper with a fingernail. "Oh yeah, girlfren. You are in for a treat today. Let's grab ourselves a couple of caramel macchiatos and cruise on over to the south side."

It turned out he wasn't kidding about the caramel macchiatos. We stopped at Rail Line Coffee where he got a grande caramel macchiato and I got an iced coffee before we headed to south Billings.

On the way, he showed me pictures of his pretty wife and regaled me with tales of his three rowdy boys, and I showed him the picture of Dancy in her red and white Christmas dress.

But we put aside our chitchat once we turned on Lumineux's street, and I grasped the irony behind Rodney's earlier comment.

Archer Street was one of those wretched communities the authorities ought to bulldoze to put it out of its misery. Tiny, dilapidated frame houses coexisted alongside clusters of mobile homes. Faded, broken toys littered the yards and spilled out into the street. Junked cars clogged the driveways and teenagers loitered on the corners, casting angry glances at the strangers trespassing in their neighborhood.

It occurred to me no matter where you traveled—Billings, San Diego, or New York City—you would find the visible wreckage of broken lives and crushed dreams.

"This is it, Wyn." Rodney angled his unmarked police car into a parking space and gestured to a house with peeling aqua paint and rusted aluminum awnings hanging in desperation from the windows.

As we approached the house, I was grateful for Rodney's company. Although I had been in worse neighborhoods plenty of times by myself, it was always nice when somebody you trusted had your back.

We were halfway up the crumbling concrete walkway when the front door of the house flew open, and a tall, thin man with greased-back hair stepped onto the porch. He was wearing a threadbare western shirt and jeans that barely hung on his bony hips.

"Yeah? What do you want?" He lapsed into a deep, rumbling cough.

I flashed my badge. "Officer Price, Perseverance Police Department." I gestured to Rodney. "This is Detective Lewis of the Billings Police Department. We'd like to talk to Charlie Lumineux."

"I'm Charlie Lumineux." He regarded us for a moment, then jerked his thumb over his right shoulder. "C'mon in."

I preferred to talk outside, but followed him into the house, anyway.

It was a pigsty and smelled of stale cigarette smoke and cheap booze. Charlie cleared a pile of dirty clothes off the sofa with a sweep of his arm, and Rodney and I sat on the stained cushions, trying to look comfortable.

Charlie pulled a wooden chair from the kitchen into the living room and sat, crossing his legs. Then he fished in his pocket for a cigarette, lit it, and took a greedy drag.

Rodney looked at me.

I said, "Mr. Lumineux, I got your address from Myrna. Myrna Flowers."

Charlie looked at the floor and flicked the ashes off his smoke.

I cleared my throat. "Last weekend, a woman named Evelyn Randall was murdered in Edgemont County. I'm trying to find out why. It may have something to do with the Brightwater Canyon Partnership. I was hoping you might answer a few questions about your relationship with the partnership and Robert Sandoval."

He took another long drag of his smoke, the tobacco hissing as it burned.

I tried to think of one reason this dissipated wreck of a human would give a damn about Evelyn Randall's death and failed to come up with anything convincing. The silence was stifling. This was a mistake. I was wasting my time and Rodney's.

Then Charlie exhaled a stream of smoke and said, "I got cancer. I won't make Labor Day."

"I'm sorry."

His sunken eyes bored into mine. "Myrna is a good friend. The best friend I have left. God knows she deserves better than I could give her."

He got up to stub his cigarette out on a saucer and hitched up his pants. "This woman who died, you think Robert Sandoval was involved?"

"We're not sure, Mr. Lumineux, we are pursuing all leads." I choked a little on that part, since this was my solitary lead and it was tenuous at best. "We got a tip Mrs. Randall may have had information about

Sandoval or the Brightwater Canyon Partnership she was planning to expose. We're attempting to establish what information she had that was sensitive or damaging enough to put her at risk."

"I can tell you Sandoval is a nasty, scheming bastard," he said with a sour face. "He cheated me. Ruined me. Everybody in Edgemont County knows that. Now you might ask why the grandson of Bud Lumineux ran off like a scared pansy, leaving behind everything his daddy and granddaddy busted their asses to build. Well, guess I'm gonna tell you why, but it's not because I give a shit about this Randall woman. It's because I would love nothing better than to see Sandoval go down."

He shuffled into the kitchen and returned with a fifth of Jim Beam Bourbon, taking a swig before he sat down. "The Sandovals are one of the most influential families in Mexico. Among other enterprises, they own a big rancho in Chihuahua and a Mexican bank.

"Sandoval went to Harvard to get his MBA. He graduated top of his class and landed a job at Blackhammer, a big US development firm that was looking to get bigger through government contracts. The way he described it, this outfit recruited him hard. He spent the next twenty years busting his ass, eventually rising to CEO of the company, and just when he was about to make a silk purse out of a sow's ear, they booted him. It was for no apparent reason, according to him, and that really pissed him off. Said he got even somehow, though. The thing is, he got one hell of a payout—a corporate 'golden parachute'—which is how he afforded the Brightwater Canyon deal.

"Relieved I wouldn't lose the ranch, I never considered getting an attorney to look at the contracts he drew up. I grabbed the papers and signed on the dotted line. What the hell, I was desperate. Afterwards, he brought in his people, and I resumed my old lifestyle. I was so damn full of myself, telling everybody I didn't have to lift a finger because my partner was taking care of it. By the time I realized something was wrong, I was in debt so deep my asshole was around my neck.

"Bill Bachmeyer from the bank came to my house himself, I guess out of respect to my daddy, to tell me I had checks bouncing all over the county. Somewhere along the line, Brightwater Partners stopped covering my expenses. So I paid a visit to Sandoval to discuss the situation.

"It turned out the contracts I signed were promissory notes

collateralized by the Brightwater Canyon property. Since I hadn't brought in a buyer since we inked the deal, the expenses the partnership was covering for me were advances."

"What did you do?" I asked.

"I said some nasty things, made some threats, and threw a couple punches—pretty sure I landed one or two. Long story short, Sandoval and his thugs taught me humility. Afterwards, I considered myself damn lucky to be alive. Sometimes I wish they would've finished the job."

"Did you report it?"

Charlie emitted a cackle that sounded like a dog puking. "What's the point? He has the law in his pocket. No offense to the present company intended. Anyway, I was never privy to the real reason he wanted Brightwater Canyon, but I'll tell you this—" He bent forward, his gaunt face intense. "It has nothing to do with attracting folks to live there. He isn't interested in building a community. In fact, if outsiders wanted to buy property to build a home, we were supposed to make sure they lost interest fast. As soon as existing owners decided to sell, we scared off realtors and prospective buyers until the sellers panicked and sold to the partnership for a fraction of what the property was worth."

"Sandoval ordered you to threaten people?"

"Not so much threaten them as make them feel unwelcome. I ripped out For Sale signs on the sly, but I was too ashamed to confront anyone who might recognize me."

"Why did he want to frighten people away from Brightwater Canyon?"

"He never let me in on his grand plan, but I figured he must be running some kind of racket he wanted to keep on the down low."

"If you were to venture a guess, what kind of racket do you think it was?"

"Drugs. With the amount of dough he flashes around, it has to be drugs."

"You think Sandoval is running a drug operation out of Brightwater Canyon?"

He scratched the stubble on his cheek. "I can't prove it, but you know how remote that territory is. It wouldn't be too hard to hide a trafficking setup."

"Is he capable of murder?"

"You know Buck Lanier's death? That wasn't an accident. Bucky got too close to something."

"Could he have been investigating Sandoval?"

Charlie gave a noncommittal shrug. "Bucky wasn't the brightest crayon in the box. Most times, he didn't ask questions because he didn't know there *were* any questions. I ain't got no proof, but Bucky stumbled on to something too close to Sandoval's personal affairs—maybe he wanted a cut of the action to keep his mouth shut—so Sandoval killed him. If you're wondering what this Randall woman knew that got her murdered, figure out what Robert Sandoval is hiding. That's all I can tell you."

He looked exhausted. Rodney and I stood up.

"Guess I did the Lumineux name proud, didn't I? I'm sure glad my daddy ain't around to see it." His tone was bitter.

"Thank you for your time today, Mr. Lumineux." Rodney held out his hand.

Charlie didn't get up, but he took the detective's hand and nodded. He looked at me. "You tell Myrna...tell her I said hello."

"I will, Mr. Lumineux."

We let ourselves out.

"You reckon this Sandoval could be your guy?" Rodney asked on the trip back to the Billings police station.

"Sure. He had the means and unless he produces an alibi for the time-frame of the crime, he had opportunity. What his motivation was, however, is a mystery unless we can nail down some substantive evidence of a drug ring."

"Have you questioned him?"

"Not yet. The guy is a local bigwig and Chief Vanderberg insists on being present when we interview him, but since politics consumes all of Vanderberg's time and attention right now, I'm treading water."

"Oh boy, I know how that goes. If the public knew how often investigations come to a screeching halt because the top brass is too busy kissing ass—"

"No, that's not what I meant," I said, cutting short his rant. "I'm talking about actual politics. Vanderberg is running for sheriff because the last sheriff—that Buck Lanier you heard Charlie talking about—died under dubious circumstances mid-term. Plus, he's also acting as interim sheriff, so he's trying to run two law enforcement shops and a campaign."

Rodney raised his eyebrows. "That does complicate things."

"Tell me about it. And if Lumineux is right about Sandoval operating a drug trafficking outfit in Brightwater Canyon, then the Wyoming Division of Criminal Investigation will step in and then the whole situation will get twice as messy."

"You're afraid the state will claim jurisdiction and trample all over your murder investigation."

I nodded. "It's like calling in the Feds—lots of inflated egos competing for a big score to boost their careers. Then the focus shifts from solving a murder to taking down a network of drug operators. Flashy drug busts are much sexier than the murders of old ladies."

"You don't know for certain drugs are involved, Wyn. Besides, I know you'll catch the murderer before the DCI intrudes—or he kills again."

"I've missed your sunny optimism, L-Rod."

Connie was gone for the day when I got back to the station, but Justin was there reading a newspaper, his feet on the dispatcher's desk.

"Good thing Connie can't see you with your dirty boots on her desk where she eats her lunch," I said, harsher than I intended.

He removed his feet. "Where have you been?"

"Billings. I interviewed a guy I hoped would have information for me about the Randall murder."

"Any luck?"

"Yes, and no. Have you ever heard of Charlie Lumineux?"

He snorted. "Everybody has heard of the Lumineuxs."

"Charlie was Robert Sandoval's partner in the Brightwater Canyon development until Sandoval ran him off. He thinks Sandoval is hiding something. He didn't give me anything specific, but he thought it might be drugs."

I picked up a piece of chalk and wrote 'drugs?' in small letters under Sandoval's name on the investigation board.

"Ka-ching!" Justin said. "I knew it."

"We don't have anything concrete yet, Justin, so keep it under your hat for now. Did you talk to Maggie McGuiness?"

He crinkled the newspaper in his hand. "I called her like you instructed me to."

"Is she coming in tomorrow?"

"Um. Well, I warned her we would visit her house again if she didn't come in, and she freaked out. I think she's afraid of her husband, Frank. She mentioned something about him being gone Monday afternoon, so I said she could come in at 2:00 on Monday."

He didn't look at me, perhaps because he was worried I would question his decision.

"Okay. I guess that will work," I said. "I don't want to incite a domestic dispute during a homicide investigation if I can avoid it. Anything else?"

"I got some information on Olivia DeWitt here somewhere—" He scrambled around in the mess of coffee cups, food containers and papers on his desk until he found what he was looking for. "Okay, here it is. Let's see...she graduated from Wellesley College and worked as a realtor in New York. Then she married Dimitri DeWitt, co-founder of Harris DeWitt Partners, but he drowned in a sailing accident in 2018."

"What does Harris DeWitt do?"

"The guy I spoke to on the phone said they develop hospitality properties, like resorts and hotels, but they also have interests in what he called 'high-end residential' and retail."

"Is Olivia still involved with the company?"

"Yeah, as far as I can tell. The guy answering the phone was new and couldn't tell me a lot, but she's listed in the company directory as a director. It looks pretty legit. Here, see for yourself."

He swiveled his computer monitor towards me.

There was Olivia DeWitt on the "Our Leadership" page, her red power suit complemented by a haughty smile and pearls.

Justin was right. It all looked genuine.

"I also searched the public records database. Other than property transactions, there wasn't much, but in 2016 Dimitri and Olivia DeWitt purchased a townhouse in New York for ten million dollars. *Ten million.*" The look on his face was a mixture of disgust and amazement. "With that kind of scratch, why would she need a couple mil from her old auntie?"

I ignored his hard-boiled detective lingo and picked up the eraser, poised to wipe Olivia's off the blackboard, then hesitated. "Did anything come in on the fax? I was expecting her to send me a copy of Evelyn Randall's will and insurance policy today."

"Nope."

"Let's follow up on that. She might have a fancy house, but the thing about reaching that level of affluence is that you need money to maintain the lifestyle. See what you can dig up on Harris DeWitt's finances, too. Olivia claimed she was in Jackson Hole on business, so check out hospitality projects and find out if Harris DeWitt is a prospective bidder."

"So you're thinking something is hinky with her story?"

"Maybe. Or maybe I don't like her. Either way, let's keep on it." I shuffled through my notes. "Has the chief been in today?"

"Yeah. He stopped by earlier."

"Did he say whether he would be in tomorrow?"

"Nope. He doesn't share his calendar with me, but he mentioned he was driving to Casper today, something about a missing maid."

"Why would a maid missing in Casper concern Chief Vanderberg?"

Justin threw an exasperated look in my direction. "No, not in Casper. It's that Perfect Touch Cleaning outfit, you know, that woman who cleans the station works for them."

"You mean Josefina? Is she the one missing?"

"Hell if I know."

"Okay, I'll call him."

"Good luck with that. He's so occupied juggling the sheriff's office calls with the campaign he doesn't answer his cell phone."

It was true. I called Vanderberg twice on the way down from Billings and left messages both times, but he wasn't returning my calls.

"When do we go talk to Sandoval?" Justin asked.

"I'm working on that."

I turned off my computer and gathered up my stuff. Gracie agreed to babysit Dancy while I went to Billings, but she had a hot date tonight and I was under strict orders to relieve her before seven o'clock.

"I'll see you later, Justin."

He grunted and put his feet back on Connie's desk.

EIGHT

My jaw dropped when Chief Vanderberg walked in the door of Shepherd of the Hills Lutheran Church.

Most folks in Perseverance didn't attend church on a regular basis, which was remarkable considering the number of churches in town. A few defunct houses of worship had been converted to housing, a trend I wasn't too keen on, but it was better than more mobile homes.

The chief was dressed in a light blue button-down shirt with a navy sports coat and tan chinos and nodded to the other congregants as he made his way to a pew in front. That was a dead giveaway he wasn't a Lutheran.

It's a known fact Lutherans didn't like to sit in the front pews. As a kid, I could never understand it. People sitting in front enjoyed the distinct advantage of being dismissed first after the service ended, but I suppose if a person was worried the pastor might look in their direction when he sermonized about a particular sin, it could be risky.

The theme of Pastor Mueller's sermon that Sunday was the importance of regular church attendance, and when he beamed at Vanderberg sitting in the first row, the chief grinned back, which I thought was hilarious since he would probably never show up at Shepherd of the Hills again.

Outside the church after the service, a small group of congregants formed a queue to shake Vanderberg's hand.

Dancy and I joined the end of the line.

When it came our turn, he said, "Price, fancy meeting you here."

"You weren't returning my calls, so I started stalking you."

The grin on his face froze, and he seemed unnerved, as if he couldn't decide if I was serious.

"That's a joke, chief. I'm a member of this church. My daughter and I attend services here every Sunday."

"Ah! I didn't know that," he said with a laugh. "It's great to see you here, anyway."

"But since you're here—"

"Chief Vanderberg." A hipster in a blue plaid suit shouldered his way through the people milling around Vanderberg and grabbed the chief's arm. "The car is this way, sir."

Vanderberg pointed to the young man pulling him towards the parking lot. "My campaign manager, Dino. We'll talk later, Price."

"But chief—"

"Later." He turned away with a wave.

Dancy made a grumpy sound and buried her face in my neck. I rubbed her back to soothe her. "Shh, shh. Let's go home for breakfast and see if Auntie Gracie is back."

The excitement of Vanderberg's visit waned, and the congregants returned to their cars. As Dancy and I followed the crowd, the family in front of me stopped without warning, and I dodged sideways, bumping into Josefina, who was moving towards the church against the flow of traffic.

"How nice to see you here, Josefina," I said.

At that moment, someone behind me called my name, and I looked over my shoulder. Myrna Flowers signaled to me as she left her elderly mother with Pastor Mueller and marched in my direction.

When I turned back to Josefina, she was already scurrying away.

"Good morning, Wyn and Dancy." Myrna patted one of Dancy's white patent leather shoes. "My apologies. I didn't mean to interrupt."

"Good morning, Myrna. No, it's fine. I saw the station's cleaning lady, Josefina, and I was going to welcome her to Shepherd of the Hills."

Myrna tsked. "If she is one of Dolores Donovan's crew, I doubt she is here for the church service. She's probably here to clean the church, poor overworked thing."

In response to my puzzled look, she said, "Perfect Touch Cleaning lost one of their cleaning women, and Dolores has forced the remaining staff to pick up the slack, which has wreaked havoc with the schedules. I know because the gal who vanished also cleaned the courthouse and we haven't had a decent cleaning in a week."

"Oh. That's too bad." I suppressed the urge to look at my watch.

"Connie said you went to see Charlie. How is he?" Her words tumbled out in a hushed rush as if someone might overhear. She glanced back at her mother, who was still bending the young pastor's ear.

"Not good," I said. "Do you know he has cancer?"

"Yes. Did you tell him I gave you his address?"

"I did. He wanted me to tell you—"

She tilted forward, eager to hear what he said.

"He spoke warmly of you, Myrna. It is obvious he considers you a dear friend. He asked me to say hello."

For a moment her characteristic poise slipped, and her eyes grew moist.

"Thank you, Wyn." She reached out and gave my hand a quick squeeze before rushing back to her mother's side.

Gracie was supposed to watch Dancy that afternoon, but she was just getting back from her date of the previous evening as we were leaving for church. As soon as she caught sight of my disapproving expression, she insisted a hot shower and copious amounts of coffee would make her right as rain, but she still looked worse for wear when we got home.

It wasn't an ideal situation, but I was burning to talk to Robert Sandoval and since it was apparent that the chief was too preoccupied, I had no other options. Besides, I was doing him a favor by taking the initiative. It was one less thing for him to cram into his hectic schedule, and if I waited until Monday, Justin Stokes would insist on coming along, and that was out of the question.

Sandoval's ranch was a decent trek from Perseverance, and neither the GPS on my cell phone nor the old map in the glove box of the cruiser was of any help in finding the place, so I ended up wandering around the backcountry for over an hour. I almost lost all hope when I topped yet another dusty hill and there it was, announced by a massive stone archway with "Sandoval Ranches" worked out in black wrought iron across the top.

The wide, smooth driveway led to a location straight out of a Hollywood movie set. On a slight rise to the south, massive pines shaded a magnificent log mansion, while multiple barns, their roofs emblazoned with a stylized red "S" brand, loomed like monoliths to the north. Thoroughbred horses frisked behind wooden crossbuck fences, and the surrounding green pastures were thick with Hereford cattle.

Sandoval might think it inappropriate for a city cop to show up unannounced on a Sunday afternoon, but if I was lucky, I might catch him off guard and he would speak with me, so I headed for the mansion and parked in the gravel drive in front of the house. When I switched off the Crown Vic, it lurched a couple times in protest before giving up with a gasp.

A dark-haired woman holding a damp dish towel answered the door.

"Hello. My name is Wyn Price," I said with a smile. "Is Mr. Sandoval home?"

"Please come in, Miss Price," she said. "Mr. Sandoval is finishing his Sunday dinner, but I will let him know you're here."

She abandoned me in the circular front foyer, which was guarded by a collection of bronze statues and almost as big as my entire house.

I bent to read the inscription on a life-sized bust of a Native American man.

"That is Conquering Bear, the reluctant chief of the Brulé Lakota. A US army trooper murdered him in a tragic dispute over a sick cow. It's an appalling story." Robert Sandoval nodded to the statue as he strode into the foyer, hands in the pockets of his jeans. "To what do I owe the pleasure of your visit, Officer Price?"

"Thank you for agreeing to see me, Mr. Sandoval. I'm investigating the death of Evelyn Randall, and I was wondering if you might help me by answering a few questions."

Suspicion flitted across his face but faded almost as soon as it appeared. "Of course, please forgive me for my lack of manners. I'm glad to answer your questions if it will aid your investigation."

"Can we speak in private without interruption?"

He tossed his head towards the main part of the house. "It's just me and our housekeeper, Lucia. My wife is visiting family in Austin. Come on, we can talk in my study. I'll tell Lucia we are not to be disturbed."

But before he could persuade the housekeeper not to interrupt us, she brought tall glasses of iced tea with sprigs of mint and little orange and rosemary-scented shortbread biscuits.

Sandoval sipped his tea and looked on as I devoured several cookies.

"Mm. Those are delicious," I said. "I appreciate your hospitality, Mr. Sandoval. I am so sorry to impose on you without calling first, but since Deputy Bartel is out injured and Chief Vanderberg is busy with—"

At the mention of the chief's name, Sandoval grunted, but then motioned for me to go on.

"Anyway, we're stretched a little thin and eager to close this case, so I am taking you up on your kind offer to help. Any information you can give me might be useful. I spoke with Mrs. Randall's neighbors, and they hold you in quite high regard. They assured me if anyone knows what's going on in the canyon, it's you."

He tipped his head back and laughed. It was genuine, as if the fact I was asking around about him was amusing. Then he put his elbows on his desk and locked his eyes on mine. "Who else did you talk to?"

I took out my notepad and flipped to the list of canyon residents. "Let's see, Mr. and Mrs. Bennett—"

He cut me off. "No. I know who you spoke to in *Brightwater Canyon*. Who *else* have you talked to?"

I hesitated. "Uh, Irene Brockman. Myrna Flowers—"

"And Charlie Lumineux."

"Yes."

"Not my biggest fans."

"No, sir. Oh, and Olivia DeWitt."

He sat back and folded his hands against his stomach. "Every single one of them might believe they have good reason to hate me, Officer Price. Whatever they told you might be true. Hell, I'm a businessman, not a politician."

"How did you know I spoke to Charlie Lumineux?"

He smirked in self-satisfaction. "I guessed. Myrna and Lumineux go way back. It's no surprise she would drag him into anything to do with me and Brightwater Canyon. She's been in love with Lumineux since high school, but he always considered himself too good for her and wouldn't give her the time of day until he squandered his chances with every other eligible woman in Edgemont County. Despite his aversion to fidelity, Myrna believed he would marry her in the end. She still blames me that he bolted without making an honest woman out of her, you know. But he's a worthless clown, and she's better off a spinster than with a two-timing loser like Charlie Lumineux."

I blinked and pretended to be eyeing another cookie.

"What else did Myrna say, Officer Price?"

"Not a great deal, other than suggesting I speak to Charlie."

"I suppose they both said I was a no-good, thieving bastard."

"Something along those lines, but I'd like to hear your side of the story, Mr. Sandoval."

His expression was wry. "I cut Lumineux a fair deal, but later, when he was down on his luck, he imagined he was cheated. You see, at the beginning, I had no intention of forcing Lumineux out of the Brightwater Partnership. I was supposed to be the silent partner, but that's before I realized the self-important ignoramus couldn't manage himself, let alone a business.

"In retrospect, I should have seen him coming from a mile away. Charlie Lumineux was all hat and no cattle, as they say. Acted like he was doing me a favor by letting me in on his exclusive grand development deal—said I would make a fortune."

I raised a disbelieving eyebrow. "You mean you haven't?"

Sandoval guffawed and slapped a hand on the table. "Hell no. I'm still so deep in the red on the Brightwater deal it would take me the rest of my lifetime to dig out if it were my sole source of revenue.

"You see, long before I came along, Lumineux hired his buddies as contractors and paid them top dollar for subpar work. The results were inadequate roads, lousy drainages, and vague property lines. Most of the parcels were unsaleable without additional development or repair. We injected a bundle of cash into Brightwater before we sold our first lot, not to mention shelling out exorbitant attorney's fees to defend lawsuits brought by existing owners over overlapping property lines and screwed-up drainages. And don't get me started on the past due bills.

"After we inked the deal, Lumineux embarked on a months-long drinking binge. The only way I gathered he was still alive was because money kept draining out of the partnership bank account. The imbecile didn't have enough sense to pay his overdue bills, but he spent money like there was no tomorrow. He bought a house for a girlfriend in Sheridan and a brand new pickup for himself in Denver, which he wrecked within a week.

"To stop the bleeding, we shut him off. A few days later, he showed up at the partnership office and assaulted one of my ranch hands. It turned out the damn fool didn't read the partnership contracts—even after I advised him to engage an attorney to go over them before we signed. He was too damn dumb to take good advice."

"He claims a couple of your thugs beat him up, Mr. Sandoval."

"I admit I ordered my men to subdue him and throw him out, and they might have roughed him up a little in the process, but I didn't have a choice. He wouldn't listen to reason and kept coming at me, swinging.

"Anyway, to recoup my losses on the Brightwater investment, I started buying up properties following the financial crisis, in particular those that were sold before we formed the partnership. With judicious planning and redevelopment, I might reverse the financial damage."

If Sandoval's version of events was true, it cast an unfavorable light on Charlie as a witness. I decided to shift gears. "What about the offer you made to Olivia DeWitt for her aunt's house? She said you lowballed her."

"I was honest with her," he said, swatting away the implication. "She'll have a difficult time selling that property because it's the scene of a violent crime. High-dollar properties in niche communities like Brightwater Canyon can be impossible to unload after a murder. Evelyn's house will be on the market for months—if not years—and still sell at thirty percent below its normal market value."

"I see your point. Folks can be squeamish about that kind of stuff."

His eyes narrowed. "What did my good friend Irene Brockman have to say about me?"

"Irene thinks Mrs. Randall had information about you, something you don't want folks to know. What do you think that might be?"

Uneasiness flashed across his face. "I can assure you I do not know what those two harebrained biddies might have conjured up in their overactive imaginations, but I can tell you this, Irene has been my sworn enemy ever since I put an end to free grazing on Brightwater's open range and insisted she pay for cattle grazing rights like any other rancher."

"I bet that didn't thrill her."

"That is an understatement. She accosted my wife and daughter on the street in Perseverance and threatened to show up here with a shotgun and shoot me. Afterwards, someone started vandalizing the Sandoval Ranches' property. It went on for years—minor-league stuff, mostly—but I always suspected it was Irene or one of her boys.

"I'll give you some advice, Officer Price. Consider the source and what their agenda might be before you believe what you hear." Sandoval made a show of getting up from his chair, as if he had been sitting too long and needed to stretch. "I hope I cleared things up for you. Now if you would excuse me, I promised my grandkids we would Skype this afternoon. I'll see you to the door."

Even though I wasn't finished asking questions, Sandoval made it clear the audience was over, and I wasn't prepared to press too hard—yet.

He ushered me to the front door and opened it.

"One last thing for my notes, Mr. Sandoval," I said as I stepped out onto the veranda. "Where were you Saturday evening before last?"

"Let me see." His smile didn't waver as he thought. "I drove my wife to the Jackson Hole airport and got back around 5:00 p.m. I was home the rest of the evening. You can ask Lucia if you like."

"No, that's all for now. I thank you for your time. I hope you won't mind if I call on you again if I have further questions."

"Of course—and tell Chief Vanderberg I said hello and good luck with the campaign. I can't say I'm surprised he's running for sheriff. Shrewd, ambitious fella like him—he will fit right in with our *illustrious* elected officials." His tone was tinged with a hint of mockery.

Unable to articulate a suitable response, I turned on my heel and marched across the gravel driveway to my cruiser. With every crunching step, I felt his eyes boring into my back.

Gracie's tanned legs were sticking out the front flap of Dancy's pop-up princess castle, which had been erected in the middle of the living room. Judging by the whistling wheezes emanating from within, she was fast asleep.

Dancy was in front of the television, her chocolate-smeared face entranced as Elsa belted "Let It Go". She had that faraway "this is the third time I have watched *Frozen*" stare.

Her face lit up with a goofy smile at the sound of my voice, but she couldn't pull her glazed eyes away from the television, so I shut it off and picked her up. She squeaked in protest, then collapsed against me as the evil spell was broken.

From inside the tent, Gracie made a sound like a pig rooting in a trough, and her toes twitched.

It was official. I was a terrible mother.

NINE

The chief was in the breakroom pouring himself some coffee when I got to work the next morning.

"It isn't often both of us beat Connie to work," I said. "What brings you in so early, chief?"

He yawned. "I keep getting further and further behind, so I came in to knock out some emails and reports before Dino hauls me back out on the campaign trail. Any joy with what's-his-name in Billings?"

"Charlie Lu—"

The front door opened, and Connie and Justin came in together.

For once, Justin didn't look hungover, so I squelched the urge to tease him by checking my watch.

"Looks like we're all chasing the same worm this morning," Vanderberg said with a grin. "There's fresh coffee in the pot."

Justin looked confused and a little disgusted by the worm remark, but Connie chuckled and pulled him into the breakroom.

The chief turned to me. "Let's go to my office and you can talk me through what you've got, Price."

I followed him and settled into a chair. "Lumineux thinks Sandoval is hiding something, but he doesn't know what it is. He mentioned a couple of incidents involving Sandoval that were dodgy, but without further corroboration, they weren't anything I would call criminal. Lumineux also mentioned a company called Blackhammer and said Sandoval was furious when they terminated his employment. Wasn't Blackhammer the name Justin brought up at the Spur?"

Vanderberg grabbed his Day Timer and started flipping through the address book. "Let's call my friend Elaine Smith down at the Colorado Attorney General's office and see what she can tell us about Sandoval and why he parted ways with Blackhammer."

While the chief negotiated with an overprotective secretary at the Colorado Attorney General's headquarters, I entertained myself by inspecting his diplomas and awards. He had more official commendations than Kanye had bling, which wasn't surprising given his years on the Chicago police force.

When the chief finally convinced the gatekeeper that he was who he said he was, he punched the speaker button and gave me an exasperated look as he sat back in his chair. "You'd think I was trying to talk to the president."

A brief interlude of canned music followed, then a sultry female voice came on the line. "Why, Lars, you tease. It's about time you called me back."

"Hello Elaine. It has been too long since we talked." Vanderberg's lips twitched, but he kept his composure and didn't give away any hints about his relationship with Elaine. "You're on speaker phone, by the way. I'm here with one of my colleagues, Officer Wyn Price."

If Elaine was embarrassed, she didn't let on.

"Hello, Officer Price," she said, cool and smooth as a Creamsicle. "How may I be of service today, Lars?"

"Elaine, have you ever heard of a company called Blackhammer?" the chief asked. "I seem to remember hearing something about them running afoul of the law down there in Denver years ago."

"Blackhammer? Let me think. Yes, I remember now. They were a government contractor that did infrastructure development work in Mexico. It was a fraud case brought by investors who were suing because they thought Blackhammer was under-reporting revenue."

"Bit of a switch there, isn't it? Most fraudulent schemes involve the over-reporting of revenue, don't they?"

"That's true, but some companies under report to avoid taxes. However, the AG speculated Blackhammer was involved in a money laundering scheme. It attracted notoriety, but the case never made it off the ground."

"You mean there wasn't enough evidence?"

"It never got that far. The investigation was over before it started. The company cut a private deal with the investors, and they withdrew their grievance and went away happy. No complaint, no foul, as far as we were concerned. Our workload is overwhelming the way it is, so if cases resolve themselves, we don't ask questions."

I leaned in closer to the speakerphone. "Elaine, do you recall the name Robert Sandoval coming up?"

"He was the scapegoat, as I remember. Blackhammer blamed the whole affair on the CEO Robert Sandoval, and then canned him."

"Did you hear anything about Sandoval after his departure from Blackhammer?" asked Vanderberg.

"Not a peep. Why are you interested in a seventeen-year-old aborted case, anyway?"

Vanderberg twiddled his thumbs. "Oh, merely curiosity, I guess. We were bored and thought we'd ask."

Elaine chortled with amusement. "Don't you Wyoming cops have anything better to do than rehash stale cases outside your authority?"

We laughed along with her.

Then Vanderberg grew sober. "Mr. Sandoval retired to Perseverance, Wyoming, and one or two folks have offered his name in connection with a murder case. He's got well-heeled supporters in this county who think his shit doesn't stink, but no one calling him a crook can produce any proof. You know that absurd 'innocent until proven guilty' rule?"

"Yes, I know. It's a pain in the ass," she said with an air of resignation.

"Let's get back to Blackhammer," he said. "Are they still around?"

"No, Corporate Dynamics acquired the company shortly thereafter."

The chief clapped a broad hand on the desk. "Right. Okay, thanks Elaine, you've been a tremendous help."

"My pleasure, but you didn't hear any of this from me, okay? Public prosecutors aren't supposed to gossip, you know?"

"Don't worry, Elaine, our lips are sealed, and I owe you one."

"I know you do. And the next time you're in Denver, I intend to collect, Lars."

"Bye, Elaine." He tapped the speaker button and ended the call.

I rubbed my temples. "So, this Blackhammer outfit, led by Sandoval, was caught laundering money—"

"And the company paid off its critics to shut them up."

"What do you suppose they were up to?"

"There were whispers in law enforcement circles that Blackhammer was in bed with the Sinaloa Cartel, but the authorities couldn't substantiate the connection."

The Sinaloa Cartel was the largest and most powerful illegal drug trafficking and money laundering operation in the world. Yesterday I was eating herb-scented cookies with a man who might have been buddies with El Chapo. It made me sick to my stomach.

I wiped my hands on my pants. "Chief, I drove out to Sandoval's ranch yesterday. Sorry if I overstepped, but on the heels of my interview with Charlie Lumineux, I needed to get a read on him."

"Was that the important matter you wanted to discuss at the church?"

I nodded.

The chief seemed unfazed by my admission. "What happened?"

"Not much. Sandoval and I had tea in his study, and he was the picture of cordiality. He didn't refute any information I got from the others except to add details. He said Charlie Lumineux was a sore loser who had himself to blame for the way things turned out with the Brightwater Partnership. Lumineux himself admitted as much. Sandoval confirmed he snapped up a bunch of properties in Brightwater when prices were low following the financial crash, but he said he suffered extensive losses in the deal with Lumineux and was trying to recover a part of his investment."

"What about the offer to Evelyn Randall's niece? How did he justify that?"

I raised my shoulders and let them fall. "He confessed the offer was low, but a property where a murder occurred can be difficult to sell."

Vanderberg cocked an eyebrow. "It sounds like Sandoval converted you to an ally."

"No, it wasn't like that," I said, waving away his remark. "I asked questions, and he answered. It wasn't an interrogation. I believed he would be more open if he was relaxed, and I was correct. At least, until I brought up Irene Brockman's claim that Mrs. Randall had sensitive information about him. He brushed the allegation off as nonsense, but then he clammed up."

"Do you think he was hiding something?"

"Yes, I do. He tried to disguise it, but it put a burr under his saddle when I brought up Irene and Mrs. Randall."

Vanderberg tapped his index finger on the desk. "Then that's the lead we pursue, Price. Talk to Irene again. See if you can get her to spill everything she knows about Sandoval."

"Okay. Sure. I was also thinking Mrs. Randall might have reported something to the sheriff's office. If something criminal was going on, wouldn't she turn to law enforcement first?"

Vanderberg shook his head. "I doubt she would have had much luck on that front."

"It might be worth it to check it out, though. Clifton Bartel seems like a pretty decent sort—perhaps she trusted him. I'd like to try it."

"Then go for it. Oh, and Price? Excellent job. I appreciate you taking the initiative on this—it takes a load off my mind. It's clear you have this under control, and I apologize for underestimating your readiness to take on a major case. From this point forward, this investigation is your baby. All I ask is that you keep me informed and let me know if you need anything from me."

The computer on his desk chimed, and his eyes shifted to the screen.

It was my cue to leave, but I hesitated. "Chief, if we suspect drugs are at the heart of this case, when do we involve the Wyoming Division of Criminal Investigation?"

He focused his attention back on me. "We can call the DCI at any time to assist in a major case if we don't have the expertise and resources to solve it. Is it your opinion we need to?"

"No," I said with more force than I intended. "I mean, not yet anyway. I'd like a crack at solving this one first. Not to disparage the Wyoming DCI, but in my experience, investigations become a three-ring rodeo once the state agency gets involved."

The chief brushed off my concern. "No need to explain. We've had our share of clashes with the DCI when they muscled in on an investigation. I'm confident we will solve this one on our own and once we do, it will be quite an accomplishment for the department and, to be honest, an enormous boost for my campaign for sheriff—"

"But if drugs are involved, we'll have no choice."

"I agree with you, but there's no reason to cry wolf before we have the salient facts. Our primary aim is to solve Evelyn Randall's murder. If we uncover a drug operation along the way, then we inform the DCI about it after closing our case."

"Okay. Thanks, chief."

"Now that's settled, we all have full plates, so let's get cracking."

Back at my desk, I called Irene Brockman, but she didn't answer, so I left a message asking her to call me back. Then I called Betty Reynolds at the sheriff's office.

Betty had worked for the Edgemont County Sheriff's Office for decades as the dispatcher and office manager. Considering her experience in the position, I imagined there must be some intelligence hiding behind her spacey façade, but she had yet to reveal it to me.

The phone rang several times before Betty picked it up.

"Hello, Sheriff's Office?" She always sounded astonished to be answering the phone, like she woke up mid-horror flick to find the phone ringing.

"Hello Betty, this is Officer Price over at the Perseverance Police Department. I'm investigating Evelyn Randall's death—"

"Yes, Officer Price, and don't I know it? My phone has been ringing off the hook with complaints. Frank McGuiness claims you trespassed on his property without permission, and I've gotten two—no, three—calls about you nosing around and disturbing the peace out there in Brightwater Canyon for no reason."

I wondered if her concern for the noble citizens of Brightwater Canyon was legitimate or if she was upset because their calls disrupted her daytime soaps.

"That's why I called you, Betty. We both want the residents of the Brightwater community to return to their normal lives as soon as possible, so I'm sure they would appreciate it if you helped me wrap this up."

"Well, I promised them I would take care of it."

"In that case," I said. "you can start by telling me if Mrs. Randall contacted the sheriff's office in the past year. If she did, I need the dates, times, and specific complaints she made when she contacted your office, and who responded to the calls. Jot the information down on a piece of paper for me, and I'll pick it up early this afternoon, say one o'clock?"

"Well, I guess I could do that." Despite her acquiescence, Betty sounded suspicious about what she was getting herself into.

"That's terrific. Now I know why everyone says you're the glue that holds the sheriff's department together. I'll see you this afternoon." Before she had second thoughts, I hung up.

While I ate lunch, I transcribed my scribbled notes into the case file and added every bit of information I could think of that might be important.

Absent physical forensic evidence or an outright confession of guilt, a successful murder charge required enough accumulated bits and pieces to make the allegation stick. But the lack of evidence at the Randall house was problematic. It suggested a meticulous and unemotional killer who was unlikely to slip up or make a mistake. Based on my interactions with Robert Sandoval, he fit that description, but he wouldn't capitulate without a fight. I would have to keep chipping away at his veneer of innocence until it cracked.

The red Ford pickup truck parked in front of the Edgemont County Sheriff's Office reversed at high speed as I pulled into the gravel parking lot, forcing me to swerve to avoid clipping the truck's bumper. Whether the driver saw me was debatable since he sped off towards town without a backwards glance.

When I entered the building, Betty Reynolds was lounging in a swivel chair, watching a flat panel television on the wall behind the booking counter. She wore a lemon-yellow polyester pantsuit with a crocheted top and white sandals, and her jet black hair was styled in a beehive. If it were 1969, she could have been the cover model for *Ladies' Home Journal*.

Despite the loud electronic buzz of the door alert, she didn't seem to notice my arrival.

"Good afternoon, Betty," I said, approaching her desk.

She picked up a piece of paper and flapped it in my direction without looking at me. "Here you go. These are all the calls we received from Evelyn Randall in the last year."

I scanned the page. It was a list of calls Mrs. Randall made to the sheriff's office from January to June of the current year, which wasn't what I asked for, but pointing that out might further aggravate Betty's frosty attitude.

The first three of the five entries were mundane, run-of-the-mill grievances. Mrs. Randall phoned in two complaints about local kids partying on the Brightwater Canyon Road and one concerning injured wildlife, but it was her last two calls that caught my attention.

On June 3rd, at 2:36 p.m., Mrs. Randall reported illegal activity on a neighbor's property. That same day, at 6:05 p.m., she called to complain about a trespasser or trespassers on her property. Deputy Clif Bartel responded to all the calls on the list except the injured deer. He sent that one to Wyoming Game and Fish.

I showed Betty the June 3rd entries. "Did Deputy Bartel file reports on these last two entries? If he did, may I see them?"

She didn't take her eyes off Dr. Phil. "You didn't say you needed copies of the reports. There's an official process for that—forms to fill out and whatnot."

"I don't need official copies. I'd just like to read them. It's in relation to the Randall case. If you're in the middle of something important, I can find them myself. Point me in the right direction."

She looked away from the tv and caught me goggling the bank of filing cabinets behind her desk. "I can't have you digging around in my filing system. I am the sole person authorized to retrieve sheriff's office documents."

"Take your time, then. I'm not in any hurry." To demonstrate my willingness to endure a long wait, I plopped into the guest chair and settled in.

Betty huffed in consternation but it was time for Dr. Phil to go on commercial break, so she levered herself up and flounced over to the cabinets, returning with a thin folder labeled "June" in bold red marker. She licked her fingers and leafed through the incident reports.

"Here we go." She handed me a report filed by Deputy Bartel on June 5th, concerning two calls from Evelyn Randall on June 3rd.

Despite the cramped handwriting, I deciphered Deputy Bartel was home when he received the calls from dispatch. The text of his report was brief.

2:36 p.m. Mrs. Evelyn Randall 1154 Meadowlark Lane, Brightwater Canyon, called to report suspicious activity on adjacent property. Checked location, no evidence of aforesaid activity. 6:05 p.m. Mrs. Randall reported someone in her backyard and requested an officer come out right away. Randall property and vicinity checked. Nothing suspicious found. Doors and windows checked at Mrs. Randall's request. All in working order and secured.

I sat back in my chair. Based on this account of events, Deputy Clifton Bartel may have been the last person to see Evelyn Randall alive.

"Is Deputy Bartel home from the hospital yet?"

She looked puzzled. "Home? Oh! Yes, but he and his wife LaVonne took off this morning for his niece's wedding in Seattle. I thought Chief Vanderberg would have relayed that to you. He's known about it for months."

I bit back a foul-tempered response. "I need to discuss this report with Deputy Bartel. Can you give me his cell phone number?"

She snatched a hot pink Post-It note from a pad on her desk and scribbled down Bartel's number.

"Thanks so much for your help, Betty."

"Mm-hmm." Dr. Phil was back, and she leaned back in her chair again.

On my way out, I encountered the cleaning woman, Josefina.

"Hello, Josefina. We meet again," I said as I spun out of her way.

Black thunderclouds roiled over the Wind River Range, and a gust of wind carried with it the smell of rain as I ran to my cruiser. Although moisture was always welcome in semiarid Perseverance, the accompanying weather was sometimes violent and unpredictable and this storm looked like a doozy. No doubt the police department would have its hands full with reports of flooding and property damage.

I dialed the number Betty gave me for Deputy Bartel and headed back to the station.

•   •   •

The storm hit in a wall of hail, followed by driving sheets of rain. Connie was on the phone and two incoming lines were blinking when I tumbled into the police station, propelled by a drenching blast of wind.

I picked up one of the incoming calls. "Perseverance Police Department, Officer Price speaking. What's your emergency? Uh-huh. Okay. Someone will be out as soon as possible, Mr. Bannon."

The caller on the other incoming line hung up as I ended the call with Mr. Bannon and I blew out my cheeks in exasperation.

"Don't worry, if it's a genuine emergency, they'll call back," Connie said with a weary sigh. "It's been crazy, so buckle your seatbelt. Someone spotted a tornado at Turkey Creek and the whole county is in a panic."

"Where is Justin?"

"He's responding to a report of flash flooding out by Glenedin."

I gestured to the chief's dark office. "Where's Vanderberg?"

"I don't have a clue."

"Okay. Well, Mr. Bannon reported a car in the creek near his ranch. I'm going to check it out."

Connie waved me out the door as incoming calls lit up the phone console.

By midnight, the storm subsided, leaving a trail of debris in its wake. Residents all over the county reported downed power lines, flooding, and broken windows. There were no injuries except for town drunk Jack Wells, who fell on Main Street trying to stagger home in the dark from the municipal bar. His only injury was a sprained wrist, but my police cruiser would smell like piss, vomit, and booze for weeks.

When I got home in the early hours of the morning, Gracie was on her back on my sofa, snoring like a hibernating bear while *The Long Kiss Goodnight* starring Geena Davis blared on the television. I shut off the tv, threw a quilt over Gracie, and tiptoed into my daughter's room.

Dancy was curled up like a kitten in her crib, clutching her purple bunny. I stroked her soft cheek for a few minutes before stripping off my foul-smelling, mud-splattered uniform and heading to bed. I was asleep before my head hit the pillow.

TEN

The next morning at the station, Justin was deep in conversation with Connie in the breakroom. I unloaded my personal stuff on my desk and walked to the back for coffee.

"Good morning, comrades. Where is our fearless leader?" I said in my best Russian accent, nodding towards the chief's vacant office.

They shook their heads in unison. I was a little disappointed they didn't find my humor amusing.

"Hey Wyn, I've got something on that company you asked me to check on." Justin took a small notebook out of his shirt pocket and flipped through the pages.

It was the first time he had exhibited any signs of organization. Maybe there was a future for him as a police officer, after all.

"Yeah, here it is," he said. "Harris DeWitt filed for Chapter Eleven Bankruptcy a couple of years ago after they got tangled up in some kind of development deal in Florida that went bad. The record says the company emerged—not sure what that means—from the plan in 2022."

"That's significant," I said. "Were you able to find out why Olivia is in Wyoming?"

"Not exactly, but according to my sister, she's been meeting with a lot of suits."

"Your sister?"

"Justin's older sister, Janice, is the assistant restaurant manager at the Four Seasons. She was always such a bright girl." Connie smiled with pride at her younger colleague. Although she was no longer a teacher, she was still proud of the kids she taught before switching careers.

I opened my mouth and closed it again, both shocked Justin had a sister and ashamed I didn't know that before now.

Oblivious to my moment of awkwardness, he continued with his report. "Olivia DeWitt has lunched with a slew of business types, but there was one meeting in particular Janice remembered because one guy was named Tug."

"Tug Stratton? I guess that makes sense," I said. "His employer, Lone Star Investors, is a venture capital firm, isn't it? That would explain why both of them are here. Any idea what the project is?"

"Nope. Jackson Hole has about two dozen commercial projects in the works right now. But is it a coincidence you saw those two Texans with Robert Sandoval?"

"It doesn't mean they're all working on the same project, and it still doesn't tie them to Mrs. Randall's murder."

"How about you? Did you find out anything at the sheriff's office?" Connie asked.

"Yes, in fact. Bartel took two calls from Mrs. Randall on June 3rd, two days before we found her body. County dispatch received the first call from her midafternoon. She reported unusual activity on a property adjacent to hers, but according to Bartel's notes, he found nothing suspicious. The other call was around six that evening when Mrs. Randall called to report a trespasser on her property. Bartel traveled out to Brightwater Canyon again, but he didn't find any signs of trespassing. I called him yesterday to see if he could remember any other details, like whose property she was concerned about."

Connie said, "I thought Clif was on vacation."

"He is. I left him a message to call me."

Justin rapped a knuckle on the breakroom table. "I bet we can figure it out on our own. Connie, where is that new aerial map of Edgemont County? You know the one they did last year?"

Connie located the map in the roll file and brought it to the table in the breakroom. Justin helped her unroll it, placing coffee cups on the corners to hold it down.

It took me a minute to get my bearings on the map. Then I remembered the maps Myrna gave me. "Wait a minute, I've got something that might help."

I found the most recent parcel map inside the Randall binder and took it to the breakroom, where I laid it on the edge of the aerial map. After locating Brightwater Canyon Road on the larger map, I followed it to the intersection with Spruce Hollow Gulch, and then on to Meadowlark Lane until I found what I was looking for.

"Okay, the Randall place is here." I pointed out the pale rectangle delineating the roof of the Randall house. "The most recent parcel map I got from the courthouse shows Brightwater Partners owns these adjacent parcels on the north, south, and east sides. It doesn't show who owns all this land to the west."

"That's because it's outside the Brightwater Canyon subdivision, but I can tell you who owns it." Justin drew an elliptical shape in the air over the western expanse. "All that belongs to Robert Sandoval. That's his ranch to the southwest—see the roofs of the barns?"

"Ah yes. It's as impressive from the air as it is in person. So that means Sandoval's property surrounds Mrs. Randall's piece on all four sides."

I bent over the map and ran my finger west from the Randall place, tracing a faint demarcation through the gulch that ran down to the stream and up the western slope, where it meandered through vegetation until it passed between two rocky outcroppings at the top.

The notch opened onto a small meadow fringed by pines. Due west of the meadow, a sloping field descended to a valley occupied by two large buildings with paved yards. The complex was enclosed by a fence, and the sole point of access was a dirt road leading north.

"What are those? They look like military barracks." I tapped a finger on the structures.

"They're storage buildings, like the ones used for grain or industrial equipment storage, but there isn't any grain production in this area. It's all rangeland," Justin said.

"True, but there aren't any corrals or livestock equipment, either."

Due south of the buildings on the other side of a table mesa was Sandoval's ranch. Besides the mesa and a dozen miles of Wyoming rangeland, there was nothing connecting the ranch and the compound, not even a horseback trail.

Justin ran his fingertips along the road leading out of the yard. "That looks like it could be old County Road 925E. It runs through Elk Heart Pass and comes out northwest of Perseverance."

"That dirt track road is the only route to this isolated location." I put my hands on the table and stared at the map. "We know Mrs. Randall was an avid hiker. I followed this trail behind her house to the bottom of the gulch and found fresh prints that appeared to cross the stream and ascend this slope, but I didn't have time to follow them."

"Maybe Mrs. Randall hiked to that meadow and saw something fishy happening at the compound," Connie said.

I thought for a moment. "That's a wild assumption, but it's possible it was one of those 'place at the right time' occurrences. I think it's time we went for a hike, Justin."

"It could be dangerous," Connie said.

Justin joined in. "Yeah, we should wait until the chief comes back."

"We are trained police officers, Justin."

He put up his hands in resignation. "It's your investigation."

The moisture from the storm, followed by the warmth of the sun, brought out the neon greens of the Brightwater Canyon cottonwoods along with a profusion of wildflowers. It was a feast for the senses and I rolled down the windows of the cruiser, savoring the smells of spring.

When we arrived at the Randall residence, I jumped out of the patrol car and shrugged on my backpack, anticipating the hike.

"Are you sure about this?" Justin drooped like a condemned man.

"Think of it as an adventure."

A raptor screeched overhead, and we both glanced up to see the russet-colored bird glide past the house and wheel in the air to take another pass.

"See that, Justin?" I pointed to the bird. "It's a red-tailed hawk. Native Americans say the screech of a red tail is a reminder to clear your mind and use your inner vision to accomplish a task. I'm taking that as a good omen. Come on."

Justin plodded along behind me as I marched around the house to the hiking trail.

"Mrs. Randall was hiking in this gulch the day she died," I said. "Tracing her path will give us insight into her life and habits. If we know her routine, we can discover what she knew, and that will help us find her murderer."

"It sounds speculative."

"It is, but a critical piece of information could wait on the other side of that gulch. Sometimes trusting your gut can make all the difference."

The hawk's shadow touched me as it drifted by again, urging me forward. I plunged down the trail.

The packed earth was slippery from the storm the evening before, and I slowed my pace so Justin could keep up in his cowboy boots. We were part-way down the path when he skidded on the slimy surface and tumbled headfirst into a tree.

Resisting the urge to chide him for his choice of footwear, I scrambled to his side. "Are you okay? Is anything broken?"

"Nah, I'm fine. I twisted my ankle a little, is all." Mud was smeared on his face and uniform.

"Do you think you can you make it to the Randall house?"

He waved a hand. "I'm not going back. No sense in wasting a trip."

"Are you sure?" Although I meant to be solicitous, part of me wished he would return to the house.

He struggled to his feet. "If I keep to the side and use the undergrowth for stability, I think I'll be all right. You go on ahead. I'll catch up."

To demonstrate his determination, he edged sideways to a shrub and grabbed it with both hands.

Afraid my presence might make him nervous, I continued down the trail alone and reached the bottom within a few minutes.

The rain had turned the area around the stream into a squishy bog and erased Evelyn Randall's boot prints, but the gurgling of the stream made a perfect soundtrack for contemplation, so I closed my eyes and leaned against a fallen log until I heard Justin slogging across the creek.

"How's your ankle, Justin?"

He stopped mid-stream to rinse the mud off his face and hands in the icy running water. "I walked it off." A rare smile split his face.

"It won't get any easier," I said. "You can wait here. I'll climb up, take a gander, and meet you back here."

He shook his head. "Nope. I'm not letting you go alone. I've come this far, and I'm determined to go the distance. If I don't make it, bury me on the trail and give my ma my badge and my pa my gun."

"Okay, okay, let's not get too dramatic."

The western bank of the gulch proved to be more of a climb rather than a hike. In places, we grabbed rocks and exposed tree roots to prevent ourselves from slipping backwards on the slippery pine needles.

As I neared the top, the notch appeared above me and I clawed my way through the opening to stand upright.

Drifts of delicate wild irises in shades of purple nodded in a meadow of tall grass, protected on the north and south sides by hulking pines and rocky cliffs. To the west, the rim of the meadow rose, obscuring the view beyond.

"Wow." Caked in mud and soaked with sweat, Justin regarded the scene with awe.

"I think this patch of flowers drew Mrs. Randall up here," I said. "When I found her body, an iris blossom lay on the floor near her hand. It must have come from this field."

For a few minutes we stood without speaking, but when I sensed Justin growing restless, I gestured to the meadow's western rim. "The buildings we spotted on the aerial map should be on the other side of that rise."

We crossed the meadow and found ourselves on the crest of a rocky slope. On either side, the pines thinned out until they gave way to open range dotted with sagebrush and native grass. A hundred yards below us in the valley stood a group of industrial buildings.

I shaded my eyes against the bright sun. "We're standing on the boundary between the Randall property and Sandoval's ranch, and below us is the compound we identified on the map."

"It looks deserted," Justin said.

I fished the binoculars out of my backpack and surveyed the area. "You're right. We could get closer, but Sandoval wouldn't be too pleased if he caught us trespassing."

Justin sniffed. "It isn't fenced, and I don't see any 'No Trespassing' signs posted."

"Hm. That's true, but it's a remote area surrounded by rangeland. Aside from that dirt road leading north across Sandoval's own property, the only other access is a steep, rugged trail on private land. Sandoval doesn't have any reason to put up fences or signs."

"So you're saying we should go back?" He squinted at me from under the brim of his cap.

"I suppose if no one sees us, it won't do any harm to investigate. We could claim we didn't know where the boundary was."

He grabbed my arm. "Wait. What's that sound?"

The roar of the engine reached us before a plain white box truck lurched through the gate into the compound below, made a U-turn, and ground to a halt.

"Get down." I dropped to the ground and pulled Justin down beside me.

A man jumped out of the truck's passenger side and pushed open the giant roll-up door of the nearest building. After the truck backed in, he closed the door behind it and stood outside.

"What's going on down there?" Justin asked.

"Not sure." I trained the binoculars on the man below. "He keeps moving. I can't get a fix on him."

Justin held out his hand. "Let me try."

I gave him the binoculars.

"I can't see a thing." He twisted the knobs to adjust the focus. "Crap. He disappeared behind the building."

"Keep your sights on the yard in front. He'll come back."

I tugged out my notepad to record the time, then made a rough sketch of our position in relation to the scene below.

Ten minutes later, the truck roared out of the building again.

"Can you see anything, Justin? A license plate maybe?"

"The angle is wrong. I can't see the building's interior either. Now he's sliding the door shut and getting back in the truck..."

The truck drove north out of the compound.

I got up and brushed the grass off my uniform. "Whatever happened down there, it seems to me they were attempting to keep it out of sight, which means Connie might have been right. Mrs. Randall was up here picking irises and saw something that didn't seem right."

Justin struggled to his feet. "What's next?"

"We need to find out what's inside those buildings."

"Back from the wars, I see," Vanderberg said when he caught sight of Justin, but his levity faded once I recounted our trip out to Brightwater Canyon.

"What gave you the idea to go there, Price?"

"I talked to Betty Reynolds, and it turns out Mrs. Randall summoned Deputy Bartel to her home twice on the night she died. The first time she reported suspicious activity on an adjacent property, but Bartel's report didn't mention whose property, so we cross-referenced the ownership maps to the aerial map—"

Justin broke in. "It was my idea to use the aerial map because it's more detailed."

"I see." Vanderberg looked back at me. "So, you looked at the map?"

I nodded. "West of Mrs. Randall's place is a compound on Robert Sandoval's property. According to the map, it's a few hundred yards beyond the Brightwater Canyon boundary. Connie proposed that was the property where Mrs. Randall reported seeing suspicious activity, so we checked it out."

"It was a hunch, but it paid off," Justin said.

"Justin is right," I said, "The path from Mrs. Randall's house leads to a meadow overlooking the compound. While we were observing, a white box truck arrived and entered one building. A short time later, it left again. What we saw could have been what prompted Evelyn Randall to call the sheriff."

Vanderberg looked unconvinced. "Maybe, but it's pretty thin."

Justin said, "We could get a search warrant."

The chief rubbed his chin. "We don't have enough evidence for a warrant. You didn't see anybody doing anything illegal, did you?"

"No, sir," I said.

"We could stake out the compound," Justin said.

I crossed my arms. "We have neither the time nor the manpower. I guess we could ask Sandoval outright—we might catch him off guard."

"Or it might tip him off," the chief said. "No, Stokes is right. I'd rather go in with a search warrant."

"Someone must know more about that place." I snapped my fingers. "Irene Brockman. She has the Brightwater Canyon cattle lease and knows a great deal about that territory. I left a message on her answering machine yesterday and she hasn't called me back, but the storm knocked out power all over the county. I'll call her again and ask her what she knows about that compound."

"Good. Did the neighbor who requested the welfare check on Mrs. Randall offer any helpful information? What was her name—McGuiness?" the chief asked.

"Justin talked to her. She's coming in this afternoon. He's also been calling the HOA board members."

Justin chimed in. "Most of them claim they knew nothing about Mrs. Randall causing trouble—but you know that bunch, butter wouldn't melt in their mouths."

"Okay. Good work, and don't get discouraged by slow progress. Something will break." Vanderberg consulted his wristwatch. "Sorry to cut this short, but I have to run. I've got another darn meeting to attend."

Connie caught my attention with a wave when I came out of the chief's office. "Wyn, Irene Brockman called right after you left for Brightwater Canyon this morning. She said it was urgent and if you call her before one o'clock, you might catch her before she heads back out to the field."

"Thanks, Connie. I'll call her right now."

Irene Brockman's personality was one of a woman in charge, forthright and fearless. After I identified myself, she cut right to the chase. "Are you any closer to nailing that bastard, Sandoval?"

"I can't discuss the details of the investigation with you, Irene, except to say we are making progress. I was hoping you could give me something to support your theory that Sandoval was responsible for Mrs. Randall's death."

"Then it's your lucky day, Officer Price, because I have information that might be what you're looking for."

"That sounds intriguing."

"I attended the Brightwater Canyon Association board meeting last night. The board meetings are by invitation alone, but our cattle lease is up this year, and it was time for me to beg on my knees again for another three-year contract. It's a mere formality, but this time it was an utter sham."

"Why, what happened?"

"The HOA board denied my application to renew the lease."

"Did they say why?"

"No, but I would bet my last dollar it was Sandoval's doing. I suspect the board is giving him the grazing lease. The Brockman Ranch lease will end at the end of the summer and the association board made it apparent they don't want to see my sorry ass—or my cattle—on Brightwater property after September."

"That's too bad, Irene. It must be an enormous blow to your operation."

She made a disgusted sound. "Nothing I can do about it now. Anyway, I didn't call for your sympathy. It was what I overheard following the meeting that I thought would interest you. Sandoval was talking to Frank McGuiness and Don Verhulst—Don is chairman of the board—and he was congratulating them on a 'grassless coup'."

"Grassless coup?"

She clucked in derision. "He was referring to the HOA board ejecting me and my cattle from the canyon. He seemed quite pleased with himself. Then Sandoval said something about Evelyn Randall—I couldn't hear all of it, but I heard her name as clear as a bell. He said she gave him a helluva fight, but they had him to thank for getting her out of their way."

"You are certain that's what you heard him say, Irene?"

"I would swear on a Bible, Officer."

"Did they say anything more after that?"

"Nothing of actual substance. They brayed like donkeys and clapped each other on the back, congratulating themselves. It made me want to barf."

"When did this take place?"

"Last night. It was all very cloak and dagger. They called a special session of the Executive Committee. I got the impression they wanted to keep it on the down low."

"Thanks, Irene. That is the most pertinent information I have gotten to date on this case."

"Glad to help, Officer."

"There is one more thing," I said. "Over the ridge to the west of Evelyn Randall's place is a cluster of buildings on Robert Sandoval's property. Do you know anything about it?"

"The name of that ridge is Brightwater Heights, and it is the legal boundary between Sandoval's ranch and the Brightwater Canyon subdivision."

"Yes, I knew that, but I wasn't aware it was called Brightwater Heights."

"It serves as a legal boundary and a natural physical one, as well. I don't have to worry about my cattle straying over on to Sandoval's land and Sandoval doesn't have to fence off access to his land—"

I cut in. "Except Mrs. Randall had access. A trail leads from her back door to this compound."

"I know nothing about the trail or the buildings on Robert Sandoval's property," Irene said. "Sorry."

"Right, well, thanks again."

After I got off the phone with Irene Brockman, my stomach growled, berating me for forgetting to pack a lunch that morning. I checked the clock on the wall. Maggie McGuiness would arrive at the station for her interview in less than two hours.

"I'm going to run over to the coffee shop and grab a ham panini," I said to Connie and Justin. "Do either of you want anything?"

Connie shook her head and Justin held up a half-eaten baloney sandwich.

I dashed across the street to the trendy little Van Gogh Coffee Shoppe, smiling at the customers as I entered.

Barb Mitchell, the owner, was behind the counter.

"I'll take one of your ham paninis and a triple latte, skinny, no flavor, Barb," I said. "Oh, and one of those doughnuts, too. I gotta do my part to keep the legend alive, you know." I patted my flat stomach for the benefit of the high school kids at the end of the counter, who groaned at my lame joke.

Barb slipped my order into a little white bag and put the latte in a paper cup. "Here you go, Hon. The total is $7.83."

I took a five-dollar bill and four ones out of my pocket and handed them to Barb, waving at the tip jar as I grabbed the bag and cup and turned to leave.

A pimply faced boy I didn't know rushed to open the door.

I nodded my thanks and was halfway across the street when I realized he was following me. "Hello. I don't think I know you. My name is Officer Wyn Price. What's yours?"

The boy offered his hand. "Randy. Randy McGuiness."

I tried not to appear startled. Assuming he was Maggie McGuiness's son, I wondered if he knew I was interviewing her that afternoon. I stuck the bag under my arm and clasped his hand. "Is Maggie McGuiness your mother?"

"Yeah. Maggie is my mom. Frank McGuiness is my dad."

He was about sixteen, thin and nervous, like his mother.

"What can I help you with, Randy?"

He glanced back at the cafe, then moved in closer. "My mother says you are investigating Mrs. Randall. Um, her death, I mean."

"Yes, that's correct." I wasn't prepared to volunteer more until I knew what he wanted.

"I have some pictures you might be interested in." His voice squeaked a little.

My mind cartwheeled into parts unknown. "What sort of pictures? I'm uncertain what you're getting at. Could you please be a little clearer?"

He looked as if he regretted saying anything.

"It's okay, Randy. I'm interested in whatever you have to say. Do you want to go inside?" I gestured towards the police station.

He looked stricken. "No! I mean...I don't think I was supposed to be on the far side of Mrs. Randall's meadow. I was taking pictures for the school paper, you know, nature stuff, and Mrs. Randall wasn't home, but I didn't think she would care."

"Go on, Randy, I'm listening." I sensed he was ready to bolt.

"I was, like, back there—"

"Back where, Randy?"

"In Mrs. Randall's meadow. I took pictures of the wild irises—some of them turned out pretty good."

"I know the patch that you are talking about. They are beautiful."

"I—I took other pictures, too, of barns and stuff. I think you should see them..."

"Okay. Do you have them with you?"

"No, see, that's the thing. My mom made me delete them. She said they would get me into trouble."

"She did?"

"Yeah, but she doesn't get digital cameras and computer stuff, you know? She doesn't understand that I store all my pictures in the cloud."

"I see. What were the pictures of?"

Randy seemed worried and confused. "I—d-d-don't—I'm not...look, do you think I could send them to you in an email? I know you have computers in there. My class toured the station last year. You weren't here then."

I put my lunch under one arm and reached into my pocket. "Sure, here's my card. My email address is below my name."

"Thanks." He shoved the card into the pocket of his jeans and ran back across the street to the coffee shop.

As I watched him go, I wondered what Randy had taken pictures of that made his mother so nervous.

ELEVEN

Maggie McGuiness slipped into the station ten minutes after one, nervous as a deer on the first day of hunting season.

I jumped up. "Hello, Mrs. McGuiness. I wasn't expecting you until two."

"I can come back later," she said, but she lingered near my desk and didn't seem inclined to leave.

"No, this is fine," I said. "Would you like coffee? I can make a fresh pot."

She shook her head, her eyes darting around the station.

"Okay. If you'll take a seat, we'll start the interview so you can get home." I pulled a spare chair over and waved Justin away. Maggie might speak more frecly if he wasn't hovering over her. "Mrs. McGuiness—"

"Maggie. Please call me Maggie."

"Of course, Maggie. Were you and Mrs. Randall close?"

Her mouth trembled with distress. "No. I mean, we were neighbors, but it wasn't like we were friends."

"Okay, right, you were not friends. But you knew her habits, at least somewhat, otherwise you would not have known something was wrong. Am I right?"

She bit her lip.

I pressed her. "What was different the day you called the sheriff's office? What did you notice?"

Maggie thought for a minute. "Our place is next door to Evelyn's and my dogs bark at her car. I was in the barn Friday afternoon before last when she came home, and I called Pippi and Sheila back because they were chasing her car. On Monday morning, I realized I hadn't seen her leave all weekend."

"Why was that unusual?"

"Evelyn's on the road all the damn time. Sometimes she goes by my place a couple times in one day, churning up dust in that fancy Lexus of hers. It's irritating."

"Where do you think she was going?"

"How would I know? I try to stay away from those harpies."

"Harpies?"

"Evelyn Randall and Irene Brockman. They're always gossiping and stirring up trouble out in the canyon."

"Trouble for who? Robert Sandoval?"

Her face colored, but she looked down and didn't answer.

"Maggie, you may be withholding something that could help us identify who killed Mrs. Randall. Are you are afraid the same person who hurt her will hurt you...or your son, Randy?"

Her eyes widened. "Randy?"

"I met him today. He's a nice kid. He told me about the pictures he took." I placed a hand on the desk in front of her. "You can be home before dinner if you tell me everything you know. Otherwise, we'll be here all night while I extract every scrap of useful information from you. It's your choice."

Maggie sagged. She knew I spoke the truth, but it was difficult to lower her guard. "I don't want my son dragged into this."

"I understand, but if you don't tell me what you know, I can't help you, Maggie."

She searched my face for a moment. Then she took a deep breath. "Okay."

"Great. Take your time."

"My husband, Frank, and I came out here from Illinois sixteen years ago and built a home in Brightwater Canyon. We were lucky and got in before prices rose sky high. My husband drove a truck for a living. It's a tough job and hard on a family, but he made a good living until the outfit he worked for went belly-up five years ago. We thought we were going to lose everything until Robert Sandoval came along and offered Frank a job."

"What kind of job?"

"A little truck driving, but mostly ranch-hand stuff and whatever else he needed done. The pay wasn't as good as his old job, but it paid our bills, and Frank was grateful for the opportunity. We owe Robert Sandoval for everything he has done for us." Maggie moistened her lips. "But then Sandoval started pressuring Frank to do stuff that made him uncomfortable."

"What kinds of things?"

"Frank wouldn't tell me and said it was better we didn't talk about it. He doesn't want to irritate Sandoval because he's worried it could cost him his job. I don't have proof, but I think it was something shady."

"And your husband agreed?"

"No. He told Sandoval to get someone else to do his dirty work, and Sandoval backed off, but something about Frank has changed. Now he's seldom home and when he is, he's always on edge and becomes angry with me and Randy for small things and sometimes for nothing at all. I do my best to protect my son. He's a good boy."

The image of Frank chasing my cruiser with a pitchfork sprang to mind. "Is Frank abusive to you or Randy?"

Her back stiffened. "Oh, heavens no. Nothing like that, but he does yell a lot."

Although the denial seemed forced, Maggie and her son were both awkward to the extreme, which could explain her evasiveness. But since she didn't exhibit any signs of physical abuse, I let the matter drop and tried another tack. "Tell me about Randy's pictures."

"He was over the moon because one of the faculty advisors for the student paper asked him to do a piece on Brightwater Canyon for a special nature issue. So one day he set off to take some pictures. He was gone for a long time and he ran straight up to his room when he got back. Near dinnertime, I realized I hadn't heard from him, so I went to his room. He had these pictures..." Her voice trailed off.

"Go on."

"Well, you see, Evelyn knew he enjoyed taking pictures of the outdoors and told him about the field of irises on the other side of the gulch behind her house. She encouraged him to visit sometime and said she would show him the path. When Randy knocked on her door that day, she didn't answer, but Randy didn't think she would mind if he walked down through the gulch. He found the field and took some beautiful photos of the irises."

"What else did he take pictures of?"

"After he photographed the flowers, he walked across the field and saw activity at a building west of Evelyn's place. For some foolish reason, he snapped some pictures—he has a digital camera with one of those telephoto lenses on it—then he took off."

She was stalling, so I prodded her again. "What were the pictures of, Maggie?"

The door of the police station banged open, and we both jumped as Molly Stensgaard, the editor of the local newspaper, *The Wind River Courier*, charged in and made a beeline for the chief's office.

Maggie's face went white with pure panic. "If Molly sees me and it gets back to Frank that I was here, officer, I will be in trouble."

"Go to the breakroom. I'll distract her, and you can slip out. But Maggie—" I grabbed her hand. "We may need to talk again soon, so don't avoid me."

After she skittered off, I approached the woman peering into Vanderberg's empty office. "Can I help you, Molly?"

Molly Stensgard wore her long red hair in dreadlocks, a tank top without a bra, baggy cargo shorts, and hiking sandals—which was her typical attire unless she dressed up and exchanged the shorts for a billowy tie-dyed skirt. She was so comfortable in her own skin that I had to admire her style, even if it was a little weird, and I wasn't certain she believed in using water for anything but drinking. Maybe it was those dreadlocks.

She peered at me through her wire-rim glasses and shifted her backpack. "I was hoping to speak with the Chief of Police—"

The door of the station swung open, and Vanderberg entered.

"Molly, it's a pleasure to see you." The chief crossed the room without hanging up his hat.

"Chief Vanderberg, I apologize for bursting in on you so late in the day." She shook his extended hand with such vigor, her scarlet dreadlocks bounced. "I felt compelled to stop in, though I'm ambivalent about this story. I'm speaking, of course, about the Evelyn Randall murder, which is the talk of the town, to our great sorrow. Are you busy, or should I come back later?"

I raised an eyebrow. Molly and her husband Bjorn—a strapping Paul Bunyan type—purchased the community gossip rag several years before and transformed it into a platform for their radical worldviews. Although the paper supported Edgemont County school activities and art festivals, Molly and Bjorn exhibited a fanatical disinterest in local news.

Vanderberg said, "Molly, I acknowledge Perseverance citizens have the right to know what is happening, but I can't discuss the murder investigation with the press. It might jeopardize our case."

"That's fair, Lars. Believe me, I don't want to make a publicity circus out of a dreadful situation, but Evelyn's neighbor Maggie McGuiness is in your breakroom right now, hiding from me, and there is a rumor floating around that Evelyn had information regarding Robert Sandoval that might have put her life in danger. If I combine what I know with rumor and pure conjecture, I could write a story that would blow your investigation—and your campaign for sheriff—to bits, even if it was unintentional." She put a hand on her heart. "But I prefer not to do that. I have a personal interest in seeing her killer brought to justice because Evelyn was my friend. Besides, I wager I have information you don't."

They stared at each other.

When Molly didn't budge, Vanderberg hung his head and motioned towards his office. "Come on in and have a seat." He shot me an irked look. "Price, please join us."

I glanced back to the breakroom, then followed Vanderberg and Molly into his office.

The chief perched on the windowsill behind his desk and gave his guest a charming smile. "Okay, Molly, I've already expressed my reservations about talking to the press, but I know if you choose to do so, you could make us look like idiots, so I will give you my word that I will not pull any punches with you. However, I expect the same from you. Do we have a deal?"

Molly measured him with a look. "Yes. Deal. I'll go first. Evelyn wrote articles on local flora for the paper. Many folks don't know this, but she was a respected botanist and a passionate conservationist. After her husband Phil died, she felt the need to stay busy and be useful, so besides her weekly column, she also helped proof the paper before it went to the printer. That's how I got to know her.

"One of our favorite topics of conversation was the Brightwater association board. Their antics were comical until about seven months ago. Evelyn was thinking about moving back east to be closer to her niece, Olivia, so she decided to sell her house. That's when things got a little warped."

Vanderberg and I looked at each other. This was new information.

"Go on," said the chief.

"She engaged Jarna Culpepper as her realtor, but the day Jarna listed it, strange things began happening. First, the For Sale signs were ripped out, and as soon as Jarna put them back up, they were destroyed or carted off, so she put up sturdier signs, but someone defaced them. Then, when Jarna brought potential buyers to the house for showings, other residents showed up and intimidated them. At one open house, an association board member informed some prospective buyers they would have to pass an interview before the board would allow them to buy property in the Brightwater subdivision."

"Do we know if that is true?" I asked. "About the interviews, I mean."

"Not to my knowledge, but the showing was disastrous. Once Jarna's contract ran out, she was relieved. Evelyn didn't sign up with another realtor."

Vanderberg nodded. "I can see why. What was Mrs. Randall's take on this?"

"She was upset at first, wondering what she did to earn such animosity. She believed she and her late husband Phil were good neighbors. They minded their own business, contributed to the volunteer fire department fundraisers, and so on. Then Robert Sandoval started calling her, patronizing her and offering to buy the property at far less than it was worth.

"After she refused his offer, Sandoval said some bizarre things about keeping Brightwater Canyon in the family and how he hated to see anyone get hurt. Evelyn didn't consider it a threat, not at first. Then she got the foreclosure notice."

The chief's eyes flicked to me.

I crossed my arms. "Foreclosure notice? Are you sure?" Myrna hadn't mentioned a foreclosure when I spoke to her about Brightwater Canyon property transactions.

Molly spread her hands. "That's what she told me. The notice from the association attorney alleged she was in arrears on her dues and that the association board was prepared to file a lien on her property and enforce its right to take possession of the property to satisfy the lien."

"I've heard about the HOA lawsuits in California," I said. "People have lost their homes to HOAs because of dues not paid."

Molly bobbed her head. "Senior citizens are the most vulnerable. Although legislation has mitigated the more egregious offenses, the new laws are sometimes optional for older HOAs under a grandfathering provision. If one dominant owner or group insists on maintaining the status quo, then the new laws are not adopted. Local and state governments often decline to get involved because HOAs are recognized as legitimate forms of government."

Vanderberg brought us back to the topic at hand. "Okay, so what happened with the foreclosure?"

"I don't know," she said with a shrug, "but County Clerk Myrna Flowers could tell you."

"We'll look into it, Molly, thank you very much for the tip," he said.

"You're welcome. I'm glad my information was useful. Now it's your turn." Molly took a notebook and pen out of her backpack and sat back.

"Let me see..." He clasped his hands behind his head and leaned against the window. "When Officer Price discovered the body on June 5th, there were no traces of a robbery or struggle and the coroner concluded Evelyn Randall died of old age. However, an autopsy later revealed she was strangled. We believe the killer staged it to look like natural causes or an accident, hence the lack of evidence at the scene."

"So you've got nothing?"

"Allow me to finish. Once we established murder as the cause of death, Officers Price and Stokes secured the crime scene and performed a thorough investigation—which turned up nothing of interest—and a canvass of the neighborhood. Several citizens offered crucial information about the case and we have followed through on all leads. I'm pleased to say that based on the evidence, we are convinced Mrs. Randall knew her killer and this was an isolated, targeted attack carried out by a single perpetrator. There is no danger to the public. We're wrapping up some loose ends, and I expect to make an arrest within the next few days."

After he finished, Vanderberg sat forward and waited for her reaction.

"It's Robert Sandoval, isn't it?" A smug expression spread across her freckled face.

He smirked, but didn't confirm or deny it. "That's off the record, but when I'm ready to go public, you will be the first person I call."

"This will be good publicity for your campaign for sheriff, Lars."

The chief pretended indifference, but I could tell he agreed.

"So, what will the headlines read, Molly?" His voice was playful as he leaned in. "'Perseverance Police Clueless in Murder of Local Woman'? Should we pack our bags and leave town before the Sunday morning edition of The Wind River Courier comes out, or can an intrepid journalist and straight-shooting lawman strike up a mutually beneficial friendship?"

His teeth were whiter than I remembered, and the distinct scent of sandalwood drifted across the desk.

I shifted in my seat. He was flirting with her—behavior uncharacteristic for the chief. Then the lightbulb came on. Instead of mild-mannered police chief Lars Vanderberg, this man was virile, larger-than-life "Lars Vanderberg, Candidate for Edgemont County Sheriff".

Molly appeared to buy his schtick. "The latter is the most desirable course of action and benefits both of us. I'll report that the investigation is progressing well, and that a suspect will be behind bars soon, but—"

He held up one hand. "And I pledge to keep you apprised of any developments."

She gave him a simpering smile.

"Awesome." Vanderberg pushed himself up from the windowsill. "Thank you for stopping by today, Molly. Let me walk you to the door."

"Of course," she said, stuffing her notebook into her backpack.

At the door, she turned, eyes twinkling, and pointed a finger at him. "Remember, I'm the first one you call, right Lars?"

"I promised, didn't I?"

He closed the door behind her and turned to me. "And that, Officer Price, is how to convince a journalist you've given her the inside scoop when, in fact, you've revealed nothing at all. Now, back to work."

"Roger that, chief."

Justin said, "Hey, Price, Maggie made tracks, but she asked if we would call her cell phone next time instead of calling her home landline. I put the number on your desk. It's like I said, she's scared to death Frank will find out she's been talking to us."

"Okay. Thanks, Justin. I'll make a note in the file."

When I logged into my computer, an email from Randy McGuiness was at the top of my inbox. Attached to the message were several images of a large white box truck entering Sandoval's compound and disappearing into the building closest to the ridge. From the angle of the photos, it was apparent Randy was standing on the ridge overlooking the compound when he snapped the pictures.

One tight close-up of the truck backing into the building caught my eye. Two men holding AR-15 semiautomatic rifles stood on either side of the roll-up door, black balaclavas pulled down over their faces. One watched the truck while the other stared towards the entrance gate.

"Whoo-hoo! Look at this, Justin."

He walked around the desk and stooped to see what I was pointing at. "Holy cow. They look like terrorists."

Alerted by our excited voices, the chief came out of his office to join us. "What's going on?"

Justin stepped aside to give him a better view.

"Where were these pictures taken, Price?" Vanderberg asked.

"This is the compound on Sandoval's property. These pictures were taken from the location I told you about this morning."

"Who took them?"

"Randy McGuiness, Maggie McGuiness's son. See those two masked guys carrying AR-15 semiautomatic rifles? It has to be drugs. What else could Sandoval be trucking in that requires an escort of armed thugs?"

Justin smacked his meaty hands together. "That's enough for a search warrant."

I looked at the chief. "What do you think, sir?"

Vanderberg clicked through the images with narrowed eyes. "AR-15 rifles are legal in Wyoming. We can't request a warrant to search the premises based on the possession of legal firearms, but we can request one on suspicion of illegal activity if we pose the argument that a lawful activity in rural Edgemont County should not require masked and armed guards. We might convince Judge Farr to issue one if we come at it from that angle."

Justin gave me a high five.

The chief raised a hand in caution. "Don't get your hopes up. Word is Judge Farr plays poker with Sandoval. It will be a hard sell. The judge is a stickler for protocol and proper paperwork, so your shit must be together, boxed, wrapped, and festooned with sparkling bows by the time the courthouse opens in the morning, Price."

"What if I can get it together tonight?"

"If it were up to me and we functioned like a regular metropolitan police department, I would expect you to get the warrant tonight, but things aren't done that way in Edgemont County. Barring an imminent threat to the public, Judge Farr will object if you show up on his doorstep requesting a warrant while he is sipping a scotch on the rocks and enjoying the latest episode of *Yellowstone*. He'll think we're over-eager amateurs. Trust me, the first thing tomorrow morning is fine. What about Mrs. McGuiness? Did you get anything useful out of her before Molly showed up?"

I shook my head. "She knows something about Sandoval, but she's too scared to talk."

"Make sure you follow that up. I would love to charge Sandoval by the first of next week."

A car pulled up to the curb of the station and honked.

Vanderberg said, "Whoops. That would be Dino. Gotta fly." He rushed out the door, grabbing his Perseverance PD Chief hat on the way.

"Wait, I have some crucial information—" I started after him, but he was already gone and I huffed in frustration. It was becoming more and more difficult to wedge investigation updates into his busy schedule.

When Justin cocked a quizzical eyebrow at me, I told him what Irene Brockman heard at the HOA meeting.

"We'll need to corroborate her version of events with Don Verhulst and Frank McGuiness," I said, "but it could be the break we've been looking for."

He thumped a fist on my desk in celebration. "With Irene's testimony, we should have enough evidence to bring Sandoval in today."

"Not so fast, Justin. We still have a problem placing him at the murder scene because he claims to have an alibi, and his motive is unknown."

"You and Vanderberg are such sticklers for rules."

"That's because a shoddy investigation will blow our entire case—especially if Sandoval has a savvy lawyer. If we don't dot our i's and cross our t's, we won't get a conviction that sticks. First thing tomorrow, I'm going to follow up a lead from Molly at the courthouse, and you're going to call Sandoval's house and ask his housekeeper Lucia to verify his alibi."

"Okay."

"If I convince Farr to give us a search warrant, we might uncover something at that compound that was worth killing for, and then we would have our motive."

Justin pumped his fist.

"You should head home and wash that uniform, cowboy. We've got a big day tomorrow."

After he was gone, I slid the pink Post-It note from under the corner of my blotter and dialed Deputy Bartel's cell.

"Deputy Bartel, this is Officer Wyn Price again. Sorry to keep bugging you on your vacation, but as I said in my earlier message, I'm investigating the Evelyn Randall murder and I have a couple of questions about the calls she made to the sheriff's office on June 3rd. You were the responding officer and I've read the reports you filed, but if you could fill in the finer details, that would help me tie up loose ends. Call me as soon as you get this message. Thanks."

•   •   •

The minute I turned my back, Dancy threw her plate of fish sticks and green beans on the floor.

"What do you want, kiddo?" I said, getting down on my hands and knees to pick up the scattered food. "I can't put you to bed hungry. There must be something you will eat."

Just then Gracie sashayed into my kitchen wearing a slinky silver mini dress and platform heels. "Hellooo!"

Dancy gave her a squinty-eyed grin. "Gwacie!"

"Hello, pumpkin," she said, ruffling Dancy's hair.

I clambered to my feet and took in her outfit. "Princess Grace McKenna, do you have a special date?"

Gracie fluttered her mascaraed eyelashes at me. "I do."

"Anybody I know?" I batted my eyes back.

"The same gorgeous guy from last week—and don't get any ridiculous ideas. He's filthy rich and money amuses me. He's got a friend, by the way. You could get Cassidy to babysit Dancy and come with us, Wyn."

"Unless you forgot, I'm running a murder investigation, and I've got a stack of paperwork that has to be done tonight."

"Yeah, yeah," she said with a bored air as she pranced to the fridge for a beer.

I tried to tempt Dancy with a peanut butter and jelly sandwich, but she slapped my hand away, whimpering, and I groaned in frustration.

Gracie shoved aside the pile of folders and documents on the counter to find the bottle opener. After taking a gulp of beer, she pointed to the heap with a glittery pink nail. "What is all this crap?"

"Didn't you hear what I said about paperwork?"

"Oh my god, you weren't kidding. Listen, instead of more hard work, what you need is a hard cowboy, Tammy Wynette Price."

Every time she called me that, I regretted the night I indulged in one too many tequila poppers at Karaoke Night and let my full given name slip. Gracie wasn't shy about using this juicy tidbit of information whenever she wanted to bully me into something.

I blame it on my dad, who was a devoted Tammy Wynette fan and could belt out "Stand by Your Man" without the slightest whiff of self-consciousness. When it came time to christen his first-born daughter, he wouldn't consider any other name, so I was stuck with it.

"I'm this close to cracking the case and I can't afford to slack off now," I said, sounding cranky. "Besides, someone around here has to be a responsible adult."

Gracie took a long slurp of beer and belched. "Alf Farr is my uncle."

I snickered despite my bad mood. "What did you say? Alf-far? That sounds like a humanitarian group—Alf-far."

She pursed her lips. "Judge Alphonso Farr is my uncle."

"You're kidding. He's your real uncle? Like, he is married to your aunt, or he's your 'uncle'." I gave her an exaggerated wink that made sleepy Dancy giggle.

Gracie ignored the wink. "He's my mother's brother."

I swallowed another smartass remark. She was serious as a heart attack.

"I bet I can convince him to give you this search warrant." She pointed to the notepad laying on top of the pile of documents on which I had written the words "SEARCH WARRANT" in bold block letters, surrounded by various macabre doodles, including an unflattering caricature of "Judge Farr" chasing a headless cop with a bloody ax.

I jumped up and scooped the notepad and files into my arms. "Geezus Gracie. That's confidential police business, and you shouldn't have read it. It could jeopardize the case if anyone finds out I talked to you about it."

She snorted in exasperation. "You can trust me to keep a secret, you know. I admire your high moral standards, but you can't get through life without trusting your friends. We get by with the help of our friends. Come to think of it, I think the Beatles wrote a song about that."

But before she launched into the chorus, a car door slammed outside. She placed her empty beer bottle on the counter and clasped her hands in front of her like a lovesick schoolgirl. "I've enjoyed our little chat, but my knight in shining armor has arrived."

"Have fun." I tried to sound convincing.

From the doorway she said, "Don't sweat the search warrant, *mon ami.*"

"Gracie—"

"Bonsoir!"

The front door banged shut behind her.

I threw the case files on the table. Dancy was asleep in her highchair, peanut butter and jelly in her hair. Careful not to wake her, I wiped the sticky goop out of her hair and put her to bed.

Afterwards, I sat down at the kitchen table and pawed through the pile of paper until I found the affidavit and application for a search warrant.

Judge Alphonso Farr enjoyed a reputation for being obstinate. Since he and Sandoval moved in the same social circles, he would be reluctant to issue a warrant based on circumstantial evidence against a man as influential as Robert Sandoval. Which meant I would need a minor miracle to wrangle a warrant out of him.

TWELVE

The landline next to my bed jangled, waking me from a sound slumber. I peered at the clock and groaned. It was five in the morning. Scrabbling around on my nightstand, I located the receiver. "Hello?"

A man with a thick accent spoke over the muffled hum of an engine. "Little Nancy, such a nice name."

My mind was still foggy with sleep. "What? Who is this?"

He hung up.

"Shit. Wrong number." I tossed the receiver on the nightstand and struggled out of bed to pull on my sweats.

With a steaming mug of coffee in my hand, I watched the sky turn light pink over dun-colored Outlaw Mesa. The stars were still visible above the mountains to the west. On the outskirts of town, a coyote howled and was answered by a series of sharp yips from his mate.

The temperature dropped into the mid-forties overnight, and I shivered in my thick sweats.

Nearby, the engine of a semi-truck sputtered to life, releasing a plume of white vapor into the air. I inhaled and caught a whiff of diesel fuel. What was it Robert Duvall said in *Apocalypse Now*? "I love the smell of napalm in the morning." For me, it was the aroma of diesel fuel.

My father used to rise early in the summer to get in a few hours of fieldwork before he left for his job in town. When he cranked up that old John Deere, the diesel fumes drifted into my bedroom through the open window. I hated it because it meant in a few hours I would have to drag myself out of bed and make his breakfast.

After he ate, dad would stand on the porch and take in the prairie vista, a cup of thick, black coffee in his hand. He said that was his special personal time to reflect on his faith and organize his thoughts for the day.

I needed a little faith of my own this morning. The investigation's lack of progress was eating away at me. Despite the growing proof of Robert Sandoval's disreputable character, we couldn't find a tangible, unimpeachable connection to Evelyn Randall's murder.

I drained the last of my coffee and shuffled back into the house.

It took me another hour to complete the warrant package for Judge Farr and tie it up with Vanderberg's proverbial shiny bow. Convinced I was as prepared as possible, I slipped out to the backyard for a kickboxing session before Dancy woke up.

While I was pummeling Jason the boxing bag into submission, Gracie sidled out of her house and drifted into my yard. She was wearing a fuzzy pink bathrobe and aviator sunglasses.

"I didn't expect to see you this morning," I said. "Bad date last night?"

"Meh. It was okay. I was home by midnight."

This was an odd turn of events. Gracie didn't go out on actual dates very often, but when she did, they were all night affairs.

"Did something happen last night? I mean, did that guy—"

"No. Nothing like that. Tug is so adorable, an absolute gentleman."

I stopped punching the bag. "Tug? You're dating Tug Stratton?"

"Yes. Do you have coffee?" She slouched to my back door without waiting for a reply.

Inside, she poured herself a cup of stale coffee and emptied the dregs in my cup. "They found another body at Ray Lake on the reservation last night," she said.

Gracie's best friend in high school, Misty Black Elk, was murdered on the Wind River Indian Reservation more than a decade ago, but the authorities never apprehended her killer. Gracie didn't talk about it very often, but I knew Misty's death still troubled her deeply.

"That's terrible. How do you know about it?"

"Tug wanted a tour of the territory around Perseverance, so we took a road trip through Edgemont County. At the Ray Lae exit south of Fort Washakie, tribal police had erected a roadblock, so we stopped to see what was going on. They were bringing out the woman's body when we got there."

"You talked to the officers on the scene?"

"Yeah. Luke Yellow Robe of the BIA police. He dated Misty in high school."

"Officer Yellow Robe told you the victim was a woman?"

She gave me a look. "Yes. He said she was a native woman in her thirties, but Luke didn't know her. She wasn't a known prostitute or a meth head. They presumed the storm washed the body up on shore, but she hadn't been dead long."

I raised an eyebrow. "Luke has pretty loose lips for a law enforcement officer."

"Luke is—was—a close friend." She seemed ready to reveal more, but appeared to change her mind. "Besides, it's not like it matters who knows the particulars. The feds will sweep it under the rug, anyway."

We both fell silent.

The FBI had jurisdiction over the most serious crimes on the reservation—including murder. Which meant the feds would send a couple patronizing city dicks out to steamroll the investigation and since tribal police didn't have the resources or incentive to cooperate, evidence would fall through the cracks, witnesses would refuse to testify, and the whole incident would fade away. That was the reason reservation murders were seldom solved.

Gracie spoke first. "It shook me up pretty bad, so Tug brought me home. We watched a movie together and then he left."

"It's a shame your special date ended on a sad note."

"Yeah, but Tug was a real sweetheart about it. He even made me hot cocoa."

"Hot cocoa, huh?" I wanted to have a conversation with her about Tug, but it would take more time than I had, so instead I drained the last of my cold coffee and got up. "I have to rouse Dancy, or I'll be late."

"Let her sleep. I'll stay and take her to daycare." She wiggled her eyebrows. "You go on and get ready. Uncle Alf is expecting you."

"Gracie—"

"I was joking, now shoo!"

Judge Farr wasn't in his chambers when I arrived at the City and County Building, so I paced the outer office of the Circuit Court, resisting the urge to chew my nails down to the cuticle.

Myrna saw me as she was passing by. "Wyn, it's great to see you again. What are you doing here so early?"

"I'm waiting for Judge Farr."

"Ah, I see." She hesitated for a moment. "I saw Charlie yesterday."

"Oh? How was he?"

"Fading fast. It won't be long now." She looked down and smoothed the lapels of her black blazer.

"Myrna, I am so sorry. I didn't know about you and Charlie—"

She stopped me. "Shush now, dear, it's all right. I know folks around here enjoy whispering about us. They think I'm a lovesick fool for standing by Charlie after he 'refused to make an honest woman out of me', as they say." She drew exaggerated quotes in the air. "He stood me up at the altar once, you know. We drove to Las Vegas to get married, but he never showed up at the chapel. I found him in the Cadillac Bar, drunk as a skunk. We had signed up for the Pink Cadillac wedding ceremony at the Elvis Wedding Chapel, and Charlie insisted he got confused. We had even paid for an Elvis impersonator to officiate."

She let out a peal of musical laughter, amused at the memory. "Let them think I'm a fool. I spent the most memorable times of my life in the company of Charlie Lumineux, and it's been worth every crazy minute. You gotta take the highs with the lows, desperado." She winked at me and strutted back to her office.

A few minutes later, Judge Alphonso Farr stumbled in, ignoring me as he fumbled with the door to his chambers. Rumored to be an alcoholic, his pale, dissipated appearance and musty, mothball-like odor suggested he was in the latter stages of the disease.

When the judge's secretary ushered me into his chambers, I introduced myself and explained the reason for my visit, but his demeanor gave me the immediate impression that his opinion about the case was already established before I showed up. He listened anyway, in that impatient way pompous big shots listen, with condescension oozing out of every pore.

After I was done, he said, "Young lady, you are asking me to grant you a search warrant on the property of one of our most charitable and illustrious community members, yet the evidence you have presented thus far is dubious and flimsy at best. Doesn't the police department have better things to do than waste my time?"

It was possible Judge Farr was giving me a hard time because he considered Robert Sandoval a friend, or maybe he was one of those old farts who felt the compulsion to tweak anyone who interrupted his navel-gazing. I couldn't tell which.

"I understand your reluctance, your Honor, but based on the facts we have, it is reasonable to suspect criminal activities are taking place on Mr. Sandoval's property. Mr. Sandoval may not be involved, but we have a duty to investigate."

I rearranged the pictures on the judge's desk and pointing out the guns again. "What kind of legitimate enterprise in Edgemont County requires masked thugs carrying semiautomatic weapons?"

He gathered the pictures and handed them back to me with pursed lips, and I lost all hope of a favorable outcome.

Then he wheezed and said, "Very well."

"Excuse me? I mean, excuse me, your Honor?"

"I'll give you your search warrant, but you will tread with care and treat Mr. Sandoval with respect. Don't turn this into a witch hunt and cause me to regret my generous interpretation of your arguments."

He leaned forward and punched a button on his antiquated desk phone.

A crackling voice responded. "Yes, your honor?"

Fifteen minutes later, I was marching out of Judge Farr's office with a search warrant in my hand.

"Is that what I think it is?" Vanderberg said when I waved the folded document under his nose.

"It is. I was shocked, too. Either my impassioned speech moved him, or Judge Farr isn't in Sandoval's pocket, after all." I dared not mention the possibility Gracie McKenna had anything to do with it.

Vanderberg strode to the big metal locker in the back of the squad room and unlocked it, throwing open the doors with a flourish.

Inside was a mini-armory of sniper rifles, semiautomatic machine guns, stun grenades, body armor, gas masks, night vision goggles and more, all courtesy of the Department of Homeland Security. The fact the Perseverance Police Department owned this arsenal boggled my mind.

The chief handed me a Kevlar body armor vest and tactical helmet, followed by a Dakota T-76 Longbow rifle and a box of cartridges.

"Do we need this much firepower and armor?" I said, struggling to hold all the stuff. "It's a search warrant, not a terrorist threat."

"You saw the guns those guys were carrying, Price. Besides, I want folks around here to know I mean business."

Vanderberg pulled on his own vest and grabbed a Bushmaster XM-15.

Connie's eyes widened as I traipsed past her desk with the armload of riot gear.

"Where is Justin?" I asked her.

"I haven't heard from him."

"Then you better call him and tell him to get his butt down to the station."

"Oh! Yes, of course."

After unloading the equipment on my desk, I inspected it. The vest covered me to mid-thigh. I would have to leave it unbuckled or I wouldn't be able to sit in the cruiser, but it would do. The Dakota Longbow had seen little use and was in excellent condition. However, it had been in storage for years and needed a thorough cleaning.

Connie was on the phone with Justin. "Oh, for God's sake, Justin. They opened the SWAT locker and got the riot gear out. Now get in here."

She jammed the receiver back into the cradle and threw a disgusted look in my direction. "I think he was still having coffee at the cafe."

She came over to my desk, fists planted on her hips. "My lord. That is one big gun. It's almost bigger than you, Wyn. Did they teach you how to shoot those things at the Police Academy?"

I ran a cleaning rod down the barrel of the gun. "No. The Academy was pretty basic. After I joined the Rapid City police force, I took special training classes in advanced firearms and tactical response. I renew my certification every year."

"Did you ever shoot anybody?"

"I've been forced to incapacitate suspects in the line of duty, but I've never killed anyone."

She wrinkled her forehead. "Have you ever been shot at?"

"Let's just say I've been in some firefights I was lucky to walk away from."

The station door banged open, and Justin stomped in, grumbling under his breath. When he noticed the sniper rifle in my hands, his face morphed from irritation to disbelief. "Holy cow. What's going on?"

Vanderberg tossed Justin a bulletproof vest. "Price convinced Judge Farr to issue a search warrant on Robert Sandoval's property. Grab one of those long guns from the cabinet."

Justin's expression of disbelief transformed into euphoria. For a moment, I thought he might wet himself.

Ignoring his subordinate, the chief ambled over to the map chest and pawed through the maps. "Where is that big aerial map we had done last year?"

"I think I have the one you're looking for." I passed him the rolled-up map that was lying on my desk.

He spread it out on Justin's desk. "Connie," he said without looking up, "if you wouldn't mind, please make some more coffee."

She hurried off, looking relieved to be doing something other than wringing her hands.

"Okay, team," the chief said, waving Justin and me over, "the warrant gives us the authority to search these buildings for potential evidence that might explain the suspicious activity captured by Randy McGuiness's photos." He pointed to the compound on the map.

Justin folded his arms across his chest. "Drugs. I know it's drugs. We're going to nail that greasy wetback."

I flinched.

The chief straightened and leveled his gaze at Justin. "You are out of line, officer. I don't want to hear that kind of talk again. Don't make me regret hiring you."

Justin paled. "I'm sorry. It won't happen again, sir."

Vanderberg went back to the map. "This location is remote, team, so let's be extra vigilant. There's but one exit and if those armed guys show up unannounced, we'll be trapped. Price, you'll stand watch while Stokes and I sweep the interiors. If anything comes down that road while we're executing the search warrant, I want to know before it's up our noses."

It was early afternoon when our cruisers slipped out of town and headed north to County Road 925E, the lone access point to the Sandoval compound by vehicle. Justin drove Unit One—which was his regular duty Chevrolet Caprice patrol car—with Vanderberg riding shotgun. I followed in the old Crown Vic, also known as Unit Two.

It was a simple plan. After we entered the compound, Vanderberg and Justin would search the buildings while I provided security on the perimeter. With luck, we would locate evidence explaining the suspicious activities caught on camera by Randy McGuiness and be out of there before anyone was the wiser.

Outside the compound's entrance, Unit One stopped and Vanderberg got out to survey the area beyond the entry point with binoculars. When he was satisfied the coast was clear, he waved us in.

The complex was tucked into a slight bowl and appeared deserted other than an audience of curious prairie dogs. Unless someone ignored the "Dead End" signs on 925E or hiked through the gulch from the Randall place, they wouldn't know this place existed.

The structures themselves were of recent construction and parallel to each other, with standard entrances next to enormous roll-up doors on the narrow ends facing the road. Each building could probably hold twelve semi-trucks with trailers arranged in three rows of four abreast.

"Okay, let's do this," the chief said. "Stokes, you are with me. We'll search the east building first. Price, you monitor the road from the yard. If you hear something, make sure we know about it before it's right on top of us."

The entry door of the first building was unlocked, and I heard their footsteps on the concrete floor fade away as they moved into the cavernous interior, then grow louder again as they returned.

The chief emerged first, with Justin close behind, and gave a negative shake of his head. "Nothing. Someone swept it clean without leaving a mouse turd behind. Let's move to the next one, Stokes."

Before they reached the second building, a deep hum from outside the compound interrupted the stillness of the afternoon.

I held up a hand. "Chief, I hear something—"

A silver Ford F350 pickup truck shot through the gate in a cloud of dust and came to a crunching halt in the yard. Robert Sandoval opened the driver's door and climbed out. He pushed up the brim of his Resistol and then sauntered in our direction with his hands in the pockets of his Wranglers.

"One of my hired hands was fixing a fence on Piney Mountain and thought he saw a couple of police cars coming up the back road," Sandoval said. "I was in town, so I thought I'd check it out. Once again, I find Perseverance's finest creeping around without invitation."

The chief ignored the needling remark. "Good morning, Mr. Sandoval. We have a search warrant for these buildings. We believe there may be illegal activity occurring in the area."

Sandoval's brow furrowed. "I hope you're wrong. The Sandoval Ranch is a sizable spread and can be hard to patrol. We're too busy to be everywhere. Hell, I don't get to this part of my property more than once or twice a year." He pointed north the way he came in. "A while back, the Edgemont County Sheriff had the harebrained notion some- one was cooking dope at the old Erickson homestead, a mile down this road here. Nothing ever came of it."

It seemed Sandoval's jibe hit a nerve, because Vanderberg's jaw tight- ened, and I remembered Justin's story about the failed investigation of the meth lab out here.

"Did you ever think about putting in security cameras?" the chief asked.

"Nah, they would be too much nuisance to maintain. After the dope thing, I considered hiring guards, but we have experienced little trouble here. Besides, I'm a cattleman, not a lawman." He hawked and spit on the ground a foot away from Vanderberg's polished black service oxfords.

The chief drew the warrant out of the inside pocket of his jacket and handed it to Sandoval. "Here's the warrant signed by Judge Farr. Now, if you'll excuse us, we'll finish our search of the premises and be on our way."

Sandoval took the search warrant without bothering to look at it, as if he couldn't care less.

Vanderberg walked towards the westernmost building and signaled for both Justin and me to follow him. "Let's get this disaster over as quickly as possible," he said.

The illumination from the overhead lights revealed the vast space was empty, but we walked through it anyway, swinging our flashlights back and forth across the concrete floor. Like the first building, this one was so clean it appeared unused.

After we returned to the front of the building, the chief strode ahead. "Get the lights, Price," he said over his shoulder as he exited with Justin on his heels.

I was reaching up to flick off the lights when something lodged in the doorframe caught my eye. It was a scrap of pale material, about elbow high.

"C'mon Price, let's go." Vanderberg's tone was sharp.

When I stepped outside, I tried to get his attention, but he was fixated on Sandoval, who was leaning against his truck with his arms crossed. The tension between them was palpable.

"Chief, there's something—" I said, running to match his longer strides.

He threw up a hand. "Whatever it is, it can wait until we're back at the station, Price. You and Stokes make a sweep of the exterior perimeters. I'll go deal with our friend Sandoval."

"But—"

He shot me a look of warning.

I dropped back to join Justin. "I'll take the outside of the western building," I said to him. "You take this one. Holler if you find anything."

We split up, working our way through the brushy vegetation surrounding the buildings. It was prime rattlesnake territory, and I moved with caution, but other than a nest with mottled eggs in it and a couple of skittish rabbits, nothing of significance caught my attention.

I completed my circuit around the westernmost building in time to see Sandoval's silver Ford roar away from the compound. Justin was already behind the wheel of Unit One, revving the engine, while the chief climbed into the passenger side.

Vanderberg waved from across the yard. "We'll see you back at the station, Price."

"Chief, wait!"

But he ignored me and pulled the door shut. Then the patrol car spun in a tight circle and sped out of the compound, leaving me behind in a cloud of dust.

With a stream of curses, I retrieved the evidence kit from the trunk of my cruiser and returned to the western building to pick the scrap of yellow fabric out of the door frame where it had snagged on a protruding nail.

Afterwards, I dropped it into an evidence bag and gave it a violent shake. "What the hell are you?"

It didn't answer, so I threw the bag onto the passenger seat and drove back to town.

•   •   •

Connie was alone in the police station when I returned.

"Where did Vanderberg and Justin go?" I asked her.

"They unloaded their SWAT gear and went to lunch. You should go home and grab something to eat. I can hold down the fort."

"Okay. I'll do that after I put my stuff away."

"I heard the search was a bust."

"Pretty much. Sandoval's compound was spotless except for this." I held up the evidence baggie with the yellow scrap in it.

"What is it?"

"I have no idea. Something brushed up against the doorjamb in one of the buildings and snagged on a nail. The material has a soft, cross-hatched texture. It seems familiar, but I can't put my finger on what it is."

"Huh," Connie said, picking up an incoming line.

I locked the scrap in my desk drawer and made a note in the case file. Then on the blackboard under Sandoval's name, I wrote "Tipped Off" and below that, "Who?"

THIRTEEN

The door to Vanderberg's office was closed when I got back from lunch.

In the breakroom, a large white vinyl banner was spread out on the table with the slogan "Vanderberg-The Right Choice for Edgemont County Sheriff" emblazoned across it in red letters. Vanderberg's face, displaying teeth like a toothpaste model, was printed on one end and a sheriff's star-shaped badge was stamped on the other.

Connie's voice at my elbow startled me. "You gotta admit, he is a handsome man."

"He doesn't plan to hang this up here, does he?"

"Of course not. Dino, his campaign manager, dropped it off. I told the snooty bugger we couldn't keep it at the police station, but he was in a rush, so there you go."

"You don't approve of Dino?"

She pressed her lips together and stifled a noise of disgust. "Since no one is running against him, I'm not sure why the chief needs a fancy pants like Dino. Seems like a waste of money to me."

"You know, we haven't really talked about what will happen after the election," I said, still staring at Vanderberg's glossy face.

"Things will change." Her tone was matter-of-fact. "When Alan left, I was devastated, but then Lars Vanderberg came along and I realized there was a difference between a cop who is a decent boss and a law enforcement professional who is an actual leader. Those same qualities will make Vanderberg a great sheriff, and thanks to the money flowing in from development, the city has the resources to replace him. Who knows, maybe there's somebody better waiting in the wings."

I considered this. "Maybe. I suppose he will continue to lead the police department until a replacement is found, anyway."

"Absolutely. By the way, I think you have a message on your desk phone. Someone called in on your direct line while you were out."

When I returned to my desk, the red light was blinking on my desk phone and I hoped it was a message from Deputy Bartel. As I picked up the handset, the door to Vanderberg's office opened, and the chief emerged with one of the county commissioners.

"I appreciate you stopping by today, sir." Vanderberg pumped the commissioner's hand.

After the other man left, he beckoned to me. "Price."

"Yes, chief?" I put down the handset.

"My office. Now." He sounded agitated.

I glanced at Connie, but she only grimaced in sympathy.

"Close the door and take a seat," Vanderberg said when I entered.

I complied, folding my hands in my lap. But if I was expecting a butt chewing for the search debacle, the chief had other things on his mind.

"We need to speed things up, Price. The county commissioners are becoming impatient with the slow pace of the investigation. There's got to be something or somebody that can help us tie Mrs. Randall's murder to Robert Sandoval. What about Irene Brockman?"

"That's what I was trying to tell you yesterday, chief. Irene heard Sandoval tell Frank McGuiness and Don Verhulst that he offed her."

"He *offed* her? She heard him say that?"

"Well, not in those exact words. He mentioned Evelyn Randall's name and then he told McGuiness and Verhulst that they had him to thank for getting her out of the way."

A slow smile spread over Vanderberg's face as he considered this.

"Okay, now we're getting somewhere. Did you get a written statement from her?"

"Not yet, but she's willing to testify. We should talk to both Don Verhulst and Frank McGuiness to validate Irene's version of events. Maggie thinks Sandoval asked Frank to do something shady for him, so McGuiness may have first-hand information about Sandoval's activities. I'd like to question him first."

The smile on Vanderberg's face faded. "Frank McGuiness is a pretty rough customer, Price. Let me handle Frank."

"I can do it, chief. Frank McGuiness doesn't scare me."

"I know, I know, but Frank and I played darts together in the dart league last winter, and I got to know him pretty well. He'll open up to me."

"Okay," I said with reluctance, "but they could have vital information and might be accessories if they knew beforehand that Sandoval was planning to kill Mrs. Randall. We still haven't pinpointed Sandoval's motive for wanting her out of the way. That leaves a gaping hole in our case against him."

He rubbed his face with both hands. "I understand, but we need to wrap up this investigation and we're running out of time. The November general election is less than five months away."

It wasn't my place to lecture the chief about his responsibilities, but it seemed like he was having trouble setting boundaries between his campaign and his job as the police chief.

"If you want to move the case along faster, then let me bring Sandoval in. Maybe if we use the evidence we have as leverage, he'll crack."

"No. Let's hold off. After the search warrant fiasco, he knows we're on to him, but he isn't a likely flight risk. His ego is too big for that. Before we pull him in, I want to gather enough evidence to bury him. Did you ever check to see if the HOA filed a lien on Mrs. Randall's property?"

"Not yet."

"Then go see if Myrna knows anything. And tell Irene Brockman we need that written statement."

"Yes, sir."

He looked up. "Why are you still sitting there, Price? Get to work."

I hurried back to my desk and called Irene Brockman. To my relief, she picked up on the second ring. "Hi Irene. Wyn Price again. You know the conversation you overheard at the Brightwater Canyon meeting the other night?"

"How could I forget it?"

"I'm accepting your offer to swear on the Bible about what Sandoval said and who he said it to. Can I email you a statement form?"

"Sure. If you send it right now, I'll fill it out before I go back to work."

"Okay, give me your email address, and thanks, Irene."

After I hung up with Irene Brockman, I entered my code to check my messages. There were two.

"First message, left today at 12:28 p.m."

Beep

"To erase this message press—"

"Yeah, yeah, yeah." I pushed the button to erase the message. I hated it when people called and didn't leave a message.

"Next message, left today at 12:36 p.m."

The greeting didn't finish before the caller started talking, which cut off part of his message.

"—your little girl. You should make sure she is okay."

"To erase this message press—"

I punched the "1" button again.

"—your little girl. You should make sure she is okay."

A man, in or near a running vehicle, with a Hispanic accent. *My little girl—Dancy?* I dropped the phone and left the station at a run.

My fingers itched to flip the siren switch although Dancy's daycare was mere blocks away, but I was in hyper-drive, and it felt like it took forever.

The owner of Tiny Tykes Daycare, Marty White, was reading a book to a little boy named Tyler when I burst through the door.

"Where's Dancy?" I asked.

"She's asleep, Wyn, what's the matter?"

I ran to the bedroom where the kids took their after-lunch naps. Little streamers of sunlight filtered in through the closed blinds and fell across Dancy's port-a-crib near the window, where she was fast asleep, lashes fanned out against her chubby cheeks.

Marty stood in the hallway, balancing the little boy on her hip and watching me with apprehension.

I slipped from the bedroom and closed the door.

"Wyn, are you okay? You look frightened," she said. "Can I make you a cup of tea? You're shaking."

She was right. My hands were fluttering like Mexican Jumping Beans. I slapped one on my forehead and fought to regain my composure. "Whew! I got one of those random crazy thoughts, Marty. The job must be getting to me."

Marty cocked her head, unconvinced.

I reached out and ruffled the hair of the little boy in her arms. "Hey, there, Tyler. How are you today? Was Marty reading you a book?"

The boy nodded and smiled, leaning his head against her shoulder.

I sauntered to the front door, attempting to appear casual. In the driveway, the Crown Vic was still running with the driver's door hanging open. Otherwise, the quiet little street was deserted.

"Marty, I suggest you keep the front and back doors locked in case one of the rug rats attempts to go on an adventure...or something, and if you ever see anyone suspicious hanging around, I want you to call me. Immediately."

"Okay."

"Right. I'll be off then." I twinkled my fingers as I backed out the door. "Bye Tyler."

Marty locked the door behind me, still eyeing me with uncertainty.

At the 5th and Main stop sign, I pounded a fist on the dashboard and cussed myself out for acting like a damn rookie—all adrenalin and no brains. I was morphing from Andy Griffin into Barney Fife.

Mrs. Barker rolled by in her Lincoln Continental, staring because I was still sitting at the four-way stop sign, babbling to myself and gesturing like a lunatic.

•   •   •

Myrna looked up in surprise when I appeared at her desk in the County Clerk's office. "We're seeing a lot of each other these days, Wyn. Not that I'm complaining."

"Yes, excuse me for barging in unannounced, Myrna. Do you have a moment?"

"Of course. Please have a seat."

She studied me as I perched on the chair. "Is everything okay? You look tense."

"No, it's nothing. I am fine, but under pressure to close this case," I said, brushing away her concern.

"Word on the street is that you are close to making an arrest." She didn't mention Robert Sandoval's name, but her eyes glinted with satisfaction.

"Which brings me to why I am here, Myrna. Molly Stensgaard gave us some information I need to follow up on."

"What information would that be?"

"Molly told us the attorney for the canyon association sent Mrs. Randall a letter telling her they were placing a lien on her property for non-payment of homeowner association dues."

Myrna looked troubled. "That's news to me, Wyn, and since lien filings come through my office, my staff would be the first to know. If the Brightwater Canyon HOA was the party submitting the filing, that is something that would attract my personal attention."

"They would sue her in court first anyway, wouldn't they?"

"Not to file a lien, no. HOAs can file liens as soon as dues are delinquent, but in order to foreclose, the association must go through a lengthy legal process. If the lawsuit is successful, the association takes possession of the property even if the owner's first mortgage is current."

I sank back in my chair. "For HOA dues?"

"Yes, and sometimes it's a small amount relative to the property's value, but a special assessment would be more apt to precipitate a foreclosure rather than annual dues. It's not unheard of for associations to assess thousands of dollars for onetime repairs or improvements. One association charged owners to build a landing strip for airplanes. I forget the exact amount, but it was close to one hundred thousand dollars per owner."

"They can do that?"

"Yes, they can, and the owners must pay the assessment or sell."

"Is it possible the homeowner association of Brightwater Canyon assessed members for a special purpose project and Mrs. Randall fought it?"

Myrna nodded. "Sure. It's possible."

"But wouldn't word of it have gotten around Perseverance?"

She looked doubtful. "Brightwater folks don't think of themselves as part of the Perseverance community. You've seen their mansions—a sizable number of them are the summer homes of wealthy owners from all over the world. They aren't likely to gossip with the locals. Evelyn Randall was one of the most engaging of the bunch because she considered herself a member of this community. Besides, the Brightwater Canyon board could have insisted on confidentiality."

"That sounds like Sandoval's *modus operandi.*"

"You could get a subpoena to force the board to open up their records."

"A subpoena would require time and resources that we don't have."

"Sorry I couldn't be of more help, Wyn."

"Well, it was worth a shot. Thanks for your time today, Myrna."

To my displeasure, a red Ford pickup occupied the Crown Vic's regular spot in front of the police station, obliging me to park in one of the "Visitors Only" spaces.

Justin met me inside the door, antsy with excitement. "You'll never guess who Chief Vanderberg has in his office."

I wasn't in the mood to try. "I can't imagine, Justin. Why don't we skip the game and go straight to the prizes?"

Raucous laughter interrupted his response and the door to Vanderberg's office flew open, disgorging the chief and two cowboys with their hats in their hands.

"Thanks for coming in, boys." The chief's face was flushed with laughter—or embarrassment.

Don Verhulst and Frank McGuiness moseyed across the squad room, giggling like a couple of schoolboys. Before he yanked the door open for Verhulst, McGuiness licked his lips and let his eyes slide down me with a salacious leer.

I waited until the two men climbed into the red Ford. "That seemed like a pleasant visit, chief. Did your friends have anything useful to say?"

"They did," Vanderberg said with a chuckle. "Both affirmed Irene Brockman's account of Sandoval's statements at the board meeting— well, sort of."

"So they knew he murdered her and failed to report it."

"Not so fast. Don and Frank swore they didn't have any idea Sandoval was talking about killing Evelyn Randall. The monthly board meetings are apparently boozy affairs, and by the time Sandoval started running his mouth, they were all pretty well-oiled."

"But they got the impression he was claiming responsibility for her death, right?"

The chief scratched his neck. "Well, see, that's the thing. Not in so many words. He made remarks alluding to the fact Mrs. Randall wouldn't be pestering them anymore, but that was about it. They assumed Sandoval was drunk and bloviating as per usual. It wasn't an explicit confession."

"Are they willing to testify in court?"

"They are, but keep in mind they both admit to being impaired. They won't be the most reliable of witnesses."

Justin cleared his throat, edging into our conversation. "Uh, I spoke with Sandoval's housekeeper." He consulted his notes. "Lucia Montez. She verified Mr. and Mrs. Sandoval set off around eleven for the airport in Jackson. Mrs. Sandoval's flight to Houston on American Airlines was scheduled to leave at 3:00 p.m. Mr. Sandoval returned to the ranch at around five and was in his study until dinner at seven. He ate a rib-eye—rare—and a green salad, then returned to his study around 7:45 p.m. Lucia said he was still in his study when she set the security system and went to bed at ten." He finished reading and looked up.

"That means we're back to square one," I said with a groan. "Sandoval has a solid alibi and no obvious motive."

"Don't be so pessimistic, Price. That's not my perspective at all,"

Vanderberg said. "This woman is his employee and will say whatever he tells her to say. If Lucia was in a separate area of the house or otherwise occupied—engaged in cooking or watching television, for example— Sandoval could have slipped away without her knowledge."

"Yeah," said Justin. "Or maybe she's an illegal alien or something. I can do some digging into her background."

"That's unnecessary," the chief said, putting up his hand, "but good job, Stokes. Why don't you clock out and grab a nice cold mug of beer at the Silver Spur? It's been an eventful day."

Justin snapped a salute and gathered his belongings.

After he was gone, Vanderberg said, "We're much closer than you think, Price. Keep gathering the pieces and we'll put together a body of evidence against Sandoval that will convince a jury. Speaking of gathering information, how did it go at the courthouse?"

"Myrna knew nothing about a lien filed on Mrs. Randall's property by the Brightwater Canyon HOA. Maybe Mrs. Randall settled her debt before it got that far."

"Or Sandoval killed her first."

"True. But why? Why would he want her dead? It had to be more than the opportunity to get his hands on her property." I sank back into my chair.

Vanderberg perched on Justin's desk, his arms crossed and concern creasing his face. "Connie said you blew out of here at a dead run this afternoon. Is everything okay?"

"It's nothing—just a couple of crank calls."

He launched himself off the desk like something bit him. "Here at the station? What did he say? Was it a threat?"

"Here, listen for yourself."

I punched the button on my desk phone and played the message for him, watching as his mouth fell open in shock.

"I picked the message up after I got back from lunch. As soon as I listened to it, I headed to Dancy's daycare as fast as I could."

"And?"

"Nothing. Marty hadn't seen anything suspicious. I asked her to keep the doors locked and call me if she saw someone she didn't know hanging around. Perseverance is a small town, and everybody knows everybody else's business. It would be pretty hard for a stranger to waltz into town..." I trailed off, reluctant to finish my sentence.

"And kidnap a police officer's child in broad daylight? This could pose a serious threat, Price. We're involved in a murder investigation that could get white hot in the blink of an eye, and someone is trying to warn you off."

"Maybe that's all it is—someone is trying to distract us from the investigation, which means we hit a nerve, chief. We've been talking to people Sandoval considers his enemies, and the search warrant unsettled him more than he was letting on. He knows you have your hands full with the sheriff's stuff and the campaign and he figures if he can sideline me, it will give him some time to cover his tracks. It means we're closing in on the truth."

"I don't know." He sounded hesitant. "I'm of the mind to pull you off the case for your protection and call in the Wyoming DCI."

"No, don't do that—not yet. We are getting close, so close I can feel it. Give me a few more days and I will bring you an airtight case. In the meantime, I'll make sure Marty and Gracie are hypervigilant."

"I'll think about it." He regarded the clock on the wall. "Look, it's almost six and I've got a couple loose ends to tie up here tonight, so why don't you knock off early? You've spent tons of time and energy on this investigation, and you need time with your family."

"Okay."

I was logging off my computer when I noticed a new email. "Chief, I have an email from Irene Brockman with her signed statement attached that recounts the conversation she overheard at the Brightwater Canyon Board meeting."

"Good. Things are starting to move in the right direction."

"Are you sure I shouldn't have another go at questioning Sandoval? I could go tonight, before word reaches him that Verhulst and McGuiness were here."

His smile faded. "After what you told me, I won't let you talk to Sandoval alone. It's too dangerous. From this point on, no more covert missions in Brightwater Canyon without another officer along to cover your ass, got it?"

I bit my lip. "So, does that mean Justin and I can go tomorrow morning?"

"I appreciate your zeal, but let's aim for mid-morning after I take care of a few campaign obligations. When we speak to Sandoval again, I want to be the one to clap the handcuffs on him. Now what are you waiting for, Price? I already sent Connie home. Get out of here. I'll stay and lock up."

I hesitated.

"That's an order. I'm serious. Now go."

Josefina entered the station as I was leaving, but in my eagerness to get home to Dancy, I didn't engage her in conversation, knowing it would be futile. Then, a few steps outside the station, I felt a twinge of regret for my bad manners and turned back.

On the other side of the plate-glass window, Chief Vanderberg was speaking to Josefina and although his back was to me, whatever he was saying must have been important, because her expression was one of rapt attention. Afterwards, she scurried away to fetch the cleaning supplies from the storage room without looking in my direction.

FOURTEEN

The next morning when I arrived at the Perseverance police station, a black Ford Explorer with a Wyoming Division of Criminal Investigation decal on the door was parked outside.

I unlocked the station and a handsome, clean-cut man dressed like a bank executive got out of the SUV and followed me inside.

After I flipped on the lights, I turned with my hand extended. "Officer Wyn Price. How can I help you—"

"DCI Special Agent Ernesto Lujan." He returned my greeting with a firm grip and a direct gaze.

Unclipping a leather case from the waist of his trim gray suit, he held it up for my inspection. Out of respect, I pretended to be dazzled by the shiny gold Special Agent badge for a moment.

"What are you doing here in Perseverance, Agent Lujan?" I asked.

"I'd be thrilled to tell you about it, Officer Price," he looked around the office, "but could I get a cup of coffee first? The stuff at the Lamplighter Inn was undrinkable."

"You stayed here in town last night?"

"Yes. I arrived around eleven."

I lifted an eyebrow. "It was my understanding Polly doesn't admit guests after 9:00 p.m."

Polly Boswell was the fussy owner of the Lamplighter Inn, an authentic piece of Americana straight out of the nineteen-fifties. Her rooms were clean and cheap, even during the high season. According to Connie, she made out better than the big chain hotels on the highway during the summer, despite her check in policies being draconian.

"Not unless you're persistent," he said with a grimace. "She refused to come to the front desk to check me in and I thought I might have to sleep in my car, but I kept buzzing. She relented once she realized I wasn't going away. After she found out I was with the Division of Criminal Investigation, she asked a slew of nosey questions, none of which I answered. Anyway, about that coffee?"

"Give me a minute and I'll start a pot." I motioned to the chair in front of my desk and scuttled to the breakroom, glad for the chance to gather my composure.

Vanderberg must have changed his mind following our discussion last night and called the DCI, but I wished he would've extended me the professional courtesy of a heads up first.

While the coffee brewed, I spied on Lujan from the breakroom. With his chiseled, smoldering Latino features, he was drop-dead handsome, but exhibited confidence bordering on machismo as he lounged in the chair, checking the messages on his phone.

I smoothed down my frizzy blonde locks, trying to remember if I put mascara on that morning, and realized I couldn't recall the last time I put on makeup—hell, I probably looked like a troll.

Five minutes later, I handed the agent a steaming cup of dark, fragrant coffee and settled behind my desk, trying not to stare.

He took a long sip and eyed the covered investigation blackboard behind my desk.

"So, you were going to tell me what you're doing here, Agent Lujan," I said.

If he noticed I was on edge, he didn't show it. "I'm here about the case you're working on."

"The Evelyn Randall murder investigation?"

He nodded. "Yeah, that's right. The Evelyn Randall murder."

"Oh. Did the DCI lab get a match on the fingerprints we sent over?"

"What finger—"

Vanderberg barged in, a bag of groceries swinging from each hand. When he saw Lujan, he dropped the bags on the floor and slung his hat on the hook without taking his eyes off him.

The agent stood up and offered his hand. "Good to see you again, Chief Vanderberg."

"I saw your car outside, Agent Lujan," Vanderberg said, eschewing pleasantries. "What the hell are you doing here?"

"I'm here about the Randall case," Lujan replied. His tone was civil, but there was a hardness to it.

"You have no authority here. Nobody asked you to get involved in the Randall murder investigation."

"From a technical perspective, you are correct, Chief Vanderberg. The DCI has no jurisdiction in murder cases unless local law enforcement requests our help."

"Exactly—"

"Except—" Lujan held up his index finger and Vanderberg halted, glaring at him. "When drugs or organized crime are involved, in which event the DCI has primary original jurisdiction and we got a tip, Chief Vanderberg, that your office is investigating the murder of a woman who was killed when she ran afoul of a drug outfit operating out of Edgemont County."

Vanderberg was at least a head taller than Lujan, but I got the feeling the DCI agent would more than hold his own if this pissing match got physical.

The front door opened again, and Connie sailed in, smiling. "Morning."

When she saw the two men squaring off in the middle of the squad room, she grabbed the grocery bags Vanderberg abandoned and skittered to the breakroom.

Lujan said, "How about we talk in your office, Chief Vanderberg?"

"Fine," Vanderberg said. "Go in and have a seat. I'm going to grab a cup of coffee and I'll be right in."

"That's fine." Lujan swaggered to the chief's office and settled into a guest chair.

I followed the chief into the breakroom. "We aren't letting this fancy suit waltz in here and hijack our case, are we?" I pitched my voice so Lujan wouldn't overhear.

The chief shook his head. "No, we are not. But if we refuse to give him any information, he may find it suspicious."

"Justin said the last time the Wyoming DCI inserted itself into an Edgemont County matter, the county's investigation was shut down cold. He swears they're in Sandoval's pocket."

The chief pinched his lip. "The story about the county's case is legitimate and I won't comment on the other claim, but I find Lujan's unannounced visit very suspicious."

"Do you think Sandoval tipped them off?"

Connie poked her head into the breakroom. "I put your campaign banner in the storeroom, chief. I figured you wouldn't want our visitor to see it." She jerked her head towards his office.

"Thanks, Connie, and good thinking. The DCI is no doubt aware I'm running for sheriff, but if they believed I was using the police station as my campaign headquarters, it would look dodgy. Damn. That reminds me. I have a meeting this morning I can't avoid."

"Can I still bring Sandoval in?" I asked.

He wagged his head. "No, let's hold off on that."

"It doesn't matter if the DCI is sniffing around and asking questions," I said, holding my temper in check. "You can't expect me to back off on this case, chief."

"I'm not telling you to stand down, Price, but we need to play our cards close to the chest. Lujan can't assert jurisdiction over our case unless drugs are involved. We haven't established they are, so here's what I am proposing you do. Fill Lujan in on the case, but leave out any references to Sandoval and his suspected illicit activities."

"That's going to be tricky. I can't lie to a DCI agent."

"Nobody's asking you to lie." Vanderberg put his hand on my shoulder. "Avoid the subject of drugs. It's unnecessary for him to know about Sandoval's compound or the fruitless search warrant—at least not right now. If he asks you point blank about something, be truthful, but don't volunteer any information."

"What if he finds out later?"

He waved away my concern. "Investigations are fluid. They change with the evidence. He knows that. If the subject comes up at a later date, we'll say we considered the possibility of a narcotics connection early in the investigation but found nothing to indicate that drugs were a factor."

"Would you like more coffee, sir?" Connie said, loud enough for us to hear her in the breakroom. "Here, let me take that and I'll get it for you."

Vanderberg shot me a look of caution. "Are we good?"

I nodded. "I think I can handle it."

Connie came into the breakroom to refill the agent's coffee cup. "Your guest is getting restless, chief."

"Yes, I know," he said. "Connie, call Stokes and tell him I want him on patrol today. Remind him the Edgemont County Farmers Market opens down at the rodeo grounds, and someone needs to put in an appearance on behalf of the police department. You're with me, Price."

I followed him into his office and took the guest chair next to Agent Lujan.

The chief's office was small and the two guest chairs were crammed together. I tucked my left elbow in to avoid rubbing it against the DCI agent, who was drumming his fingers on the arm of the chair.

"Agent Lujan," Vanderberg said, sounding more cooperative, "I apologize for keeping you waiting. I was ironing out a few scheduling details so I could free up some of Officer Price's time for you today. She is an experienced homicide detective that came to Perseverance from the San Diego Police Department and has been running the Randall murder investigation from the beginning."

Lujan reacted to this information by giving me an appraising look, followed by a subtle nod of approval.

To my horror, I felt the color rise in my cheeks.

The chief continued. "I want to make it clear this is a Perseverance Police Department case. I do not need the DCI's help nor am I asking for it. Before I consent to allow you access to the information that my team has gathered, Special Agent Lujan, I want your assurance that you understand the limits of my largesse. We are at a critical juncture in this case. Officer Price's time is valuable, and I trust you won't take more of it than is necessary. Are we on the same page?"

"Yes. Yes, I believe we are," the agent said, "and I hope you understand

I have a responsibility to follow up on the tip. But don't worry, I have no intention of stepping on your toes, Chief Vanderberg."

"That settles it, then." Vanderberg pulled his lips back in a stiff smile. "I'll leave you two to it." He stood and opened the door.

I stood as well. "Let's convene at my desk, Agent Lujan, and we'll get this over with."

Eyes narrowed, Lujan considered us both before rising to follow me.

He was no doubt accustomed to throwing his weight around in the backwoods of Wyoming, but Vanderberg put him on notice he wouldn't stand for it in Perseverance, and I vowed not let him browbeat me, despite him being easy on the eyes.

"More coffee, sir?" I asked.

"No, thank you. Now, what can you tell me about Evelyn Randall's death?"

"A little over a week ago," I said, "we received a call from one of her neighbors requesting a welfare check. When I entered the Randall home, I found Mrs. Randall dead at the bottom of the stairs in her living room. At first, the coroner believed the victim suffered a heart attack or stroke and ruled it a natural death."

He nodded. "Go on."

"During the autopsy, the medical examiner didn't find any evidence of a natural death, so the next logical conclusion was that she died in a fall down the stairs—and she did in fact fall postmortem—but in the end he identified manual strangulation as the official cause of death. Her assailant fractured her larynx and hyoid bone." I arranged my arms as if strangling an imaginary victim but realized that was weird and dropped my arms. "Which is consistent with injuries precipitated by manual force rather than a fall. Therefore, it was the coroner's final opinion that the perpetrator strangled her manually."

Lujan looked bored. "That was the coroner's opinion?"

"Well, it was Doctor Appleton's opinion, but Gleason—ah—County Coroner Ricky Gleason concurred."

"Gleason is a loser and a drunk, isn't he?"

I felt my anger rise. There is something grating about someone outside your community making snide remarks about one of your own, although what they say might be true. It doesn't sit right.

"Gleason has been the county coroner since 1986, and we have had no complaints," I said. Then I remembered the way he flipped over Evelyn Randall's body and winced, but Lujan didn't catch it.

"Okay. So, you're looking for someone strong enough to strangle someone manually. That rules out a female killer."

"Not necessarily. Mrs. Randall was small and elderly. A strong woman could have overpowered her."

"True, but statistically unlikely."

I conceded the point with a slight inclination of my head.

"Where did the victim live?" he asked, examining his fingernails, which were immaculate.

I glanced at my own broken nails, some of which were chewed down to the nail beds. One was a deep violet because I crushed it in the car door yesterday and I was a little worried I might lose it. I slid my hands off the desk to my lap. "Mrs. Randall lived in Brightwater Canyon. It's an exclusive gated community about fifteen miles out of town in unincorporated Edgemont County."

"How did the Perseverance Police Department end up with a county case?"

Given Lujan's familiarity with Gleason, I presumed he knew all about the saga of Buck Lanier, so I dispensed with the details of the calamities that beset the Edgemont County Sheriff's Office. "Deputy Clifton Bartel was providing security at a fire in Union Pass when the call came in and county dispatch forwarded the call to us."

"They contained the fire early last week. Why didn't Deputy Bartel take over?"

"Uh, someone injured him while he was on duty at the fire—a minor injury—but then he had a family wedding to attend in Seattle."

In the background, I watched Vanderberg tiptoe out of his office, staying out of the agent's line of sight. He pulled on his hat and gave me a thumbs up before slipping out the front door.

"Bartel is in Seattle?" Lujan sounded a little testy.

"Yes."

The agent pinched the bridge of his nose with a thumb and forefinger. "That's a shame. I was looking forward to working with Deputy Bartel again. In that shitshow you Edgemont County folks call a sheriff's department, he does his best to hold the institution together. But I digress. Go on, Officer Price, tell me about the murder scene. You mentioned fingerprints. Did you find anything else of interest?"

"It gets a little complicated."

"Complicated? Do tell."

I detected a note of sarcasm, but I forged on. "On the day I discovered Evelyn Randall's body, the coroner determined her death was from natural causes, so there was nothing to investigate." I spread my hands as if my logic made sense. "But after the autopsy revealed it was a homicide, we returned to the scene of the crime and discovered someone scrubbed the premises before we could gather evidence."

The narrative oozed incompetence, and I knew it, but to my astonishment, Lujan didn't say a word. In fact, the incongruities seemed to slip right by him.

"What about witnesses? Did the neighbors see anything?"

"Officer Stokes and I canvassed the entire neighborhood. The houses are spread out, and the terrain is rugged and heavily wooded. Even if someone looked in the Randall property's direction the evening of the murder, they couldn't have seen anything given the natural environment."

Lujan rotated his neck. "What about the neighbor who requested the welfare check?"

"Maggie McGuiness. She claims she knows nothing. It was what she didn't see that caused her to call county dispatch on Monday, June 5th. During a normal weekend, Mrs. Randall was on the road several times a day, but Mrs. McGuiness realized she hadn't seen her since Friday."

"Is she a person of interest?"

"No."

He steepled his fingers and peered at me over the top of them. "But in theory, a neighbor could have killed Mrs. Randall, right? If they were a resident, no one would have thought it suspicious if they saw them near the victim's home."

"Maybe." I halted short of revealing we had a potential suspect, remembering Vanderberg preferred I keep Sandoval's name out of the conversation for now.

But Lujan didn't pursue the issue. Instead, he asked, "Any thoughts on why someone might want to kill an elderly woman?"

"She may have seen something she wasn't supposed to see—damaging information that someone wouldn't want exposed."

"Do you have any leads on who this someone might be?"

"We're working on it."

He gave me an incredulous look. "But you have an idea."

"We're looking into it and have identified a potential suspect."

"Why haven't you brought this potential suspect in for questioning?"

"Because I'm sitting here talking with you, Agent Lujan." I attempted to sound Dirty Harry cool, but came off as snotty.

He spread his hands. "Don't let me stop you, officer."

The truth of the matter was Vanderberg would blow a gasket if I approached Sandoval on my own. Until he got back from wherever he was, my hands were tied.

"Chief Vanderberg and I intend to do that as soon as he gets back," I said.

Lujan glanced over his shoulder at the chief's vacant office, then sat back in his chair and scrutinized me.

I placed my hands on my desk. "Are we done here, Agent Lujan?"

"I would love nothing more than to get the hell out of here myself, Officer Price, but it's going to be damn near impossible to convince me that the tip was unfounded until *I'm* satisfied you have disclosed all the relevant information."

He pulled back his coat sleeve to reveal a gold watch. "Now, all I ate for breakfast was a stale doughnut and I don't know about you, but I become unpleasant and irrational if I haven't eaten. As I recall, the truck stop serves a pretty decent lunch. How about you join me for a sandwich, and we can discuss how to wrap this situation up to our mutual satisfaction?"

It was a reasonable request. Then he smiled at me and little crinkles appeared around his dark brown eyes, which were fringed with black lashes.

Good Lord. What would Gracie McKenna think if she spotted me having lunch with him?

"No." I said. "I mean, the truck stop's food isn't half as good as it once was. How about the Perseverance Cafe? It's closer and we can get a quiet booth in the back."

•   •   •

"I'll have the club sandwich on whole wheat with a side salad and an unsweetened iced tea," Lujan said as he handed Dottie the menu.

"You got it, honey." She flapped her eyelashes at him. "Will you have the usual, Wyn?"

She had never addressed me so politely.

I gave her a curt nod. "Sure."

Lujan and I were seated in a semi-private booth at the rear of the cafe, but as we had made our way through the gregarious lunch crowd, every pair of prying eyes followed us.

"Wyn—do you mind if I call you Wyn?—is an unusual name. Is it a nickname?" he asked.

"Of sorts. My full name is Wynette."

His eyes twinkled. "Wynette, huh? As in Tammy Wynette?"

"Yes. Tammy is my first name." I threw him a look that dared him to laugh.

Sensing it was a touchy subject, he changed course. "Tell me about yourself, Wyn. Vanderberg said you were with the San Diego police force."

I knew the drill. He wanted to know my bona fides. My street cred. What type of police work was I doing before Perseverance?

I rattled it off like I was in a job interview. "I earned my bachelor's degree in criminal justice at the University of Wyoming and served four years on patrol and three years in the criminal investigation unit with the Rapid City Police Department. In California, I spent four years in the homicide division of the San Diego Police Department, and six months' light duty. Pregnancy."

The last part left a bitter taste on my tongue. It was the profession's dirty secret that most police departments didn't know what to do with pregnant cops. I spent the last six months of my stint with the San Diego PD making coffee and filing reports for guys who used to call me boss.

"I'm impressed. Perseverance was lucky to snag you."

I recoiled, assuming he was patronizing me, but his expression seemed sincere.

"Thank you. I'm lucky to be here, Agent Lujan." It wasn't an honest answer, but I couldn't think of anything else to say.

"Please, call me Ernie. Everybody does."

Dottie brought our order, and he gave her a rakish grin.

After she was gone, he asked, "Do you have kids?"

It was impossible to pinpoint the moment our conversation had veered into the personal, but if it meant I didn't have to talk to him about the Randall investigation, I would play along.

"Uh, yes. A daughter. Danica Dawn. She's two."

"Danica Dawn, huh? Another unusual name."

"Yes, but I call her Dancy, which some people confuse with Nancy. She's probably going to hate me when she grows up."

He took a sip of his iced tea and contemplated the glass. "I have two. Sierra is fifteen and Nicholas is seventeen."

"Oh."

"What about Dancy's father? What does he do?"

I went stone cold, which is what happened every time someone asked me about him, but this time an inexplicable void appeared where Jason's face should've been. How was it possible to forget what my husband looked like? I quailed, searching for an appropriate response to Lujan's inquiry—one that wouldn't give too much away.

Lujan noted my obvious disquiet. "My apologies, I didn't—"

"No, it's all right. Ernie." It was awkward to use his given name. I took a gulp of my Coke. "Dancy's father is no longer in the picture."

"Oh. I see."

"We were childhood sweethearts," I said. "After we got married, he—Jason—joined the Marine Corps."

Lujan didn't fuss with his napkin or swig his iced tea as I rambled on despite every self-preservation mechanism in my brain screaming to stop. "When he finished MOS, I quit my job with the Rapid City police force to join him at Camp Pendleton. We were in California about a year when the San Diego Police Department offered me a job in homicide as a detective."

"Was Jason supportive of your decision?"

"No. He was furious because I applied without asking him first. It was a constant source of contention. Shortly after he got out of the

Marines, he left me and San Diego didn't seem very classy anymore, so I answered an advertisement for a law enforcement officer in 'a rebounding little village where you can raise your family'. It sounded ideal, so here I am, living the Mayberry dream in Perseverance, Wyoming."

He cocked his head.

"Forgive me, that sounded sarcastic," I said in a rush. "As a single parent, I was looking for a quiet, safe environment to raise my daughter while trying to stay in law enforcement."

"There is nothing wrong with that."

Dottie cruised by, winking at Lujan as she ripped a receipt off her order pad and threw it on the table. "I can take you up front when you're ready, hon."

"What about you Ernie?" I asked. "What does your wife do?"

Hell, sauce for the goose is sauce for the gander.

"Ex-wife."

"Oh."

"She loathed being a cop's wife."

"I see."

"After a brutal divorce and custody battle, I decided being a married man wasn't in the cards for me."

"I'm sorry."

Lujan laced his hands behind his head and stretched out his legs. "Me too, Wyn. But you've heard the statistics, around seventy percent of law enforcement marriages end in divorce. Some call it quits for the same reasons civilians split up, but most wind up divorced because the spouse can't handle the fear and uncertainty.

"As police officers, every time we walk out that door, we accept the risk that we won't come home. But regardless of the peril, we continue to do it. Hell, the best cops are adrenalin junkies, but Human Resources doesn't let us list that qualification on the job description. We thrive on danger and people who aren't in law enforcement struggle to wrap their heads around that mindset. The only human beings on earth who understand us cops are other cops. Am I right?"

It was a rhetorical question, and he gazed into my eyes while the comment hung in the air like a puffy cartoon question mark. Under normal circumstances, I could produce an intelligent—perhaps even witty—response, but I lost myself in his liquid brown eyes and my conversational skills vanished.

Vanderberg jolted me out of my trance. "Looks like I'm too late."

Without skipping a beat, Lujan said, "We were just leaving Chief Vanderberg. Wyn suggested we visit the crime scene in Brightwater Canyon."

"Wyn suggested that, did she?" Vanderberg scowled at the agent's casual use of my first name.

Ignoring my stare, the DCI agent shrugged and stuck out his lower lip. "So I can get the lay of the land, so to speak."

The chief raised an eyebrow. "Lay of the land?"

Lujan took a couple of bills out of his wallet and laid them on the receipt before sliding it across the pockmarked Formica table. "Would you mind taking this to the cash register for me while your boss and I have a quick word, Wyn? Tell Dottie to keep the change."

I hesitated, wondering who in the hell he thought he was, then grabbed the cash and marched to the front of the cafe.

There was a line at the register and when I returned to the table, Vanderberg was folding a white paper napkin into a tight, neat triangle while Agent Lujan chewed on a toothpick and studied the ice in the bottom of his glass.

As soon as he saw me, Vanderberg stopped smoothing the small white packet. "I have agreed to let Agent Lujan accompany you to Brightwater Canyon so you can show him the 'lay of the land', but make it quick. We have a case to close."

"Yes, sir," I said.

"Good. Let's go." The DCI agent discarded the toothpick and stood up.

After we exited the cafe, I said, "What was that all about, Agent Lujan?"

"Your boss showed up before I got around to discussing it with you."

"You manipulated me."

He sucked his teeth and looked away.

•   •   •

"Agent Lujan and I are headed out to Brightwater Canyon," I said when we entered the police station.

Connie was dusting the filing cabinets, and Justin was pretending to be a professional police officer by clacking away on his keyboard with a stern expression on his face. If I wasn't so furious with Lujan, I would have snickered.

Justin struggled to his feet when I announced our intentions, but I raised my hand. "It's okay, Justin—Officer Stokes. We won't be long, and the chief is keen to keep department resources focused on the Randall case. You can stay here and work on...uh, whatever you have been working on."

I retrieved the key to the Randall house from my desk drawer and walked outside to my cruiser. No doubt Special Agent Lujan expected us to take his fancy new Ford, but driving my cruiser would make me feel more in control of the situation.

At first, he hesitated when he saw the lumbering Crown Victoria, but then pulled open the creaking passenger door and slid in, a slow grin spreading over his face as he ran a hand over the vintage upholstery.

I turned the key and the pounding beat of Eminem's "Alfred's Theme" from his *Music To Be Murdered By* album thumped out of the stereo.

I slapped the power off. "Sorry."

"I like that song," he said, "but I'm more of a Pitbull fan myself."

"So, your boss is running for sheriff."

It wasn't a question, and I didn't dignify it with a response.

Lujan surveyed the scenery out the window. "For someone new in these parts, it's a gigantic leap from town cop to the sheriff of a big county. He's from Chicago, right?"

I gripped the steering wheel tighter. "Yes."

Brightwater Canyon Creek flashed and sparkled to our right as we drove down the winding road flanked by towering evergreens and shimmering cottonwoods. Inhaling the spicy scent of the cottonwoods, I willed my tension to dissipate.

"Nice," said Lujan.

"Yes, it is," I said, guiding the wide-bodied Crown Vic around a hairpin turn. "It used to be the Lumineux Ranch. A renowned name around these parts until the Lumineux boys pissed it away—pardon my French."

We entered through the Spruce Hollow Gulch gate and took a right on Meadowlark Lane. I pointed across the meadow. "That white house behind the gate over there is Frank and Maggie McGuiness' place."

"How do they fit into this narrative?"

"Mrs. McGuiness—Maggie—is the neighbor who called in the welfare check."

When we reached the Randall residence, I pulled into the driveway and switched off the car. "You want to go in the house?"

"I think we should."

He whistled under his breath when he got out of the cruiser and took in the 360-degree panorama.

The house boasted a spectacular view in any direction. To the west, the foothills of the Wind River Mountain Range rose behind the house and to the north and south, majestic pines swayed in the ubiquitous Wyoming breeze. An emerald-green meadow stretched out to the east, a kaleidoscope of flowers flourishing among its native grasses.

Lujan turned back to the house with its wrap-around veranda and xeriscaped yard. "Looks like a pretty high-end neighborhood."

"The average home price out here, with acreage, is around $1,200,000, which isn't affordable for most Perseverance folks, but not as outrageous as Jackson."

I was referring to Jackson Hole, Wyoming, where multi-million-dollar homes owned by affluent outsiders were abundant and working class locals struggled to find affordable housing.

At the sound of an engine, we turned to watch a red Ford pickup creep by slowly on Meadowlark Lane.

"It's a small community. Everybody's nosy," I said.

Once inside, we proceeded to the great room, which was spotless, like a photo shoot for *Better Home and Gardens*. Even the leather gleamed, but underneath the scent of Lemon Pledge, the house still reeked of decayed flesh.

Lujan sniffed. "What was it you said? Someone swept the floors and ran the dishwasher after the coroner removed the body?"

"Yes. A plate in the kitchen had the remains of Mrs. Randall's last meal on it. It was gone when I came back, and the dishwasher was empty."

"What kind of murderer returns to the crime scene and empties the dishwasher?"

"One that's trying to get rid of evidence?"

"Or we're off base and whoever cleaned the house afterwards was not the same person who committed the crime."

"I'm not following."

"Look at this place. The amount of physical work it takes to keep a large house in this condition is overwhelming." He swiped a finger across a side table and held it up. "These surfaces are pristine—polished and dust-free. Either Evelyn Randall was a geriatric dynamo who spent all her time keeping house, or she employed a professional cleaning person."

It hadn't crossed my mind that Evelyn Randall employed a house cleaner.

"Who else would have a set of keys to the house?" Lujan said. "A family member? A neighbor?"

I shook my head. "Not family. We know of one relative—Olivia DeWitt, a niece that lives in New York. But she doesn't have a key, and she made it clear she would not be coming out here to Mrs. Randall's house."

"Like I said, she had a cleaning lady."

"Yes, perhaps. But how could she be ignorant of the fact Evelyn Randall was dead?"

"C'mon Wyn. Most of the cleaning ladies I know don't speak English or pay attention to the local news. If Mrs. Randall had a cleaner, I bet the same person cleaned other homes in the area."

I nodded. "There is a Casper cleaning company that provides services to the businesses in Perseverance. I think Vanderberg knows the owner. I'll ask him."

"All right. Now, walk me through the scene from the moment you entered the home."

I motioned to the spot where I found the body. "That's where Mrs. Randall's body was lying."

"Stop right there. Close your eyes and tell me what you see."

He moved in, so near I felt his body heat and smelled his aftershave, even above the residual odor of a rotting corpse. It was distracting.

As if he could read my mind, Lujan said, "Focus, Officer Price."

I cleared my throat. "Okay. She's lying on her stomach and her head is turned to the right. Her left arm is twisted behind her back, but her right arm is stretched in front of her, palm up. A wild iris is near her outstretched hand."

"A wild iris?"

"Yes, it's wilted but intact."

"What else?"

"She has short gray hair and there are liver spots on her hands. She's wearing a pink silk blouse and cropped denim pants."

"What about her feet?"

"She is wearing...one tan moccasin."

"Did you find the other shoe?"

"No. She probably lost it in the struggle with her killer, but it wasn't on the floor by the body—" In an involuntary reflex, my eyes flicked to the loft.

We jogged up the staircase together. At the top, Lujan rotated in a semicircle, surveying the layout.

I pointed to the carved table against the railing. "This table was crooked, and the stem of a wild iris was under its leg. Everything else was as you see—"

In unison, we turned towards the back wall and saw the tan moccasin beneath the built-in desk.

I sucked in a gulp of air. "That shoe wasn't there when I found the body or after we returned later to gather evidence. Officer Stokes and I covered every inch of this place. We would have seen it."

"Perhaps you and Officer Stokes were standing in the wrong place."

My scalp prickled. "No, I am certain it wasn't there when we processed the scene."

"Despite the skylights, this corner is dark, and the craft table obscures the area beneath the desk unless you're standing in the right spot."

His keenness to give me an easy way out annoyed the hell out of me, and I ignored him. There wasn't any point arguing about it.

He snapped pictures of the moccasin from different angles with his cell phone, then pulled it forward with a handkerchief. "We'll need to bag this up as evidence."

I crouched down beside him. Something jammed behind the desk drawer caught my eye. "What's that?"

A red plastic folio was wedged two-thirds of the way behind the drawer, suggesting whoever stashed it was rushed. I took a latex glove from my pocket and retrieved it.

It was an inch thick and fastened with an elastic string. Inside were a few old magazines, newspaper clippings, and a yellow legal pad filled with cramped handwriting.

I spread the contents out on the desk and selected a magazine, reading aloud from the cover, "Fortune, April 25, 2005, The Fortune 500. The Largest US Industrial Corporations." One page was marked with a paperclip, so I flipped it open to the page and scanned the article.

A smug, handsome man with a Cuban cigar clenched in his teeth grinned from behind a mahogany desk, the Denver skyline in a dramatic silhouette behind him.

Lujan peered over my shoulder. "That's Robert Sandoval, and so is this." He picked a newspaper clipping out of the pile with his fingernails and held it up.

The headline read, "Blackhammer Under Scrutiny". A sullen Robert Sandoval glared at the camera, flanked by two solemn men in dark suits, one of whom had a hand up to block the photographer's shot.

The other clippings chronicled the investigation's progression and Sandoval's eventual ouster from the company.

Lujan riffled through the pages of the yellow legal pad, squinting at the tiny handwriting. "It appears the victim was tracking someone's movements. These are detailed notes on the target's activities and location—dates, times, places, and the people he met with. The notes say 'RS', which, given the other evidence, I would guess is Robert Sandoval."

I saw the wheels turning in his head, putting two and two together. Snatching the notepad from his hands, I stuffed the documents into the folio and fastened the closure. Like the shoe, I could swear the red folio wasn't there last week.

Lujan unbuttoned his coat and loosened his tie. The butt of a Glock 19 protruded from a holster under his left arm and his white dress shirt was snug across his muscular chest.

"Sandoval. Robert Sandoval is your murder suspect," he said in a measured cadence.

I avoided his eyes, declining to corroborate his suspicion.

"Oh, now see there? You looked away as soon as I spoke his name, which confirms it." He threw up his hands. "What is it with you people and Robert Sandoval?"

"I'm not sure what—"

"You heard about the big meth lab hoax? I wasted two weeks of my life out here in Edgemont County chasing rumors and half-baked theories, and you know what we found? Nothing."

"Maybe you weren't trying hard enough." I stopped myself before I said something regrettable. It was one thing to get into a pissing match with a fellow officer over jurisdiction, but a different matter altogether to call someone a dirty cop. You couldn't take an accusation like that back once it escaped your lips. Besides, it was Justin who alleged the Wyoming DCI accepted bribes from Sandoval to look the other way about the suspected methamphetamine lab, and Justin wasn't the most impartial—or sensible—person I knew.

Lujan's eyes widened in disbelief. "Wow. Okay. Tell me Officer Price, what's the connection here? You said Evelyn Randall saw something. So put it together for me. How did you jump from a wilted flower to the conclusion Robert Sandoval is a murderer?"

I told him about Robert Sandoval's sudden appearance at the crime scene on the day I discovered the body and his previous interactions with the victim. Then I explained about the trail behind the house and the pictures Randy McGuiness took of Sandoval's compound, glossing over the details he didn't need to know. If he were as clever as he thought he was, he could connect the dots himself.

After I finished, he said, "Is that everything?"

"More or less." I avoided his eyes.

He raised his eyebrows as if questioning the veracity—or at least the completeness—of my narrative, then brushed it off. "Okay, let's bag up this evidence so you can take it to the Perseverance station. I want to see that trail before it gets any later."

Shaded in vibrant hues of green, the trail was cool and pleasant. I took it at a fast pace, daring Lujan to keep up, but when I slowed at the bottom near the creek, he veered to avoid running into me.

As I caught my breath, I pointed to the moist earth near the creek. "I found footprints here made by small hiking boot, about the size Mrs. Randall wore, implying she was here a day or two before she died."

Lujan squatted and inspected the ground. "A herd of cattle was through here recently."

"The homeowner's association leases the land out to local ranchers for summer pasture and uses the money for roads and general upkeep of the public areas. Irene Brockman of the Brockman Ranch has leased the Brightwater Canyon range for the last several years. The lease allows Donna's cattle free-range within the bounds of the subdivision, but don't worry, I got pictures of the prints."

"How much farther is it to the compound you were talking about?"

I eyed his stylish suit and polished shoes. "It's over that ridge, but the path is difficult."

He interpreted my expression and snorted. "Don't worry about me, Officer Price. It's all part of the job."

I shrugged and started up the steep embankment.

The slope was slippery from the rain, forcing me to grab rocks and shrubs for handholds so I wouldn't tumble backwards on top of him. When I reached the top, I stopped to brush soil and dried leaves off my uniform while I caught my breath and waited for Lujan.

The field of irises was past its peak, but here and there, pockets of delicate lavender flags still fluttered in the afternoon breeze.

"This is beautiful." A smile curled his lips. He wasn't even breathing hard. "It's worth the climb."

"The Sandoval compound is over that rise." I pointed.

We trekked across the meadow to the lip of the slope and surveyed the compound below.

Lujan swept his arm from left to right. "Sandoval owns all of this?"

"Yes. He owns this entire swath of land on the western side of Brightwater Canyon. His ranch is south of that mesa."

He nodded and stroked his chin. "Were that kid's pictures taken in this vicinity?"

"Yes, Randy was standing in about this exact spot."

"I want to see his pictures," Lujan said. "Let's head back to town."

"Of course, Agent Lujan."

"I thought we settled that matter already. Since we're going to be working together, you need to call me Ernie."

"Of course, *Ernie*."

He led the way back to the Randall house, which gave me the opportunity to admire his athletic build from behind until I gave myself a mental slap for moral turpitude and resolved to keep my eyes on the trail. As he pointed out, Special Agent Ernesto Lujan wasn't going anywhere soon, and I didn't look forward to explaining that to Vanderberg.

On our way out of the canyon, Lujan made several attempts to connect with someone at DCI headquarters in Cheyenne. Finally, one of his calls went through. "Hey, Bonnie, I need you to do something for me, sweetheart."

I gritted my teeth. What a narcissistic jerk. If someone I worked with said that kind of shit to me, I'd give him a piece of my mind.

"Bonnie? Bonnie? Can you hear me?" He pulled the cell phone away from his ear and looked at it with irritation.

"The service out here is pretty spotty," I said. "You'll have better luck once we turn onto the county highway."

"Right." He slipped the cell phone back into his suit pocket and rolled down the window to prop his elbow on the door frame.

The smell of cottonwood spice drifted in through the open window and the late afternoon sunlight sparkled through the green leaves, creating a surreal, golden ambiance. It might have been romantic except I was with a colleague—an egotistical special agent at that—and we were investigating a murder.

Lujan took off his blue silk tie and put it in his pocket. "What do we know about Evelyn Randall's killer?"

"He knew what he was doing. I think we can rule out a crime of passion, since he carried it out with precision and left no trace. It has all the hallmarks of a premeditated act of violence."

"Exactly. Almost like a professional hit, which leads me to believe it wasn't the killer's first time. He might have been watching her—or stalking her. He could have followed her to the house on that footpath."

"Or he drove up to the front door. If he was well known in the canyon, no one would think twice about it. All the information we have points to Robert Sandoval as our prime suspect—"

Lujan made a clicking sound with his tongue, cutting me off. "You won't be arresting Sandoval soon, not until I can look at the photos anyway, because everything you told me reeks of an organized crime operation. If it is, then my agency has jurisdiction and we will not let you wade in without our explicit authorization, but I suspect you knew that already."

He was right. Some of the biggest homicide cases I worked on in San Diego involved crime syndicates. Conducted jointly with the California Bureau of Investigation, those cases took months to unravel, which meant justice for victims like Evelyn Randall often fell by the wayside in the pursuit of bigger and flashier fish. Sometimes, it also meant that the right palms got greased and the entire case evaporated.

But although he was correct. I wasn't about to stand down.

"I hate to break it to you, *Ernie*, but this is my murder investigation and I have no intention of backing off." Flicking a glance in his direction, I tried to gauge his reaction, but his expression remained impassive.

"I respect that, but we're on the same team," he said in a soothing manner. "Given what you told me about your background, you didn't rise to the rank of homicide detective without a solid understanding of how these operations work. They get complicated fast. What starts out as a straightforward murder investigation of an isolated death develops into a multiple agency investigation into organized crime. The whole damn operation is a chess game, with every move weighed carefully be-forehand. We have to think five to ten steps ahead of the bad guys in a complex case such as this because if we act without considering the consequences, we could destroy our chances of taking down the big players."

"I'm aware of that, but the upshot could be that Evelyn Randall's murderer goes free."

"If it serves the greater good—"

"That's bullshit and you know it."

"Look, we need to work together on this investigation, Wyn. If we identify Evelyn Randall's killer along the way, I promise that justice will be done, but you have to trust me."

That was the problem. I wasn't sure I could trust him. "Well, Ernie, if we're making promises, then this is what I can promise you. I am going to catch her killer. I'll stay out of your way and do my best to aid your investigation, but my priority is Evelyn Randall."

We rode in silence after that. I could feel him studying me, but I didn't give him the satisfaction of acknowledging the attention. Instead, I concentrated on maintaining a steady speed on the twisting road.

Lujan pulled out his cell phone as soon as I swung the cruiser onto the highway. "Bonnie? It's me again. Sorry about that, gorgeous. The reception here is sketchy."

I rolled my eyes.

"He is a total jackass."

"That's the third time you said that," Gracie said, checking her phone again.

"I'm closing in on Evelyn Randall's killer. I can feel it. Why Lujan thinks he can waltz in and railroad my investigation now is beyond me."

She put her phone down on the table and crossed her arms over her chest. "What did this special agent do to get your panties in such a bunch?"

My face reddened.

She let out a squeal. "Oh, my God. You dig this guy—"

"Shh! You'll wake up Dancy—and I do not. He's macho—sexist—arrogant..." I spluttered.

Her phone vibrated, but she ignored it.

"Aren't you waiting for a call from Tug?"

"Tug can wait."

Tired of her interrogation, I steered the conversation away from Lujan. "You know, the first time I met Tug Stratton, he was in the company of Robert Sandoval."

"Yeah, of course. Tug's company is negotiating a business deal with him."

"What kind of deal?"

She smirked. "How should I know? We don't talk that much about work. In fact, we hardly talk at all, if you get my drift."

"It doesn't bother you that your new beau is associated with a notorious crook?"

She put her palms on the table. "Here's what I know. Tug Stratton is the most sincere, honorable, and trustworthy man I've ever met. If he thought Robert Sandoval was a bad person, he wouldn't be doing business with him. Full stop." She rubbed her hands together, a salacious glint in her eyes. "Now, you were telling me about Special Agent Ernesto Lujan."

"Gracie, there is nothing to tell."

"How did you describe him? Macho? Arrogant?" Her eyes twinkled. "In other words, he's sexy, confident, and masculine. No wonder he's got you all hot and bothered."

I sighed. What irked me was she was right.

After Gracie went home, I retrieved the red folio from Evelyn Randall's house and poured over it, looking for clues that might explain what why she was killed, but none of it made any sense. Why would she hide this stuff? There was nothing damning here. It was all public knowledge and old news. Water under the bridge.

Even the legal pad filled with notes was nothing but a generic log of dates and times. It could be a record of the occasions when Mrs.

Randall spotted activity at Sandoval's compound, but if that was accurate, she was camping out on the ridge day and night, which seemed unlikely. Without additional documentation, it was useless.

It was possible that Justin and I overlooked the folio in our sweep, but I could swear the moccasin was not there when we processed the crime scene. It was placed there later for us to find, but why?

I shivered, goosebumps prickling along my arms. Someone was playing a game with me.

FIFTEEN

I was thirty minutes late and running on less than two hours of sleep when I stumbled into the police station the next morning balancing a travel cup and binder on one arm and my backpack, holster, and hat on the other.

Vanderberg caught sight of me and tapped a long finger on his watch with a frown.

The front window shades of the station were pulled down, which made the interior gloomy, despite the overhead lights. Near the break-room, two uniformed men were drinking coffee with Lujan, who thrust his chin out in greeting when he saw me, but I was too foggy to acknowledge him.

A striking Black woman in her mid-thirties was on my desk phone, listening to someone on the other end and taking notes. Now and then she said, "Mm-hmm."

I dumped my stuff on the desk and mouthed a half-hearted apology when she looked up, startled.

She ended the call and stood to extend her hand with a brilliant smile. "I'm Special Agent Lynette Hobbs, DCI. Thanks for letting me use your desk, Officer..."

"Price, Officer Wyn Price," I said with a slight stammer, feeling myself shrink as I clasped her warm hand in my clammy one.

Hobb's glossy hair was twisted into a neatly braided bun at the crown of her head, and under her form-hugging navy suit, she wore a silky white blouse that complimented her dark skin. She was almost six feet tall, and gorgeous. I felt like Barney next to Andy.

Lujan approached my desk with the two uniformed men. "Officer Price, I'd like you to meet Sergeant Dennis Buchowski from the Sheridan County Sheriff's office, and Captain Andy Watson from the Wyoming State Highway Patrol. Sergeant Buchowski and Captain Watson are Task Force Officers with the Northwest Enforcement Team."

I uttered a polite greeting as I took each man's hand.

Forty-something Buchowski had a handlebar mustache that reminded me of an old western lawman while Watson was younger by a decade and buff, with a ramrod straight posture and quick smile. I pegged him as ex-military.

"Okay." Lujan rubbed his hands together. "Let's get the ball rolling. Agent Hobbs was kind enough to bring us a couple of whiteboards, which we can use to document what we know and keep the team on the same track." He gestured to the back wall, where two giant whiteboards formed a screen across the room.

As I snuck a furtive glance at the rickety old blackboard behind my desk, Vanderberg came out of his office and stood beside me, arms crossed in a defensive posture.

Lujan perched on the edge of Connie's desk and addressed the group. "Lynette, Dennis, and Andy are old hands at this, but since this is the first Wyoming DCI rodeo for Officer Price and Chief Vanderberg, I'll explain how this works in The Equality State."

What followed was an explanation of the DCI's special investigations and how regional task forces operated. The special agent was full of himself, but I was mesmerized despite my determination to resist his charms.

Thirty minutes in, Vanderberg returned to his office to check his email and didn't return.

After talking for over an hour, Lujan called a recess. Hobbs and the two officers walked across the street to the Van Gogh Coffee Shoppe for breakfast, and I sat down at my desk to check my voice mail and email.

"Anything new?" Lujan draped himself in the chair across from me.

"Ahh, no. Nope."

"It looked like you were expecting something."

"I'm waiting for a callback from a source. It may be another dead end, but I thought I would follow up."

"Did you have time to look at the stuff we picked up at the murder scene yesterday?"

I smacked a hand on the red folio on my desk. "With a fine-tooth comb, twice. It's all outdated, generic information. Even the hand-written notes were a bust."

"Huh. So we still don't know what we're up against. All we have are some inconclusive photos and sketchy details." He waved a hand at the whiteboards.

"And a murder," I said, unable to mask my irritation with his dismissive attitude.

"Of course, and a murder."

Lujan picked up my stapler and fiddled with it. "Would you have dinner with me once the investigation is over?"

His question knocked the breath out of me. "Excuse me?"

"Dinner. After we wrap the case. I know a terrific steakhouse in Dubois."

I swiveled my head, praying no one overheard, and said between gritted teeth, "No. Thank you, Agent Lujan. I don't think that's a good idea."

Before he managed a reply, the others returned from the coffee shop.

"Has anything exciting transpired?" Hobbs asked.

Lujan tilted back in his chair and looked her up and down. "Not until you got here."

I flushed and pretended to adjust my monitor to hide my bewilderment.

Hobbs noted my obvious discomfort and chided him. "You haven't changed a bit, have you, Ernie?"

"You know you would hate it if I changed, *chula*." His faint Hispanic accent grew more pronounced as he flirted with her.

Hobbs laughed and shook her head before switching back into professional mode. "I got some interesting news from Barnes. A couple of days ago, the DEA picked up a conversation in a gaming chat room frequented by wannabe and known drug traffickers. Someone was looking to move goods already in transit to Wyoming in a hurry. They're monitoring the channel, but the users in question have gone quiet."

"Good work, Hobbs. That could be our pals out in Brightwater Canyon. Let's verify the intel and stay on it. Tell Barnes to make it his priority and fill in the other team members."

"You got it." She moved away to join Watson and Buchowski.

"It's not that I don't trust the DEA," Lujan said to me, his demeanor professional yet amicable, "but we aren't exactly their priority. I prefer to get intel direct from the source—if I can do it without stepping on the DEA's toes. Who knows, it very well could be a major drug cartel moving product."

It was as if the invitation to dinner had never happened. I should have been relieved, but my insides twinged in disappointment.

"Or maybe it's merely some small-time crooks fencing stolen video games," I said.

"True. All we can do is to be patient, and hope things break our way. Which reminds me, yesterday you mentioned something about fingerprints. I checked with the State Crime Laboratory in Cheyenne. They haven't received prints, or any evidence related to the Randall case."

"That can't be right. Chief Vanderberg sent them in himself."

He shrugged. "Perhaps he got too busy with his *campaña* and forgot, darlin'."

My cheeks grew hot, but before I could deliver a scathing reply, the front door opened and Justin tripped in, his hair still damp from his morning shower.

Lujan ignored Justin. "Did anyone ever tell you how beautiful you are when you get mad?" Without lingering for a reply, he rose to his feet and winked at me.

It wasn't a wink one could dismiss as a simple blink. It was a bold, suggestive wink. When Justin caught the exchange, he stopped dead in his tracks, a look of confusion on his face.

To cover my humiliation, I said, "Where have you been, Officer Stokes? The doughnuts are in the back. Better hurry before they're all gone."

Vanderberg was on the phone when I rapped on the door to his office.

"I don't care what you have to do, just take care of it, Dino. Until we finish this task force business, the campaign is going to have to wait," he said, rolling his eyes for my benefit. "Listen, I have to go. Don't call me, I'll call you."

Pale stubble covered his jawline, and he looked exhausted. His uniform shirt was the same one he wore the day before because I recognized the mustard stain above the pocket.

He hung up the phone and beckoned me to enter.

I took a seat opposite him, tipping my head towards the crowded squad room. "I'm sorry about this chief—"

He waved off the apology and leaned back in his chair. "No, I'll have none of that. It's not your fault."

"I informed Lujan I wasn't backing off on the murder investigation. Of course, I'll help the task force out where I can, but I'm not asking Lujan's permission to do what I need to do to close the case."

"How did he respond?"

I rolled my eyes. "He gave me the old party line about being a team player and seeing the bigger picture. Blah, blah, blah."

"That sounds like par for the course."

"He also told me the DCI lab didn't get the fingerprints Justin lifted off the back door of the Randall house."

The chief frowned. "What is he playing at? I sent them in myself."

"That's what I told him. Should I ask him to check again?"

Vanderberg's eyes flicked to the squad room. "No. I'll take care of it. You should be cautious about what you share with him, Price. I don't trust him—or any of them."

"Roger that, boss. There's a lead I need to follow up on this afternoon, and it would be easier if Agent Lujan wasn't breathing down my neck. Will you cover for me?"

"I guess I can do that, but take Stokes with you."

I wrinkled my nose. "It would look suspicious if we both disappeared. They need a local guy, and Justin's eager to make a good impression on them."

The chief drummed his fingers on the desk, still eyeballing Lujan in the squad room. "Okay, but keep me apprised of your whereabouts."

"I will. I'm going to talk to the woman who owns Perfect Touch Cleaning. What's her name?"

He looked surprised. "Dolores Donovan?"

"Yes. Whoever cleaned Mrs. Randall's house was a professional. I doubt Mrs. Donovan has any connection to the murder, but the logical method to find a local cleaner is by asking the owner of the janitorial company that cleans most of Perseverance's businesses."

"You know Dolores is in Casper, right?"

I nodded. "Whatever it takes."

He opened a drawer and handed me an ivory business card. "Here, this is Mrs. Donovan's contact information. I will warn you she isn't the friendliest person you'll meet."

"Thanks, chief." I gave him a lazy salute.

Lujan's eyes were glued on me when I came out of the chief's office and followed me until I gathered up my stuff and left the station.

It wasn't as if I was obliged to tell him where I was going. I made it clear to him that my investigation into Evelyn's death would progress regardless of the DCI's plans. Vanderberg would simply have to keep him distracted until I got back.

Josefina was sitting on a patch of grass outside the coffee shoppe across the street, staring at the police station. I waved in her direction, but as usual, she ignored me.

I made the three-hour trip to Casper in two and a half, pulling into the dirt parking lot of a rundown industrial park north of town in the early afternoon.

The corporate headquarters of Perfect Touch Cleaning and Maid Service was housed in a cinder block building in what was otherwise a deserted section of the park. The structure's paint was once hot pink, but now was faded into a color resembling Pepto-Bismol.

In front of the building, a silver Cadillac Escalade sporting the pink Perfect Touch Cleaning decals and a black Chrysler 3000 with tinted windows were parked side-by-side. Near the entrance, a thin woman wearing a black polyester smock and pants set was propped against the cinder block wall, smoking a cigarette. She narrowed her eyes as I parked the Crown Vic next to the Chrysler and got out.

"You're early," she said with a rasp.

The claws of the hand holding her cigarette—which she didn't bother to put out—were lacquered in silver glitter accented with pink swirls. It was a safe bet she didn't do any heavy cleaning with that manicure.

I'd never met Dolores Donovan in person. I merely knew her as the boss of the Perfect Touch Cleaning crew and a disembodied voice who called Vanderberg several times a week, but in the flesh, she personified the old cowboy expression, "rode hard and put away wet". She was somewhere in her fifties, with heavy makeup and a lustrous dark wig that didn't flatter her worn, pitted face.

She squinted, giving me the once over. "Lars said you were looking for information about that dead woman's cleaner. There wasn't any reason for you to drive all the way to Casper. I could've told you everything you needed to know about her over the phone." Her prickly manner suggested she was put out by the intrusion.

"She works for you?"

Dolores blew out a long stream of smoke. "She used to. She went missing over a week ago. I figured she scurried her skinny little ass back to the reservation. You know how they are, unreliable as the Cleveland Browns on a Sunday. It's a wonder I can keep a crew running at all, but if you're in this line of business, you get used to employees coming and going. It's a shame, though. She was a damn good worker."

"Could I get a name and home address? I have a few questions to ask her."

She tossed her head with a snort of disgust. "Good luck finding that one. Her name was Angie Smith. She was a transient, so I don't have an address. While she was working for me, I let her live in one of my properties in Edgemont County, but I can guarantee you she isn't there anymore."

"Did she leave anything behind?"

"Nope." She stubbed the cigarette out on the concrete step and put the butt in the pocket of her black smock.

"Was it Angie who cleaned Mrs. Randall's house Tuesday or Wednesday last week?"

"Hmm..." Dolores thought about this. "Nope. That wasn't Angie."

"If Angie didn't clean the Randall house, do you know who did? Was it one of your other cleaners?"

She lifted one shoulder and let it drop. "It wasn't one of my girls."

"Did Angie have a roommate or was she friends with other cleaners? If so, is there any chance I could talk to them?"

She touched her top lip with her tongue. "My girls work alone, Officer. I wish I could give you more information, but I told you everything I know. Now, I run this place by myself, so I gotta get back to the phone. If I think of something, I'll call you."

"There is one more thing. Have you ever done any work for Robert Sandoval?"

Dolores's hand was on the door. "Nope," she said, but something flickered in her eyes at the mention of his name.

I stifled the urge to pressure her. "Okay, thanks for your time."

"Mm-hmm." She slipped back into the building and locked the door behind her, leaving me standing outside in the dusty parking lot.

In my gut, I suspected she knew more about Evelyn Randall's death than she was letting on. When I got back to the station, I would do some digging into Dolores Donovan's background.

My cell phone buzzed. It was Connie.

"What's up, Connie?"

"Where are you?" she asked in a hushed voice. "Vanderberg and Agent Lujan and have been going at it like a cobra and mongoose ever since you disappeared."

"I'm in Casper, following up on a lead."

"Casper? Oh my God, you need to get back. Now. The DCI got information about a shipment coming from Mexico. It has everybody jumping and Lujan has been asking about your whereabouts. He's pissed you aren't here."

"I'm on my way, but it'll be a couple of hours." I slid into the front seat of my cruiser. "Stall him if you can."

"I'll do my best," she said before disconnecting.

As I exited the parking lot, I glimpsed two dark-complected men coming out of the Perfect Touch Cleaning office in the rearview mirror. Dolores Donovan, face suffused with anger, appeared in the doorway behind them, gesticulating wildly. Her rage must have spurred them into action because they scrambled into the black Chrysler and exited the other side of the lot in a cloud of dust. I got the prickling feeling they were up to no good.

The station was a noisy hubbub of activity when I returned.

Vanderberg collared me the second I came in the door. "Any luck?"

I grimaced. "Not much. Angie Smith was the woman who cleaned Mrs. Randall's house, but Dolores Donovan said she ran off a week ago and didn't leave a forwarding address. Dolores wasn't uncooperative, but I sensed she knows more than she's saying."

"Oh? Why would she hold back information?"

"I don't know. I'm going to talk to Josefina, the station's cleaning lady. Dolores claimed Angie wasn't friends with any of the other Perfect Touch Cleaning crew, but I find it hard to believe."

"It will have to wait." He inclined his head towards Lujan, who beckoned us to join the group around the whiteboards.

"What's going on here, anyway? Connie said something about a shipment."

"The DEA confirmed to the DCI that a shipment of contraband crossed the border from Mexico last night. Lujan thinks it's headed this way."

"Last night? If it's headed to Sandoval's compound, it could arrive tonight."

He nodded. "Things are moving pretty fast. I understand you're determined to focus on the murder case, but put it on a back burner. It's all hands on deck tonight."

Before I could express disagreement, my cell phone hummed, and I scowled at the screen. It was Gracie.

"Officer Price, will you please join us?" Lujan said from across the room.

"I'll be there in a second. I have to take this first."

It turned out Tug wanted Gracie to go out to dinner with him, but she was supposed to babysit Dancy, so she called to ask if it was okay if Cassidy watched her instead.

"Fine," I said, "But remind her to lock the doors. Make sure you tell her." I hung up and joined the others.

"This task force will be based here in the police station," Lujan said. "A remote surveillance unit is on its way to monitor activity in the Sandoval compound. Agents Barnes and Drexler will keep us apprised of any developments."

"Where are you going to put a surveillance van?" Vanderberg asked. "There's one road into that compound and for all we know, it's being watched. We don't know who else is involved in this besides Sandoval."

Lujan gave him a smug look. "That's why we'll do it in stealth mode. The Perseverance police have been involved in the Randall case from the beginning, so we'll use your team as a cover, Chief Vanderberg. The surveillance team will arrive in Brightwater Canyon in your patrol vehicles and pack the equipment in via the trail on the Randall property. We'll set the equipment up in this area." He crossed to a map on one of the white boards and pointed to the notch above the compound. "I want one of your officers posted at the Randall house around the clock. If anyone asks, say you're stepping up your efforts to wrap up the investigation into Evelyn Randall's death. Are you on board with that, chief?"

Vanderberg chewed his lip and nodded once.

"At the first sign of activity, the surveillance team will inform the task force, and Hobbs and Watson will rendezvous with the duty officer at the house, who will lead them to the location via the gulch trail. After the first group is in position, they'll wait for me and Buchowski to arrive via the north road."

Justin raised a hesitant hand.

Lujan gestured to him. "Yes, go ahead, Officer Stokes."

"Will more law enforcement officers be arriving to assist?"

Buchowski snickered and elbowed Watson. Justin saw the exchange and flushed, which made me feel sorry for him. It was obvious the other officers intimidated him.

"No, it's a good question," Lujan said. "Everyone needs to have a solid understanding of how this operation will proceed. The task force team will be primarily composed of the officers in this room, plus two surveillance personnel. The Riverton Police Chief is also joining us, but he's assisting tribal police on a case and could be delayed. We also expect support from the DEA. However, I'm not sure when they will show up. I'm still waiting to hear from them."

Justin squirmed, uncomfortable with Lujan's answer, but the agent walked over and put a hand on his shoulder. "I promise we have all the personnel we need. Hobbs and I have run bigger investigations with fewer people, and Buchowski and Watson are seasoned Task Force Officers. Hell, I think you've been doing this longer than I have, haven't you, Andy?"

Watson gave him a look of feigned injury. "Are you calling me old, Ernie?"

Everyone chuckled, including Justin, albeit self-consciously. During the momentary distraction, Hobbs pulled Lujan aside for a private conference and Connie brought a fresh pot of coffee from the breakroom to refill our cups.

Lujan broke off his conversation with Hobbs and addressed the group. "Okay, listen up. Some of our DEA pals spotted the suspected truck carrying the shipment near Boise City, Oklahoma. We believe Sandoval's compound is its destination, and we plan to be there to intercept it. This could be a big score, team. If our information is correct, we have the opportunity to shut down a major drug pipeline into the Midwest—and solve the Evelyn Randall murder case at the same time."

The last part was an afterthought, no doubt appended for my benefit.

I studied the grainy black and white photo of Evelyn Randall tacked to the whiteboard behind Lujan. It was of such inferior quality it distorted her face, but the glossy color publicity shot of Robert Sandoval next to her was recognizable from across the room.

If Lujan noticed my distraction, he ignored it. "Also, Hobbs heard from Special Agent Jake Barnes and the DCI surveillance team will be here within the hour. Chief Vanderberg, one of your officers will take Barnes and his team out and take the first shift at the Randall house."

Vanderberg pointed at Justin, who blanched but nodded back. I was about to volunteer for the second shift, but Vanderberg said, "I'll relieve you at midnight, Stokes."

"Unless something pops before then." Anticipation glinted in Watson's eyes as he said this.

Lujan nodded. "That's settled, then. We'll maintain radio silence with the surveillance team and communicate by satellite phone. The Perseverance officers should carry on normal radio chatter. And remember, not one word of this to anyone outside this room. Not even your family, folks. Let's keep each other safe. Hobbs and Stokes, keep me in the loop. Unless something pops, as Andy says, I'll see you around zero hundred hours when Vanderberg and I come out to relieve you."

The group dispersed, but Lujan caught my arm. "I don't know where you disappeared to earlier, but I need your devoted participation in this undertaking, Price. After the surveillance team is in place, we'll need twenty-four seven monitoring of their communications. Hobbs will fill you in on the details."

My eyes flicked to Vanderberg, but he was talking to Connie.

"Of course, *sir*," I said to Lujan.

He searched my face for a moment before releasing my arm and walking away.

Justin rushed over, flapping an eight by ten photo. "Hey Wyn, I wanted to show you this before I left. Remember that gal at Lone Star Investors, the one who said she would let me know if they found anything on their security video?"

"Yeah, I remember," I said, still stung by Lujan's reprimand.

"Well, she came through." He handed me the picture.

It was a low-res, low-light image of a light-colored sedan in motion. The decal on the door was blurry, but I recognized it at once. "We already knew Perfect Touch cleaned Mrs. Randall's house. When was this taken?"

He leaned in, pointing to a set of fuzzy numbers in the lower corner that were partially cut off. "Uh, I think it's June third. I must have cut those off when I enlarged the photo, but I asked her to—"

I stabbed the photo with a finger. "June third was a Saturday. That's the night Evelyn Randall was killed."

Justin and I stared at each other for a moment.

"Have you shown this to anyone else?"

"Only the chief."

"Okay, I'll take from here. Thanks, Justin."

"Not a problem." He jammed on his Perseverance PD cap. "It looks like the surveillance guys just got here. I'll talk to you later."

As I carried the photo back to my desk, my thoughts raced. Was Angie, the missing cleaner, somehow involved in Evelyn Randall's murder? Is that why she disappeared?

"Officer Price? Is that your cell phone?" Hobb's voice broke through my concentration, startling me back to the present.

The DCI agent was staring at me. "Your cell phone."

"Oh yes. Right." I fumbled at my belt.

The caller ID displayed my home phone number. In my rush to answer before the caller hung up, I almost dropped it. "Hello?"

It was Cassidy, and she was shrieking.

"Cassidy, calm down. I can't understand you. Stop screaming and tell me what happened."

Lujan rushed over to my desk. "What is it?"

I silenced him with a raised hand, focusing on the distraught girl on the phone. "Cassidy, listen to me. Take Dancy to the bathroom and lock the door. I am on my way. Okay? Cassidy, are you listening to me? Cassidy? Cassidy?"

Lujan dogged my steps as I dashed towards the door. "Wyn, tell me what's going on."

I jangled my keys, searching for the Crown Vic among the law enforcement vehicles lined up outside the station. "That was my daughter's babysitter." My voice was unsteady.

He took me by the shoulders. "Is your daughter all right?"

"I'm not sure, but I think she's in danger. Cassidy said two strange men are sitting in a car outside my house. Just sitting there—" My voice cracked.

He shoved me towards the passenger side of his Ford Explorer. "Get in."

I did as he commanded, my mouth dry and heart thudding against my ribcage.

"Which way?" he asked.

I pointed north.

The SUV's tires squealed on the pavement as he swung it around and flipped on the lights and siren.

"Take the next left," I said. "In five blocks, turn right on Cinnamon. It's the little yellow house on the right. There's a brown Honda Accord in front."

"Okay, Wyn, what aren't you telling me?"

"I got a couple of weird phone calls. I don't know if they were threats—"

He frowned at me. "You've been getting threatening phone calls? Tell me about them."

"The first one was Wednesday morning, I think—"

"Wednesday? You're sure?" Lujan took a corner without braking and the high-profile vehicle yawed like a yacht in the Americas Cup.

I nodded. "Yes. I'm sure. It woke me up. It was early, about five o'clock."

"Man? Woman?"

"Man."

"What did he say?"

My voice trembled as I raised it to be heard above the siren. "Uh, he said 'Nancy is a nice name', or something along those lines. I thought it was a crank caller, but—" I drew a deep breath. "Then the same afternoon, I picked up a message on my answering machine at the police station. It was a man. The greeting cut off part of his message because he started talking before it finished. He told me to make sure my daughter was okay."

"To make sure she was okay..." Lujan pondered this as we careened onto Cinnamon Street. "Did you recognize his voice?"

"No. It wasn't anyone I know."

"Was it the same guy both times?"

"I can't say for sure. They didn't speak more than a few words." I screwed up my face and thought about it. "I heard a motor running in the background both times."

"Did you save the messages?"

"Yes."

"Well, at least that's something."

There were no other vehicles on Cinnamon Street when Lujan brought the SUV to a skidding halt outside my little yellow house and my stomach clenched with foreboding. "Would they—do you think—"

"If these men are connected to the Brightwater Canyon smuggling outfit—and I suspect they are—then we're dealing with some ruthless and most likely desperate people, Wyn." His face was grim.

SIXTEEN

While Agents Lujan and Hobbs questioned Cassidy, I sat on the front porch step, unable to move or form a coherent sentence.

Gracie brought me a mug of coffee and I took it without comprehending what it was.

She sat down and wrapped her arms around me. "Do you know what happened?"

"Cassidy forgot to lock the door. She said she was sorry—" I swiped at my nose with a soggy Kleenex. "She called me after she saw the car outside, but she didn't remember the door was unlocked until they burst in while we were on the phone together. One threw a blanket over Dancy and carried her out of the house while the other jerk pointed a gun at Cassidy. The kidnapping took less than a minute."

"Did Cassidy get a good look at them?"

I twisted the Kleenex in my hands. "They were wearing dark clothing and bandanas over the lower parts of their faces. They grabbed Dancy and left without saying a word to Cassidy. She said there was nothing she could do..."

"You can't blame her, Wyn. She's a kid, and this is Perseverance. Nothing bad ever happens in Perseverance—at least not until now."

Lujan traipsed down the steps, turning back to look at us from the sidewalk. "How are you holding up, Wyn?"

"She's doing as well as expected under the circumstances," Gracie said.

He flashed his even white teeth and extended his hand. "I don't think we've been introduced. I'm Special Agent Ernesto Lujan, Wyoming DCI."

She stood to take his hand. I worried she might utter something embarrassing, but she said, "I'm Wyn's neighbor Gracie McKenna."

Vanderberg's white Yukon pulled up to the curb in front of the house and Lujan tilted his head in the chief's direction. "Does he know?"

"Know what?" My head was a solid block of concrete.

"About the calls."

"Oh. Yes. He knows."

Lujan moved away to intercept Vanderberg, pulling him to the side before he reached the porch. I couldn't hear what the agent said, but the chief's face remained rigid and expressionless. Once Lujan finished, Vanderberg pushed him aside and walked towards us.

He nodded at Gracie and then said to me. "I want you to let us handle this, Price. That is a direct order. Sandoval has made this personal, and I cannot allow you to remain in harm's way. As of right now, I am placing you on administrative leave. You're off the Randall case—and the task force—until we find your daughter and bring her home safe."

My lips moved, but my tongue was too numb to form a response.

A Wyoming Highway Patrol vehicle arrived and parked behind the chief's Yukon. Watson and Buchowski got out and engaged in an animated conversation with Lujan, who nodded in my direction as he spoke, explaining the situation. After he finished, they turned their somber faces to me, and I flinched at the pity in their eyes.

Out in the nether regions of Wyoming, where the constellations shine brighter than the meager lights from the scattered towns, the luminescent smudge of the Milky Way spilled across the sky against a spangle of stars. "The Trail of Tears" the Cherokees call it. That night it kept a vigil over the little yellow house on Cinnamon Street.

Slumped against Gracie, I squeezed my eyes shut so my own tears wouldn't escape. I dreaded the moment the law enforcement unit withdrew and abandoned me to a house that was empty without the tiny human who made it a home.

After the DCI crew finished interviewing Cassidy, they cleared her to leave, and as she squeezed by us with her parents, she peered back at me, her eyes red and swollen from crying. It crossed my mind that I should say something reassuring to her, like "It wasn't your fault" but the words of consolation stuck in my throat and then she was gone.

The DCI team came out of the house, followed by Vanderberg and Lujan who were quarreling. Although they kept the volume down so we wouldn't hear what they were saying, the burning fury in Lujan's eyes was evident as it clashed against Vanderberg's stony glare. Then the chief's cell phone rang, and he ended the conversation with a chop of his hand.

Lujan ran a hand through his hair and spun to us. "You can go back inside. I'll send someone over to stay with you, Wyn."

Gracie pulled me up and reached out to open the door, but I hesitated. "Wait. What is your plan to find Dancy, Agent Lujan?"

"We've issued an Amber Alert and notified all state law enforcement agencies to be on the lookout for the suspect's vehicle. We'll bring her home, Wyn, try not to worry." He walked away.

My hands balled into fists. His answer was rehearsed. A canned, boilerplate response to a panicked parent. I yearned to lash out, to make him hurt as much as I did, but Gracie pushed me into the house and closed the door behind us.

"Let me get you something to drink," she said. "Do you want more coffee, or should I make you some tea?"

I bent over to retrieve Dancy's floppy bunny from under the coffee table and hugged it to my chest, stroking the soft purple fur. "Did I ever tell you Dancy was a fussy baby?"

"I don't think we've ever talked about it."

"She cried all the time. Jason had already bailed on us, so I didn't have anyone to lean on. I was exhausted and felt so alone that I almost lost my mind. Eventually, Dancy grew out of that stage and now I can't imagine a day without her. She's the one thing that keeps me from falling off the edge of the world and tonight, someone took her right from under my nose in this quiet little town where I was supposed to keep her safe."

I choked back a sob.

Gracie hugged me. "Oh, sweetie. Shh. It's not your fault. Besides, they have every cop in the state looking for Dancy, and I know they'll find her."

"I pray you're right." I wiped away a tear with the back of my hand.

"Do you think Sandoval took her?"

"I don't know." I drew away from her to sit on the sofa. "Maybe we're getting close enough to the heart of this whole situation and Sandoval is panicking. Or we're complete fools, and Dancy's abduction is an unrelated act by some pervert." The thought made me feel worse, and my eyes grew hot again with tears.

Then there was a knock at the door, and Gracie hurried to answer it.

"Hi Gracie, may I come in?" It was Vanderberg.

He crossed the living room to perch on the chair closest to the sofa, twisting his navy hat in his hands. "I promise we will do everything we can to find your daughter, Wyn."

My given name sounded weird coming from his lips. He always called me Price.

He bent down to look me in the eye. "Let us do our job. Stay here with Gracie and remain calm. If anything happens, you have my word that you'll be the first to know."

"Knock, knock." Agent Lujan entered without asking for permission.

"Agent Lujan," Vanderberg said, "I was telling Officer Price it's in her best interest, and that of her daughter's as well, if she agrees to let us handle this." He gestured between himself and the agent.

Lujan regarded him. "I concur."

The chief leaned forward and gripped my shoulder. "Believe me, if it were my child, I'd fantasize about tracking down the creep who took my kid and make him pay in blood, but that isn't rational. A person crazed with fear and anger makes poor decisions, and when you're a cop, that's dangerous. Cops lose their jobs, and their lives, once they let their emotions take over. We don't want anything bad to happen to you or your daughter, Nancy—"

"Dancy," I said, correcting him.

"Yes, of course, Dancy. I don't think Dancy is in any jeopardy. This is a distraction to stall the investigation. Nothing in Sandoval's past suggests that he's a child molester."

I blanched.

Lujan shot Vanderberg a scowl. "We don't believe she's in any danger of that."

"No, of course not," the chief said.

The agent cleared his throat and steered the conversation in a more positive direction. "We issued an Amber alert at 8:30 p.m. A few minutes ago, we got a tip that a black sedan matching the description of the kidnappers' car was seen headed east on US Highway 26 near Morton. We're scrambling to get roadblocks in place at Shoshoni and Riverton."

"That's a gigantic area," Gracie said, "and it's unpopulated. Anybody with knowledge of that territory could take the back roads to avoid the roadblocks. Hell, they could go cross-country and stay off the roads altogether."

"We know that Gracie," Lujan said. "That's why we alerted the BIA police and law enforcement agencies between here and Cheyenne to be on the lookout, too. We know what we're doing. A member of the DCI surveillance team is on his way here to set up listening equipment on Wyn's phone line. The instant the kidnappers make contact, we'll be ready to mobilize."

Vanderberg stood and put on his cap. "Since Special Agent Lujan has this end under control, I'll head down to the station and fill the task force in on the situation. We're going to get the bastard, so hang in there, Wyn."

The agent stepped aside to let the chief pass. After the door closed, he approached the sofa and sat beside me, his eyes locking on mine.

Gracie cleared her throat. "I'm going to run next door and check on Sarge. I'll be right back."

Sarge was Gracie's finicky, aging cat. He despised humans, including Gracie, but I suspected she needed an excuse to have a cigarette and a beer. The charismatic presence of Special Agent Ernesto Lujan was no doubt making her twitchy.

Lujan and I both began to speak, halting when our words collided with each other. After an awkward pause, he motioned for me to continue.

"That's fine, Gracie," I said. "Go check on Sarge, then grab beer and a smoke. The minute I know anything, I'll call you, okay?"

The thought of being alone with Lujan made me uncomfortable, but if I begged Gracie to stay, he might think I was clinging and pathetic.

"I'll come right back I prom—"

Lujan cut her off. "Wyn and I have some sensitive things to discuss, Gracie. It might be easier if you weren't here."

She wavered, then disintegrated under Lujan's direct gaze. "Um. Okay. But call me if you need me, Wyn, and I'll be here in a flash."

"I know, Gracie, thanks," I said.

After she was gone, I turned to Lujan. "What's so sensitive we couldn't talk about in front of Gracie?"

He shrugged. "She was making me nervous, that's all. Someone needs to stay with you until Drexler gets here with the equipment and there was no reason for both of us to hang around."

I felt foolish for assuming he might have something more on his mind, but also stung by the implication we had nothing to talk about. "What about the task force, Lujan? You will postpone the raid until after we find Dancy, right?"

His eyes darted away.

I jumped to my feet. "It's obvious the kidnappers are attempting to throw us off the scent, so the shipment from Mexico can be delivered without interception. If you go forward with this operation, you will put my daughter's life in danger. Call it off."

"Wyn, I can't call it off, there is far too much at stake—"

"Can't? Or won't? I may not know you well, but I understand your methods, Lujan. You're too damned conceited to listen to anybody. All you think about are the commendations or financial gains you'll reap from a flashy drug bust. You don't give a shit about Dancy or anybody else."

"I know you're upset, but that is not true—" He broke off, a frown creasing his brow. "This situation is not what you think. I can't tell you more than that, but I am asking you to trust me."

"Trust you? Trust *you*? Give me one good reason I should trust you with my daughter's life."

He pulled me down beside him. "You should trust me because I'm a damn good cop and father. I'll do everything in my power to bring Dancy home safe, but don't ask me to call off the operation. We have to let it play out. I can't tell you more because if I'm wrong, the blow-back could be blistering."

"And if you're right?"

He got up and straightened his tie. "Let's focus on the present. Where's your landline?"

I threw up my hands and slumped back on the sofa. "It's in the hall."

He unplugged the phone from the hall jack and moved it to the living room, arranging it on the coffee table. Then he moved through the house, scoping out the vantage points from the windows and checking behind doors.

I watched him, hugging Dancy's bunny to my chest.

When he was satisfied with his preparations, Lujan returned and switched on the television.

A news alert from Casper WGWY flashed across the screen.

Amber Alert: Manhunt underway for two men suspected of abducting Dancy Price from her home in Perseverance, Wyoming. Dancy is two years old with blond hair and blue eyes. She is wearing light blue pajamas with the word 'Frozen' on the front. Suspects last seen traveling east on US Highway 26 in a large dark-colored sedan with tinted windows. The Wyoming Division of Criminal Investigation asks anyone with information to contact the Division at 800-999-1515. We will keep you updated as this story develops.

Lujan checked his watch, switched off the television, and sat in the armchair.

"I'm going to make a pot of coffee," I said. "Do you want a cup?"

"That sounds good."

I managed to pour the water and measure out the coffee before the tears overwhelmed me. Gripping the lip of the counter, I hung on as anguish surged through me like hot lava.

"Are you okay?" Lujan asked from the doorway.

"All I had to do was protect her and keep her safe. I messed up." My voice was hoarse with grief. "I am the world's worst mother."

He crossed the kitchen to stand next to me. "You are not a bad mother. This isn't your fault, Wyn. You can't beat yourself up about it."

"It feels like I have been sloppy—even careless. Ever since I found Evelyn Randall's body, I've been one step behind whoever is doing this."

"I didn't foresee this happening in quiet Perseverance either, but let's maintain a positive attitude and concentrate on what we need to do to get your daughter back."

A car door slammed outside. Lujan walked to the living room and pulled back the drapes. After ascertaining the visitor was not a threat, he admitted a beefy young man wearing a black DCI cap.

"Wyn, this is Special Agent Drexler, one of our surveillance specialists," Lujan said. "He's going to set up the listening equipment on your phone line."

"Ma'am." Drexler removed his cap and flashed a toothy smile before moving into the front room with a satchel of equipment.

While Lujan returned to the kitchen to finish making the coffee, I watched the agent set up the devices on the coffee table.

"Hobbs told me you're a police officer," Drexler said.

I inclined my head. "Yes. Perseverance Police Department."

Drexler stole a glance in the kitchen's direction. "I'm sorry about your daughter, but don't worry. If anyone can get her back safe, it's Special Agent Lujan."

"Oh. Well, that's good then."

By the time Lujan came back with three cups of fresh coffee, Drexler had explained each piece of equipment and how it worked, and I was a quasi-expert in the DCI's phone listening technology.

"Would you like me to stay, sir?" the junior agent said after he finished the setup.

"No. Check in with Hobbs at the station. If nothing's happening in Brightwater Canyon, get some shuteye."

"Yes, sir."

Lujan locked the door behind Drexler and began scrolling through his text messages.

I collapsed on the sofa and rolled my neck to ease the tension in my back and shoulders, but it didn't work, so I sat forward and stared at the phone.

"Don't worry, Wyn, they will call," Lujan said.

• • •

By 11:00 p.m., the kidnappers still hadn't called, but Lujan received a call on his cell phone and when he hung up, he had a peculiar look on his face.

"That was Chief Vanderberg," he said. "Someone spotted a black Chrysler 3000 at the Exxon in Lander. The two males in the vehicle fit the description of the kidnappers."

"So much for your roadblocks," I said. "Gracie was right. They took a detour at Kinnear through Ethete."

"Well, at least they're back on our radar, and Vanderberg thinks he knows where they might be headed."

"What are we waiting for? Let's go." I stood up.

"Listen, we already talked about this." Lujan put a hand up to stop me. "You're staying here."

"But Dancy—"

"I'll call you the minute she is safe in my arms." He scrutinized my face. "Remember what we talked about earlier? Please. Trust me, Wyn."

With a reluctant sigh, I said, "I'll try."

As I watched Lujan's Explorer leave, a dark sedan pulled into the driveway behind my cruiser.

"Hey, I'm back." Drexler sounded almost cheerful about it. "Vanderberg asked me to keep you company."

"Keep me company?"

"Oh, and run the listening equipment if the kidnappers call, of course. Um, do you have more coffee?"

What he wasn't saying was that he was there to prevent me from tailing Lujan, which had crossed my mind, but Drexler was a big, strapping guy and I couldn't get by him without getting physical, so I went into the house without an argument.

Inside, I chewed my nails and paced the living room like a bobcat.

Drexler stopped me when I reached for the television remote. "It might be better if we didn't, ma'am—um, Officer Price. If anything happens, they will contact us right away. Sometimes the local news station gets it wrong, you know." He gestured to the kitchen. "Is it okay if I make more coffee?"

"Sure."

I rechecked my watch. The kidnappers were at least an hour ahead of Lujan, and their destination was anybody's guess. I prayed he knew what he was doing.

SEVENTEEN

Drexler was dozing on the sofa when the telephone jolted us both to attention. He jammed the headset on and motioned to me to pick up the receiver.

"Price residence, this is Wyn speaking." My words came out in a rush as I fought to control the tension threatening to launch me off the armchair like a rocket.

It was Hobbs, and she asked for Drexler. I handed the phone to him and blew out a stream of breath in frustration.

He removed his headphones and took the receiver. "Hello, Hobbs. What's up?"

In an instant, his relaxed manner evaporated, and he sprang to his feet.

My chest constricted with fear. "What is it?"

Drexler held up his hand, concentrating on what Hobbs was saying. "Yes, ma'am. On my way."

"Oh, my God. What is it? Is it Dancy? Is she okay?"

"No. It's not Dancy. We still don't have any news about your daughter."

"Then what the hell is it, Drexler? What has happened?"

"It's Special Agent Lujan, ma'am. He's been shot. They need me in the task force center."

My heart dropped like a stone. "Is he going to be okay?"

"That's all I know. Now if you'll excuse—"

"Surely they'll call off the raid now?"

He shook his head slowly. "I don't think so, ma'am. Now I really have to go. Oh—" He stopped on his way to the door. "Hobbs clarified you are to stay here. The kidnappers might still call."

I chased him outside. "Drexler!"

He left without looking back while I stood in the street, cursing at the receding taillights.

The commotion woke Gracie, and she ran out of her house to join me in the street. "What's going on? Have they found Dancy?"

Her long strawberry-blonde hair was a snarl of tangles and mascara was smudged under her eyes.

I ground the heels of my hands into my eyes with exhaustion. "No. Not yet. Lujan has been shot."

"What? Oh, my God." She grabbed my arm. "Is he dead?"

"I don't know."

It was then I noticed the LadySmith 357 Magnum revolver thrust into the waistband of her jeans. "Gracie, wha—"

The loud rumbling throb of an engine caused me to halt mid-sentence.

"Who is that?" Gracie pointed to the decrepit maroon pickup chugging down Cinnamon Street. Her other hand gripped the handle of the revolver at her waist.

"Stop that." I swatted her hand away from the gun.

"But—"

The pickup grumbled to a stop in front of the house, brakes screeching. Behind the wheel was an elderly man I didn't know, and in the passenger's seat was the figure of a woman wearing a black hoodie.

The old man got out and leaned against the truck's rusted fender. Fumbling in his pocket, he extracted a pouch of tobacco and rolled a cigarette. The passenger hesitated, then exited the vehicle and checked the street in both directions before pulling off her hood.

"Josefina?" I took a step in her direction.

Gracie plucked at my sleeve. "Wait. Who?"

At that instant, Josefina saw the gun in the waistband of Gracie's pants and froze, her eyes wide.

Out of the corner of my mouth, I hissed at Gracie. "Get your hand off that gun or I'll take the damn thing away from you."

"Okay, okay. Geez." She put her hands up in submission.

"It's okay," I said to the timid cleaning woman. "No one will hurt you."

Josefina shuffled forward until she was a couple of steps away and searched my face with her sad black eyes.

"What are you doing here, Josefina?"

She answered, but her voice was very faint, and I couldn't make out the words.

"I didn't understand that. What did you say?"

She thought for a moment. "Uh...niñita."

"Niñita?" I struggled to grasp the meaning of the Spanish-sounding word, and then it hit me. Josefina wasn't Shoshone or Arapaho. She was South American. During my stint in San Diego, I became rather fluent in Spanish, but the vernacular Josefina was speaking wasn't Mexican Spanish. It was some other South American dialect.

"Hablas inglés, Josefina?"

She shook her head and kept saying, "Niñita."

I scrunched up my face in concentration. "Little girl. Niñita means little girl, doesn't it?"

Josefina's face lit up, and she spoke in a torrent, but I still couldn't understand a word she said. Baffled, I shrugged and raised my palms.

When she recognized we weren't making any progress, she pointed at me and made the motion of rocking a baby in her arms. "Niñita."

I squinted, struggling to comprehend. "Me. Rocking. Rock-a-bye, baby. Me. My. My little girl?"

She bobbed her head. "Si."

Then I understood. Someone told Josefina about Dancy's kidnapping, and she was trying to console me. "Ah! I see. Yes, someone took my little girl. Thank you for your concern, Josefina."

"No." She shook a finger in my face, then gestured as if wiping a slate clean and pointed to the pink embroidered Perfect Touch Cleaning logo on the breast of her black hoodie.

I puckered my brow, but Gracie said, "Perfect Touch Cleaning."

Josefina beamed and nodded at Gracie, then pointed again at me.

"You," said Gracie.

The woman nodded and made another rocking motion with her arms.

"Uh...baby?" I said.

"Si." Josefina's eyes were bright with excitement. She pointed again to the logo on her breast and repeated the motions, pointing to the imaginary baby in the crook of her arm and then the logo. "Okay. Niñita okay."

Gracie said, "The...baby...is at Perfect Touch Cleaning? And...she...is...okay."

Josefina's face blossomed into a broad smile, and she bobbed her head. "Si! Baby okay. You go." She pointed east.

"Wyn!" Gracie grabbed my arm in excitement. "Josefina is telling us Dancy is at this Perfect Touch Cleaning place. All we have to do is track down the address and go get her."

I scrunched up my face in confusion. "I know the address. It's in Casper, almost three hours away. How did she end up there?"

"Ethete," the old man said.

"Excuse me?" I was unsure if he had sneezed or if he was trying to communicate something.

He spoke again, louder this time. "Ethete. That Perfect Touch outfit has a bunk house there, south of the casino on Big Eagle Road."

The place he spoke of was on the Wind River Indian Reservation and uneasiness spread across Gracie's face. "You're sure she's in Ethete?"

The old man regarded his cigarette and said nothing, but Josefina repeated the word. "Ethete. Si."

When it was apparent her mission was a success, Josefina wrapped me in a Pine-Sol scented bear hug and climbed back into the maroon pickup. After throwing his cigarette in a patch of cactus on my lawn, the old man joined her.

"What are you going to do?" Gracie asked as she watched the pickup make a u-turn on Cinnamon Street.

"I'm going to get my daughter. If we deciphered what Josefina told us correctly, then Dancy is less than an hour away."

"*If* she was telling us the truth. Shouldn't you wait for backup or something?"

I whirled to face her. "The DCI task force cares more about taking down Sandoval than rescuing Dancy. Besides, Vanderberg ordered me to stay put. If I tell him what Josefina told me, he'll rush off to Ethete and I'll be stuck waiting. It's been hours since those goons took my daughter, and all this time she's been in—in—*Ethete*, for Pete's sake. God knows what they have done to her and now that Lujan's been shot, if I don't rescue her, nobody else will because nobody else gives a damn."

Gracie's eyes teared up. "That's not fair, Wyn. You know I give a damn. I would do anything for Dancy. I love her like she's my own."

Ashamed of my outburst, I put my arms around her. "I'm sorry, I know you do."

"Good." She pushed herself away. "Now that we're on the same page, let's go find the dickheads who kidnapped her."

"Oh no, you aren't going with me, Gracie. It's too dangerous—"

"Like hell I ain't. You're not going after these guys alone." She patted the revolver. "But don't worry, I won't shoot anybody unless they piss me off."

Saliva had dried at the corners of her mouth, and her hair was a tangled mess. She looked batshit crazy, and she had a gun to boot.

"What are you looking at?" She pulled up her jeans and straightened her tie-dyed t-shirt with "This Ain't My First Rodeo" spelled out in pink rhinestones across the front. Then she licked her index finger and wiped off the smeared mascara from under her eyes.

"Are you wearing a bra?"

"Nope."

"I'm so going to regret this," I said, heading for the house.

Inside, I grabbed Dancy's diaper bag from the hook behind the front door and shoved it into Gracie's hands. "Fill that with peanut butter cookies and a couple of bottles of water. Put in diapers and her purple bunny."

While Gracie stocked the bag, I went to the bedroom and changed into a plain long-sleeved shirt and tactical pants, then stuffed my hair under a paint-splattered University of Wyoming cap.

In my mind, it was pretty clear Dancy's abduction was intended to make us back off the Sandoval investigation, which meant Sandoval already knew—or suspected—that law enforcement was preparing to make a move on his operation despite our best efforts to keep a lid on our plans. That meant someone on the inside alerted him—but who?

I retrieved my Sig Sauer P365 pistol from the gun safe in my closet and shoved it into the side pocket of my pants. In a duffle bag, I threw two extra magazines, a box of cartridges, and some zip ties.

Gracie was snoring on the sofa when I returned to the living room, one arm thrown over her head like a swooning damsel and the revolver still tucked in the front of her jeans. Uneasy it might discharge while she slept, I reached out to relieve her of it, but her hand shot out like a bullwhip and stopped me.

"Geezus. I thought you were sleeping."

She sat up and rubbed her eyes. "I was catnapping. Are we ready to go?"

"You don't have to come with me. I need to locate Dancy fast and get her somewhere safe before they raid Sandoval's place."

"They're going to raid the Sandoval Ranch?"

"I wasn't supposed to tell you that. It's top secret."

"Will they go ahead without Agent Lujan?"

"I don't know, and I don't have time to ask. If they proceed with the raid, it will put Dancy in grave danger, but if I tell them my plan to rescue her on my own, Vanderberg will try to stop me, and I can't let that happen."

Gracie struggled to her feet and jammed her cell phone into the pocket of her rumpled jeans. "Then what are we waiting for, girl? Let's roll."

Before I could stop her, she charged out the door and climbed into the Crown Vic's passenger seat.

I tapped on the window and motioned for her to get out. "We can't take a Perseverance PD vehicle. This isn't an official police action. Besides, since Ethete is on the reservation, tribal police will be in a snit if we conduct a rescue op on tribal land without asking them first. We'll have to go incognito."

"In your car?" Gracie stared at my broken-down Honda Civic. "Did you get the radio and air conditioning fixed?"

"No, I didn't have time."

"Then we'll take my truck. I'll drive." She ignored my protests as she marched to her garage and pulled up the door.

I had to admit, Gracie's brand new air-conditioned Dodge Ram TRX pickup was a much better option than my beat-up old Honda. Besides, Gracie drove like Dale Earnhardt Jr. and was a Houdini at avoiding speeding tickets.

"Okay, you can drive," I said, hoisting myself into the passenger seat and fastening my seatbelt, "but stay out of my way—and wear your seatbelt."

Gracie stuck out her tongue and put on her seatbelt with exaggerated motions.

"Oh, real mature," I said.

She ignored the comment and gunned the truck out of the garage. Popping it into drive, she spun out on the asphalt. It felt like something out of *Starsky and Hutch*—or *Turner & Hooch.*

"Where are we headed to in Ethete?" Gracie asked, turning on the overhead light and checking her face in the rearview mirror.

"Big Eagle Road. And keep your eyes on the road."

Ignoring me, she rummaged around in the center console, extracted a tube of pink lipstick, and began applying it in the mirror.

"Watch out," I said as a startled deer skittered across the road.

But Gracie kept her eyes on her reflection until she was satisfied. Then she tossed the tube back in the console and switched off the overhead light just in time to take the turn onto the highway.

I loaded the magazines for my pistol with bullets, wishing I had brought along the Sig's extended clip. Slapping a magazine into the gun, I double-checked the safety and placed it on the seat beside me. Then I stashed the spare magazines in a pants pocket and shoved a couple of zip ties in another.

Preparations complete, I sat back against the seat and exhaled.

Except for the hum of the truck's engine, the cab was quiet.

Gracie reached out to squeeze my hand. "She'll be okay. We'll find her."

The speedometer hovered around ninety-five miles per hour. At that rate, we would be in Ethete in forty minutes.

I checked the side mirror. There was nothing but emptiness behind us as we crossed into the Wind River Reservation. Tribal police didn't have jurisdiction over non-Indians speeding on the reservation, but if they stopped us, it could be a nightmare.

The clock on the dash caught my eye. "You were supposed to be at work by five o'clock, weren't you?"

Gracie made a face. "They'll get by without me."

"What are you going to tell Rusty?"

"I'll think of something. If Rusty has a problem with it, he can kiss my lily-white ass. So, what is the plan? The actual one, I mean." Gracie gave me a sideways look.

"The plan is for you to remain in the truck."

"That's bullshit. Seriously, is that your grand plan? For me to stay in my truck? Bullshit."

I rolled my eyes. "Look, I don't know what we're headed into. We don't know the precise location of the Perfect Touch bunkhouse or what sort of opposition we'll encounter when we get there. After we locate Dancy, we'll have to extricate her and get out of there fast, which means you need to drive the getaway vehicle. But I want you to promise me you will not use your gun, Gracie. Not under any circumstances."

She opened her mouth to argue, but snapped it shut when I shot her an icy stare.

As the sun rose on the sagebrush steppe, a golden eagle lifted off a wooden fence post alongside the road, its powerful wings stroking like pistons, carrying the enormous bird higher and higher. Native Americans believed the Golden Eagle represented strength, courage, and freedom. It was a good omen.

Even without the strawberry-blonde bombshell wearing mirrored aviators behind the wheel, Gracie's tricked-out cobalt blue truck was conspicuous in Ethete. I pulled my ball cap down and slid lower into the seat.

Big Eagle Road was a narrow dirt loop winding through the native scrub. Most of the residences were frame houses, but neglected mobile homes, dilapidated sheds, and junked machinery were sprinkled in between.

On the second pass around the loop, I noticed a white car parked in the driveway of a ramshackle house.

"Hold up," I said. "Was that a Perfect Touch Cleaning vehicle? Back there, the white Chevrolet sedan behind the padlocked gate."

Gracie lifted her sunglasses and shifted into reverse to get a better look. "That must be the bunkhouse the old guy was talking about. Looks like it's locked down pretty tight."

As we studied the shabby house, the front door swung open, and two women and a man emerged.

"Pull ahead and park in the next drive on the left," I said. "Hurry, before they notice us."

She pulled the truck into the driveway of a battered green mobile home, where a pit bull strained against the chain tethering it to the axle of an old tractor, barking furiously at the intrusion.

Over my shoulder, I watched the man open the gate and, after a brief conversation, the two women got into the sedan and drove west on Big Eagle Road. Before reentering the house, the man locked the gate again.

I opened my door. "Okay. You stay here, and I'll go find Dancy. Be ready to pick us up when you see me come out of the house with her."

"Mm-hmm. Sure." Her eyes were glued to the pit bull that was salivating a foot from the pickup's front tire.

I slid out of the pickup, jamming the pistol into the back of my jeans before sauntering down the gravel road, trying to look casual. As I neared the bunkhouse, I surveyed the immediate area before scaling the metal gate and dropping into the driveway.

I crouched low as I crept closer, staying out of sight in case anyone inside the house looked in my direction.

Part of the interior of the house was visible through a screen door. In the front living room, a man lay on a sofa with his back to the door. To the left, a hallway led to a dimly lit kitchen.

If going through the front door was the only way in, I would risk it, but I preferred to gain entry without being detected, so I followed the dirt driveway to the rear of the house and ducked behind a black Chrysler 3000 sedan. The backyard was taken over by tall weeds, but a well-worn footpath led to a back door with a small diamond-shaped window covered in duct tape.

The back of the house featured three main floor windows and two smaller ones on the basement level. Dingy sheets doubling as curtains obscured the interior, but the fabric sagged on one window at the lower level, leaving a small gap.

The weeds behind me crackled, and I reached for the pistol at my back.

"Wyn?" Gracie said in a stage whisper.

I exhaled and released the grip on my gun. "What happened to staying in the truck, Gracie?"

"The guy who owned the trailer came out to walk his dog."

"The pit bull?"

"No, the other kind of dog." She made a rude gesture with her hand.

"Oh."

"I moved the truck. Do you see anything?"

"Not yet. Maybe I'll be able to see something through that gap in the basement window covering. Stay here."

I left the shelter of the car and scuttled through the weeds, crouching beside the window to peer through the opening.

Only a portion of the basement was visible through the grimy, cracked pane. A fraying piece of brown carpet covered a section of the concrete floor, and in the corner, a red and yellow star quilt was spread over a cot.

A slender, dark-haired girl wearing faded jeans and a baggy pink t-shirt swayed into view, cradling a tiny baby in her arms. She spoke in Spanish to someone I couldn't see.

Then a child jabbered in English and another woman said, "Shh! *Sólo cállate.*"

My breath caught in my throat as I recognized Dancy's babbling. I pressed my face against the dirty glass, but she was outside of my line of sight.

I was so absorbed in trying to glimpse her I didn't hear the gangbanger's footsteps until he rambled around the corner of the house, gazing at his cell phone and dragging on a cigarette.

He was about two hundred pounds, Hispanic, with a shaved head and gang tattoos on his neck and bulging biceps. As an accessory to his white wife-beater and Nikes, he packed a .38 revolver in the waistband of his baggy jeans.

I sucked in my breath, and that's when he saw me.

Using my arms to launch myself from a crouch, I hurtled sideways in the air, striking him in the left knee with both feet. Under the full force of my weight, his knee bowed backwards with a loud, stomach-turning snap. He opened his mouth to scream, but before the sound came out, his head snapped to one side and blood splattered across my face.

Gracie towered above us with a bloody come-along winch in her hands.

I wiped my face with a sleeve. "Geezus, Gracie. I told you to stay put."

"And let this thug crush you with his bare hands?" she said with a hiss.

I checked his throat for a pulse. He was alive, but he would be madder than a rattler when he woke up with a shattered knee and a pounding headache. I scrambled to my feet, plucking the gun out of his waistband and emptying the bullets out of the cylinder. Then I hurled the gun into the sagebrush behind the house.

"Help me move him behind the car." I motioned to the Chrysler.

We dragged him around the car by his arms and I zip tied his hands to the tire rim.

When he moaned, Gracie flinched, readying the winch for another blow.

I laid a hand on her shoulder. "Okay, Gracie, you wanted to know the plan, so here it is. Dancy is in the basement with at least two adult females and an infant. If they didn't secure the back door, we'll enter that way. If it's locked, we have no choice except to go in through the front. A guy was asleep on the sofa in the front room, but he appeared smaller than our brawny amigo here, so if we're lucky, sleeping beauty is the sole opponent we'll have to contend with. I'll keep him busy while you go downstairs and get Dancy. You might meet some resistance from the women—and lethal force isn't an option." I eyed the winch in her hands.

She raised one shoulder, trying to recover some of her trademark self-confidence. "Not a problem."

"After you locate her, take her to the truck. Don't stop, no matter what happens. If I'm not right behind you, you must leave without me. Get Dancy out of there to safety. Got it?"

Gracie nodded, but her eyes flitted back to the unconscious man and her lower lip trembled a little.

I patted her arm in encouragement. "Let's go."

To my dismay, the back door was locked, which meant we would have to confront the man in the living room head-on. I jumped off the crumbling concrete steps and ran to the front.

Gracie, still wielding the gory winch, followed on my heels.

The man on the sofa didn't stir despite the squeal of the storm door as I pulled it open. He probably assumed it was his *compadre* coming back from his patrol of the premises.

"That way." I mimed to Gracie, pointing down the hall to the kitchen.

"Emilio?" A woman appeared in the hallway and screamed at the sight of two strangers standing in the living room.

In a cobra-like motion, the man uncoiled from the sofa, knocking over the low table and scattering beer cans and empty food containers across the floor. He seized me by the front of my shirt and, before I could spin away, punched me in the side of my head. He struck me again, this time in the left eye, and pulled me into a headlock to pummel my ribcage.

I sagged in his grasp, dazed, and struggled to breathe as his arm crushed my windpipe.

Then Gracie rushed him, howling at the top of her lungs and swinging the winch around her head like a medieval mace. He put out a hand to deflect the assault, but she landed a cracking blow on his forearm.

The distraction was enough. I pivoted out of the headlock and twisted his arm into a wrist lock, forcing him down on the sofa with my knee on his back.

He swore at me in a stream of Spanish.

"I'll try to hold him," I said. "Remember what you need to do, Gracie. Now go."

She dropped the winch and ran towards the hallway, but when she tried to shove past the cowering woman in the narrow corridor, the other woman clawed at her, screeching something unintelligible.

"Ow! Bitch." Gracie grabbed a fistful of the woman's hair and hammered her head against the wall. Buckling, the woman fell to the floor. Gracie shoved her aside and dashed to the kitchen. A door creaked open, and Gracie's footsteps thudded on the stairs as she descended to the lower level.

Voices drifted up from the basement, and I strained to hear what they were saying, but my opponent was strong and wiry, and I didn't dare lose focus or my grasp on him would falter. We were both sweating from the exertion and my arms ached. I wouldn't be able to control him much longer.

After what felt like an eternity, Gracie returned clasping Dancy in her arms.

The man beneath me shifted, sensing a lessening in the tension, and my grip began to slip.

"Don't stop, Gracie. Keep moving," I said with gritted teeth. "Get Dancy to the truck. I promise I'll be right behind you."

She sprinted out the door, shushing a tearful Dancy.

The instant they were out of the house, I shoved away from my adversary and extracted the Sig from my waistband, leveling it at his forehead as he spun to seize me again.

When he saw the gun, he met my eyes with a sneer and raised his hands.

I backed away, stepping over the upended table to put myself beyond the range of his lightning-fast grasp, and made a slight movement with my pistol. "Lie face down on the floor and put your hands behind your head."

He didn't move.

"Boca abajo! Hazlo!"

As he lowered himself to the floor, he said in accented English, "I will come after you, bitch."

When his stomach touched the floor, I flipped the table over on top of him and ran.

Gracie was struggling to scale the gate with Dancy in her arms. Shoving the gun into the pocket of my pants, I climbed over and took my daughter from her.

The man ran out of the house waving a gun and shouting.

"Gracie! Where's the truck?"

"Down there." She pointed with her chin as she clambered over the gate.

About ten yards down the dusty road, the grille of the big Dodge protruded from behind a cluster of lilac bushes. I took off at a sprint with Dancy clinging to my neck. She smelled like refried beans and urine.

When we reached the truck, I heard a gunshot and twirled around, my stomach lurching.

Gracie was midway between the gate and the truck, the LadySmith revolver in her extended hands.

I yanked open the driver's door and clambered in, heaving Dancy over the backrest into the rear seat.

My hand fumbled at the ignition. No keys.

Two more shots rang out. Gracie was backing towards the truck, but she was still a couple yards from the lilacs.

Heart thumping against my ribcage, I remembered Gracie liked to stash her keys in the ashtray and breathed a prayer of relief when my fingers closed around the metal.

Jamming the key into the ignition, I started the truck and shoved it into gear. It mounted the road with a furious roar.

As I drove by Gracie, I bent over to thrust open the passenger door. "Get in."

She tumbled halfway in and I seized her by the neck of her shirt, dragging her the rest of the way into the cab as a bullet pierced the rear passenger window. After glancing over my shoulder at Dancy, who was happily clutching her bunny and looting the diaper bag, I stomped on the accelerator.

Gracie lay on the seat beside me, panting, the rhinestone shirt pulled up around her neck.

The dirt track in the rearview mirror was thick with dust, but the gunman was nowhere in sight. I suspected he was in the backyard trying to free his friend from the tire rim of the Chrysler.

Glimpsing my blood-smeared face in the mirror, I did a double-take. My left eye was swelling shut and one side of my face was turning a nasty shade of purple. A two-inch gash above my eyebrow oozed blood and would need stitches.

Gracie grabbed the dash and pulled herself up like a zombie rising from the dead. Hauling the door closed, she collapsed against it and looked at me. "Holy shit."

One lens was missing from her aviators.

"Are you okay?" I asked.

"Me?" She pulled her shirt down and made a feeble show of examining herself. "No bullet holes, so I'm good."

"Then buckle up buttercup. We're getting out of here."

"Fine by me." Her voice cracked a little.

From the backseat Dancy said, "Mommy, look. Cookies!"

We both turned. Dancy was wearing Gracie's $400 Stetson, a gooey peanut butter cookie in each hand. Crumbs wreathed her sweet little face.

A lump formed in my throat. "Gracie—"

She stopped me with a shake of her head. "Don't, or we'll both start blubbering."

I didn't ease up on the gas until we reached Fort Washakie, my eyes flicking to the rearview mirror every few minutes. Satisfied the gangbangers weren't in hot pursuit, I slowed on the periphery of the town and let the truck rumble along at a sedate pace.

At a stop sign, we encountered a Fort Washakie Police patrol car, and Gracie raised a languid hand to the officer in greeting. "Think he'll notice the bullet hole?"

"Think he'll notice the missing lens in your aviators?" I said, but my attempt at lightheartedness fizzled.

"What was that sideways supersonic flying ninja thing you did to take out that badass dude's knee? Did you learn that move in police training?"

"No. They don't teach that stuff at the academy. I took some Krav Maga classes in San Diego, but that move today was part kickboxing and part cheer stunt powered by pure adrenalin."

She gave me a sideways look. "Cheer stunt?"

"Yeah. I was a cheerleader—"

"You were a cheerleader? You gotta be effing kidding me. I can't imagine you as a cheerleader—all perky and feminine in midriff tops and short skirts."

"Well, me neither now you mention it, but we were pretty hard-core. It was a serious sport, not a popularity contest. We won the state High School Cheerleading Championship twice and placed third at nationals."

"You mean that jumping and tumbling and throwing each other around stuff like on that *Cheer* TV show?"

"Uh, sure, except at the high school level."

"Huh." She stared at me like she thought I was kidding.

I glared out the window, hoping she would get the hint and drop the subject. For some dumb reason, it hurt my feelings that she didn't think I was feminine enough to be a cheerleader.

It was a period of my life I didn't like to think about because Jason and I were inseparable in high school. I checked Dancy in the back seat, who was singing to her purple bunny. She was so much like her daddy that it made my heart hurt. That jackass didn't know what he had missed.

Gracie punched on the radio and tuned it to Wyoming's Big Country, KTAK 93.9 FM. Raelyn's "Keep Up" warbled out of the speakers.

She turned up the volume and sang along, slapping a rhythm on the dash.

EIGHTEEN

Folks with regular daytime jobs were already at work when we arrived back in Perseverance, and people who didn't were still sleeping or eating breakfast. The streets were quiet, which was preferable, since prying minds might wonder where we were last night in Gracie's truck and how we got that bullet hole in the window.

Gracie slumped against the passenger door, fast asleep with Dancy cradled in her arms. I parked the truck outside her garage, resisting the urge to lean back and doze myself.

Now that Dancy was safe, I couldn't help thinking about Lujan and the status of the investigation. It was time to get back into the action.

As if on cue, my cell phone buzzed. It was Deputy Clifton Bartel.

I sat up straight. "Hello, Deputy Bartel. Glad you finally got back to me."

Bartel got right to the point and after the call ended, I sat in stunned silence, facts clicking around in my brain like a safecracker tumbling through the cylinder locks, listening for the right combination to crack open the safe.

The details in this case never quite added up, but after speaking with Bartel, an unsettling suspicion that had been lurking in my subconsciousness took shape.

"Gracie," I said, shaking her. "Wake up."

She yawned and rubbed one eye.

"Gracie, listen to me. I want you to take Dancy to your grandma's. Once you get there, lock the doors. Don't let anybody in. Tell your grandma not to let anyone in either, okay? Not anybody. Even if you know them—especially if you know them. Do you understand?"

She blinked at me. "What? Why?"

"I don't have time to explain. Promise me you will keep Dancy safe until I get back."

"Umm, okay. Where are you going?"

"To the police station." I reached over to stroke Dancy's pale hair before I got out. "The keys are in the ignition. You can't stay here, it's not safe. Now go."

I ran into the house to change into my uniform and retrieve my service weapon. After pinning my Perseverance Police Department badge to the front of my shirt, I appraised my battered reflection in the bathroom mirror.

I took this job with humble expectations—for the position and myself. When this homicide case came along, it dredged up painful memories of some stuff I didn't want to face, but it also reminded me of who I used to be and why I became a cop.

From the moment I found Evelyn Randall's body, this case unsettled me. Then the truth about how she died emerged, and a straightforward murder inquiry splintered into a treacherous and ever-growing web of deceit. Every time I got a grip on the plot—or at least thought I did—it slipped out of my grasp. Somewhere along the way, I lost faith in myself, which clouded my ability to discern who was telling the truth and who was lying. But now the fog had cleared, and I was pretty certain I knew who the liar was.

The Perseverance police station was deserted except for Connie, who jumped in surprise when I walked in. "Oh my God, Wyn, what happened to your face?"

"I'll explain later, Connie. Where is everybody?"

"You missed them by a few minutes. Vanderberg called the task team out to Brightwater Canyon."

"Okay, thanks." I tugged open the SWAT locker and grabbed the small Kevlar vest and Dakota sniper rifle. "Tell the DCI headquarters and the local new outlets to cancel the Amber Alert. Dancy is okay."

"Oh, thank God, where is she?"

"She is somewhere safe."

Connie twisted her hands together. "There must be something more I can do to help."

I paused in the doorway, still uncertain who I could trust. "There is. When you contact the DCI headquarters, tell them the DCI operation has been compromised and the task force team is headed into an ambush at the Sandoval compound. Tell them to send reinforcements. It's urgent."

Chief Vanderberg's white SUV was parked in the driveway of the Randall house next to a brown Dodge Charger with Wyoming Highway Patrol decals. I pulled the Crown Vic in behind the SUV and got out to survey the area.

Except for a couple of stellar jays squawking at me from the peak of the garage, the neighborhood was peaceful. Then the front door of the house flew open, and Justin Stokes lumbered out in a rumpled uniform, his hair sticking up in tufts at the back.

"Justin. What are you doing here?"

He yawned and scratched his belly, putting a hand up to block the sun from his eyes. "No one came to relieve me last night. Then, about twenty minutes ago, that state trooper came storming through here and ordered me to stay put. I'm supposed to guard the gulch and stop anybody from going down there or leaving."

"Okay. Good." I slipped on the vest and tucked the sniper rifle under my arm, watching him. He wasn't wearing his gun.

He squinted at me. "I thought you were supposed to be on administrative leave, Price. What are you doing here?"

"Vanderberg called," I lied, trying to sound nonchalant, "he needs—" I reached into the cruiser and snatched up a folded piece of paper, tucking it into a pocket of my vest before he could get a good look at it, "—this map."

"But—"

Without waiting to hear his objection, I snapped a half-salute in his direction and headed to the path behind the house. By the time he realized something was wrong—if he ever figured it out—I would be halfway to the compound.

The sun wasn't high enough yet to illuminate the depths of the gulch, forcing me to descend with care until my eyes became accustomed to the light. Part of the way down, I startled a deer, and it crashed off into the trees.

At the bottom, I splashed across the creek and scaled the steep bank on the opposite side. When I climbed out through the notch at the top, I searched for signs of the task team, but all I found was a deserted surveillance camp under the trees near the rocky outcropping, so I crouched and ran to the lip of the ridge overlooking the Sandoval compound to peer over the edge. Below, half a dozen armed men were positioned in the front yard of the nearest building, facing the northern entrance of the compound.

Out of the sight of the gunmen, Captain Watson and Agent Drexler crept along the outside wall of the building, guns drawn.

Sandoval's silver pickup was parked in the yard. I shouldered the rifle and used the scope to scan the men below, but Sandoval was not among them.

Moments later, a Sheridan County Sheriff Department's SUV and a DCI sedan rumbled into the compound, lights flashing. Inside the gate, the vehicles maneuvered into a nose-to-nose position to block the exit and sounded a "whoop-whoop" on the sirens to make sure they had everyone's attention.

The gunman scrambled for cover in the building as Sargeant Buchowski opened the driver's door of the SUV and braced himself behind it, his shotgun balanced on the doorframe.

Hobbs emerged from the DCI vehicle with a bullhorn in her hand. "This is the Wyoming Division of Criminal Investigation. Put down your weapons and come out with your hands behind your heads."

Her demands were met by a barrage of bullets.

The task force officers took shelter behind their vehicles but didn't return fire.

"This is the Wyoming Division of Criminal Investigation. We have you surrounded. Put down your weapons," Hobbs said again.

The gunmen shouted obscenities and offered another volley of gunfire from the building, but the law enforcement officers continued to hold their fire.

Watson and Drexler were in position at the front of the building. Suddenly Watson lunged forward, lobbing something around the corner through the open door. The stun grenade detonated with a flash and deafening boom. Drexler followed up with two rubber ball grenades in quick succession.

Inside the structure, men cursed and shrieked in pain.

But before the task force could press their advantage, a red pickup thundered through the gate, smashing aside the blockade and scattering the team.

Armed men spilled out of the vehicle, guns blazing, and the officers returned fire. Hobbs was hit in the shoulder and tumbled to the ground, but from her prone position, she dropped a gunman with one shot from her pistol.

Exposed and with limited cover, Watson and Drexler pulled back.

I dropped to one knee and sighted in my rifle. *Steady. Exhale. Pause.* I squeezed the trigger, and a gunman tumbled to the ground. I searched for another target.

One of them spotted me above him on the slope and raised his rifle, but before he could get off a round, I buried a bullet in his shoulder, and he dropped the weapon. The other new arrivals dispersed, firing shots at random as they took shelter.

I scrambled down the hill and joined Watson and Drexler, who had retreated from the front of the building.

Watson swept his pistol from left to right, searching for a clean shot amid the dust and chaos in the yard. "I should ask what you're doing here, Officer Price, but we're glad you joined us. We're up to our necks in shit."

An object sailed out of the structure and exploded against the cab of the Sheridan Sheriff's SUV, engulfing it in flames.

"Drexler," Watson said, "see if you can get to Barnes on the other side of that far building. I want the two of you to move forward to close the gap on the west side of the yard. We don't want them escaping across the range or flanking us from behind."

The gas tank of the sheriff's SUV exploded, and the gunmen sprayed the compound with another round of bullets.

I shouted to be heard above the noise. "Where is Chief Vanderberg?"

"Last I knew, he was hunkered between the buildings," the highway patrolman said. "You can go help him hold that center corridor."

I slung the rifle on my back and ran. As I rounded the rear of the building and entered the center corridor, the wind shifted, blowing the smoke from the burning vehicle into the narrow alley. Acrid fumes burned my eyes, obscuring my vision, but through the haze, I glimpsed two figures in the passage up ahead.

They stood about five feet apart. One man had his weapon drawn, and the other held his hands up in surrender.

Then man with the gun stretched out his arm, and the gun bucked.

In horror, I watched the defenseless man fell backwards, his hands still raised in submission, but instead of standing down, the armed man advanced until he was straddling the wounded man and leveled his weapon for another shot.

There was no mistaking that profile—the confident stance—the angle of the hat.

I drew my service pistol.

Then the smoke cleared, and he saw me.

"I got the bastard, Price." Vanderberg smirked as he looked down at Robert Sandoval.

A patch of scarlet was blooming on the front of Sandoval's white shirt from the bullet hole in his chest.

"Drop your gun." I stepped closer and raised my weapon.

"What has gotten into you, Price?" He delivered a vicious kick to Sandoval's ribcage. "Sandoval is our man—he's the murderer."

"Drop your firearm and step away from him, Vanderberg."

"Oh. It's *Vanderberg* now, is it? Didn't you understand what I said? I got him. God knows you weren't ever going to get around to it." He spit his words out like nails.

I ignored the dig. "I think you killed Evelyn Randall."

He curled his lip in disgust and let the hand holding the gun drop to his side. "I don't know what you're talking about."

"I spoke to Deputy Bartel. He didn't go to Evelyn Randall's place that night. You were the one who took the calls from County, and you forged those reports to make it look like it was Bartel. Mrs. Randall worked it out that you were running a drug operation out here, didn't she? You killed her before she could squeal on you and then staged it to look like an accident, but that ruse didn't work out, so you cooked up the fictitious case against Sandoval. Then Lujan came along and started asking too many questions, so you kidnapped my daughter—"

"Oh, now she thinks she's some kind of genius detective—" he said, ridiculing me in front of an imaginary audience.

"Shut up, you miserable piece of shit. You kidnapped my daughter to lure Lujan into a trap and force me out of the investigation. You believed Agent Hobbs would back off with Lujan sidelined, but she pressed forward and the only way out of your dilemma was to slaughter the entire team."

Vanderberg was silent for a moment, then with a swift movement he brought up his gun and pointed it at me, his eyes chips of blue ice. "You ungrateful little bitch—cripes, what a pathetic excuse for a police officer. It was an open and shut case against Sandoval, but you couldn't let it unfold. I spoon fed you the clues. All you had to do was follow my lead.

"Who gives a damn about the Randall witch, anyway? The elderly fall down stairs or drop dead of old age all the time and nobody cares. No one would have been the wiser, but then you and that idiot Gleason allowed her uppity niece to talk you into an autopsy. This is all your fault—"

A thunderous bang echoed from within the building and a thick black cloud of smoke rolled out, followed by more gunfire.

He displayed his teeth in a hideous grin. "Do you hear that, Price? That's my crew, following orders like obedient soldiers."

At first, I didn't understand, then it hit me between the eyes. "You're destroying the evidence of your smuggling operation."

Gun still trained on me, he said, "Gee, I don't know what you are talking about, officer. This is Sandoval's operation, remember?"

"Shh!" I lifted my chin. "Do you hear that?"

Judging by his expression, he heard it. It was the shriek of sirens, lots of them, and they were getting closer.

I tightened my grip on the pistol. "That's the sound of our reinforcements. I instructed Connie to call DCI headquarters and tell them the task force was headed into a trap. It's game over, Vanderberg. Now drop your weapon."

"You don't have the nerve to shoot me," Vanderberg said with a sneer. "But don't worry, Price, I'll tell them you died a hero."

His finger twitched against the trigger, but mine was faster.

NINETEEN

lifted the handkerchief to check Sandoval's wound and compressed it again.

He took a sharp breath and gritted his teeth. "That bastard tried to kill me in cold blood."

"Shh. We need to stop the bleeding to keep you alive, Mr. Sandoval. Now lie still."

He was pale, but his pulse was strong, and he was belligerent as ever. The bullet passed through the upper left side of his chest, but it didn't appear he suffered any internal injuries.

"Who are these other goons? And why did he shoot me?" He pointed at Vanderberg's lifeless body.

"Stop moving around. If I can staunch the blood and keep you from going into shock, I think you'll recover."

Behind me, part of the burning building's roof fell in with a crack, and flames licked through the hole.

Sandoval nodded towards the blaze. "Never mind me, Officer. You get that truck out of there before it's too late or there will be a lot more lives lost today."

At first, I didn't understand. Then the last pieces of the puzzle clicked into place.

"Hold this," I said, pressing Sandoval's right hand down on the handkerchief.

I leaped to my feet and sprinted to the front of the building.

The noises of the compound were muted except for the roar of the fire. Watson was cuffing a man near the burned-out shell of the Sheridan Sheriff's SUV.

To get Watson's attention, I waved my arms and pointed to the box truck inside the burning building. "We can't let the truck burn. We have to get it out." But he didn't seem to understand what I was telling him.

A wooden beam groaned inside the building, sending up a shower of sparks. The entire roof would crash in at any minute.

I charged inside, covering my mouth and nose to avoid inhaling the thick smoke, and wrenched open the driver's door of the truck. Clambering in, I said a prayer under my breath as my fingers fumbled at the ignition. Then the shape of the key materialized under my fingers, and I twisted, bringing the engine to life.

As the beam collapsed, the truck heaved out of the building and cannon balled across the yard, ramming the red pickup out of the way and narrowly missing several officers before I brought it to a stop short of the gate.

Alarmed by the violent commotion, a state trooper advanced with his gun trained on the cab. "Get out of the vehicle and keep your hands where I can see them."

I slipped down from the cab, my hands still raised. "I'm Officer Wyn Price, Perseverance PD. We have to get the box of this truck open."

The trooper hesitated, but didn't lower his weapon until Hobbs ran towards us, clutching the bloodied arm of her blazer and shouting that I was on the task force team.

When I was certain he wouldn't shoot, I ran to the back and struggled with the padlock on the box. "Help me open this."

The trooper disappeared and returned with a pair of bolt cutters, making quick work of the padlock. I slipped it off and threw it aside, but when I attempted to pull the door up, it was too heavy.

"Stand back." With a mighty heave, the trooper shoved open the door.

Fifteen terrified women crowded together behind a stack of boxes and wooden crates, their faces smudged with soot, sweat and tears. When they saw the officer, they screamed and cowered against the truck's back wall.

Hobbs moved forward and gripped the edge of the container. "Don't be afraid. We are friends. Are you okay?" She repeated herself in Spanish.

Finally, one of the women replied, and Hobbs conversed with her for several minutes.

After reassuring the women that no harm would come to them, Hobbs turned to the trooper. "Lieutenant Falk, radio for additional resources. If I understand correctly, they've been in this truck for several days without food or water. We'll need transportation and a couple more EMTs."

When she finished speaking, Hobbs faltered and clutched at the frame of the truck for support.

"You need medical attention, Agent Hobbs." I reached out to steady her.

"I'm headed that way now." For a moment, she rested against me and scanned my face. "You've seen better days yourself, Officer Price."

I touched the butterfly strips I applied in haste to close the gash over my swollen eye. "It's not serious. Besides, I found my daughter and brought her back home, so it was worth it."

"That is fantastic news, but I'm not surprised. Agent Lujan said you were a force to be reckoned with."

I swallowed, unsure if I could trust my voice. "Do you have any news of Lujan?"

"The last I heard, he was on life support." Her composure slipped, and she bit her lip.

My heart stuttered. A million questions rushed to the tip of my tongue, but they melted away again.

Noting my expression, Hobbs leaned in. "It's always hard to see the bigger picture amid chaos, but Agent Lujan would have been proud of us today, and of you in particular. Some of us wouldn't be alive if it wasn't for you. You're a hero."

I gestured to the blood seeping between her fingers as she clutched the wound in her arm. "You should have that looked at."

She nodded in agreement and shuffled away.

A *hero*. Would Hobbs believe that after she heard about Vanderberg?

Bullet casings tinkled against my dusty oxfords as I trudged across the yard of the compound towards the law enforcement vehicles clustered outside the gate. It was high noon and the pungent smell of smoke and gunpowder hung in the air.

Every inch of my body ached like I'd rushed for four quarters against the Pittsburgh Steelers. I opened my bulletproof vest and palpated my ribcage. Nothing seemed to be broken, but I wouldn't be doing any roundhouse kicks for a while.

I searched the brilliant blue Wyoming sky for the red-tailed hawk, but it was empty. Perhaps he found happier hunting grounds, far away from this place.

Two ambulances were parked under the shade of cottonwood trees near the gate, and Robert Sandoval lay on a gurney behind one of them.

On impulse, I made a detour instead of continuing on to the DCI vehicles.

When he saw me approaching, he pushed his oxygen mask aside. "Officer Price, good to see you again, although I didn't expect it so soon. Shoot any more of your fellow cops today?"

His attempt at levity set my teeth on edge. "That was unnecessary."

"Sorry, it's the drugs. I meant no disrespect."

"How's your shoulder doing?"

"The EMT said I was lucky. The bullet went straight through. After he got the bleeding slowed, he pumped me full of painkillers and left me here to languish while he attends to someone more important. I plan to give him a piece of my mind when he gets back."

"What were you doing out here today, Sandoval?"

He sighed. "I got a call from Vanderberg. He asked me to meet him. He said it was urgent."

"Were you in the habit of meeting with him?"

"Aren't you supposed to read me my rights before you interrogate me, Officer—or do I need a lawyer here?"

"Calm down. I shot my boss to save your ass, so you owe me some answers."

He pursed his lips but remained silent.

"You and Vanderberg were working together, weren't you?"

"What? No. That crazy bastard—" He made a sputtering noise and coughed violently.

Before I could call the EMT over to check on him, he cleared whatever was in his throat.

"That crazy bastard tried to kill me," he said with a gasp.

I stepped closer to the gurney. "You weren't involved in the trafficking ring?"

A look of utter disgust came over his face. "Are you asking me if I was smuggling human beings into the country and selling them off like cattle? Hell, no!"

"What about Mrs. Randall? Irene Brockman said she was going to make trouble for you. Did you and your pal Vanderberg kill her to protect your operation?"

"I didn't have any involvement in Evelyn's death. Besides, that creepy prick Vanderberg was no pal of mine. He's been a thorn in my side ever since he showed up in Edgemont County—always skulking around where he shouldn't be."

"But you wanted her gone, didn't you? You were so determined to remove her from the picture you rigged up an excuse for the Association to foreclose on her property."

He waved away the accusation. "The foreclosure notice for delinquent dues is standard practice. Our attorney sends them out if a landowner is late. It's a scare tactic, nothing more. We never planned to file anything."

I narrowed my eyes. "Or it was another tactic in your plot to wrest her land away from her. Her niece Olivia DeWitt said you were trying to coerce her into selling, but Mrs. Randall wouldn't budge."

Sandoval's expression turned remorseful. "Okay, okay, I tried to get Evelyn to sell to me."

"And when she wouldn't sell to you—or because she found out you and Vanderberg were planning to use the land to expand your trafficking operations—you had her killed."

"I did not kill her, nor did I have her killed. She was getting on in years and I figured the place was a burden to her after her husband died, so I approached her about selling me her piece, and I expected she would jump at the chance. I didn't want anybody else—" He stopped.

"You didn't want anybody else to what, Sandoval?"

"Folks have accused me of many things, Officer Price, and I'm guilty of a fair number of them, but I didn't kill Evelyn, and I don't traffic in human beings."

"How did you know about those women?"

"I was arguing with Vanderberg when the truck showed up," he said. "The sick bastard opened the back doors and cackled with perverse delight at my shocked face. We got into a shoving match, then you folks showed up and all hell broke loose."

He clammed up when an EMT arrived to retrieve medical equipment from the ambulance. After checking Sandoval's vitals and adjusting the IV bag, the technician left again.

Sandoval made certain he was out of earshot before continuing. "See, I've got this business deal that will be very lucrative for Brightwater Canyon Partners, but I needed the Randall property."

"What kind of deal?"

He looked at the sky. "A golf course."

"A golf course?"

"Yes. An exclusive golf course, country club, and luxury resort. I had these buildings constructed last spring to store construction equipment and building supplies, but other things came up and they sat empty. At least, I thought they were empty."

I crossed my arms. "The homeowner association board is going to let you build a resort in Brightwater Canyon?"

"Hell, the HOA board is in on it. The financial rewards will be substantial and pay for improvements the Association has been trying to raise money for, including enhancements to roads and security and a new fire station. But before you accuse me of anything underhanded, be assured my attorney went over the resort deal with a fine-tooth comb, and it is one hundred percent above-board."

"Did Mrs. Randall know about your luxury resort?"

He rubbed his jaw. "I thought she was on to us. She called me, raving mad about something. I thought it was about the foreclosure letter the Association attorney sent to her, but now I wonder."

"What do you wonder?"

"She ranted about it being a criminal offense to treat humans like that. It was impossible to follow her because she was upset and carrying on like a lunatic. I tried to calm her down and talk sense into her, but she wouldn't have any of it. After a while, I grew tired of arguing with the old bat and advised her to call law enforcement. Hell, I had done nothing illegal, and I told her so."

"Did you tell anyone else about the conversation?"

"I think I mentioned it to the board when we were in an executive session discussing the golf resort," he said. "I let them know Evelyn might have gotten wind of our little project, but I didn't go into specifics. As I recall, everyone agreed to keep their damn mouths shut until we completed the deal."

"Mrs. Randall was the lone holdout?"

"No. Mrs. Edelman hasn't agreed to sell—she owns two adjacent lots on the south side—and Jameson Warner, who has a piece on the north. None are as key as the Randall property, but it's a matter of time before Edelman and Warner die. Both are getting on in years, and their grasping heirs won't refuse a cash transaction."

"Like Olivia DeWitt?"

"Well, Ollie's a whole other deal."

He noted my puzzlement when he called Olivia DeWitt by her familiar name. "Ollie and I go way back. Anyway, she took the deal I offered to her."

"She agreed to sell her aunt's property to you?" I asked, surprised by this news.

"Yes. She flew out from New York, and we inked the deal over dinner. Ollie is a sharp businesswoman. She wanted more money and a cut of the action from the development deal."

"In exchange for keeping her mouth shut?"

His expression turned inscrutable.

That would explain why Olivia DeWitt was in town. She made it sound as if she would never sell to Sandoval, but as they say, money talks and bullshit walks.

I said, "Irene Brockman claims she overheard you bragging to Don Verhulst and Frank McGuiness at an association meeting last week that they had you to thank for getting Mrs. Randall out of the way."

He snorted in amusement. "She heard no such thing. I was talking about the deal with Ollie. Once she consented to sell her aunt's piece to me, most of the obstacles were out of our way, and we could begin development."

"I see." I glanced towards the group of DCI officers. "That's it then, Mr. Sandoval. I have no more questions."

"Good. Now it's my turn."

I considered walking away, but Sandoval disabused me of the notion. "Don't screw with me Price, we both know you're not supposed to be cross-examining me without legal representation and I'd be willing to bet the DCI would disapprove if they knew. This is a private conversation between you and me. I won't tell if you won't."

Robert Sandoval had more money to spend on attorneys than the city of Perseverance. I was already in hot water with the DCI and the last thing I needed was Sandoval screaming about the infringement of his legal rights.

"Okay, but make it quick. Someone is waiting for me."

Sandoval fixed me with a stern stare, like a lawyer grilling a witness. "Why did you kill Vanderberg?"

"Because he had just shot an unarmed man and was pointing his gun at me."

"But he was the chief of police. Your boss."

I rubbed my face and frowned at the blood and soot on my hands. "I know. It's complicated, but I had a hunch Mrs. Randall's murder, my daughter's kidnapping, and this trafficking operation were all related, but it took me a while to figure out Vanderberg was in the middle of it."

I stopped short of telling Sandoval I suspected Vanderberg was trying to frame him from the beginning. Of course, at some point, that information would come out and the authorities would question why I almost allowed Vanderberg to get away with it, but Sandoval didn't need the sordid details.

"That was your child who was kidnapped?"

"Yes. But we found her and she's okay."

"That's good news." Sandoval's eyebrows furrowed again. "So you think Vanderberg was the mastermind behind this whole trafficking operation?"

"Maybe. I believe he orchestrated the ambush today."

Sandoval gave me a sharp look. "So that's what happened—an ambush."

A commotion caused us to look towards the entrance gate where a state trooper was shoving a handcuffed, yet still combative man into a transport van.

Sandoval grunted in disgust. "Frank McGuiness. I knew that was Frank's truck. That double-crossing bastard was trouble from the day I laid eyes on him. Wish I never would have offered him a job. My foreman reported he doesn't show up for work most days."

I heard someone call my name. Near the gate, a stern DCI agent beckoned to me.

"I have to go," I said. "You take care of yourself, Sandoval."

"You as well. If you see that pimple faced EMT, tell him my pain meds are wearing off."

I walked to the man waiting for me at the gate.

"Officer Price? I'm Stan McCloskey, the DCI Region 1 Commander." He sized me up as he spoke. "First, let me express my appreciation for tipping us off about the ambush and rescuing the prisoners in that truck. The losses here today would have been unacceptable if it weren't for your bravery and quick thinking."

"Thank you, Sir."

"However, it is my responsibility to inform you there will be a full investigation into the shooting of Chief Lars Vanderberg."

I nodded. I killed a fellow law enforcement officer who was also my superior. There were bound to be questions—lots of them.

When I told Commander McCloskey my version of events leading up to the moment that I put a bullet in Vanderberg's heart, it sounded fragmented and absurd. To his credit, he avoided casting me as a newbie or outsider and asked unbiased questions without editorializing, which I appreciated because it kept me grounded in the present.

Afterwards, I made my way back through the gulch as soft light sifted through the bright green leaves of the cottonwoods, their piquant perfume reminding me of the day Lujan and I were here together. Part of me wanted to lean against the fallen log and close my eyes for a while, but I had a daughter at home who needed me and loose ends in want of tying.

On the final ascent to the Randall house, I looked up. A disheveled Justin Stokes stared at me from the top of the trail, an expression of shock and disbelief on his pale, doughy face.

I ignored him and cut around the south side of the house.

In the driveway, Molly and Bjorn Stensgaard waited with a half dozen others—some of whom I recognized as Brightwater Canyon residents.

At the sight of me, Molly charged across the gravel, her flowing pink and purple tie-dyed skirt flapped around her ankles. "Officer Price!"

Bjorn was close on her heels and began snapping pictures of me with an enormous camera.

When I sidestepped to avoid them altogether, Molly grabbed my arm. "What happened back there, officer?"

I pulled my arm away and opened the door of the Crown Vic to throw my cap on the seat. My hair was plastered to my head with sweat, but the shutter of Bjorn's camera kept clicking away like a giant, deranged cicada.

"I can't give you any information at this point, Molly," I said. "The DCI will notify the newspapers when they're prepared to give a press briefing. That's all I have right now."

"Chief Vanderberg promised—"

"Yes, I know, and I'm sorry." I unbuckled the Kevlar vest and got into the cruiser.

Molly was still talking as I started the engine.

After I maneuvered around the cluster of curious onlookers, I shoved a tape of Eminem's Greatest Hits into the cassette player and floored it.

TWENTY

The magazine rack in the waiting room of the Cheyenne Regional Medical Center's Intensive Care Unit offered a variety of magazines, none of which interested me but I didn't want to look like a stalker so I selected an issue of *This Old House* and pretended to read it.

A thin, well-dressed blond woman paced the floor in Lujan's hospital room, chattering on her cell phone. A boy and a girl, both in their teens, sat on either side of his bed. The girl stroked Lujan's hand, looking miserable, while the boy stared at the television hanging from the ceiling in the corner. They both resembled their dad, with fine features and dark wavy hair.

It was a five-hour drive to Cheyenne from Perseverance, and I didn't leave until Gracie got off work, so it was already late afternoon when I arrived. Now I was hanging around outside Lujan's room, trying not to bother the family or attract attention to myself while I waited.

The intensive care nurses might not let me see Lujan since I wasn't a relative, but I wasn't leaving until I gave it my best shot and although I was on administrative leave, I wouldn't hesitate to use the Perseverance police badge in my pocket if it gained me access.

Finally, Lujan's ex-wife and kids left, and I got up and walked with determination towards his room.

The ICU room was dim and cooler than I expected, a bank of glowing monitors casting a strange greenish light on Lujan's face. Even swathed in bandages and intubated, he was handsome, yet his face was so peaceful that if it weren't for the soft rise and fall of his chest and steady beeping of the heart monitor, I would have sworn he was dead.

In a dark, abandoned parking lot in Casper, Lujan's attacker shot him four times, once in the head and leg, and twice in the back. He would have died at the scene if the noise hadn't woken a trucker sleeping in his nearby semi, who called 911.

The ambulance arrived within minutes and the EMTs stabilized Lujan enough to get him to the hospital for surgery. Afterwards, the doctors put him in a drug-induced coma to give his brain an opportunity to heal, but they were tightlipped about his chances for a full recovery.

I bent close to his ear. "Hey Ernie. I came to tell you that Dancy is safe at home. Gracie and I found her in Ethete. I know it sounds crazy, and after you get out of here, I'll tell you the whole ridiculous story. You'll get a big kick out of it, trust me."

The nurse came in to adjust his breathing tube and gasped when she noticed me. "Oh! I didn't see you in here."

"It's okay, I'm a colleague." I flashed my badge with a confidence I didn't feel.

She squinted at my proffered credentials.

"I won't disturb him, I promise," I said. "I just want to sit with him."

"Okay, but only for a little while."

When she was out of earshot, I leaned in again. "There's something else I need to tell you, and I wanted you to hear it from me first. Lars Vanderberg is dead. I shot him. That's another long story, but I did it to save Robert Sandoval's life—and my own. That's crazier than me and Gracie rescuing Dancy, I know, but don't judge me before you hear my side of the story, okay? I'm still working it out in my head, but when I tell you everything, I think you will understand. Hell, you no doubt had it figured it out long before I did."

One machine hummed like an air compressor and the blood pressure cuff on Lujan's arm inflated. Reluctant to raise my voice above the noise, I waited until it shut off.

"I didn't thank you for lunch and doing what you thought was right to rescue Dancy—" I looked around at the terrifying array of machines, my voice failing. "And I'm sorry I suspected you of being a dirty cop. I should've trusted you to do the right thing, and I didn't. It's just—well, I have a trust problem.

"Remember in the restaurant—when I told you Jason abandoned me? That's true, but not wholly accurate, and I can't bear the thought of a lie coming between us—not that there is an 'us'—I mean..."

I stumbled over my words and blushed, although he was unconscious and couldn't hear a word I was saying.

"After Jason got out of the Marine Corps, I hoped we could make a fresh start. He seemed different, and I chalked it up to maturity. He still didn't like the fact that I was a homicide cop, but I thought we were finding our new normal in the wake of military life. I couldn't have been more wrong. Even though Jason looked and acted fine on the outside, inside he wasn't fine at all.

"Two years to the day after he came home from Afghanistan, my squad answered a call about a body in a downtown flophouse. It was Jason. The official cause of death was fentanyl overdose. You can't imagine what it was like to find my husband's body and try to wrap my head around the fact that he was a junkie. Afterwards, a couple of his friends told me he had been abusing drugs for years.

"In hindsight, my Jason—the sweet, outgoing high school boy I fell in love with—didn't come back from Afghanistan. When I tell people he deserted me, that's the stupid euphemism I use to deflect the feelings I can't deal with." A tear slid down my cheek and I wiped it away.

I took Lujan's hand in both of mine.

"Jason dreamed about starting a big family after he got out, but I couldn't make him understand I didn't want to stay home and raise babies. I'd never be that kind of wife and I couldn't make him recognize that.

"I loved Jason, but it's like you said, Ernie. The only people who understand cops are other cops. He committed to the Marine Corps without asking me, but I didn't insist that he give up that commitment. He wouldn't accept, though, that I couldn't give up being a cop for him.

"The day of his funeral, I found out I was pregnant and it seemed like

Jason's revenge. The chief stuck me behind a desk and let me stay on, out of pity, I suppose. But because of everything else that had happened, I didn't handle it well and after Dancy was born, my boss hinted I should look for another job. Since there was nothing remaining for me in California and I couldn't go home to South Dakota, backwater Perseverance seemed like the ideal location to drop out of sight and life—"

The nurse stuck her head in the room. "My shift is ending. The night duty nurse knows you're here, but it's getting late."

I glanced at my watch. "Five more minutes and I'll be out of here, I promise."

"Okay, I'll tell Kate," she said. "Good night."

I rubbed my eyes. I was tired and dreading the long trip home to Perseverance, but I still had something important to say before I left.

"Every day, I feel guilty, Ernie, because I couldn't be the woman my husband needed and because I didn't want Dancy—even though now she's the center of my universe, and I can't imagine life without her.

"The anniversary of Jason's death is coming. He died almost three years ago and sometimes it feels like a hundred, yet I'm as broken as the day I found his body in that flophouse.

"Then you showed up and turned my miserable existence inside out. That day in the cafe I felt embarrassed and exposed because the person reflected in your eyes was a desirable woman and talented cop, not the dull, invisible drone I had become. She was an echo of the person I once was, and to my surprise, I missed her and mourned her almost as much as I grieved the loss of my husband and my career.

"It was like being shocked back to life after being braindead. I realized maybe it was time to forgive Jason—and myself—and somehow start over. Perhaps along the way I will reclaim the authentic version of myself. So stick around, Special Agent Ernesto Lujan. Someday, I'd like to introduce you to the real Tammy Wynette Price."

His fingers twitched. I kissed him on the forehead and slipped out of the room.

TWENTY-ONE

Gracie and I were drinking beer on my front porch while Dancy played on a quilt spread out on the dirt. Although I spent all summer trying to grow a real lawn, the grass was still pretty sparse. But at least she wasn't sitting in a patch of cactus.

It was a cloudless September afternoon in the upper Wind River Basin. The sun was warm on our skin, but the breeze held the hint of a chill. Fall was coming. The nights were already dipping into the thirties. Soon it would be winter, and we'd be stuck inside for months, playing card games, and trying to stay cozy. But for now, while the sun was high, we pretended it was still summer.

In an hour or two, we'd go inside for dinner and after I put Dancy to bed, we'd pull on our fleece jackets and sit outside talking.

"You don't have to leave," Gracie said.

I smiled at Dancy, who was kissing her bunny. "I know, but I might not have a choice."

To be honest, at that moment I was in limbo. The investigation into the Brightwater Canyon incident was still ongoing, and even if I was cleared in the shooting, I wasn't sure I would stick around Perseverance afterwards.

Gracie put her arm around me and squeezed. "It'll be okay, Wyn. He deserved it and everybody knows it." She didn't say his name, but we both knew who she was talking about.

If I spent too much time mulling over the events of that fateful day, I got depressed. Sometimes my mind tricked me into believing I made a mistake and murdered an innocent man, but I didn't mention these misgivings to Gracie. Saying them aloud might make them true.

One thing that would stick with me for the rest of life was the look of shock on Vanderberg's face when the bullet entered his heart. Before I could squeeze off a second shot, he was already falling backwards. Then all I could remember was grief and relief washing over me like a tidal wave.

I had been on administrative leave since June. Any day now, a Wyoming Division of Criminal Investigation special agent would show up and slap me in handcuffs or cut me loose. Either way, I longed for that day to come because I felt like a caged bobcat.

"Those poor women—and to think Josefina was one of them." Gracie frowned, looking introspective. "All that time, they were enslaved right under our noses, and we didn't notice."

"The thought troubles me too. I ran into Josefina all the time, but I didn't really see her."

"It wasn't only us, though, was it? The newspaper said the trafficking ring was suspected of supplying sex and labor slaves to major hospitality hubs throughout the west, including Jackson Hole. God knows how many women and children were run through Vanderberg and Donovan's bondage mill—or how many locals were in on it."

Gracie was right, of course, but it didn't assuage my guilt. I was a police officer who was trained to spot the signs of trafficking, and I ignored them.

I shook my head slowly. "Part of me knew that little scrap of yellow fabric was a piece of a baby's swaddling blanket the instant I saw it. Why didn't I trust my gut instincts? Sometimes I wonder what happened to that baby."

"You can't think like that, Wyn, or it'll make you crazy. You figured it out in time to save the women in that truck."

Gracie got up and shuffled down the walkway in her fuzzy pink bunny

PERSEVERANCE 269

slippers, which oddly complemented her skimpy daisy dukes and white midriff top. When she reached the end of the concrete, she lit a cigarette.

"I guess so," I said with an air of defeat, "but how many were we too late to save?"

"Those bastards." Gracie blew a stream of smoke toward the street and shook her head.

The day after the shooting, *The Wind River Courier* published Bjorn's picture of me along with the headline "Officer Slays Perseverance Police Chief in Shoot Out". I was sure I would be lynched or die of mortification, but somehow neither happened.

The story of the South American women rescued at the compound made national headlines. Photos featured them—faces blurred for privacy—peering from the windows of the bus taking them to a shelter in Colorado, while the journalists speculated whether the shell-shocked people of Perseverance were complicit or simply dumb, racist rednecks and stoned new-age freaks.

In the hullabaloo over the trafficking ring and attempted assassination of a state agent, the nationwide news outlets didn't latch on to my role in the mess, probably because the DCI had a tight lid on the internal investigation.

Some Perseverance residents still shunned me on the street, but I couldn't blame them for that. I shot the chief of police, for goodness' sake. It was disturbing, even if he did deserve it.

The first locals to offer their support were Pastor Mueller and Myrna Flowers. After Charlie Lumineux died in mid-August, Myrna began visiting me almost every day. We joked about forming a grief support group for widows, but it was closer to the truth than we let on.

The general election was a few months away, and since no one else had stepped forward as a candidate for Edgemont County Sheriff, Justin was contemplating running. While Connie insisted his chances were excellent, I couldn't envision the sheriff's star pinned on his chubby chest. However, I didn't dissuade him. Everybody needed a goal in life, especially Justin.

Mrs. Barker drove by in her Lincoln and gawped at me sitting on the porch.

"Hi Mrs. Barker." Gracie struck a provocative pose and gave the old busybody her best Rodeo Queen wave.

"Hi Barky!" Dancy echoed in a cheerful voice.

Gracie and I giggled.

I summoned the courage to tell Gracie the whole truth about Jason the day after I visited Lujan in the hospital. But to my relief, she didn't make a big deal of it or accuse me of lying to her. Instead, she listened without judgment and then put her arms around me while I cried.

So amidst the whirling aftermath of the Brightwater Canyon incident, the third anniversary of Jason's death passed, and with the help of Dancy, Gracie, Myrna—and half the town—I got through it.

"Are you expecting someone?" Gracie said, scrutinizing a black Explorer that was approaching on Cinnamon Street.

"Nope."

My stomach somersaulted when the SUV with a DCI decal on the door parked at the curb in front of my house and Special Agent Ernesto Lujan got out.

Silver streaks glinted in his wavy black hair, and he was thinner, but was still sexier than any guy I'd ever seen in my life, except Jason in his Harding County High School football uniform. Of course, I would never tell him that.

After giving him the once over, Gracie asked in a sultry drawl, "Are you here in an official capacity, Special Agent Lujan?"

"I am." He smiled at Gracie and gave Dancy a wink before turning his gaze to me.

I stood up and put a hand on the railing to steady myself, feeling self-conscious in my tight Sturgis Motorcycle Rally t-shirt and shorty-shorts, although Gracie said I looked smoking hot in them.

Gracie stubbed out her cigarette and ran over to Dancy. "Hey, Fancy-Dancy, you wanna help Auntie Gracie eat some ice cream?"

Dancy squeaked an affirmation and held out her arms so Gracie could scoop her up.

After watching them go, Lujan limped to the foot of the porch steps and studied my face. "Hello, Wyn."

Without thinking, my fingers flew to the scar on my brow. "Should we go in?" I gestured to the door behind me.

"That would be good, thanks." It was impossible to tell if he was being polite or if something else lurked behind his nonchalant manner.

I opened the door and followed him in.

Before he sat on the couch, he unbuttoned his suit coat and smoothed his tie.

I perched on the opposite end, hoping my nervousness didn't show.

"I apologize for this taking so long. It was far more complicated to unravel this case than the DCI review panel expected. But I won't hold you in suspense. Tomorrow, the DCI will issue a report saying you were justified in using lethal force against Perseverance Police Chief Lars Vanderberg. The review panel has cleared you to return to duty."

I opened my mouth, figuring it was a good time to tell him I planned to resign from the Perseverance Police force, but he kept talking.

"In fact, the investigation team was so impressed with your actions during the Brightwater Canyon incident that they wanted me to make special mention of it. Your decisive actions prevented a massacre. Although Dennis Buchowski's injuries will force him into early retirement, it's a miracle everyone else escaped serious injury."

He was talking about the good guys, of course. The bad guys didn't fare so well. Five of them were critically wounded or killed. I shot three of them myself, including Vanderberg.

Lujan put a hand on the cushion between us. "What I'm about to tell you now is off the record. It's doubtful this information will ever be made public, but I believe you have a right to know everything—or at least what we've established as the truth."

I nodded. "About Vanderberg."

"Yes, about Vanderberg." His eyes turned flinty. "Lars Vanderberg was a dirty cop long before he came to Perseverance. He ran petty graft schemes in Milwaukee before moving up to the big leagues in Chicago. Then he got greedy and devised an ambitious extortion scam that stepped on the toes of some big players in the city's bureaucratic machine, but according to our informants, he knew too much to be prosecuted. So instead of cutting him loose or killing him, his superiors decided he would be far more valuable as a boss of one of their organized crime units.

"Alan Sloan's retirement from the Perseverance police force couldn't have come at a better time for their plans. The Perseverance city council fell all over themselves to hire Vanderberg following the Chicago PD's glowing recommendation, and his handlers, pleased with the arrangement, sent him to Wyoming."

While I digested this news in stunned silence, Lujan got up and walked to the kitchen. The refrigerator door thumped, followed by the opening and closing of multiple cupboard doors. "Don't you have anything stronger than beer?"

I joined him in the kitchen. "There's a bottle of Jack on top of the fridge."

He retrieved the bottle and poured the whiskey into glasses, pushing one across the table to me. "Do you need water with that?"

"No." I picked up the glass and drained it.

He chuckled and took a gulp of his own.

I said, "Are you saying the whole time Vanderberg was in Perseverance, he was operating a trafficking ring?"

"Yes, but it was more than a human trafficking racket. They were running drugs, too. Do you remember the meth operation? It was Vanderberg's venture, but the operation was put in jeopardy when Sheriff Lanier caught wind of it. I can't prove it—yet—but I expect Vanderberg was involved in Buck Lanier's death."

I blew out my breath. "So Lanier might not have been dirty after all?"

"Possibly. That's not to say he wasn't a sleaze on the take, but we've found nothing that puts him in bed with Vanderberg."

"And what about Sandoval?"

"Vanderberg devised a plan to set Sandoval up as the scapegoat if things veered south. I almost admire Vanderberg's audacity. It was a clever move, implicating Sandoval. Outside of Brightwater Canyon, Sandoval has enemies in the county, and he's ruthless enough that it wouldn't take much to convince the public of his guilt. After Vanderberg killed him, it would be easy to make sure all the evidence pointed to Sandoval."

A lightbulb switched on in my head. "Everyone would assume Vanderberg was a brilliant lawman, and he'd be a shoo-in for sheriff."

"Precisely." Lujan laughed at the look of astonishment on my face. "As sheriff, he could do whatever he wanted in Edgemont County, and no one could stop him. He also planned to close the Perseverance Police Department under the ruse of cost savings, but his actual intention was to eliminate anyone who might be unwilling to turn a blind eye to his criminal operations."

He poured me some more whiskey.

I took a swallow of the amber liquid and relished the burn as it slid down my throat. "How did Evelyn Randall get caught up in all this?"

"Mrs. Randall saw something incriminating at Sandoval's compound and Vanderberg had to shut her up before she snitched." He gave me a respectful nod. "But he messed up and didn't count on your tenacity. After his designs spiraled out of control, he orchestrated Dancy's kidnapping to distract us and derail the raid so he could execute the final plan."

I shivered at the recollection of Dancy in the basement of the Perfect Touch bunkhouse. "When did you figure out it was him and not Sandoval?"

He looked thoughtful. "Early on, I sensed something was off. I didn't suspect Vanderberg at first, even though he made a big stink about the DCI getting involved—cops are territorial—but as soon as we found the moccasin and that other stuff at the Randall house, my gut instinct told me they were planted. Then there were the elusive fingerprints you kept needling me about—which were Vanderberg's, of course. He never sent them to the lab. We found them in his desk drawer."

"Why didn't he destroy them?"

"It beats me. Maybe he was keeping them as some sort of macabre trophy." A look of disgust crossed his face. "It sounds weird, but when he called your daughter Nancy, it was the nail in the coffin. I thought, what a dick of a boss. He couldn't be bothered with getting your daughter's name right."

"The first caller said Nancy, too, remember? But there were a dozen small things that didn't fit and seemed like coincidences until I spoke with Bartel, then all the details that didn't fit began gravitating to Vanderberg."

We both drank and I could feel Lujan's eyes on me as he tipped his glass back.

I swirled the remaining whiskey in my tumbler. "He couldn't have done it all on his own, though, could he?"

"You already know about Dolores Donovan and her crew. Frank McGuiness and Don Verhulst were his henchmen inside the Brightwater Canyon Association. Verhulst and McGuiness have lawyered up, but I think they'll both talk once we get closer to trial. It will be tricky to unmask Vanderberg's bosses, but I am going to try."

"You'll be in court for the next hundred years."

"We'll be in court, you mean. Your testimony is key to securing convictions. Besides, what else will you do to entertain yourself in Perseverance?" he asked in a teasing tone.

I snorted with scorn and we both grew quiet.

Clearing the whiskey from my throat, I said, "You look good. I mean, it's good to see you recovered from..." I gesticulated with my hand, unsure if I should speak of the shooting.

He was in an induced coma for weeks because of the horrific nature of his injuries. When they brought him out of the coma, he didn't remember the ambush or who shot him. Perhaps he never would, but there was no question in my mind it was Vanderberg.

Lujan smirked, running a hand along his smooth jawline. "At least they didn't damage this face," he said with mock hauteur, "but I got scars elsewhere."

"Don't we all." The instant the remark slipped out, I regretted saying it. It sounded so cynical.

To cover my embarrassment, I said, "I came to see you in the hospital, but you were unconscious."

"I know."

My mouth went dry.

"Wyn. Look at me."

I looked at him.

"I can't imagine how difficult this situation and its aftermath have been for you," he said. "However, you have more support here than you know. Perseverance isn't perfect, but these people need your strength to help them heal and move forward as a community. If you give them the chance, someday they will show you how much they appreciate you."

He was speaking of Perseverance, of course, but his eyes seemed to be saying so much more.

"I don't deserve their appreciation, Ernie. Angie and Evelyn Randall would still be alive if I hadn't been such an idiot. It was almost too late when I grasped what was happening."

"Don't be so hard on yourself." He touched my hand and lingered there for a moment. "Besides, Josefina and the women in that truck are grateful you didn't give up."

"It was too late for Angie Smith, though. She was the body they found out at Ray Lake, wasn't she?"

"Yes. Her real name was Angelina Tamay, a Guatemalan. She was Evelyn Randall's cleaning woman and likely another one of the victims that Vanderberg killed to cover his tracks."

"What's going to happen to Josefina?"

"She's on her way back to her family in Guatemala. Before Vanderberg's associates kidnapped her eighteen months ago in Santiago Zamora in the Sacatepéquez on her way home from work, she was a weaver." The Spanish names rolled off his tongue like honey.

"No wonder she was always so despondent. I'm glad she's going home."

"Oh, I almost forgot." He retrieved an envelope from the inside pocket of his suit and put it on the table in front of me. "Open it."

It was a cheap, neon green card with "Thank You" spelled out in yellow daisies across the front. Inside, below the flowery verse, was Josefina's full name, "Josefina Maria Ruiz Garcia", written in bold, flowing cursive.

"I see the haunted look in your eyes, Wyn," Lujan said, "and I know you're scared, but you have genuine friends here. It's time to forgive—not only yourself, but those who have hurt you in the past—and give yourself permission to start over. Even a badass chick like yourself needs a place to call home and in my humble opinion, Perseverance is a better choice than most."

I blinked back unwanted tears and attempted a feeble laugh. "Badass chick, huh?"

He gave me a lazy wink and drained the last of his whiskey. "Well, I better be going. It's a long drive back to Cheyenne. I'll see you around."

I followed him outside and watched from the porch until the black SUV's taillights disappeared.

A muley doe and her fawn, its spots already fading, regarded me with nervous curiosity from the vacant lot across the street, but when I didn't move, they dismissed me as a threat and went back to nibbling among the tall weeds.

To the west, the September sun sank behind the Wind River Range, painting the cirrus clouds crimson against an azure sky. Amplified by the stillness of dusk, laughter carried to the little yellow house on Cinnamon Street from a neighbor's open kitchen window.

Lujan was right. It was time to forgive Jason—and myself—and start over. Perhaps untamed Perseverance was the perfect place for a badass chick to do exactly that.

P.A. TREMBLAY writes stories set in the forgotten corners of the American West and Midwest. On the South Dakota farm homesteaded by her great-grandparents in the early 1900s, she grew up listening to her father Glenn's wild, but true, stories about local characters. The descendants of those courageous people populate her books.

She lives in the Colorado mountains with her husband Topper and standard poodle, Rogue.

Perseverance is her first novel and was inspired by her niece, who is a police officer in North Dakota.

Visit her at www.patremblayauthor.com.

Printed in Dunstable, United Kingdom